Praise for Minerva Spencer & S.M. LaViolette's

"Spencer creates characters w........................
Phoebe's sister:....................

-Publishe...

THE BOXING BARONESS

"Swooningly romantic, sizzling sensual...superbly realized."

–Booklist STARRED REVIEW

A *Library Journal* Best Book of 2022

A Publishers Marketplace Buzz Books Romance Selection

"Fans of historical romances with strong female characters in non-traditional roles and the men who aren't afraid to love them won't be disappointed by this series starter."

–Library Journal STARRED REVIEW

"Spencer (*Notorious*) launches her Wicked Women of Whitechapel Regency series with an outstanding romance based in part on a real historical figure. . . This is sure to wow!"

-Publishers Weekly STARRED REVIEW

THE DUELING DUCHESS:

"Another carefully calibrated mix of steamy passion, delectably dry humor, and daringly original characters."

—Booklist STARRED REVIEW

VERDICT: Readers who enjoyed *The Boxing Baroness* won't want to miss Spencer's sequel.

–Library Journal STARRED REVIEW

A *Library Journal* Best Book of 2023

This book is dedicated to Vanessa Kelly, my Christmas Yoda.

A Very Bellamy Christmas

The Bellamy Sisters
Book 5

Minerva Spencer

writing as
S.M. LAVIOLETTE

Crooked
Sixpence
CS
P
Press

CROOKED SIXPENCE BOOKS are published by

CROOKED SIXPENCE PRESS

2 State Road 230

El Prado, NM 87529

First printing October 2024

10 9 8 7 6 5 4 3 2 1

Printed in the United States of America

Prologue

A llow me to introduce you to Viscount Clayton's daughter, Miss Eustacia Martin," Lady Crowley said, beaming at the Marquess of Shelton.

Lord Shelton smiled at Stacia, took her hand, and bowed over it. "It is an honor to meet you," he said, smiling down at her, the skin crinkling delightfully at the corners of his unearthly blue eyes.

The air left Stacia's lungs in such a rush that she felt as if he'd punched her. She was vaguely aware that her mouth was agape but could not shut it. An elbow in her side reminded her to drop a shaky curtsey. She said, in a voice that was all but inaudible, "It is a pleasure to meet you, my lord."

But the glorious golden god had already released her hand and moved on.

"And this is Lady Louisa, the Earl of Cumberland's daughter," Lady Crowley continued, introducing yet another of the four wallflowers the poor woman had been engaged to chaperone that Season.

The loss of Lord Shelton's attention—brief as it had been—left Stacia with a chill, as if clouds had covered the sun.

The Marquess of Shelton had arrived at the ball so late that Stacia and her friends had given up hope that he would make an appearance. He had scarcely entered the ballroom when a clutch of chaperones and marriage-minded mamas had fallen upon him like crows flapping around a corpse, although the simile was a poor one. The chaperones actually looked more like tropical birds and there was nothing whatsoever corpselike about the Marquess of Shelton.

He was without a doubt the most beautiful man Stacia had ever seen. He towered above her—although that was not so unusual given that she was barely over five feet—and possessed hair that really did look like spun gold. His face was classical perfection with a chiseled jaw, lips that were firm and shapely, and eyes that defied description. And then there was his figure. Stacia swallowed as she yanked her hungry gaze from his face and stole a quick but thorough look at his broad chest and shoulders before moving down to his skintight pantaloons which displayed his muscled thighs and calves in a way that should have been illegal.

Not only was he physically stunning, but whenever she saw him socializing—usually from afar, unfortunately—he was always smiling and laughing, emanating warmth even beyond the fortunate female he might be speaking to.

As if that was not enough, he was also a highly decorated officer and heir to the Duke of Chatham.

It hardly seemed fair for one man to be so blessed.

Stacia was still ogling his magnificent body when it moved on to the next clutch of debutantes awaiting an introduction.

"He is even more perfect up close," Lady Louisa said in a breathless voice.

"A person or thing cannot be *more* perfect, Louisa," Miss Edith Barkley chided.

"If anyone could be more perfect, it would most certainly be Lord Shelton," Stacia felt compelled to say.

"He is so perfect that he does not look real," Miss Sarah Creighton said.

All of them nodded at the truth of her statement.

Lord Shelton did not dance with any of them that night. Indeed, he didn't dance at all. After he'd been introduced to upwards of forty young women a collective sigh of disappointment went up in the ballroom when he disappeared into the card room and was not seen again.

A week later, at yet another ball, Stacia happened to be standing with two different girls and their chaperone when the older woman introduced her charges to Lord Shelton.

Stacia opened her mouth to say they had already met, but Shelton graced her with the same glowing smile and crinkled eyes, bowed over her hand, and said, "It is an honor to meet you," before moving on to the next girl.

Stacia could scarcely manage a curtsey and mumbled a response in such a quiet voice that even she could not hear the words.

He had forgotten her. She was *forgettable.*

Did she cry a little that night when she was in her bed and re-living the night? Yes, just a little.

Fine. More than a little.

Four nights later Lord Shelton did something even worse. He looked through Stacia yet again—and *most* of her other friends—but this time his brilliant gaze snagged on one of them.

Sarah Creighton.

"Will you do me the honor of dancing this waltz with me, Miss Creighton?"

Sarah's cheeks pinkened and she stammered, "Y-yes, my lord. I have—I have permission to waltz."

His full lips twisted in gentle amusement. "It is my lucky night."

Sarah cast a stunned, almost apologetic glance at Stacia as she was borne off on the golden god's arm to join the other dancers.

She knew that Sarah's hasty glance had been meant kindly. After all, Sarah knew just how terribly infatuated Stacia was.

Rather than soothe her, however, her friend's pity was like a knife in her breast.

Stacia turned to see if the other wallflowers had witnessed the exchange. But they were staring in open-mouthed bafflement at Sarah and Lord Shelton.

Sarah, the daughter of a country baronet, was neither gorgeous nor an heiress, and yet Shelton had not only singled her out—*and* remembered her name—he had asked her to dance. This from a man infamous for appearing at a ball and departing half an hour later without leading even a single partner onto the floor.

Stacia and Sarah had been schoolmates, and she had always liked the other girl, who was sweet and unassuming. Sarah was passably pretty but utterly unlike the sort of beauty who usually attracted the attention of England's most eligible, handsome war hero.

Lord Shelton's choice of Sarah was the ultimate irony as she had never seemed as slavishly smitten by gorgeous marquess as the rest of them.

Indeed, of all the girls who languished together at every ball, she would have said that Sarah was the one who was least interested in finding a husband. She would have gone so far as to say that Sarah pined for her home and family.

And yet Sarah had somehow managed to do the impossible and attract Lord Shelton's interest. What had she done to make him notice her?

What you really mean is, why can't it be you?

Yes. That is exactly what she meant!

Have some pride! He doesn't even remember who you are. How many times does he need to forget you before you stop yearning for him?

The voice of self-preservation was right and Stacia debased herself daily—hourly—by worshipping at Shelton's altar, even if he never learned of her adoration.

But she could not make herself stop.

Watching him bestow his attention on Sarah—dancing and laughing with her—was like quaffing acid and she felt something very close to hatred for the mild, inoffensive woman.

Stacia took comfort—albeit slight—in the fact that she was not the only woman unable to control her unwanted reaction.

3

By the time Shelton asked Sarah to dance with him a *third* time—scarcely a week later—the small clique of wallflowers who had once been Sarah's friends were so bitter toward her that she no longer sat with them.

Stacia couldn't blame her. Neither could she stop herself from hating her.

The fourth time Stacia was introduced to Shelton and he didn't recognize her, she was no longer breathless with awe in his presence. Instead, she felt an almost irresistible urge to do something he *would* remember. Like club him over the head with her reticule.

"It is an honor to meet you," he murmured after Lady Crowley had made the introduction, his beautiful eyes aimed at somebody over Stacia's shoulder.

Irked beyond bearing, Stacia said, "We have been introduced before, my lord."

Lady Crowley gasped and Lord Shelton's gaze *finally* snapped to Stacia's face.

A slight notch formed between his jewel-like eyes. "I beg your pardon?"

"I said, *we have been introduced before.*" Stacia gave him a tight smile. *Four times,* she might have added. *Which doesn't include the dozens of times you've stood as close to me as we are now and flirted with some other woman.*

His gaze sharpened, like a man who'd just been stung by an insect he'd heretofore believed benign. His befuddlement gradually shifted into amusement. "I see. I beg your pardon, Miss, er…"

"It is Miss Martin," Stacia said after letting the silence drag out a few extra seconds. "However, I've learned to answer to Miss Er… ."

The golden god barked a laugh. If Stacia hadn't already girded herself against it, she would have been reduced to a quivering blancmange by the sheer splendor of such a sight. Fortunately, she had been subjected to his male beauty several nights a week at that point, although the full force of his attention had never been focused on her as it was at that moment. While her exposure to him had not inoculated her against his devastating looks, it had mitigated the severity of the symptoms and she no longer gawked and trembled.

"My dear Miss Martin," Lady Crowley murmured in a chiding voice, giving a nervous laugh. "Whatever has come over you?"

Stacia did not respond, her gaze locked with Lord Shelton's.

You look away first, she silently challenged.

"I apologize, my lord," Lady Crowley said. "I do not know what has got into—"

"I am the one who should apologize," Lord Shelton countered, still holding her gaze.

The ice around her heart began to melt, slightly, and her lips began to form a smile.

And then the cad's eyes flitted back to whatever he'd been looking at before!

You obnoxious, vile, insufferable—

"Miss Martin?" The Earl of Townshend's diffident voice interrupted her internal diatribe.

"What?" Stacia snapped, still staring at Shelton, willing him to *notice* her.

"Er, I believe this is my set."

"My dear?" Lady Crowley's hand settled on Stacia's shoulder and gave a slight squeeze. "Lord Townshend is here to claim his dance." The older woman barely lowered her voice and, when Stacia did not respond quickly enough, hissed, "Your *only* dance."

Shelton's eyes slid back to hers. Naturally, the odious heel had heard *that*. His perfect lips quivered faintly and his eyes glinted with amusement.

It was mortifying.

But at least he was looking at her.

Lady Crowley's fingers tightened painfully on her shoulder. "*Stacia.*"

Stacia gritted her teeth against the interruption.

You are a detestable cad, she silently flung at Lord Shelton.

But his attention had already drifted away. This time, Stacia could not help but follow it.

He was smiling across the room at Miss Sarah Creighton—who was fluttering and blushing. And why shouldn't she?

Stacia's foot twitched to kick him in the shin.

"Am I mistaken, Miss Martin?" the Earl of Townshend asked.

"You are not mistaken," Stacia said, her words so clipped that the timorous peer flinched. She took the earl's arm, cut a last withering look at Shelton—not that he noticed—and loudly said to the underside of his chin, "I beg you will excuse me, my lord."

And then she all but dragged the earl onto the dance floor.

Townshend led her into a waltz, his jerky motions bringing to mind an automaton.

"I'm sorry, Miss Martin—but did I interrupt something?" Townshend asked after they'd waltzed—badly—for a moment.

She dragged her attention from the man behind her to the one in front of her and smiled, because the gentle earl did not deserve a scowling dance partner. "Not at all. I apologize if I appeared distracted."

Townshend didn't look entirely convinced, but the subject held little interest for him, so he raised another topic, this one dear to his heart. "Have you seen Lord Buckley's newest acquisition?"

It was all Stacia could do not to run screaming from the ballroom.

But Townshend was a kind young man, if boring and pedantic, and she needed to remember that, even though his obsession with illuminated manuscripts—an interest he shared with Stacia's father—was not a subject she cared to discuss in the middle of a ballroom.

"I have not yet seen it, but my father has." That sounded too abrupt, so she added, "He believes it may be the work of Gerard Horenbout."

Lord Townshend became as illuminated as one of the manuscripts he loved so much. "It is the most beautiful work I have ever seen. One hundred and forty pages. Just imagine that, Miss Martin!"

Stacia didn't have to imagine it; her father had spoken of the newly discovered prayerbook until she felt sure she'd start bleeding out of her ears.

As always when the subject of illuminated manuscripts was raised, Lord Townshend nattered on quite happily without any contribution from her, leaving Stacia to her own thoughts.

Thoughts which were, unfortunately, still fixated on Lord Shelton.

She had no right to mock Townshend's mania for ancient manuscripts when she was so obsessed with the Marquess of Shelton.

It was always easy to spot the marquess, no matter how crowded the function. All one had to do was follow the yearning gazes of at least half the young ladies in attendance.

Tonight was no exception, and Stacia easily located her quarry in the tightly packed sea of humanity.

Predictable, corrosive jealousy churned in her belly at the sight of Shelton dancing with Miss Sarah Creighton.

Stacia was heartily sick, not to mention ashamed, of how badly she wanted to be in Sarah's slippers. But she could not make herself stop.

The only thing that kept her from going mad was the fact that so many of her peers were watching the pair dance and suffering from the same affliction.

Misery was not the only thing to love company. Jealousy appeared to be fond of it as well.

"—the scrolling alone is unparalleled!" Townshend's joyous voice broke into her jealous musings.

Stacia nodded and smiled vaguely, which was enough to keep her dance partner chattering happily.

Bitterness churned in her belly. *Sarah is not that much prettier than I am. Why can't he laugh and smile at me? Why doesn't he seek me out to honor with a dance? Why, why, why?*

Infatuation, Stacia decided unhappily, was exhausting.

Five weeks later, after Lord Shelton had destroyed Sarah's reputation and future by spending an entire evening with her *alone* and then refusing to marry her, Stacia tried to convince herself that she had been fortunate to have avoided such a scoundrel's attention.

But jealousy and envy far outpaced any relief she experienced. Sarah, for all that she could never show her face in public again, would at least have *some* pleasant memories to reflect on when she was old and gray.

That was more than Stacia would ever have.

A month later, when the *ton* gossipmongers discovered that Sarah Creighton was with child, Stacia felt certain that no vestige of adoration for Shelton could survive such damning news.

And yet…

And yet her yearning for a man she barely knew—and which the intellectual part of her despised—was in no way attenuated by his atrocious behavior.

So, who really was the greater fool? Sarah for capitulating to Lord Shelton's wiles, or Stacia for wishing it had been her?

How could infatuation be so tenacious? How could she *want* him so desperately even though he was, in every way that mattered, so unworthy?

The thought obsessed her for weeks, ruining any chance of enjoyment for what remained of what would be her first and only Season.

Ultimately, the only thing that managed to put a stop to Stacia's obsessing was the unexpected and devastating death of her father.

Her grief at the loss of her kindly, absent-minded parent was compounded by the horrible discovery that she'd been left with a legacy that was scarcely enough to keep body and soul together.

Her cousin Geoffrey, the new Viscount Clayton, made it clear there would be no home, at least nothing long-term, for her under his roof.

Stacia would have to work for a living and her choices were simple: companion or governess.

And then—two weeks after her father's death—a third choice presented itself.

The Earl of Townshend called on her and the shy, tongue-tied lord haltingly proposed marriage.

Here was a chance to escape a life of servitude!

Townshend was a kindly man and wealthy, besides. He possessed more than enough money to pursue his only passion—illuminated manuscripts—and also support a wife in luxury.

He believed, erroneously, that Stacia shared his passion.

If she accepted him, she would need to continue lying for the rest of her life.

If she accepted him, she might have children to satisfy her need for love. After all, what was romantic love when compared with that of a child?

If she accepted him, she could continue to move in society—to socialize with the only people she knew.

If she accepted him, she could continue to see Lord Shelton, who had already returned to London after destroying Sarah Creighton's life, unabashed and unashamed of his infamy.

It was that last thought that tipped the scales and cut short her one avenue of escape. How could she marry a man when her mind—and perhaps even her heart—was always on another? It would not be fair to the earl, and it would not be fair to herself.

And so Stacia politely declined Lord Townshend's offer.

A week later, she accepted a position far away from London—somewhere a man like Shelton would never be caught dead: Bath.

Two Years Ago

Stacia smiled and nodded to numerous people as she navigated the crowded Pump Room, a glass of the famous healing water in her hands.

In the months that she'd worked as a companion for the very elderly Lady Hamilton, Stacia had come to the Pump Room five days a week, rain or shine—excepting the few days earlier in the year when her employer had been bed-bound with a head cold.

Her employer was a kind lady who was easy to work for—certainly when compared to some of the other employers she'd seen.

And if Stacia's days were boring and all blurred together with daily visits to the Pump Room, cards at Lady Lydia's on Monday and Mrs. Markham's on Thursday, and a half dozen other routinized activities? Well, boredom was better than the alternative, which was serving as a governess to an unruly brood of brats.

That's what she was telling herself that morning as she performed the same ritual for what she calculated to be either the 199th or 200th time.

And then, in the midst of the predictable tedium, a face she had only seen in her dreams for almost two years appeared before her.

Time seemed to slow, and the glass began to slide between her limp fingers as she stared, gaping, at what surely had to be an apparition.

A hand closed around hers and a familiar, jocular voice boomed in her ear, "Careful, Miss Martin! You almost lost your precious burden."

She wrenched her gaze away from the Marquess of Shelton and turned to Colonel Kelley, who grinned down at her.

"Oh, thank you, sir," she murmured, taking the glass back.

He clucked his tongue. "What is this *sir* business?"

"I am sorry…Richard."

Colonel Kelly smiled, the genuine expression making his handsome, weathered face even more attractive. "That's better, my girl."

But no matter how attractive the colonel was, her eyes slid toward where Lord Shelton stood talking to Lady Hamilton and her friend, Lady Lydia Gregg, who seemed to be leaning on Shelton's arm, almost as if she had some claim to him. Were they related? Stacia's employer visited Lady Lydia every week—sometimes twice—so why hadn't Stacia heard of this connection? What was Shelton doing in Bath at this time of year? What—

Colonel Kelley leaned close and tried to whisper—something that wasn't possible for a man who'd spent thirty years barking orders at subordinates. "Shelton will have all the doves in a flutter, the rascal." He gave an indulgent chuckle.

"You sound as if you admire the man."

The colonel had the grace to appear sheepish. "Oh, I know he has done some things of late that do not reflect well on him, but—"

"That is certainly *one* way of putting it. A mild way, I must say."

The colonel looked pained. "What you need to understand, my dear, is that Shelton is one of Britain's most highly decorated soldiers."

"Are you saying that excuses his reprehensible behavior?"

"No, of course not. However, it does not erase his heroism, either. He"— the Colonel shook his head, visibly conflicted— "Shelton did things for this country that not many men would, or could, make themselves do. I cannot think of a braver man."

Stacia frowned and turned back to find Lady Hamilton gesturing for her to come closer.

The colonel offered his arm and for once, Stacia was glad of her elderly admirer's presence.

"My dear Miss Martin, you must come and meet Lady Lydia's nephew. And you too, Colonel."

Stacia had a moment to collect her wits as Colonel Kelley pushed forward, as eager as any debutante to meet one of England's foremost war heroes.

"A pleasure to meet you, my lord," he gushed.

Shelton smiled politely. "Colonel Robert Kelley? You were with Fletcher, weren't you?"

The Colonel's ruddy face darkened with pleasure. "By Jove! You've heard of me, have you? That is a treat, sir! Yes, I did serve under Fletcher." He nodded enthusiastically and opened his mouth, no doubt to continue gushing, but Lady Hamilton had other plans.

"And this is my companion, Miss Stacia Martin, Viscount Clayton's daughter," she said, thrusting her way into the conversation.

Lord Shelton turned away from Kelley, took Stacia's reluctantly proffered hand, and bowed over it. "It is an honor to meet you, Miss Martin."

Stacia stared up into his eyes, disbelief and fury breeding like rabbits when she realized that—yet again—the blasted man did not remember meeting her.

It felt as though she stared into the blue depths for at least a minute, but it couldn't have been longer than a few seconds. Shelton, obviously accustomed to women gazing at him fatuously, gave her a faint smile—nothing that could be misconstrued as encouragement, of course—released her hand, and then turned to answer something his aunt was asking.

All the way home from the Pump Room her employer chattered happily about Lord Shelton's unexpected visit to his great aunt and what treats Lady Lydia was planning for his visit.

Over the following two weeks and four days that Lord Shelton remained in Bath—feted by all and sundry, his deplorable treatment of Sarah Creighton completely forgotten, as if the denizens of Bath had collectively suffered amnesia—Stacia was at no fewer than nine functions with the man.

Not once at any of those dinners, parties, assemblies, and yes, one picnic, had Lord Andrew Shelton exhibited any indication that he recalled meeting Stacia in London.

She *hated* him.

When he finally left town, she breathed a sigh of relief, her muscles unclenching for the first time in weeks.

Good riddance to bad rubbish!

That is what Stacia told herself.

And yet...

And yet when Colonel Kelley offered Stacia marriage—and a life of leisure with a man who if she did not love, at least she liked and respected—Lord Andrew Shelton's beautiful face rose up in her mind like a specter.

For the second time in her short life Stacia found that she could not accept an offer of marriage, and at least part of the reason could be laid at the feet of Lord Shelton. Oh, not because she loved him—she did not even *like* the man. And certainly not because she held out even the faintest hope that he would ever notice her.

No, the reason she could not tie herself to one man, while so mindlessly infatuated with another, was because she would not be able to bear it if somebody did the same thing to her.

Six-ish Months Earlier

Somewhere on the Great North Road

Andrew Derrick, the Marquess of Shelton, looked from his cousin the Duke of Chatham, to Baron Angus Fowler—the man who had just blackened Andrew's eye—to Lady Hyacinth Bellamy, who was apparently the brand-new Duchess of Chatham.

11

All three were regarding him as if he were an especially noxious toadstool that had sprung up in their midst.

"Where is my sister?" Her Grace demanded through clenched teeth.

Andrew dabbed some blood off his lower lip and winced—there would be swelling in addition to his black eye—and then looked up at the new duchess and smirked in a way he knew made people want to hit him. "Congratulations on your nuptials, Your Grace. No hard feelings, I hope?"

"You tried to *blackmail* me," she seethed.

"If we are being precise, it was Chatham I blackmailed." Andrew smirked. "And I didn't just try; I succeeded."

The duchess took a step toward him.

Chatham hastily placed his body between Andrew and his tall skinny wife, a woman currently, and convincingly, garbed in men's clothing.

The duchess was not a pretty woman, nor even a handsome one, but she was distinctive looking with her bright orange hair, pale as milk skin, and gaunt, tall body. Her most attractive feature by far was her eyes which were not only a striking pale green but also broadcast her keen intelligence to anyone who bothered to look.

Andrew met his cousin's gaze. Sylvester, the Duke of Chatham, was a man he'd known since Chatham's father, the old duke, had taken Andrew into his home when he'd been orphaned at the tender age of four.

For a good chunk of his life, Andrew and Chatham had been as close as brothers. Andrew had idolized and worshipped the other man up until the day Sylvester had married Mariah, the woman Andrew loved.

That had been eleven years ago, and Andrew had hated his cousin with a passion every day since.

"Married, hmm?" Andrew met the older man's gaze and sneered. "Congratulations, Syl."

An explosion of white sparks and a crack of pain were Chatham's answer.

Andrew, suddenly flat on his back, blinked up at his cousin through stars.

"I told you not to call me *Syl*," the duke said in a cool voice.

Lord Fowler gave a hoot of laughter. "I have been waiting for you to plant him a facer for years, Chatham."

The duke ignored his friend's cheering and held Andrew's gaze.

Andrew shifted his jaw from side to side to make sure it still worked before saying, "You wouldn't have got in that hit if both my eyes were working."

"Where is Lady Selina?" Chatham asked, extending a hand to help Andrew up.

Andrew considered stringing his cousin along for a bit—he'd not gotten under Chatham's skin so effectively in years, and it wasn't for a lack of trying, either—but he was bloody exhausted and, quite frankly, the jig was up.

He disregarded his cousin's hand and pushed to his feet without any assistance. The room tilted, but he managed to not embarrass himself by falling onto his arse for a second time.

"I don't know where she is," he admitted. "But wherever she went, she emptied my pockets first."

Fowler sneered. "She wouldn't have got far if she'd been forced to rely on that. But she emptied mine, too, and I had enough money in my purse to get her to Moscow and back."

Fowler was a bloody mountain of a man—outweighing Andrew by at least three stone—and Andrew felt a burst of pride when he noticed the giant baron had swelling over one eye and a nasty cut on his cheek from their little set-to.

Any pride he felt, however, was dashed when he recalled just why they had been fighting.

Andrew was used to being viewed as a villain—hell, he cultivated it—but this time he was truly ashamed of his behavior. He had abducted Lady Selina Bellamy and would have ruined the woman—maybe he already had—if Fowler hadn't stumbled onto the two of them at this inn and commenced to thrash Andrew for the woman's honor.

While they had been fighting like a pair of street curs, Lady Selina had rescued herself by robbing them both and absconding, leaving Andrew to face the wrath of his cousin and Selina's sister.

Was he ashamed?

Yes. But not because of *what* he'd tried to do—elope with Lady Selina—but because of *why*.

If he had loved Lady Selina as he had pretended all Season, then abducting her would have still been scandalous, but not cruel. Instead, Andrew had absconded with her to get back at Chatham because he had mistakenly believed the duke was in love with Lady Selina.

The moment Andrew had been scheming toward for years—depriving his cousin of a woman *he* loved—had finally presented itself. And Andrew had seized the opportunity with both hands.

It turned out he'd been right about Chatham being in love, but he'd mistaken which Bellamy sister his cousin had lost his heart to.

A Very Bellamy Christmas

Somewhere between sitting in the carriage with Lady Selina and listening to her disparage his character, and getting knocked unconscious—briefly—by one of Fowler's Christmas ham sized fists, Andrew had accepted what a complete and utter arsehole he was for using Lady Selina in his ongoing war against Sylvester.

Selina had done nothing but behave with kindness toward him, and Andrew had abused her trust and friendship horribly.

Why he suddenly understood that *now* was beyond him. Perhaps he had needed to be struck in the face repeatedly by a massive fist before coming to his senses?

In any event, Andrew was ashamed. Deeply.

But he had no intention of allowing Chatham or Fowler to see that.

"If she took our money, it is a fair bet that she left on the stage that stopped here," he said when it was obvious the other three were not finished glaring. "Have you asked any of the ostlers if she bought passage? She is not exactly easy to forget."

Fowler's scowl deepened. "I'm not a fool. That is the first thing I thought about. Unfortunately, none of them recall anything about who got on or off the stage."

"Let me guess. They were too busy watching us fight?"

Fowler's hands flexed at his sides and Andrew readied himself for another punch.

The duke turned to his friend. "Go to the next stop, Fowler. And the one after that. Keep going until you find out where she is bound."

Fowler wrenched his glare from Andrew nodded. "Aye." He hesitated and gave the duke a sheepish look. "Er, but I'll need some blunt since—"

"Yes, of course," Chatham said. He reached into his coat, pulled out his notecase, and took what looked to be half the money and handed it to his friend.

Fowler took the notes and shoved them into his pocket. "I'll send word— you'll be in London?"

The duke looked at his wife.

"I want to help look for Selina," the duchess said.

Sylvester hesitated only a few seconds before nodding at his wife and turning to Fowler. "Send any news to Chatham House. They will know how to find me."

"Aye," Fowler said, clearly eager to get on his way. But then he paused, a look of anguish on his face as he turned to the duchess. "It is my fault that she left. She didn't want me to fight. If only I had listened to her and taken her back to your aunt then—"

14

"Just find her, Fowler," the duchess said quietly. Her pale green eyes slid to Andrew. "We can assess blame later."

Once Fowler had gone, the duke turned to Andrew and held out his hand. "This should get you back to London."

Andrew looked at the money in his cousin's palm. "I'm going to help you look for—"

"I don't want him with us, Chatham," the duchess said.

Andrew's face heated at her scorn. "I thought the aim was to find your sister? Or is venting your spleen more important than her well-being, *Your Grace?*"

"Do not speak to my wife in that tone," the duke said, taking a step toward him.

Andrew closed the gap between them, until they were chest to chest. "Do not think to hit me again, Chatham," he said, every bit as coldly as his cousin. "I will not be caught unaware a second time."

Chatham opened his mouth, but the duchess spoke first.

"You are right, Shelton. Finding Selina is the goal, and we should accept all the help we can get." She left the words *even yours* unspoken. "I will be in the carriage, Chatham." The duchess pivoted on her heel and headed for the door, moving too quickly for either the duke or Andrew to open it for her.

When she had gone, Chatham sighed, his shoulders slumping. "This needs to stop, Drew. How many more people need to get hurt? Enough is enough."

The duke had not used Andrew's pet name in over a decade. If he thought that would endear Andrew to him, he was sorely mistaken.

Fury crackled through him at the other man's words. "I will decide when and how much is—"

"I am sorry, Drew," the duke said quietly.

"For what?" Andrew demanded through clenched teeth.

"I am sorry about Mariah. I am sorry I was selfish and cruel. I am sorry that you both paid the price for my behavior. I am sorry I did not do the right thing all those years ago and set her free. I am sorry it has taken me so long to admit just how awful I was to you both. I am sorry for all of it. *Everything.* And I am even sorrier that I cannot go back and do the right thing. But I cannot, Drew. I can never fix the damage I caused. Not only to you and Mariah, but to Sarah Creighton and Lady Selina and anyone else who has been caught between us. How many more people need to get hurt?"

Andrew stared into the eyes of the man who had once been a brother, best friend, mentor, and idol to him.

The man who had married the woman Andrew loved.

And then allowed her to die in childbed.

With your child.

The quiet accusation sent a shudder through his body and Andrew's vision turned blurry.

Mariah and your *son.* You *were the one who got her pregnant, not Sylvester. It was because of* you *that she was weak and sick with worry and brought to bed a month early.* You *are the one who killed her.*

A hand landed on his shoulder and Andrew jolted at the touch. He tore himself away from grief that was old—ancient—and yet as sharp as the day the blade first cut.

He met Sylvester's anguished gaze.

"I am so sorry, Andrew, and I will never stop regretting what I did. But I don't want to spend another decade hating you. Or being hated. Is there no way we can salvage… something? You were closer to me than my own brother. We might never be able to rebuild that bond, but must we go on hating?"

The words were like the first cracks in a dam. The anger and despair behind the crumbling edifice took *so much* effort to keep in place.

Andrew was tired—exhausted. So bloody sick and tired that he ached from it, body, mind, and soul.

Chatham's hand tightened on his shoulder. "Andrew?" His cousin leaned closer, concern in his eyes. "Are you—"

"I am fine," he said, sounding less than convincing to his own ears. He gave a small shrug, and the duke removed his hand. He swallowed several times and then spoke before he could stop himself. "What you just said—what you admitted about M-Mariah?"

"Yes?" Chatham prodded.

"Your apology means something to me—I—Christ," he muttered, shoving a hand through his hair and then wincing when he encountered a goose egg from his fight with Fowler. He cleared his throat. "I am mindful of what it took to say those words, Chatham. And—and I agree with you." Andrew was momentarily stunned by his own admission. Had those words really come out of his mouth?

He swallowed down his amazement and then said, "It will take time. Time to—" He stopped, not sure how to phrase what he meant, the enormity of this sudden shift in his world overwhelming.

"I agree," the duke said. "You will come stay with me at Chatham Park...after this?"

Andrew hesitated and then nodded. "I will come."

"Good. We will need time to repair this breech."

Again, Andrew nodded.

"We will take that time. All the time we need, Drew. But that is for later."

Andrew was almost weak with relief that the time wasn't *now*.

He jerked his chin toward the door the duchess had just used. "Let us go and find Lady Selina. I have some apologizing of my own to do."

Chapter 1

Wych House
Little Sissingdon
Early December

Phoebe, Viscountess Needham, hurried through the portrait gallery, her hand beneath the swell of her belly. At seven months pregnant her hurried pace was no longer very fast.

If Nanny Fletcher could see her, she would shout down the roof. Her childhood nurse believed that expecting mothers nearing their eighth month should do no more than sip fortifying cordials while reclining on a chaise longue.

That would drive Phoebe mad within a week.

She was thrilled to have this family Christmas party to plan, even though her husband, Paul, chided her daily about over-exerting herself.

"Hire somebody to do all this for you, darling. You know Dixon would be happy to help. He has more time than he needs now that Dennehy has taken over most of his burdens."

Phoebe knew that was true. Her husband's longtime secretary, Mr. Dixon, was a wizard. Although Dixon would be leaving shortly after the New Year—to take up residence at an estate he'd inherited from a great uncle—he had an apt pupil in Paul's new secretary, Colbert Dennehy.

Phoebe did not know Mr. Dennehy very well, but her husband's long-term protégé, was clever, dedicated, and had readily soaked up Dixon's instruction over the last few months.

So, yes, the two men could have managed the preparations far better than Phoebe.

But how did one explain to one's husband that some things—like overseeing the preparation of her sisters' and brother's chambers for their return to their ancestral home after an absence of more than six years—was *not* something she wanted to delegate?

Nor could Phoebe delegate the errand that was bringing her to the south wing, the part of Wych House that was home to Ellen Kettering, a woman all and sundry believed to be her husband's former mistress and mother of his illegitimate child, Lucy.

Ellen, against all odds, had become Phoebe's dear friend over the past months. Their friendship had begun even before she had learned that Ellen and Paul had never been lovers and Lucy was not his child.

In the months since learning the truth about Ellen and Lucy, Phoebe had come to love both of them. It pained her greatly that Ellen—who had been ill for years—was dying. And dying soon. Every day the other woman looked weaker and weaker. Phoebe suspected Ellen was only clinging to life because she didn't want to die before Lucy's birthday, which was Christmas Day.

Phoebe visited Ellen every day, right after Lucy went up to the schoolroom to have her lessons with her governess.

They would enjoy a cup of tea, chat, and Phoebe would read bits of the newspaper aloud as Ellen could no longer see well enough to focus for long. Afterward, Phoebe went about her day and Ellen returned to her bed. She slept a great deal in order to be awake for those hours when Lucy would join her.

But lately, Ellen had slept through Phoebe's visits. Rather than leave her friend, Phoebe stayed and sat beside her while she slept because Ellen had once confessed that Phoebe's presence was a comfort to her.

Phoebe also stayed because she worried the fragile woman would go to sleep and not wake again.

Something hot slid down her cheek and Phoebe dashed away the tear with the heel of her hand, disgusted with herself. The last thing Ellen needed to see was her weepy face. She stopped in front of an ancient looking glass that hung just outside Ellen's spacious apartment and made sure her eyes weren't red. And then she practiced a smile—not stopping until it looked natural—and knocked softly before entering.

An almost crippling wave of relief rolled over her when she saw the other woman was awake and, for a change, sitting upright rather than reclining on her chaise longue.

She smiled. "Good morning, Phoebe." If a person did not look too closely it was easy to believe Ellen's flushed cheeks were a sign of health rather than feverishness. "You are just in time to help me go through all this."

All this was the jumble of jewelry boxes, wrapping paper, and spools of ribbon on her secretaire desk.

Phoebe grinned and this time she did not have to force it. "Oooh, wrapping gifts? My favorite! What is all this?" she asked, pulling a chair close to the desk.

"Nothing especially valuable, just some treasured trinkets." Ellen opened a pretty blue lacquer box. Inside was a delicate gold chain with a lovely filigree cross.

"Beautiful," Phoebe said.

"I gave Paul the more valuable pieces to keep in his safe. I hope you will help him choose what to give to Lucy on her birthdays and other special occasions in the years to come."

Phoebe nodded, her eyes prickling. "Of course."

Ellen set her hand over Phoebe's, her fingers like frozen twigs for all that her color was so high. "Thank you so much for agreeing to have a special Christmas with just the four of us, Phoebe. I promise I will not keep you and Paul away from your family for long."

Phoebe gently squeezed Ellen's hand. "I am delighted to have an intimate celebration. But remember that you are more than welcome to join the larger gathering, too."

"Thank you. If I feel well enough, I will."

But Phoebe knew that would not happen, and not just because of Ellen's illness, but because the rest of the Bellamy family still believed that Ellen was Paul's former mistress.

Paul, Phoebe, and Ellen had agreed to maintain the fiction until Lucy turned eighteen, when Paul would tell her the truth about her parentage. Only then would Phoebe tell her sisters the truth.

It was for the best, although it did make matters awkward in the meanwhile.

Unfortunately, Phoebe thought with a painful stab as her friend chattered happily about the small gifts littering the table, Ellen herself would not be around for long to suffer that awkwardness.

Suddenly, the mound of paper and ribbons moved, and a furry head emerged.

"There you are, Silas!" Ellen said, the words scolding but her tone affectionate as the little rodent yawned, strutted across the desk, and then strolled up Ellen's arm, giving Phoebe a daring look as he snuggled against the sick woman's neck.

Her brother Dauntry's squirrel was a furry bundle of mischief that had plagued Phoebe for years. Lucy had begged to care for the pet while Doddy was away at school and Phoebe had, reluctantly, agreed. Although the little beast often caused havoc when he escaped Ellen's apartment and ran amok in the huge house, Phoebe could not regret his presence for how much joy he gave not only Lucy, but—unexpectedly—Ellen, too. Whenever Silas was near it seemed to Phoebe that the ill woman looked less fragile.

If the squirrel helped keep Ellen alive longer, then Phoebe could almost like the animal.

But as she watched Ellen's pale, shaky hand stroke Silas's thick winter fur, she feared even the squirrel might not be enough to keep her with them until Christmas.

Several days later...

Phoebe stared across the massive desk at her husband Paul and bit her lip to keep from speaking because she was too angry to trust herself. Not angry at Paul, but what her parents were constantly forcing him to do.

"Don't be angry, darling." He smiled at her, his rugged features irresistible and charming. It still astounded her that they had been married less than a year. In fact, she had not even known him last Christmastime and yet now she could not imagine life without him.

"I'm not angry at you, Paul. I just wonder when it will all stop." She did not mention how ashamed she was of her parents—she had admitted that to him times beyond counting—because she knew it distressed him. Any person who looked at Paul Needham's massive body and harsh-featured face would not believe he could be so sensitive. But he lived and breathed for her and Phoebe would never stop thanking God that she had been fortunate enough to meet him in a dusty lane last spring.

The source of her chagrin was a letter Paul had received from Phoebe's father, the Earl of Addiscombe, just that morning. Not only had the earl cancelled his plans to spend Christmas with them—the letter arriving the very day he was supposed to arrive—but included with the brief missive was a sheaf of bills.

Paul removed his spectacles and tossed them onto the desk before pushing his chair out from his desk and striding toward the door.

Phoebe twisted in her chair and watched as he locked the door.

Her lips parted and her heart began to beat faster as he strode back to his chair and sat. "Come here," he said.

"Paul, we can't. It is too—"

"Come here, Phoebe." He patted his massive buckskin clad thigh with an equally massive hand.

Phoebe bit her lip, barely hesitating before heaving herself to her feet. Even before she'd become pregnant, she had not been a petite woman. Now that she was eating for two, she felt like a lumbering cow.

Or at least she would have felt that way if not for the adoring, lustful gaze in her husband's eyes as she lowered herself onto his lap.

"*Mmm.*" He wrapped one muscular arm around her hips to draw her closer to the hard wall of his chest while his other hand came to rest on her swollen belly.

21

Phoebe loved the look of masculine pride that stole over his face.

"Mine," he murmured, stroking from her bulging midriff up to her ridiculously swollen breasts. His lids lowered over his penetrating gray eyes as he palmed her, his huge hand actually making her look small. "How long did the midwife say we could keep—"

"As long as it does not hurt," Phoebe hastily interrupted, before he could say something vulgar and wildly arousing. After all, they were expecting the first of their Christmas guests within the next few hours. It would not do to give in to her body's relentless demands for him in the middle of the day, no matter how much she might like to do so.

She glanced at the long-case clock, calculating the hours before she could feel his bare skin and huge body pressed against her own.

Paul grinned at her, fully aware of the thoughts running through her mind. "Well?" he taunted.

"We don't have time," she said, unable to keep the whiny disappointment from her tone. "By the time we make our way up—"

"We don't need to go up to your chambers. We don't even need to get undressed. I could just slide my hand beneath this pretty gown," he demonstrated exactly that, his warm fingers caressing up her stocking-clad calf to her bare thigh. "Open for me, Phoebe," he said, his voice gruff with desire.

Her gaze slid to the clock. "Are you sure we—"

"Spread your thighs for me," he said, giving her the stern look that turned her knees to jelly, his dark eyes capturing hers. She swallowed and slowly spread her knees.

His nostrils flared as his hand stroked up her thigh until one big finger encountered the lips of her sex. His eyelids fluttered when he felt how swollen and wet she was. "Good God! You are drenched," he accused, dipping his finger into her slick heat as he looked up to meet her gaze. "You poor needy darling," he said, circling the source of her pleasure with just the perfect amount of pressure. "You need to come, don't you?"

She widened her eyes at him. *"Paul."*

He grinned smugly at her outraged reaction. Even though they had been married for nine months, his vulgar words still made her face heat.

And she loved it.

"Can you feel how hard you make me, Phoebe?" he asked, shifting beneath her.

"As if anyone could miss *that*," she muttered as a thick, iron-hard ridge dug into her fleshy bottom.

He laughed. And then, before she knew what he was doing, his hand slid out from beneath her skirt and he took her by the hips and lifted her onto his desk as if she weighed no more than a book, making Phoebe fall even more in love with him.

"You should not lift me like that! You are going to hurt yourself."

He made a scoffing sound and shoved up her skirt and petticoat, baring her to her hips.

"Where are Dixon and Dennehy?" she asked nervously. "They aren't going to—"

"Open for me," he barked.

Her knees instantly jerked apart. Irked at her body's reaction, she began to close them again.

"*Uh, uh, uh.* I don't think so, darling." He easily pushed her thighs apart. "Lie back for your lord and master."

"I am serious, Paul. They have keys, do they not? Are they going to—"

His eyes, now a dark, hungry slate gray, snapped from her sex to her eyes. "Lie back, or I will summon them both here to watch while I strip you naked and pleasure you right here on my desk."

Phoebe's jaw sagged at the vulgar suggestion—and not only with surprise, either.

"Why, you naughty thing!" he teased, reading her fiery blush and guilty look with an ease that both disconcerted and aroused her. "That made your tight little pussy clench, didn't it? You would like to be watched while I licked and fingered and fu—"

"I would *not*," she insisted, mortified.

His grin disappeared and the dangerous look that replaced it made her shiver. "Good. Because I won't share you. Ever. And I will kill any man before allowing him to look at what belongs to me."

Was it wrong that his violent, primitive words made her sex clench and throb even harder?

"Now," he said, his voice silky. "I am only going to say this one more time. Lie down."

She swallowed and then carefully complied, feeling incredibly exposed as he pulled her to the edge of the desk and proceeded to drape one leg over each of his shoulders.

"Paul—"

"Hush," he ordered.

Phoebe bit her lip to keep from making embarrassing noises when he spread her lower lips and his hot, wet mouth closed over her sex.

"Oh, God," she muttered. How could something so naughty feel so very, very, very good?

He groaned, noisily licking and sucking as if he would consume her. "Your juicy, delicious cunt is going to be the death of me one of these days."

"Paul!"

He ignored her exclamation and clamped her legs tighter with his arms to stop her squirming, burying his tongue deep inside her, the warm pad of his thumb rhythmically stroking her engorged nub in exactly the right place.

All plans to remain silent flew out the window the moment the coiled bliss inside her exploded. She was vaguely aware of loud, animalistic cries—hers—and the feel of his hair between her fingers as she first ground against him and then, after her climax began to ebb—tried, and failed—to pull his head away.

"Paul! It's too much," she whimpered.

"Just once more." He lightly sucked her throbbing peak between his lips.

Phoebe had thought she was too sensitive—painfully so—to climax again, but he proved yet again that he knew her body far better than she ever would.

When she was quivering and limp from her second orgasm she tried to close her thighs, but he easily held her open.

"I won't touch anything sensitive," he promised between licks. "I just want to make sure I didn't miss anything." He was as good as his word as he carefully, and thoroughly, laved and kissed every part of her. "So good," he murmured, his tongue lightly probing the entrance to her body. And then he groaned and plunged deeper.

Phoebe's face was on fire as he feasted on her. She considered trying to get up but knew he would not release her until he was good and ready. In fact, any sign of resistance only made him dig in.

Besides…she *loved* this part, when he worshipped her body, which he—inexplicably—continued to be obsessed with. Indeed, he seemed to want her more, despite how horribly ungainly she'd become.

Her lips curved into what she was sure was a fatuous smile and she gave herself up to the bliss of the moment.

An indeterminate time later he heaved a reluctant sigh, gave the source of her pleasure one last, lingering, sucking kiss and then gently lowered her legs before standing. "I would do this all day—if not for the fact that I have a blasted meeting with Bixby and I've not read over his report yet." Bixby was his man of business who'd come all the way from London, otherwise she suspected Paul would have made the poor man wait.

He smiled down at her, his lips red and swollen from his labors. "Did I hurt your hips?" he asked when she brought her knees together and winced.

"It was worth it," she said as she straightened her skirts.

He laughed and then strode to the door and unlocked it before returning and slipping his arms beneath her and returning to his chair, holding her cradled in his lap.

"There, you see? You have pleased your husband greatly and nobody is the wiser." He lifted her close enough to kiss her, a faint, musky scent lingering on his lips.

"You like tasting yourself on me, don't you?"

Predictably, she blushed.

He chuckled smugly, kissed her hard, and then leaned back in his chair, wincing as he adjusted the long, hard ridge that was jammed into her hip.

Phoebe slid a hand between their bodies and lightly squeezed the thick bulge. "May I help you with this, my lord?"

His eyes kindled and she could see he was seriously considering it. But, after a moment, he sighed and shook his head. "Unfortunately, there is no time. But rest assured that I will save it for you."

"Save it?" she asked with a wide-eyed look, continuing her stroking, purposely goading him because she loved it when he was filthy, no matter how much it shocked her.

"I am saving it for tonight, when you will beg for every inch." His gaze flickered to her mouth and his eyes narrowed. "I fact, I think you will take me *twice.*"

"Paul!"

He raised a black velvet eyebrow, one of his big hands suggestively stroking the crease between her buttocks, a thick finger pressing against that most taboo part of her. "Perhaps even three times."

Phoebe gasped. They had done *that* on only two occasions, and she had, to her intense astonishment and mortification, enjoyed it.

"My wicked wife," he said, chuckling at whatever he saw on her scarlet face—probably her unladylike eagerness—and kissed her hard, taking her hand by the wrist and firmly removing it from his manhood. "Behave."

"I thought I *was* behaving?" she said, pouting.

He kissed her again. "What a little monster I've created."

"Ugh. Not so *little*." She shifted uncomfortably and glared at her bulging midsection.

He took her chin and tilted her to face him, his expression unexpectedly stern and even more domineering than usual. "As it happens, I love your body."

Phoebe's breathing quickened beneath his piercing gaze, and she couldn't look away.

His eyelids lowered slightly, and he set his free hand on her belly and caressed her, a slow, sensual smile spreading across his face. "I intend to put you in this condition as often as is safe for you."

"*Paul!*"

He kissed her lingeringly. "You don't know that you are perfect, do you?"

She gave a scoffing laugh. "You are the only one who thinks so."

"I am the only one who matters."

"Yes, you are," she agreed, caressing his jaw, the love she felt for him so overwhelming it sometimes scared her.

He was leaning down to kiss her again when the library door banged open.

Both their heads whipped up.

"Papa?"

Phoebe clambered off her husband's lap—or at least tried to, but Paul kept her in place easily with one arm.

"Oh, I'm sorry—I didn't realize you weren't alone," Lucy said. "I can come back later and—"

"You did not interrupt anything," Phoebe lied.

"Come and sit." Paul gestured to the chair that Phoebe had briefly occupied.

Phoebe tried to get up, but Paul continued to hold her.

Lucy did not appear to find it odd that Phoebe was sitting on Paul's lap. As usual, Silas's glittering black eyes peeked out from the curtain of Lucy's curly blonde hair.

"Did you need something, sweetheart?" Paul asked his daughter.

"Miss Capshaw wants me to go into the village with her, but—" she broke off and slid Phoebe a shy look. "But I didn't want to miss Doddy's arrival—because Silas is so excited and misses him," she added, blushing fierily. "Do you know what time he might get here?"

"Not until much later, sweetheart," Paul assured her. "You can go with your governess and still be home in time to meet his carriage."

"Oh, good. Miss Capshaw is taking me for my last fitting." She turned to Phoebe. "It is the pale pink gown, Phoebe—the one you suggested—and it will be ready just in time for the Christmas fete."

"Excellent! It is perfect for your first dance," Phoebe said.

Although Lucy was not yet fourteen, she would not be the only one her age at the dance, which was part of the annual village Christmas celebration and occurred early enough in the day to be more of a family gathering than a traditional assembly.

"Miss Capshaw said that I must ask you whether I could purchase proper gloves, Papa." Lucy's huge blue eyes, so much like Ellen's, fixed on Paul. "Please," she added softly.

"Proper gloves?" Paul repeated, obviously confused.

"Yes—long ones. The sort ladies wear to balls."

"Oh." He frowned. "I am not sure—"

"Please, Papa," she wheedled.

Paul turned to Phoebe. "What do you think?"

"It is true that she is young, but you will be there. I think, under the circumstances, it would be unexceptionable."

Paul nodded. "You may have them."

"Huzzah!" Lucy leapt to her feet. "I had better go and find Miss Capshaw. The sooner we leave, the sooner we can return." She darted from the room in such haste that the two of them chuckled.

Paul sighed. "One minute she is wanting gloves like a young lady, the next she is still a child." He raised his eyebrows. "I trust you know that it is not reuniting your brother with his squirrel that is making her blush and smile so much. I am

Phoebe laughed. But her laughter dried up faster than a drop of water on a hot stove when Arnold—one of her favorite footmen—opened the massive metal-strapped door and her mother's voice pierced the chill December air like a cutlass through flesh.

"—what could you have been thinking to leave behind that bag, Martin?"

"I'm so sorry, my lady, I thought—"

"I am sure that I do not care about your addled mental processes. Just fetch the bag. *Right now.*"

Phoebe took a deep breath, fixed a smile on her face, and stepped out into the frosty air to greet the first of her guests.

"Mama," she said, hurrying through the chill afternoon to embrace her mother. "I am so sorry nobody was out here to meet you. We thought—"

"Phoebe!" her mother shrieked. "What in the *world* are you doing outside looking like that?"

"Uh—"

"You are as big as a house!" The countess's gaze slewed left and then right. "What if somebody were to see you in such a condition? Get inside *immedia*—"

"Mama." Phoebe spoke the word quietly but firmly. "I am not hiding myself away because I am pregnant"—her mother hissed at the word, as if it were a vile curse, but Phoebe ignored it. "You had best become accustomed to my presence in public over the coming days."

The countess blinked, for once at a loss for words.

"You must be chilled to the bone, Mama." Phoebe gestured for the footman to bring the fur cloak. The servant hurried over and draped the luxurious garment over her mother's shoulders. The countess eyed the costly cloak as if it were a live animal. For a moment Phoebe thought her mother would reject the thoughtful gesture.

Instead, she pursed her lips into a sour scowl and then strode toward the foyer without a word of thanks.

Phoebe turned and saw a slight figure hurrying toward them, laden with baggage. At first she thought her mother had brought a girl, the person was so small. But as she came closer Phoebe realized she was a full-grown woman. She was even shorter than she first appeared given that her head was piled with masses and masses of dark brown hair.

"Welcome, Miss Martin," Phoebe said, having to look down—albeit not by much—to smile at the other woman.

"Thank you," she said in a breathy voice.

Arnold reached for the bags in her hands. "Let me take those, Miss."

Miss Martin opened her mouth, but before she could speak the countess barked, "Do not touch that!" She jabbed a finger at the smaller of the two valises. "It contains delicate items, and I don't want a clumsy oaf dropping it. *You* carry that one, Martin. Come along now, quit dawdling."

"Yes, my lady," Miss Martin said, giving Phoebe a shy smile and deep curtsey before hurrying after her mistress.

"I will show you to your rooms," Phoebe murmured, her face hot with shame at the way her mother had spoken to the obviously genteel young woman.

The countess's head swiveled from side to side as Phoebe led her through the massive entry hall.

"*Hmmph*," she muttered as they ascended the main staircase, which had been built in the late thirteen hundreds. "I see that *some*thing has been done about the wood rot." Her words might have been taken as a compliment if her tone had not been so reproachful.

"Needham found woodworkers who'd done work on the great cathedral in York, and they recreated several new sections," Phoebe said. The amount of money her husband had spent on Wych House continued to flabbergast her. Especially considering they were only leasing the house while their own was being constructed a few miles away.

As if her mother had read her thoughts, she said, "I saw the monstrosity Needham is having built."

Stay calm, Phoebe counseled herself.

"But your route from Bath should not have taken you past Needham Park."

"*Needham Park*," her mother repeated with a snide huff. "It looked to have at least fifty rooms."

"There are seventy-one," Phoebe corrected.

The countess scowled. "You are determined to make spectacles of yourselves."

Phoebe smiled serenely, refusing to be drawn.

"I see you are taking me to the east wing," her mother said when Phoebe did not respond. "I do hope Needham has had the sense to fix that wretched draught that howls down the corridor."

"Indeed, he has. I think you will be pleased." Although Phoebe doubted it. Had she ever seen her mother pleased about anything? If she had, she could not remember it.

"*Hmph*," the countess muttered.

Phoebe's smile frayed around the edges. It was going to be a long day.

***

Stacia smiled as she looked around the luxurious suite of rooms. "This is lovely, my lady."

"I am pleased you like it," Lady Needham replied, her good-humored smile so different from any expression that Stacia had ever seen on the countess's face that she might not have believed the two women were related, if not for the physical resemblance.

"Blue is my favorite color," Stacia blurted like a fool.

"It is my husband's, too," the viscountess admitted. "Whenever I was at a standstill when it came to the decoration of yet another suite of rooms and consulted him, his suggestion was invariably *make it blue*." She chuckled. "So there are at least ten blue bedchambers, which makes it difficult to decide which one of them is the real *blue suite*."

Stacia felt her face creasing into an expression that hadn't happened very often of late: a genuine smile.

"I have assigned a maid to you—Dora is her name—so please do feel free to call on her services."

"Thank you, my lady. That is most generous."

"If you need anything, please don't hesitate to—" She stopped when Miss Ackers, the countess's maid, appeared in the doorway.

The older woman curtsied to the viscountess. "I beg your pardon, my lady, but Lady Addiscombe wants Miss Martin." She cleared her throat and added, "Immediately."

"Oh." Lady Needham looked nonplussed.

"Thank you, Miss Ackers. I will be right there," Stacia murmured and then turned to her hostess. "I am sorry to run off, but—"

"It is wise not to keep my mother waiting. We shall all assemble in the drawing room a half hour before dinner. I shall see you there, if not before."

Stacia waited until the other woman had left the room before untying her cloak, stripping off her gloves and bonnet, and then hurrying toward the suite where they had left her ladyship a mere five minutes earlier.

Just because her hostess had put Stacia into a guest room and was treating her like a guest did not mean she *was* a guest.

Stacia was there to serve Lady Addiscombe, and she would do well not to forget that.

Season. "I cannot resist teasing them. Shelton is so accustomed to being feted and worshipped everywhere he goes that he cannot see that he is being tweaked. As for Fowler?" Katie rolled her eyes. "I think Doddy probably knows more about the opposite sex than poor Angus."

Hy suspected that Katie was right on both counts. Still, it had unnerved her that her sister's assessment had been so succinct and mature. Certainly, more astute than anything Hy could have come up with.

Even though she'd not understood Katie's motivations, she'd been relieved by her answer and had passed it along to Sylvester.

"Oh, poor, poor Drew," he'd said, once he had stopped laughing. "I almost feel sorry for him."

Hy had begun to agree with her husband as the weeks had passed. Her little sister was devious and made the two men suffer in endlessly ingenious ways. She seemed to know exactly what taunts would incite them to behave like idiots. The three squabbled, fought, and wagered like a trio of adolescents.

Even Hy, who did not possess much of a sense of humor, could not help being diverted by some of Katie's antics. She felt a twisted sort of pride in how easily her seventeen-year-old sister consistently bested the two seasoned *ton* veterans.

One of the main reasons she had agreed with Sylvester when he had suggested bringing Shelton to Wych House for the Christmas holiday was because she didn't think the man deserved weeks of peace and quiet away from Katie.

She still didn't trust Shelton, but he was Sylvester's only close family aside from his horrid mother and the men had once been as close as brothers. Sylvester believed with all his heart that Shelton could still be salvaged.

Hy was not sure she agreed, but she loved her husband fiercely, and if having Shelton along made Sylvester happy, then tolerating the handsome rake's presence was a small enough price to pay.

***

Outside the Duke of Chatham's Coach...

Andrew shivered as a chill wind cut through his heavy layers of clothing. The journey had been a frigid one, the weather uncharacteristically cold even for December. The sky was a relentless slate gray, and the sun burned sullenly, unable to penetrate the leaden clouds and offer any warmth.

Their ducal cavalcade of three coaches and six outriders—including Andrew and his cousin—was drawing ever closer to the ancestral home of the Bellamy family. With every mile that passed the unease in his belly grew stronger.

He had been a fool to accompany Sylvester, his duchess—a woman who hated Andrew, and rightfully so—and the duchess's pestersome little sister to their family's country house to spend Christmas.

But Sylvester, who appeared to be so mellowed by marriage as to have gone soft in the head, had engaged in underhanded dealing to force Andrew's compliance.

"You are my only close family, Drew, and I would like to spend Christmas with you. We have not done so in years, and I have greatly missed you. Surely you yearn for those long-ago celebrations when we were lads as much as I do?"

Andrew had been alternately shamed, embarrassed, and pleased by his cousin's candid affection. And also nearly reduced to tears.

He had attempted to conceal his emotional response by quipping, "Your mother is family and *she* is not going." When Sylvester had merely raised an eyebrow, Andrew had felt a genuine stab of alarm. "Good God, Sylvester! The Dowager is not accompanying us, is she?"

The duke had laughed. "How easily you snapped at my bait, Drew. No wonder Kathryn enjoys teasing you so much. I think you have forgotten that my mother despises me even more than she does you."

Andrew hadn't forgotten because the Dowager Duchess of Chatham had given them all—Sylvester, Andrew, the new duchess, Kathryn, and that fool Fowler, as well as all the servants and neighbors—daily proof of what a disappointment her son was to her. It was bloody irksome to sit by and watch the Dowager insult Sylvester in every imaginable way.

But it had been amusing to see how Sylvester had *not* permitted his mother to engage in the same belittling behavior toward his new wife. Indeed, it was the first time Andrew had seen actual anger flare in his cousin's eyes. And that was an emotion he had been trying to goad out of Sylvester for eleven years.

"Not only will it be good to spend time together, but it will give you an opportunity to begin mending the breach between you and Lady Shaftsbury."

Ha! A breach. More like a canyon.

And yet here Andrew was, quickly approaching the ancestral home of a woman he'd wronged terribly. Even though his abduction of Selina Bellamy had led to her meeting her husband—a marriage that was evidently a love match—that still didn't excuse his cruel behavior.

Andrew felt the telltale prickle of somebody watching him and turned toward the coach. He immediately regretted the impulse when he met the malicious green gaze of the duchess's fiendish sister.

Kathryn smirked, puckered her lips as if she were blowing him a kiss, and then winked.

Andrew was annoyed when his face heated. He scowled at the little monster and swiftly looked away.

Christ! How could he constantly be unmanned by a seventeen-year-old country chit?

He was nearing five-and-thirty years of age and yet he found himself *incessantly* lured into arguments and wagers and competitions with the little viper. Even worse was the fact that he had lost almost every single argument or verbal joust with the maddening hellion, who possessed the olfactory senses of a bloodhound, tracking him down no matter where he had hidden on his cousin's vast estate.

The only consolation—and it was slight—was that she tormented Sylvester's blockheaded best friend Baron Angus Fowler just as relentlessly.

Unfortunately, Fowler would not be at Wych House to draw the redheaded witch's fire for the next few weeks. Chatham had invited the man, but Fowler had wisely rejected Sylvester's offer and scuttled home to Scotland with some pitiful excuse of spending Christmas with his own family.

The coward.

Andrew sighed.

"Why the heavy sigh?" Sylvester asked.

"No reason," he lied, shifting in his saddle with a grimace. His arse had become accustomed to easy living after months of luxury at Chatham's. This was the first ride of any duration he'd had since the summer.

Andrew had been a soldier for more than eight years, which had meant living in the saddle. Even after he'd sold his commission and returned to England he'd rarely stayed put for more than a few weeks. In fact, Andrew couldn't recall the last time he'd remained in the same place so long.

It was back during those heavenly, and eventually hellish, few weeks with Mariah.

He hastily shoved away the unwanted memory and turned to Chatham. "How much farth—"

The sound of the carriage window sliding open interrupted his question and he and Sylvester turned as Kathryn thrust her gloved hand out the opening and pointed. "There is Queen's Bower."

Both she and the duchess were staring at a small manor house in the distance. Kathryn was always beautiful, but right then—with a wistful, fond smile on her face—she was breathtaking.

Andrew thought it might have been the first time he'd seen her look genuinely happy. As frequently as she laughed or smiled there was always a brittleness to both. He had always thought her high spirits were youthful enthusiasm, but now he wondered if there wasn't something a bit... desperate about her behavior.

Before he could ponder the matter any further, the carriage rounded a gentle curve.

"And there is Wych House," the duchess said.

Like her younger sister, Her Grace sounded different. Excited, Andrew decided, although it was so subtle that it would probably evade the notice of a person who hadn't lived the last few months in the same house with her.

Sylvester's new wife was not a conventionally attractive woman, but there was a strength of character in her face that made a person look twice. Her pale green eyes were brilliant even in the weak winter sun, the shade of green as close to peridot as he had ever seen.

She cut him a glance, as if feeling his gaze, and Andrew quickly turned to look at the building they were approaching.

He was no stranger to magnificent houses. Not only had he grown up at Chatham Park, but his own property—Rosewood—was an ancient, if ramshackle estate that was grand enough, at least from a distance, to rob a person of breath.

But Wych House, a rare example of Gothic architecture that wasn't a church or monastery, was quite something else. Like York Minster, Wych House had been built in a style commonly referred to as Perpendicular Gothic. The long, gently curving drive made the most of the structure's four-centered arches, buttresses, and towers. There was even a grand rose window set in a pointed arch with tracery.

"The South Tower has a new roof and is no longer boarded up," the duchess said in a wondering tone. "They must be brand new as the old lozenge windows had all but rotted away."

"And it will all be for Doddy," Kathryn added, awed.

Andrew had heard that Viscount Paul Needham, who'd married Phoebe Bellamy, was one of the wealthiest men in Britain. The man must have deep pockets indeed if he was able to pour thousands of pounds into a house he was only leasing. Kathryn was correct: Lord Dauntry Bellamy—Doddy as his sisters called him—was the heir to the Addiscombe earldom and would one day benefit from all the money his wealthy brother-in-law was spending on Wych House.

"I would like to see the house Needham is building," Sylvester said, turning to his wife. "Is it far from here?"

39

"Less than five miles. We must ride over and see it," Her Grace answered, her voice eager.

Andrew knew the duchess hated going anywhere in a carriage when she could be on horseback. She was only sacrificing her pleasure on this journey because Sylvester had put his foot down. The tall, gangly woman was several months pregnant—although it was difficult to tell just looking at her—and his cousin was already hovering and fussing around her like a mother hen with one chick.

It was nauseating.

You're just jealous.

Andrew didn't bother to deny it. Who would *not* be jealous of such deep affection—nay, such *love*?

Servants were already milling around two carriages and footmen were bearing valises and trunks into the house when Sylvester's retinue rolled up.

A *very* pregnant woman waddled down the terraced flagstone steps, smiling broadly, one hand waving wildly while the other supported a belly that looked large enough for twins.

"Katie! Hy!"

"Pheeb!" Kathryn shrieked, the door to the carriage flying open before it had even come to a halt.

"Damnation, Hyacinth!" the duke barked when it looked as if his wife might vault out after her younger sister. "You will wait for the steps to be let down," he commanded, using his *ducal* voice.

To Andrew's astonished amusement the duchess meekly obeyed her husband, waiting until he could help her from the coach before hurrying to join her siblings.

Kathryn flung herself into the arms of the very pregnant Lady Needham hard enough to make Andrew wince.

But the viscountess just laughed. "Katie! Where has my scruffy little sister gone? Who is this grand, elegant woman who has replaced her?"

Choked sobs answered her and Andrew looked away, unexpectedly moved by the obvious love between the siblings.

There it was again: *love*.

Andrew sighed and slid from his mount. He stretched his aching muscles and stayed back from the flurry of activity, feeling distinctly *de trop* as Sylvester greeted not only his new sister-in-law, but also her husband, Viscount Needham, a tall, powerfully built man who came out of the house trailed by a golden-haired, blue-eyed stripling who looked so much like Selina Bellamy that he could only be the heir, Dauntry Bellamy.

Behind the young viscount trailed a girl a few years younger. Andrew knew that Kathryn was the youngest Bellamy sister so this must be one of the other guests.

"Might I take him, sir?"

Andrew turned from the joyous reunion to find a groom politely waiting for Drake's reins.

"Ah, yes, thank you. Give him an extra helping of oats," he said, flipping the servant a coin that earned him a smile.

Andrew was just wondering if he could sneak past the cluster of embracing, laughing, crying Bellamy siblings when the sound of approaching carriage wheels made him turn.

Another grand coach, as large as Sylvester's, was rolling toward them. The postilions and outriders wore black and silver livery and the team of six pale gray horses was as well-matched as any Andrew had ever seen.

Unease uncoiled in his belly as the coach neared. It had to contain one of the only two Bellamy siblings not currently squealing and hugging on the steps.

He swallowed as the carriage approached, his gaze flickering over the massive black lacquered equipage in search of an escutcheon.

But his eyes stopped dead in their tracks when they met a pair of celestial blue orbs in a face that could probably have launched a thousand ships, had Lady Selina Bellamy ever cared to engage in naval warfare.

As the coach rolled to a smooth stop the new Marchioness of Shaftsbury locked gazes with Andrew, her full, shapely lips pulling into a wry smile that made Andrew's ears burn.

He sighed and strode toward her carriage, motioning the footman aside and opening the door himself.

It was time to face the music.

Chapter 3

Andrew was just finishing dressing when there was a light knock on the door.

"Come in," he called out, giving his cravat one last tweak.

The door opened and Sylvester strode into his room. "I am glad I caught you before you went down."

"Are you doing reconnaissance for your wife?" Andrew teased, turning away from the looking glass and picking up his tailcoat.

Sylvester chuckled as he came up behind Andrew and helped him into the snugly tailored garment. "It is true that Hyacinth is very curious about how your conversation with Lady Shaftsbury went—so is Kathryn. So am I," the duke added, and then flicked a piece of lint off Andrew's shoulder before stepping back. "I do wish you would engage a valet, Drew. You know I will gladly pay."

"While I appreciate your offer, I must yet again respectfully decline. I'm already so far in debt to you that I will never dig my way out," Andrew said, slipping on his father's signet ring before turning to his cousin. "Besides," he added with a slight smile, "if I engage a valet then I won't be able to crow that I have a duke waiting on me hand and foot."

Sylvester rolled his eyes.

Andrew strode toward the door. "As for my meeting with Lady Shaftsbury, I am afraid you are precipitate," he said, opening the door for the duke and then following him out of the room. "She gave me short shrift earlier, informing me that she was too busy to waste time on me. I am on my way to her and Shaftsbury's chambers to have the momentous summit now."

Sylvester nodded but said nothing as they strode down a magnificent corridor that boasted pointed transverse arches soaring overhead.

"This is spectacular," Andrew said, his voice hushed, as though he were in a church.

"Hyacinth told me the entire south wing of the house had been a ruin the last time she saw it. Needham has evidently brought tradesmen from all over Europe to have the house ready by Christmas, sinking a fortune into the place."

"From what I've heard the man has a fortune and more to spare."

Sylvester's mouth pulled down on the side that was not rendered too stiff by the huge scar, his expression pensive. "It is true he is wealthy. But he has already done more than his fair share for the family."

Andrew groaned. "I know that look, Sylvester. Please tell me you aren't planning to take on part of the Bellamy burden?"

"Needham has been bearing the burden of Papa and Mama Addiscombe for half a year. They have four married daughters now; it only seems fair that the rest of us should shoulder our share."

"Four married daughters? But I thought the one working up in Scotland was unmarried?"

"Ah, you did not come for tea earlier, so you missed it."

"Missed what?" Andrew had gone directly to his chambers rather than join the family reunion. The last thing the Bellamy siblings needed was their sister's abductor taking tea with them.

"Lady Aurelia arrived."

"She was not expected?"

"Her brother and sisters believed she was not coming. Only Needham and his wife knew." Sylvester smiled slyly. "And she did not arrive alone, either."

"I can see you are almost bursting with news."

"She is now Lady Crewe and came with her husband, his daughter from his prior marriage, and two other guests."

"Crewe?" Andrew repeated, frowning. "Lord!" he said as he matched a face to the name. "You don't mean—"

"Yes, it is the same Crewe you are thinking of. Indeed, the only one I know of."

"This has to be his third or fourth marriage. I thought he was half dead from being mauled by a tiger?"

"It is his third marriage, and it was a panther." Sylvester reached up and stroked the savage scar on his own cheek, the gesture unconscious. "He is badly scarred, and not just on his face, but appears recovered."

Andrew recalled Crewe from years gone by. The man had a reputation for raking that did not equal Andrew's, of course, but he was a near rival. Or at least he had been. Andrew had not seen Crewe in ages.

He turned to his cousin, leaving aside the matter of the sudden marriage, and returning to the subject of Papa Bellamy and who should frank his expensive lifestyle. "You, Shaftsbury, and Crewe might be downy, but none of you can hold a candle to Needham's wealth."

"Thank you so much for pointing what an impoverished beggar I am."

Andrew smiled. "Now you know what it feels like to be compared and found wanting. And no, you have never made me feel like an impoverished beggar. I did that to myself." He stopped and frowned at the green and gilt door in front of him. And then he strode back down the corridor to the door he had just passed, which was scarlet and gilt. "This is where we must part ways, Sylvester."

The duke gave him a look of sympathy. "Er, do you know what you are going to say?"

"I am going to beg her forgiveness and grovel."

"That seems an excellent plan. Come find me in the billiards room when you are done."

"I will if Shaftsbury leaves me walking and talking," he said, only partly jesting. He waited until his cousin had disappeared down the stairs before knocking.

The door opened a moment later and Andrew found himself face-to-face with the Marquess of Shaftsbury himself rather than a servant.

The older man smiled. "Good evening, Shelton."

"Er, Shaftsbury," he said, sounding like an idiot. Andrew didn't know why he was so stunned that a blind man would answer his own door. "I suppose your wife told you I was coming?"

"No."

"Then how did you know it was me?"

"I recognized your smell."

Andrew's jaw sagged.

A squawky laugh that Andrew remembered well came from somewhere behind the marquess. "Caius, are you tormenting my guest?"

"No, that is your job, my dear. I am just teasing him a little." Shaftsbury's lips tilted up on one side. "It has been a long, long time, Shelton. I think you must have been ten or eleven the last time I saw you."

"Yes. I remember that summer well."

Shaftsbury's smile turned into a grin. "You used to follow Chatham and me around like a lovelorn chit."

"Thank you for reminding me."

The marquess threw back his head and laughed.

Andrew had expected the other man to call him out for what he'd done to his wife. He supposed mockery was better than being punched in the face. Although it was a near thing.

As if reading his thoughts, the humor drained from the marquess's face and he stopped chuckling, leaned closer, and hissed, "I can't bring myself to hate you since your caddish actions brought Selina into my life." He lowered his voice even more. "You behaved like a scoundrel, Shelton. If this wasn't a family get together and I wasn't in another man's house—and if I had not promised my wife that I would behave—then I would be sorely tempted to kick your arse for you."

Andrew swallowed at the menace in the other man's voice, pinioned by the intensity in his sightless silver-gray eyes.

"I deeply regret my behavior, Shaftsbury." He hesitated, and then added, "I am only grateful that something good came out of it."

"No thanks to *you*," the other man retorted.

"No thanks to me," Andrew agreed.

The marquess hesitated for a long moment before taking a step back. "You might as well come in," he said, his gaze fixed somewhere over Andrew's shoulder. "I hope you have a taste for crow, Shelton."

"I have come prepared to dine, Shaftsbury."

The marquess snorted and Andrew entered a suite that was far grander than his own. The fireplace was almost as tall as he was, the high, coffered ceiling glinting with gold.

As spectacular as the trappings were, they were still eclipsed by the woman who occupied the room. Like a priceless jewel on a magnificent crown, Lady Shaftsbury sat in the middle of a gold brocade settee. Her delft blue eyes were cold and distant.

Heat surged up Andrew's neck at her scathing look.

The marquess made his way to the settee with the use of his cane and lowered himself beside his wife, who continued to stare at Andrew, keeping him standing like a supplicant for at least a minute before saying, "Lord Shelton."

Andrew was impressed by how much scorn she could inject into just two words. As he studied her beautiful face, he realized she wasn't the same soft kitten he'd abducted last summer. She had been a girl—regardless of the fact that she'd been at least twenty—last Season. Now she was all woman and had fully come into her own. Andrew doubted he would have meddled with *this* woman if he'd met her last spring.

Lady Shaftsbury inclined her head. "Have a seat, Shelton."

Andrew flipped back his coat tails before lowering into the big armchair across from the couple, not sure whether he should be flattered or alarmed that she was allowing him to sit rather than kneel.

"I was astounded when my sister wrote to me about you coming to my family's home for Christmas."

He'd not believed his face could get hotter, but the cool mockery in her tone made him feel an inch tall. "You were not the only one astounded," he admitted, smiling wryly.

She merely stared, unmoved by his attempt at humor.

Andrew discarded any hope of charming her. "In the main, I came here because my cousin asked me to. But I also came because I wanted to see you; to apologize to your face for the wrong I did you." When he paused, she gave a slight gesture for him to continue. "I am profoundly grateful that you were not irreparably damaged by my actions. I don't expect your forgiveness. You have already been more than generous just giving me this hearing and I thank you for that." Andrew stood. "I won't take any more of your time." He nodded at the marquess, recalled the man couldn't see and murmured a quiet, "My lord," and then turned on his heel.

"Lord Shelton." He had just reached for the door handle when her voice stopped him.

He forced himself to turn. "Yes, my lady?"

"I stopped being mad at you a long time ago, right after I met Shaftsbury for the first time." Her expression softened as she reached over and took her husband's far larger hand, entwining their fingers. Her lips suddenly quirked into a mischievous smile, this one more like the innocent young woman he'd known before. "Perhaps it wasn't the *first* time I met him, but surely by the third or fourth."

Shaftsbury laughed. "Thank you, my dear." He lifted his wife's hand to his lips, the love on his face so raw that Andrew felt shaken.

He jerked his gaze away from the other man and inclined his head to the marchioness. "Thank you. You are very generous, my lady. Far more than I deserve."

"I have one question, Lord Shelton."

"Of course."

"If the duke had not fallen in with your plans, would you have abandoned me like you did Miss Sarah Creighton?"

Her soft words were like a knife to his belly. And not entirely unexpected, nor undeserved.

46

"It was my plan that we would marry regardless of what happened, my lady."

She held his gaze for a long moment, and then nodded. "I believe you. And I also forgive you."

Andrew gaped, too dumbfounded to do more than say, "Thank you, my lady."

"I forgive you, but I cannot say the same for my family." She paused and then added, "Especially my mother." She gave him a look that was almost pitying. "Lady Addiscombe does not yet know you are here. I am afraid you have a confrontation awaiting you that will be far more unpleasant than this one has been."

Andrew felt like running down to the stables, hopping on Drake, and riding away as fast as his horse would carry him. Instead, he nodded and said, "It is no less than I deserve."

Lady Shaftsbury laughed. "Oh, trust me, my lord, nobody—and I mean *nobody*—deserves my mother's wrath."

***

If Stacia hadn't been hurrying so fast, and not looking where she was going, she would have seen the large man who stepped out of a door right in front of her.

But she *was* hurrying—her mind on her disgruntled employer rather than what she was doing—and so she plowed right into the man, the impact slamming a yelp from her and a low, masculine "*Ooof!*" from her victim.

It was like running into a wall and she bounced back, arms flailing as she struggled to stay upright.

Big hands closed around her upper arms, steadying her.

Stacia craned her neck until she could see the face of her savior.

The world seemed to shift on its axis.

"Steady on," the apparition murmured, his voice like something from a dream. If his hands had not been holding her, her knees would have buckled.

No, it could not be!

She jerked one arm free from his grasp and rubbed her eyes. Hard.

But when she took her hand away, the god-like face still loomed over her. It was a face she'd imagined in her dreams more times than she could count.

It was older now—there were lines fanning out from the corner of his eyes and the perfect bone structure seemed more chiseled, as if he had lost weight—but it was undeniably the man of her fantasies: Lord Andrew Derrick, Marquess of Shelton.

"You!"

The blazing blue eyes blinked and his golden-brown brows descended, his perfect features shifting into a mask of perplexity. "Er, I'm sorry, do we know each other?"

Although she should have expected them, his words were like a slap, and she reeled back a step, her head buzzing and her gaze blurry.

He reached out again to steady her.

"Don't touch me!" she snarled, swatting away his hands.

Shelton jerked back. "I beg your pardon," he said stiffly. "I thought you were going to faint."

He was right, she had been feeling faint. Only her fury had revived her.

Stacia held his gaze, *glaring* with all her might, as if she could force recognition into his beautiful eyes.

But he just regarded her with a look of confusion that was quickly turning to an expression of impatience—as if he had somewhere more important, and interesting, to go.

How…lowering.

"You are not hurt?" he asked brusquely, glancing down the hallway, his attention already somewhere else.

Some things never changed.

"Of course I am not hurt," she retorted, ashamed when the misery that was crippling her leaked into her voice.

Not that Shelton noticed. He gave her a smile that was perfunctory at best and dismissive at worst. It was a smile she was more than familiar with, the sort she had received often. Only a few times had a man looked past her short stature and unfashionable coiffure to the person within.

And Shelton was not one of those men.

Without a second glance, he strode off down the corridor.

Naturally, Stacia turned to watch him, loathing herself as she did so. The familiar hunger—which she had foolishly believed she'd rooted out of her system—gnawed away at her as savagely as ever.

She shook her head in wonder. He was just so unspeakably *gorgeous*, even walking away. He moved with the athletic grace of a man entirely at home in his body. And why shouldn't he be? Who wouldn't like to occupy that body?"

Stacia blushed at the thought, even though nobody else was there and they would not have heard if they had been.

They might not have heard your thoughts, but they would have seen the naked lust on your face clearly enough.

Stacia wanted to argue against the truth of the accusation. After all, what in the world did she know about *lust?* She who had never even kissed a man. And yet as hazy as her desire for him might be, there was no denying the visceral sensation in her belly—and lower—as she all but consumed him with her eyes.

You know exactly what those excruciating, unladylike urges you feel in the middle of the night are. And we both know what you've done to find relief from—

"Shut. Up," she said. And then glanced around to make sure nobody had overheard her.

Stacia might not know what it was she wanted from Shelton, but there was no doubt that she wanted him.

Disgusted with herself, she forcibly pushed and shoved Shelton's image out of her mind and collected her rattled wits. Why was she still slack-jawed, standing in the middle of the corridor while her employer was probably fuming about her lengthy absence?

She hurried back the way she'd been going before she literally ran into the object of her fantasies.

Lady Addiscombe had sent her down to the kitchens to fetch a posset that evidently only the housekeeper at Wych House could make.

"It needs to stew for hours, and I want it to be ready when I come back after dinner," she had explained, even though Stacia had not asked why the countess couldn't just ring for a servant to deliver the message. She had learned over the past seven months that she'd worked for the older woman that it was easier to do what the countess wanted without asking questions.

She scratched softly on the door to Lady Addiscombe's room—one was never to knock—before opening it.

"What in the world *took* you so long, Martin?" the countess demanded as Ackers dressed her hair.

"Er, I got lost, my lady."

Lady Addiscombe fixed her with a piercing, suspicious look before making a loud *hmmph* noise. She scowled at her expression in the looking glass and then slapped away her maid's hands. "Quit fussing, Ackers," she snapped when the other woman attempted to adjust the turquoise velvet and silk turban that complemented her rich chestnut hair.

Miss Ackers cut Stacia a wry look and even gave a slight eyeroll that had Stacia dipping her chin to hide her smile. The countess would be furious if she ever discovered that her employees often shared a laugh or smile at her irritable temper tantrums.

"Come, come, Martin! Don't dawdle." The countess strode toward the door, which Stacia hurried to open for her. "I know my children will meet down there before dinner even though *Lady Needham*"—she sneered as she said the words, her mouth twisting into an ugly pucker that bore an unfortunate resemblance to the back end of a pug— "neglected to impart that information."

Stacia had no response for that. What could she say? That she sympathized with the countess's daughters in wanting a few moments without their mother's critical observations and crushing expectations?

It was difficult to imagine growing up with such a parent. Her own mother had been sweet, vague, and ill for most of the eight years Stacia had known her.

"—that is not something I shall take part in. Martin? *Martin*! Are you paying attention?" The countess stopped in the middle of the corridor and whirled on her.

Too late, Stacia realized she'd missed the first part of her employer's words. "I'm sorry, my lady. I—I'm afraid my mind wandered for a moment." She forced herself to meet the older woman's annoyed gaze.

"Is this too much excitement for you, Martin? Are you overwhelmed? Perhaps eating dinner in the dining room is more than you can manage? I could arrange for a tray to be brought up to your room. Or perhaps you would rather eat in the servants' hall?"

"No, my lady. I'm sorry, I was just trying to memorize the surroundings, so I would not get lost again."

The countess's nostrils flared slightly, as if she smelled a falsehood. Finally, after what felt like a hundred years, she resumed walking. "What I *said*—if you had been listening—was that I have no intention of getting caught up in any after dinner foolishness." She lightly touched her temple with one elegant hand. "I already have a slight headache just *thinking* about the evening ahead. Protracted exposure to my children's boisterous and relentless enthusiasm would only make it worse."

"I understand, my lady." *Why would you want to socialize with your children after not seeing them for half a year? And how appalling that your offspring and their families are exhibiting* boisterous and relentless enthusiasm *so close to Christmas?*

The countess's head whipped around and for one horrifying moment Stacia wondered if the sarcastic words had accidentally slipped out of her mouth.

But the other woman merely gave her a brooding look before saying, "I want you to stay with them when I go up to my chambers."

"Er, you do?" The words were out before she could catch them.

She gave Stacia a withering look and said, in the tone one would use with an imbecile, "You have not heard a word I said, or you would know that I am not only horrified by the presence of Needham's illegitimate spawn in the house, but there is the added aggravation of my oldest daughter's...*entourage*," she spat the last word.

Stacia had been astonished to learn the newly minted Countess of Crewe had brought along not only her husband and his daughter, but her husband's illegitimate son as well as the young man's mother. From the little she had seen the quintet seemed to adore each other.

How bizarre. And fascinating.

"—neither my son, nor Kathryn, associate with either. You will inform me of whatever they are plotting and planning for the upcoming days so that I might quash anything that is inappropriate before it is too late. My daughter Phoebe has all the sense of a toddler when it comes to propriety. *Somebody* must be the voice of sense and reason." The countess's mouth flexed into a petulant frown, the deep furrows in her pale cheeks indicating this expression was habitual.

Stacia felt profoundly sorry for the other woman. Even though she was attractive, healthy, and surrounded by family, Lady Addiscombe was not happy. Indeed, she had not been happy the entire time Stacia had worked for her.

Why was the woman so miserable all the time? Stacia would forfeit years of her life just to have a few more hours with either of her parents. Was there nobody in the world the countess loved or liked? If there was, Stacia had not met them yet.

A footman leapt to open the door to the drawing room and Lady Addiscombe sailed past him without sparing him so much as a glance.

Stacia gave the handsome servant a smile of thanks and hastened after her employer, almost slamming into her when the countess screeched to a halt in front of Lord Shelton. "You!" she accused, unknowingly echoing Stacia's exclamation from earlier.

Lord Shelton's eyes went comically round as Lady Addiscombe leveled an accusatory finger at him. "What on earth are *you* doing here?" she demanded in a voice that could probably be heard in the village.

Shelton's eyes slid right and then left, as if seeking an avenue of escape. When it was apparent there wasn't one, he bowed to the countess and said, "I am—"

"He is a guest in this house, Mama," Lady Needham said, speaking from one of the settees.

Lady Addiscombe's head whipped around and she glared at her daughter. "Have you lost what little sense you once possessed?"

The viscountess looked pained by her mother's words, but not—Stacia couldn't help noticing—especially hurt. "Mama, this is hardly—"

"I know he was living with your sister, but I don't expect any better out of Hyacinth as she has never had the sense to recognize what is proper behavior. But I *did* hope for better judgement from you, Phoebe."

"Hyacinth and His Grace wrote to Selina first and asked if it would be acceptable to bring Lord Shelton. Lord Shelton apologized to Selina in a letter months ago—and would have done so in person long before now if Selina had invited him to Courtland. As it is, he just left her and Lord Shaftsbury's chambers where he apologized."

"Of *course* he is apologizing! He was caught red-handed. No doubt Chatham has curtailed his allowance and now he is hanging on his cousin's sleeve for every penny he receives." She sneered. "Naturally Needham is so lacking in all decency that—"

"Mama." The viscountess spoke the single word in a quiet, calm tone, but the command in it was enough to stop her mother's diatribe. "You may say whatever you like about me but never utter a disparaging word about my husband in my presence."

Lady Addiscombe's jaw sagged at the quiet chastisement.

Stacia wanted to cheer. Although she had only exchanged a few words with the intimidating looking Viscount Needham she had quickly seen how kind he was to his wife and her family, not to mention that all the servants at Wych House absolutely adored their employer.

Lady Addiscombe glared at her daughter for a long, fraught moment.

The younger woman lifted her chin and stared back, the dull flush that crept up her throat the only sign she was agitated.

"Very well," the countess said. "As you are evidently determined to run your reputation into the ground by handing it over to a man who has no clue how to go on—an *ironmonger,* for pity's sake—I will speak to Needham myself. Where is he, pray?"

"Mama, I don't think—"

"No. You don't think," her mother snapped. "I wish to speak to your husband. If you don't tell me where to find him, I shall ferret him out myself. You will come with me, Martin," the countess said.

Stacia's jaw sagged. "Er, my lady? Should I summon a servant to—"

"That won't be necessary. I will take you," Lady Needham said wearily, and began to push to her feet.

Shelton, who was still standing in the middle of the room, hastened toward the viscountess and offered her his hand.

"Thank you," Lady Needham said, cutting him a swift, distracted smile before turning to her mother. "Needham was called to the library for some urgent business only a short time ago. I will accompany you."

"*Business*," the countess sniffed. "I hardly require an escort; I know where the library is."

"Nevertheless," Lady Needham said firmly, "I will take you there."

Lady Addiscombe swanned from the room without responding, Lady Needham behind her.

Stacia glanced from face to face, meeting looks of sympathy, embarrassment, and—from Lord Bellamy's young school friends, open-mouthed befuddlement.

The countess's voice came from the corridor, "*Martin!* Do quit dawdling! I am waiting for you.*"

Stacia briefly squeezed her eyes shut.

And then she hurried to catch up to her employer.

Chapter 4

Viscountess Needham did not speak as she led the countess and Stacia down two corridors and up a flight of stairs before knocking on a particularly elaborate door and then opening it a few inches. "I'm sorry to interrupt, Needham, but I need a few moments of your time."

A low voice replied and Lady Needham opened the door wider to allow Lady Addiscombe and Stacia to enter.

Stacia dragged her feet but could think of no way to avoid what was likely going to be an excruciating experience. Surely the viscount would send her away?

The towering lord was standing beside a younger man who was every bit as tall but so lean he was almost gaunt. Both men were dressed in their evening blacks but were engaged in something that involved piles and piles of documents spread out over a massive desk.

Lord Needham strode toward his wife, an expression of concern on his harsh features. "What is it, darling? You look flushed. Is something—"

"I am fine," she assured him. "I know you are in the middle of something important, but my mother wanted a word with you."

The viscount looked from his wife to his mother-in-law, his face hardening. "I have a few minutes but not many. I must have this letter out within the hour if it is to reach Bristol in time." The abrupt words were directed toward the countess, rather than his wife. "Have a seat, my lady." He turned back to Lady Needham, his expression instantly softening and cupped her cheek in one giant hand. "Are you sure you are all right, my love? I suspect you have been over-exerting yourself. I could have dinner sent up to your chambers and you could rest if you—"

"No, no, that isn't necessary. But thank you, Needham. I should get back to our guests."

His eyelids drooped as he lowered his head and proceeded to thoroughly kiss his wife.

The sight caused a pleasurable pulsing between Stacia's thighs, and she quickly dropped her gaze to the floor, the yearning inside her chest overpowering the sudden bolt of desire. Desire not for Needham, but for the way he so obviously loved and adored his wife. Lady Needham had an engaging smile and a lovely nature, but she was not an especially beautiful woman. And yet this powerful, attractive, wealthy man clearly worshipped her. It was impossible not to be at least a little bit envious.

The countess, evidently, thought otherwise. She heaved an exaggerated sigh. "If this revolting display is meant for my sake, you are wasting your time, Needham."

Needham didn't seem affected by the countess's scathing words, but the viscountess stiffened.

The viscount gradually released his wife and stepped away, giving her cheek one last caress before escorting her to the door and ushering her out.

When it was closed, the big lord turned back toward them and the temperature in the room plummeted.

The viscount's hard-edged gaze did not leave the countess as he strode back to his desk. Only when he was seated did he speak. "How may I serve you, my lady?"

"Please dismiss your servant," she said, jerking her chin at the other man, who was seated at a smaller desk, his quill rapidly scratching across parchment.

"Mr. Dennehy is my secretary and privy to all my business, ma'am. And right now, he is involved in business that is extremely important." *Unlike you.* Although the words were unspoken, his meaning caused the countess's face to darken. "Mr. Dennehy will remain here. If you do not care for that, you are welcome to leave."

"Business!" The countess spat the word as if it were a fly she'd found in her tea.

"How may I serve you today?" Lord Needham repeated, his voice as mild as ever, but his gaze as cold as an arctic wind.

"Were you aware the Marquess of Shelton would be a guest here?"

"Of course."

"Are you not aware that is the same man who abducted one of my daughters and destroyed her life?"

The viscount set his hands on the desk and laced his fingers. "I just saw Lady Shaftsbury and her husband a few hours ago and she did not appear to be a woman whose life was ruined."

"And what would you know of the matter?" the countess snapped, her voice pulsing with loathing.

The change in Needham was so slight that Stacia was amazed she saw it. His expression was still as bland as before, his posture just as relaxed, but Stacia knew—without being able to articulate it—that the viscount was angry. Very, very angry.

As if he'd heard her thoughts, his sharp gaze turned her way, and it was all she could do not to cower beneath the weight of it.

"Why have you decided to subject Miss Martin to this conversation, my lady?"

"I've brought her along because this concerns her."

Stacia's jaw dropped. How in the world did Lady Addiscombe know about her feelings for—

"How so?" the viscount demanded.

"Miss Martin is an unmarried girl of gentle birth. That is exactly the type of woman Shelton prefers to victimize. By having that—that *villain* in my family's home you are jeopardizing my companion's reputation. She deserves to hear your excuse for placing her in such danger."

Stacia opened her mouth to assure Lord Needham that she had no such concerns, but the viscount's rapier-like gaze was riveted on Lady Addiscombe.

"The only person in this house who has the right to object to Lord Shelton's presence here is Lady Shaftsbury. Before the Duke and Duchess of Chatham asked my wife if they could bring Shelton as a guest they wrote to Lady Shaftsbury, who gave her consent. My wife then added him to our guest list. Phoebe is mistress of this house and has complete control over domestic matters." He cocked his head slightly. "I find it interesting that your own daughter—an unmarried one—has been living in proximity to Shelton for months and has come to no harm. Are you not concerned for Lady Kathryn's wellbeing?"

The countess gave a derisive huff. "Kathryn rejected my home in favor of her older sister's. Short of physically dragging her away, there is little I can do."

"It was my understanding that you sent Kathryn to her aunt's rather than invite her to live with you in Bath. I specifically recall Kathryn being upset that she was being sent to live with your sister rather than accompanying you to your new home."

Stacia stared at the countess, waiting for her to deny such a thing. Instead, the older woman seethed, thwarted.

The viscount turned to Stacia and his expression gentled. "I do not want you to go about my house in fear for your reputation or your person. If you find Shelton's presence in any way concerning, you need only nod and I will make arrangements for him to leave. You will not be implicated in the decision, and nobody will ever know of your part in it except the four of us in this room."

If Stacia said *no*, her employer would not be pleased with her. If she accepted Lord Needham's offer, then she would be admitting that she feared Lord Shelton when she didn't. If anything, she feared her own behavior around him, but she did not believe he would abduct or compromise her.

More's the pity...

Stacia turned to Lady Addiscombe. "It would be a lie to claim that I fear for my reputation, my lady."

The countess fixed her with a look that did not bode well for continued employment.

Needham evidently thought so, too. "If Miss Martin's answer is unacceptable to you then I will be pleased to pay her a generous severance, provide a glowing letter of reference, and arrange for her transportation back to Bath—or anyplace else she wishes to go."

Stacia stared, warmed by the man's generous offer.

"Miss Martin will remain in my service," the countess snapped. "You will not rid the house of this scourge?"

"If by *scourge* you mean Shelton, then no."

Lady Addiscombe surged to her feet and marched toward the door in a flurry of skirts.

Stacia scrambled to open the door for her, but the viscount's voice stopped her just as she reached for the handle.

"One more thing, my lady."

Stacia sensed a titanic struggle taking place inside the countess and wondered, for a moment, if she would simply leave without listening to what he had to say.

But self-preservation overwhelmed her pride, and she inhaled deeply and then turned around.

The viscount had come closer and was standing only a few feet away.

"Yes?" the countess demanded rudely.

The big man came even closer, until he was standing mere inches from his mother-in-law, who had to crane her neck if she wanted to meet his gaze.

"If you ever upset my wife again—or cause her so much as a flicker of annoyance—you will not be welcome in any of my homes. Ever. Do you understand me?"

The hairs on the back of Stacia's neck stood endwise at the quiet menace in his tone.

For the first time, she saw uncertainty on Lady Addiscombe's face. Although the viscount hadn't threatened to cut off her allowance—which everyone knew was how the countess managed to live so well when her husband had gambled away all the family money—she must have realized just how tenuous her position would be if she were barred from attending future family functions.

The older woman swallowed, opened her mouth, but then closed it and jerked out an abrupt nod.

Rather than smile in triumph at having routed his foe, Lord Needham gave Stacia a speaking look when the countess stormed from the room. He quietly said, "Remember that you have choices, Miss Martin." And then he turned and strode back to his desk, leaving Stacia to ponder his words as she hurried after her employer.

Chapter 5

Lady Addiscombe re-appeared in the drawing room no more than ten minutes after she had left it.

Judging by the high color in her cheeks and the flames shooting from her eyes—and also the fact that Andrew wasn't currently standing out front of Wych House with his bags piled around his feet—he was apparently not going to be tossed out of the house.

He could not decide if he was glad or disappointed.

The mood at the dinner table was stilted, all the guests unable to ignore the dark cloud hovering over Lady Addiscombe's head. Not until almost the end of the meal—and the impending prospect of getting away from the unpleasant woman—did the atmosphere begin to lighten and the guests start to converse without restraint.

Andrew enjoyed the half-hour of port and cigars after dinner. Especially interesting to him was listening to Needham describe—at the behest of Shaftsbury and Chatham—his initial steps to revivify the estate the Earl of Addiscombe had spent the prior twenty-years decimating. As the owner of a criminally neglected estate—a great deal of which was Andrew's doing—he appreciated Needham's pragmatic approach and had taken more than a few pointers from the businessman turned landed gentleman.

He had been dreading returning to the drawing room, where he assumed the morose shadow cast by the countess would be casting the entire assemblage into gloom and doom.

Fortunately, Lady Addiscombe had eschewed the promised entertainment. She did not retire quietly or gracefully, of course, but made her displeasure at the prospect of games and amateur musical performances known—*loudly*—before rudely rejecting her companion's offer to accompany her back to her chamber.

"Oh, do stop clinging, Martin. I am far too fatigued to entertain you tonight" the countess snapped before leaving the room.

Andrew considered doing the very same thing—albeit far less noticeably—but one look at Sylvester's hopeful face decided him against it.

Only by claiming mental fatigue from the journey did he manage to avoid being roped into either whist, chess or—God forbid—the noisy game of Casino taking place at a table full of boisterous youngsters.

Instead, he sat in a comfortable wingchair with a book he'd found tucked under the chair cushion.

Chatham, blast him, had almost choked on his tongue when Andrew had claimed that he preferred to read. His cousin knew that Andrew had not voluntarily opened a book since he'd left school to join the army. Unless one counted betting books or stud books.

He lazily examined the other guests as he pretended to read, his gaze flickering over a trio of men who were talking quite loudly about a new tariff agreement currently in the works—business acquaintances of Needham's—to where Shaftsbury appeared to be playing chess with an elderly squire from a neighboring village.

Shaftsbury leaned forward, lightly touched the pieces on the board and then moved his knight. "I believe that is checkmate, Sir John."

His opponent gave a good-natured chuckle. "I fear I am not giving you much of a challenge, my lord. Will you allow me another chance to retrieve my dignity?"

The marquess smiled. "Of course—if you do not mind setting up the board."

Who would have believed that a blind man could play chess?

There was a cluster of three older ladies talking quietly in front of the fireplace, all of them industriously engaged in needlework. Andrew thought they might be the spouses of the three businessmen.

His eyes moved on, flickering over a lone female sitting beside a brace of candles.

And then returning to her again.

It was the Countess of Addiscombe's dogsbody, the same woman who'd slammed into him in the corridor before dinner. She had been something of a shrew, hectoring Andrew even though she had been the one who'd not looked where she was going.

She was not the sort of female Andrew usually noticed. That is to say she was neither pretty nor ugly but just…there. He probably would not have taken any notice of her right now if not for the fact that she was the only person in the room who was alone. Other than Andrew, of course.

She must be some poor Bellamy relation who had the unfortunate luck to be tapped as the countess's companion. He couldn't recall the woman's name at the moment but had a nagging feeling that he'd seen her before.

The most interesting thing about her, as far as he could tell, was her ability to occupy a room without anyone else noticing her.

But *he* noticed. And he wasn't sure why. Perhaps because he, too, was an outcast—a leper who'd not yet been captured, contained, and transported to isolation. While the Bellamy siblings and their spouses had been amiable enough, they were obviously in no rush to associate with him.

The other guests were either of the merchant class or the sort of bourgeois gentry who would have read about Andrew's antics over the years and been disgusted. As a result, there was an invisible barrier around him that kept anyone except his cousin—and, unfortunately, Kathryn—from coming too near.

He lost interest in the colorless companion and turned his gaze to Chatham, who was currently paired with his wife in a game of whist against Lord and Lady Needham.

Andrew's lips twitched. He didn't need to ask to know how *that* was going. Needham would be fortunate to leave the room tonight still in possession of his shirt. Andrew had had his arse kicked by the duke and duchess times beyond counting in the months that he'd been forced to cohabitate with them. He would almost prefer a night in the stocks to sitting across the table from the formidable, merciless duo.

Not that life at Chatham Park was any great hardship. With over two hundred rooms he could have arranged his life so that he had only encountered his cousin and his wife at meals, if he so chose.

Avoiding Kathryn, however, had not been so easy. Andrew suspected that he would not have been able to escape her if there had been a thousand rooms.

His gaze slid to his tormentrix. The green-eyed vixen was sitting across from one of Needham's secretaries, a morose-looking young man whose name escaped him, and the two were playing chess.

Andrew would not have believed that Kathryn could sit still for long enough to concentrate on such a complex game.

Not that he was one to talk. Chess had been the game of choice among many officers during the war and Andrew had been forced to play at a superior's *request* on more than one occasion. He had never voluntarily played the game and was awful at it.

Kathryn's eyes slid from the board up to Andrew, as if she felt his stare. For once, she did not poke out her tongue or blow him a kiss. She did not taunt him in any way, but merely gave him a cool look—although he could not decide *what* her expression said—before turning to glare at the chessboard as if it had personally insulted her.

Why was she playing the game if she hated it?

Needham's secretary said something, and Kathryn laughed, her sophisticated carefree expression once again firmly in place.

But the moment the secretary turned back to the board her smile faded. What was it that seemed to be repressing Kathryn's seemingly irrepressible spirits?

Perhaps it was being in proximity to her mother?

Andrew decided that could certainly do it.

Lady Addiscombe was perplexing. With her handsome features and shapely body, the countess should have been a desirable woman. Instead, just looking at her was enough to give Andrew a bowel weakening sensation he'd not experienced since riding into battle. The woman combined the worst characteristics of both a Cit and aristocrat to create something entirely new and twice as noxious.

The way she had publicly harangued Lady Needham earlier had made Andrew's own face heat in sympathy.

And then, during dinner, she had not once, but *twice,* sent her companion to fetch something from her chambers. What could she have possibly required so desperately? Twice.

He looked up from his thoughts and straight into Lady Shaftsbury's cerulean eyes.

The marchioness held his gaze for a moment and then turned her attention back to the people clustered around her, which included Viscount Bellamy, the little blonde girl, whom he'd discovered was Needham's natural daughter, twin girls from one of the neighboring estates, and Bellamy's young school chums whose names he'd already forgotten.

Lucy—that was Needham's daughter's name—was perhaps thirteen and chattered ten to the dozen while casting yearning looks at Addiscombe's heir. Clearly the lass was smitten.

Andrew prophesied that Needham would have a problem with that in a few years. Lady Addiscombe might have allowed a mere daughter to marry an ironmonger, but she would draw a hard line at allowing her heir to take an illegitimate bride.

He turned away and encountered the dark brown eyes of the Countess of Addiscombe's companion.

Rather than look away like the mouse she resembled, she held his gaze, her own pulsing with censure, just as it had in the corridor when she had plowed into him.

So, she was yet another woman who knew of his scandalous, wicked deeds.

Or at least she thought she did.

Andrew snorted at her censorious look and was amused when she recoiled, her face flushing.

He glanced at the longcase clock in the corner—barely fifteen minutes had passed since the last time he'd looked.

Christ. He could not leave just yet; he had to hang on for at least an hour more.

It was…purgatory.

His gaze slid to where the oldest Bellamy child—the newly minted Countess of Crewe—sat surrounded by the small menagerie she'd brought with her.

Evidently her marriage had been a revelation to almost everyone. Not even her mother had been told. Judging by Lady Addiscombe's horrified scowl at the dinner table she had *not* been pleased to discover her daughter had married the Earl of Crewe, despite the fact that Crewe was well larded.

Aurelia Bellamy—now Lady Crewe—was a lovely, lithe woman with intelligent eyes and the slightly startled expression of a newly married young lady.

Interestingly, Crewe also looked a bit startled, even though he must be forty and had been wed twice before. If Andrew had been forced to wager, he would have bet that Crewe, a hardened rake, was truly smitten with his new wife.

More remarkable than their sudden marriage was the identity of two of the three guests they had brought along.

The presence of Lady Celsa, who was Crewe's daughter and heir—the Crewe earldom could pass to a female—was not unusual. But the appearance of Crewe's natural son, Captain Guustin Walker—a man who bore an extraordinary resemblance to his father—had caused a stunned silence in the drawing room. Most dumbfounding of all, the young man's mother, Mrs. Nora Walker was also among their party.

Who, in the name of all that was holy, brought not only their husband's bastard to their family Christmas house party, but also the mother of that son? Just…*who* did that sort of thing?

The Bellamy women, evidently.

Andrew couldn't help the grin that twisted his lips as he furtively regarded the merry bunch. Honestly, he felt as though *he* was the normal one among this collection of people.

To their credit, Crewe, his wife, son, and Mrs. Walker were laughing and obviously enjoying themselves in a game of whist that pitted the women against the men.

Crewe's ex-paramour—at least Shelton assumed she was a *former* lover—for all he knew there might be a very interesting erotic arrangement between Crewe, his wife, and Mrs. Walker—was a truly lovely woman who had some sort of debilitating disease that had curled her hands into gnarled fists. She could only play cards by utilizing a wooden card holder that her son had designed for her.

Andrew looked down at his own hands, which were shapely and elegant—or so every lover he'd ever had had told him—and felt a sharp stab of shame. His hands were perfect and yet he'd done very little good with them in his life. At least not since the War ended.

A just God would have turned Andrew's hands into gnarled stumps and spared Mrs. Walker, who was obviously an affectionate mother and had raised a son who appeared dutiful and loving.

And yet it was Andrew who sat there in a body that functioned just fine, with a cousin determined to forgive him and forgive him and forgive him, no matter what an utter monster Andrew had been for the past eleven years.

What had he ever done to deserve any of it?

People do not always get what they deserve, do they? a voice taunted.

No, evidently not.

Andrew looked at Chatham. His cousin was currently grinning at his wife, the pair of them having just finished drubbing Lord and Lady Needham—who looked as though they had just been savaged by a storm—and was struck with a painful stab of guilt at how horribly he had treated the other man for years and years.

And still Sylvester had forgiven him. Not only that, but his cousin loved him and had taken great pains to show his love over the past months.

Suddenly, the room felt small and claustrophobic.

It was bloody hard to breathe.

Andrew pushed to his feet, shoved the book back beneath the seat cushion, and made his way to the door, not caring what anyone thought about his hasty departure. Not that he believed anyone would notice. The people around him were far too happy to pay attention to him.

***

Stacia surreptitiously studied the other denizens of the large room. Was it odd to be surrounded by people and yet feel utterly alone?

She supposed it was not so unusual given that she was an outsider at a family Christmas. Not that the Bellamy siblings and their spouses had been anything but kind to her today, treating her the same as they did any other guest.

Doubtless their treatment would change after seeing how Lady Addiscombe ordered her around like a feudal serf.

Stacia sighed. She tried not to care about such things. Besides, the woman might treat her badly, but she treated her own children even worse. As much of an outcast as she might be, the Bellamy siblings were still warmer to her than they were to their own mother.

Of course Lady Addiscombe had a hide like an old goat and did not notice how little her children liked to be around her. Or if she did notice, she didn't care.

Stacia wasn't sure why the countess had even made the journey to Wych House as she seemed as unhappy as she was in Bath.

In any event, the countess had gone up to her chambers, claiming exhaustion from her journey. When Stacia had risen to accompany her, she'd given her an irritated look. "Oh, do stop clinging, Martin. I am far too fatigued to entertain you tonight."

Those around them who'd heard the sharp comment had looked embarrassed.

Stacia was grateful they had not seen the countess's lips moving with her soundless message, *I told you to stay here!* reminding her that she was to spy on her hosts.

She swallowed down her distaste. After all, she didn't *have* to report everything she learned, did she?

Buoyed by that thought, she resolved to enjoy her brief liberty from servitude. She'd brought her basket of needlework down earlier so at least she could appear occupied.

A quick survey of the room showed that only Stacia and Lord Shelton sat alone.

While she was engaged with her embroidery Lord Shelton had a book in his lap. It took her only a few minutes to discern he was not reading it. Instead, he stared at the other denizens of the room with a brooding expression that made him look like a sulky angel.

A *gorgeous* sulky angel.

Over and over again her eyes were drawn to him.

It was almost two years since she'd last seen him. The years had robbed Stacia of the only attraction she had ever possessed—the dewiness of youth—while they had, unjustly, served to make Shelton even more desirable.

The lines around his eyes gave him a depth he had lacked the last time Stacia had seen him. Or at least it afforded him the *trappings* of depth while Stacia merely looked like a spinster rapidly spiraling toward maiden aunthood.

Yet another of the hundreds of ways in which the world was so cruel toward women.

Stacia wasn't the only one who stared at the brooding lord. Even though he was not paying attention to anyone, the young girls playing Casino, and even the older married women gossiping and working on their cross-stitching, constantly stole glances at the handsome lord.

As much as Stacia hated to agree with her employer on any matter, Lady Addiscombe was correct when she said Lord Shelton was nothing but trouble for any woman—rich or poor, young or old, married or spinster.

She wondered how Sarah Creighton—Shelton's most notorious, if not most recent, victim—was faring in exile. Stacia had not heard another word about the other woman after she'd married a nameless farmer. Sarah would have given birth to Shelton's baby long ago. Was it a boy or a girl? Did her husband accept the child? Did Sarah think of Shelton and yearn for him still, even though she knew the truth about his character?

You still do, why shouldn't she?

Perhaps when the holiday was over, Stacia would write to Sarah. Maybe they could resume their acquaintance now that both of them were essentially outcasts from their former society.

And maybe you can ask her what happened when Sarah disappeared with the handsome lord for one entire night…

Stacia could not deny that she had long felt a burning curiosity to know what had transpired between the pair.

Why don't you ask Lord Shelton?

Stacia snorted at the thought.

Lord Shelton suddenly turned her way, his eyes landing on her directly rather than skittering dismissively over her.

Almost as if he were privy to her thoughts.

Rather than modestly lower her gaze as a good girl should, she stared at him as she'd done the time she confronted him.

He returned her gaze for a moment and then gave a huff of amusement and turned away.

Stacia bristled. How *dare* he treat her so dismissively?

And why should he be allowed to feel at home in the drawing room of a family he had shamed with his abhorrent behavior?

You had your chance to get rid of him. Instead, you chose to alienate your employer.

Stacia chewed on her lip, not wanting to think about the confrontation waiting for her when the countess eventually decided to strike.

It had been foolish to oppose her demand earlier in Lord Needham's library.

But you could not bear the thought of being the cause of Shelton's banishment.

Stacia hated that the accusation was true. She was so pathetic! Still yearning for him after all these years.

Lord Shelton suddenly stood, shoved the book he'd been holding beneath the seat cushion, and made for the door.

Just where was he off to in such a hurry?

Stacia was still pondering her relentless attraction for the biggest cad in England when Lady Kathryn Bellamy, who'd finished playing chess and was idly observing the raucous Casino game, strolled in a leisurely way toward the door, leaving without saying anything.

Could Lady Kathryn and Lord Shelton be having some sort of assignation?

Stacia hated to think that was the case. Lord Needham had essentially vouched for the man's character.

It is your duty to make sure the girl is not in danger of being compromised.

Stacia hesitated only a second before setting aside her basket and heading for the door, which opened just as she reached it.

She waited for three maids, all laden with heavy trays, to enter before slipping out of the room and asking the footman. "I don't suppose you know where Lord Shelton went? Er, I have a message for him."

"He asked where he could have a cigar and I directed him to the conservatory. It is just down the main staircase and then follow the corridor that leads west. You cannot miss it."

"Thank you," Stacia said, her mind whirring as she hurried off. If they *were* having an assignation, just what would she say or do?

Chapter 6

Andrew stared through the conservatory glass at the moon and inhaled until his lungs could hold no more, waiting for the tobacco to surge through his body.

It was a cold clear night. He thought it might actually be too cold to snow, although somebody at dinner had been sure there was a storm on the way.

Lord. The only thing that would be worse than spending Christmas and New Year at Wych House was if he were snowed in and couldn't take his daily ride.

He reluctantly exhaled, the smoke heavy in the humid air, mingling with the scent of dirt and vegetation.

There was an interesting halo of sorts around the moon and the sight momentarily diverted his thoughts.

Andrew squinted as he tried to recall what the phenomenon was called.

"It is a *moondog*."

Andrew bit back a groan at the unwanted voice. "Why are you following me?" he asked, not caring if he was being rude. "We're here—in the bosom of your family and friends—and yet you still must persecute me. Can't you find a more interesting target?"

Kathryn laughed, the throaty, sensual sound far older than her tender years. "I think you underestimate your appeal, Shelton." She waved her hand in front of her face and gave an exaggerated cough. "Must you befoul the air?"

"Yes, I must. Perhaps you should find somewhere else to be if you do not care for it?"

Undaunted by his bad manners, she said, "How are you enjoying your first evening at Wych House?"

Andrew would have liked to ignore her question—and her, as well—but several months of enforced proximity with the youngest Bellamy sister had taught him that ignoring her only invited more persecution. For whatever reason, she delighted in bedeviling his every waking hour.

"I am having a delightful time," he said, not bothering to hide his sarcasm.

"Liar. The only person here who looks more unhappy than you is my mother's companion."

Andrew thought about the woman who'd just scowled at him in the drawing room. He'd been too agitated to notice much about her when she'd run into him outside Lady Shaftsbury's chambers. But seeing her again at dinner, and afterward, he'd felt a strange twinge of memory. Had he met her somewhere before?

He'd never had a head for names, but his ability to recall faces had become even worse after he'd returned home from the War.

"Who is she?" Andrew asked.

"She is my mother's companion."

"I know that," he said, giving her a withering look. "What is her name?"

"Why?"

Andrew lifted an eyebrow at her suspicious tone. "Why what?"

"Why are you asking?"

"Why do you think I'm asking?" he demanded testily, although he could no longer remember why himself.

"Is she your next target for seduction?"

"Very droll." How did the little witch manage to draw him into these conversations?

Kathryn laughed. "Or *ab*duction, I suppose."

Andrew knew he deserved her mockery, so he kept his mouth shut and endured it.

But he also took a deep draw on the slender cigar and then exhaled, not being too choosy about which direction he blew his smoke.

She coughed. "Is she, Andrew?"

"Is she what, *Kathryn*?"

"Your target."

He gave vent to an explosive sigh. "Lord, but you're persistent! You're like a walking, talking, nagging burr in skirts."

"And you are avoiding the question, which can only mean I've hit on the truth. I should probably warn our host of your intentions."

"Bloody hell!" he muttered, pushed beyond civility by her harping. "You can stop teasing yourself on the subject, Kathryn. I'd have to be desperate indeed to foist my attentions on such a drab, downtrodden little dab of a female." Shelton scowled, furious that she had driven him to utter such unkind words. While it was true the countess's companion had given him a look of near loathing in the drawing room, there was no excuse for what he had just said.

69

"That was a cruel thing to say, Shelton." There was no humor in her voice now.

Andrew's ears heated and he hoped it was too dark to see the flush that was no doubt coloring his face. "Haven't you heard that I'm an unprincipled cad?" he taunted. "What else do you expect?"

"Even for you that was low."

It had been.

"Her name is Miss Martin," Kathryn said. "Don't you know her?"

"Would I have asked you if I did?" he shot back irritably.

"I'm not sure about that," she murmured.

He frowned. "Just what do—"

"I know she is a desperate woman," she went on, talking over him as if he was not there.

The woman he'd seen earlier had looked scornful and haughty, but not especially desperate. "Why do you think she is desperate?"

"Only a desperate woman would take a position working for my mother."

He barked a laugh. "Such filial devotion. That's rather a, er, grim assessment of your mother."

"Is it?" She gave him a slyly amused look. "You met her earlier in the drawing room."

"Touché."

"So, what do you think of her?"

"I think she has good reason to dislike me."

"I don't mean my mother. Even an idiot could guess that. I meant Miss Martin."

"*Should* I think something about her?"

She shrugged.

He picked a shred of tobacco off his tongue and flicked it away before saying, "I assume she is some poor relative?"

"No, her father was Viscount Clayton."

Clayton. Andrew vaguely recalled the name but could bring no face to mind. "What's she doing working as a companion?"

"Her father died without a son and the new viscount—a distant cousin—is a cheeseparing villain who tossed her out. And so she had to leave her family home and earn her crust."

"I thought you said you didn't know her," he said, amused by her description of the man.

"I don't, but I know about her situation."

Andrew grunted, bored with the subject of the companion. "Will your father be joining us?"

"Thankfully, we will be spared that gruesome event as he is spending the holiday at Oatlands with the Regent."

He wasn't exactly thunderstruck to hear that Addiscombe had chosen to carouse with the profligate prince rather than play chicken stakes whist with his family. Doubtless the earl would lose a packet over the holiday; money that Needham would have to pay.

"Do you know my father, Andrew?"

"I've met him, but I wouldn't say that I *know* him." The man owed Andrew money from years before, but it seemed indelicate to mention that.

"You mean you've played cards with him."

He hesitated before saying, "Once or twice."

"Did he lose?"

"He might have. I can't recall," he lied.

"When was this?"

"Ages ago. You would have been in leading strings." Andrew could still recall what a dreadful cardplayer the man was. Doubtless he was greatly enjoying himself now that he could loot Needham's bottomless pockets.

It wasn't any of Andrew's concern, but he hoped Sylvester didn't get drawn into supporting the profligate old rooster. The dukedom might be wealthy, but a man with Addiscombe's ability to waste the ready could drive it into the dirt fast enough.

He took a last draw on his cigar, pinched off the glowing end, and exhaled before saying, "I'm going back inside. Are you coming?" he added, his manners getting the better of him.

"No. I'll stay here for a while," she said, sounding oddly subdued.

"Suit yourself," he said, and then left the moody adolescent to whatever was eating away at her.

71

***

I'd have to be desperate indeed to foist my attentions on such a drab, downtrodden little dab of a female!

Stacia couldn't stop hearing the words, which echoed like the ring of an especially unpleasant bell.

I'd have to be desperate indeed to foist my attentions on such a drab, downtrodden little dab of a female!

The description had frozen Stacia to the spot, far more unpleasant than the smoke from Lord Shelton's foul-smelling cigar.

Stacia had always considered herself to be a practical person. She was not beautiful, but neither was she ugly. Perhaps being average was even worse than either of those things? She'd never believed that to be the case until tonight.

Drab, downtrodden little dab of a female.

Was that really how people viewed her?

Stacia quietly eased from the conservatory and hurried back toward the ancient staircase, as if she could outrun the nasty words.

She glanced down at her gown as she climbed the stairs. Yes, it was a serviceable shade of brown, but what was wrong with that? As a matter of fact, brown suited her!

I'd have to be desperate indeed to foist my attentions on such a drab, downtrodden little dab of a female!

"Enough!" she hissed upon reaching the landing.

Lord Shelton's head suddenly popped around the corner. "What was that?"

Stacia shrieked.

Shelton winced. "Er, sorry. I heard somebody say something behind me and assumed you were talking to me."

"What is *wrong* with you?" Stacia's hand had jumped to her heart, as if by laying a hand over it she could soothe its frantic rhythm. She glared up into a face that would make angels weep, her eyes colliding with a pair that were an unearthly shade of blue.

I'd have to be desperate indeed to foist my attentions on such a drab, downtrodden little dab of a female!

"Are you all right, Miss Martin?"

The sound of her name on his tongue snapped her from confusion and misery to icy control. So. He had finally remembered it after all these years, had he?

Rather than please her, it only made her hate him more. "I am *fine*, my lord. At least I was until you leapt out of nowhere and all but stopped my heart."

He recoiled at her harsh tone, momentarily taken off guard. But he recovered quickly enough, his eyelids lowering and his unfairly perfect lips pulling up into a lazy smirk that was, even after all these years, enough to snatch the air from her lungs. "I normally prefer to stop a lady's heart using more… pleasant means."

Her jaw dropped.

The knowing expression on his face said he was accustomed to robbing women of words and laying waste to their wits. He gifted her an amused, condescending smile and held out his arm. "Allow me to make up for my boorish behavior by escorting you back to the drawing room."

I'd have to be desperate indeed to foist my attentions on such a drab, downtrodden little dab of a female!

The words snapped her from her besotted fugue.

"Oh, dear me!" she said in an exaggerated, gushing tone. "Such a treat would likely make my head swell, my lord. I'm sure it is far safer for my peace of mind to walk into the room unassisted."

His expression of stupefaction was so complete that she was tempted to linger and enjoy it. But Stacia knew the value of a well-timed exit and took advantage of the stunned silence to sail past him, her chin high.

Only when he was behind her did she allow herself a triumphant smile. *Take that you insufferable, arrogant toad.*

Chapter 7

Several Mornings Later

As usual, Andrew rose before dawn and was the first of the houseguests to arrive at the stable.

What had not been usual, however, was the dream that had woken him that morning. It had been shockingly vivid.

It had been arousing.

And yet all he could recall of it was that Miss Martin's hair—which had to reach well past her arse—had been unbound and spread across his chest, abdomen, and cock. His *hard* cock.

That was all, and yet he could not recall being so hard in years.

It was…disturbing.

Naturally, he'd needed to take himself in hand.

Andrew scowled, shoved the memory from his mind, and focused on the breaking dawn. As sunrises went it wasn't especially remarkable, but the pale-yellow sun made the frost glitter on every surface, turning the morning into something almost magical. Indeed, the enchanting scene filled him with an odd feeling of optimism.

Are you sure the reason for your elation isn't the result of boxing the Jesuit first thing in the morning?

Andrew ignored the mocking reminder.

Being astride a horse was one of his favorite places in the world. It allowed him to clear his mind and order his thoughts.

This morning, he had good thoughts to ponder.

Like silky coffee-brown hair and—

Andrew jerked his errant thoughts back to the *real* reason for his happiness today: the letter he'd received right before he'd left Chatham Park. It had come from Jem Moore, the man who managed Andrew's stud enterprise. Jem had filled all but two of the slots they had remaining for their prize stallion. Thanks to several excellent colts from last year's mares the operation was, if not booming, at least flourishing. And all without requiring any large infusions of money.

Andrew smiled at the thought, the tension leaking out of his body as he rode through trees so ancient he felt as if he might encounter Arthur and Guinevere any moment.

He'd ridden every morning since he'd been a boy. It was a ritual that helped clear his head and prepare him for the day ahead.

These past months at his cousin's house he'd ridden with Sylvester, too, but those jaunts took place a bit later in the day and were often shared with the duchess who was as skilled in a saddle—side or astride—as anyone Andrew had ever met.

He had never invited anyone else to accompany him on these early rides.

Not even Mariah.

She had been a slapping rider and had often begged him to come along.

After her death, Andrew had regretted that he'd not relaxed his rigidity and invited her. Especially since he had lost more and more of her with every year that had passed, his memory no more resilient against the incursion of time than a sandy beach against the tide.

Alarmingly, the *forgetting process* seemed to have sped up since he'd begun to reconcile with Sylvester, as if he had only room in his memory for one of them: his cousin or his dead lover.

Andrew was glad that he'd accepted his cousin's invitation to spend time with him at Chatham Park. It was past time to let go of the hatred that had fueled him for more than a decade. But he'd not expected the giant void that had appeared in his life once he'd relinquished his vendetta.

It would have been all too easy to run from his cousin's home and return to the familiar, almost comforting, cycle of retribution and hatred.

But Sylvester had said something during Andrew's second week that had kept him at Chatham Park.

"You're my brother, Drew—the only one I have left. Having you back in my life is worth some awkwardness and discomfort as we make up for lost time."

Sylvester was right. It *had* been painful to reacquaint himself with a man who'd once been his closest friend. Part of that pain was admitting just how many years he had wasted—because there was no denying that the majority of their estrangement had been his doing—and would never—

A sharp yelp pierced the early morning air and cut off his thoughts.

Andrew reined in Drake and listened, but there was nothing other than the sound of his horse's breathing. He was about to nudge his gelding into motion when he heard the sound again. It was undeniably a canine cry—a dog in pain—and it was coming from somewhere in the trees.

"Let's go and see what this is all about, Drake," he murmured, guiding the horse off the path. A quick glance at the ground showed a disturbance in the frost that covered the fallen leaves, branches, and bracken which had somehow managed to grow in the shadows beneath the tree canopy.

The next time the yelping sound came it was followed by the murmuring of a voice. A female voice.

Andrew dismounted when he encountered a huge rotting log. "You stay here, boy," he said, looping Drake's reins lightly over a branch before following the disturbed detritus toward the canine whining and human cooing.

"Hello?" he called out.

Both the dog and human sounds ceased and then a head popped up above a thick cluster of ferns.

It was the companion—Miss Martin—the very woman he'd been dreaming about, although she looked nothing like the temptress who'd aroused his sleeping body.

Her small face was a study of emotions: worry, relief, indecision, reluctance, and a dozen others. "I've got an injured dog. His foot is caught in a trap. I tried to free him, but I am not strong enough to pry it open."

"I will have a look," he said, climbing over lumps of old deadwood so thickly covered in moss they looked as if they'd grown green fur. When he reached the patch of bracken, he parted the tall fronds and found her kneeling with a wiry-haired mutt that looked to be chiefly terrier.

Miss Martin's gray walking costume was liberally smeared with blood and dirt, and she was holding the shivering animal on her lap, along with a very nasty snare.

"That's a cruel looking thing," he said, dropping to his haunches. "We'll get that off you in a trice, you poor little blighter," he said to the dog and then looked up at her. "Hold him firmly and keep talking to him. He's going to want to pull his paw away when I open the trap."

She nodded, her attention on the dog. "There's a good boy," she praised. "Just another minute and Lord Shelton will take away that awful pain. Be a good boy for a little while longer."

Andrew looked for a release plate that was sometimes on such devices, but this was a rustic trap that was hardly more than a tangle of metal with spikes. He was going to have to wrench it open.

"Here I go," he warned.

The dog whined and twitched as he began to pull the jaws apart, but Miss Martin held him steady.

"Be ready to lift his paw off the spikes before he can jerk it away."

She nodded and moved one hand to the dog's haunch.

Andrew gritted his teeth—more against the pained animal sounds than the effort required—and the jaws grudgingly parted. He'd barely opened it an inch when Miss Martin carefully freed the paw.

"Well done," he said, closing the trap and tossing it aside before turning to look at the dog. "Hold him steady and I'll check the leg for a break."

"There's a good boy," she said, gently but firmly holding the little beast still.

"I know, I know," Andrew said when the dog made a pitiful whine as he felt the limb. There was a lot of blood coming from two deep punctures. "I don't feel a break," he said after a moment, releasing the leg and looking up. "But I'm sure it hurts like the dickens."

Her cheeks were stained with tears and her eyes red and swollen. She was not the sort of woman who could cry prettily and looked almost as bedraggled as the poor creature she held.

Andrew pulled out his handkerchief and wrapped it around the wound while the little dog stoically watched without making a peep. "There," he said, scratching the dog behind the ears. "That should hold it until we get back to Wych House. Although I'm afraid your gown is ruined."

She raised a hand to her cheek and wiped away the tears with the back of her trembling hand.

"How long have you been here?" he asked.

"I don't know; it feels like a long time."

"I imagine it does. It is a little early for a walk, isn't it?"

"You are out walking," she shot back.

Andrew bit back a smile at her sharp retort; a little hostility was better than weeping anguish.

He held out his hands. "Let me hold him while I help you up."

She hesitated, but then gently lifted the little dog.

"No squirming," Andrew admonished, cradling the dog in one arm and offering his other hand to Miss Martin, who ignored it and pushed to feet with a harsh intake of breath that told him her legs had probably fallen asleep.

He gestured to the fallen tree trunk. "Sit for a moment and allow the feeling to return."

"No, I am ready."

"I want to dispose of the trap first," he said, handing her the dog.

"Oh. I'd forgotten about that."

Andrew found the nasty piece of metal and used the hard heel of his riding boot to crush the trap, over and over and over, until it was so bent and twisted it could never be repaired.

He looked up to find Miss Martin watching him with wide eyes.

"I loathe those things," he said, feeling his face heat a bit in the cold morning air. "It is a coward's way to kill and oftentimes the poor animal languishes for hours or days before the hunter returns."

She nodded.

"My horse isn't far," he said after an awkward moment. "I can take you both back."

"On your *horse?*" She looked so scandalized that one would have thought Andrew had just informed her they were heading for the Scottish border. "I can walk, my lord. It is not—"

"I was riding for almost a quarter of an hour, Miss Martin. It will take you at least twice as long afoot."

She opened her mouth, clearly bent on arguing, but then heaved an exasperated sigh and said, "Oh, very well," employing the ungracious tone of a person who was doing *him* a favor.

Andrew was amused by her prickly nature. How did she manage to efface herself to Lady Addiscombe when she was so combative? Or perhaps it was only Andrew who brought it out of her?

The little dog bore the jostling in stoic silence, and they reached his horse without any fuss from either his canine or human companion.

Andrew turned to the woman and saw that she was gazing up at the big gelding with an uncertain look. "Don't worry—he looks big, but he is a gentle giant and shan't hurt you."

She pulled her gaze from the gelding to glare up at him. "I am not afraid of horses, my lord."

He grinned at her withering tone. "No, of course not. I will mount and then you can hand him up."

Still looking dubious, she nodded.

Once Andrew was astride, he leaned low and scooped the dog up with a minimum of squirming, holding it as he'd done before.

He turned to Miss Martin and extended his free hand. "Take my hand and put your foot on my boot."

Her brow furrowed and she bit her lower lip, a lip he couldn't help noticing was nicely plush in contrast to her far slimmer upper lip.

After studying him for a moment, she set her gloved hand in his and lifted her foot.

"The other one," he said.

The furrows in her forehead deepened briefly before a sheepish look flickered across her features. "Oh."

She was small—indeed, tiny was a more fitting word—but as stiff as a plank, which made it awkward to maneuver her with only one arm. Still, Andrew managed to get her hip onto the saddle.

"Take our patient," he said, shifting so she could collect the dog. Once she had, he looped his arm around her waist and pulled her closer, until she was securely tucked between his thighs. She might be small, but she had a pleasingly full, soft backside.

His brain wasn't the only part of him to take note of how nice she felt, and warmth pooled in his groin. Christ! He had definitely been without a woman for too long if a plush arse was enough to get him excited.

She whimpered.

"Am I hurting you?" he asked.

"Hurting? No, but it is rather, er, cramped."

Andrew laughed. "I'm afraid there is no avoiding that."

"No, I suppose not." But he felt her try to shrink away, regardless.

"Stop squirming," he said, tightening his arm around her midriff.

"I am not squirming," she said, stilling her squirming.

They rode in silence as Drake picked his way through the trees. Only when they reached the path did Andrew feel some of the tension leave her body.

"So, you are an early morning riser, too," he said when it was clear she would not speak.

"Yes."

He thought that was all he'd get, but then she went on.

"It is the only time of day when my services are not needed."

"When does your mistress usually wake?"

"Not until eleven, sometimes even twelve."

"And then you are at her beck and call until you retire?"

"That is the life of a companion," she agreed, a certain wry amusement in her tone.

Odd how Andrew had never given any thought to companions before. Well, not really odd, he supposed. Why would he think about such people? Companions were, in his experience, wraithlike women who flickered insubstantially around either very old ladies or young girls in their first Seasons. The only time he had really noticed a companion or chaperone was when he'd needed to conceive of ways to get around them and steal time with their charges.

"Do you like working for Lady Addiscombe?"

"She pays a generous wage."

Andrew was amused by her evasive answer. "Is she your first employer?" he asked, recalling what Kathryn had said about her father dying.

"Do you really care? Or are you just asking questions to pass the time?"

He blinked at her hostile response. "I don't think you like me, Miss Martin. Why is that, I wonder?"

"I should think the answer to that question is perfectly obvious."

He had been expecting a polite denial and was nonplussed by her direct answer. "You refer to my notorious debauchery, I suppose."

"Debaucher*ies.*"

He couldn't help grinning. When was the last time a chit barely out of the schoolroom—or any woman—had scolded him to his face?

Andrew couldn't think of a single episode. Ever. It was his experience that women giggled, stammered, or lowered their eyes in his presence. Even those matrons who disapproved of him never made a peep of protest if he asked their daughters to dance.

Lady Selina had not giggled or blushed, but neither had she given him a proper raking. At least not until he had behaved abominably toward her.

You behaved abominably last night in the conservatory. Or have you forgotten what you said about Miss Martin?

Andrew felt a pang of embarrassment at the memory of his unkind words. But she had not been there—

He suddenly recalled how they had encountered each other on the stairs. He assumed she had been fetching and carrying for her employer, but the countess had gone up to bed earlier.

Just what had Miss Martin been up to wandering around the house?

Was it possible that she'd been in the conservatory—although it was certainly not on the way to anywhere else—and heard him?

His stomach clenched at the appalling thought.

Unfortunately, it seemed like the best explanation for her dislike.

"You will forgive me if I point out that your animus sounds almost personal in nature, Miss Martin."

"Your past behavior should be a personal affront to every decent woman, whether she knows you or not," Miss Martin retorted heatedly. "But it just so happens that I am friends with Sarah Creighton."

Any sympathy or guilt he'd been feeling toward her drained away. "Indeed," he said dryly. "Friends with Miss Creighton, are you? Surely, as you are such *dear* friends, you know that is no longer her name?"

She twisted around until her nose was touching his chin, her dark brown eyes burning into his. "You are smiling!"

"Am I?" he asked.

"You are not even ashamed or regretful of what you did, are you?"

"Ashamed? No. Do I regret it? More often than you would believe," he muttered, and then laughed at her look of horror.

"You are—you are—"

"What am I?" he asked, although he could guess.

Her jaw worked, but she clamped her lips tightly together, drawing his attention to her mouth again, which was quite lovely. Indeed, this close to her he had to admit her features were not without charm. She had no stature to speak of and would never be called beautiful, but she was not unattractive. Her eyes, which were large and well-formed, were a warm shade of dark brown. Or at least he thought they might warm up when she was not regarding a person with outraged loathing.

Interestingly, Andrew decided that her most appealing trait—aside from her lush bottom, sweet lower lip, and big brown eyes—was her keen, albeit hostile, intelligence. It had been Sylvester's new wife who'd shown Andrew that a woman's appeal could sometimes be enhanced by a magnitude if she was clever.

81

Who would have guessed?

Hyacinth Bellamy was such a scrawny, unprepossessing female that she'd had no problem convincing half the *ton*—the male half—that she was a man. For months she had rubbed elbows with dozens of men in London's gambling dens and yet nobody had guessed her gender.

After living in proximity with the duchess for several months, Andrew could not deny the woman emanated a magnetism—not to mention significant sexual appeal—that was far more compelling than a pretty face.

"What? Why are you looking at me like that?" Miss Martin demanded.

Andrew realized he'd been staring rather than watching where they were going. Not that Drake needed any help on this well-trodden path.

"Like what?" he asked. Andrew silently willed her to say the word; he wanted to see what her lips looked like when they formed the word *lustful*.

She frowned, visibly irked. "I don't know. But I don't like it."

Andrew grinned. "Why are you so angry at me?"

"I'm not—"

"Were you in the conservatory that first night?"

The scarlet wave that flooded her face was answer enough.

God damn his wretched mouth! What an arse he was. "I deeply regret what I said, Miss Martin. It had nothing to do with you. It was just a thoughtless—"

"You must think I am stupid as well as a *drab little dab of a woman* if you think I will believe that!" she all but snarled.

"My words weren't just unkind, they were untrue, as well. No—" he said when she opened her mouth, probably to argue—"just listen a moment and allow me to finish. I was being flippant and disagreeable to Lady Kathryn. We have a—a, well, let's just call it an adversarial relationship and I was looking for something to say that would put her back up, hoping it would drive her away." He stared into her disbelieving eyes. "It is the truth, Miss Martin. Your clothing is, I think you would have to admit, not exactly colorful, but your person is not drab. Surely you must know that?"

Her blazing gaze, pink cheeks, and flaring nostrils told him that his words had failed to appease her.

Andrew couldn't blame her. He'd behaved like a cad.

He suspected that she was about to launch into a proper raking, but they were near enough to the stables that a lad came trotting over to take Drake's reins and interrupted whatever she was about to say.

"Leave the horse for a moment and take the dog," he said to the boy. "Have a care, it is injured."

Once Miss Martin had handed over the dog, Andrew took her hand. "Use my boot again and I'll lower you."

Andrew was amazed by how much he missed the soft warmth of her body once it was gone.

She smoothed out her gown, as if that would rid the garment of blood and muck, and then looked up at him and—very grudgingly—said, "Thank you for helping me."

"Shall I go with the lad and—"

"I will see to the dog, my lord." *Go away!* her hostile eyes shouted.

"As you wish," he said, and then watched as Miss Martin, the boy, and the dog disappeared into the stables.

***

By the time Stacia had finished binding the dog's leg—with the help of not only the stable boy, Gerald, but also the kind stablemaster Mr. Higgins—settled him into a vacant stall, fetched some milk and a bone from the kitchen, and then sat with the quivering little dog until he dropped into a restless sleep, it was already past ten o'clock. She hurried up to her quarters to change before heading to Lady Addiscombe.

It was the friendly maid Dora who delivered her hot water. "Goodness!" she said when she saw Stacia's gown. "What happened?"

Stacia told her about the dog—leaving out Lord Shelton's rescue—and then said, "I don't suppose there is anything that can be done to save the dress?"

"You leave it to me, Miss."

"Thank you, Dora." Stacia quickly stripped off the gown, politely declined the maid's help to dress, and then donned her dark brown morning dress, the newest of any of her clothing.

She paused to regard her reflection in the mirror. The gown was suitable and the color was not unattractive on her.

But it is, undeniably, drab.

She scowled at her reflection as she speedily unpinned, brushed, and then re-plaited her hair. There. That was good enough. As good as she ever looked.

As she made her way toward Lady Addiscombe's chambers Stacia told herself to forget Lord Shelton and anything he'd said. Unfortunately, her body clung to the man as tenaciously as her brain and kept reminding her of what it had felt like to be pressed up against his gorgeous body as tightly as paint on a wall.

Even through all the layers of clothing she'd felt the warmth of hard muscles, his far bigger body easily enclosing hers, his strong arms gently but firmly holding—

Enough. Stacia gritted her teeth against the distracting clenching between her thighs.

She had been a fool to not take Lady Addiscombe's side and encourage Lord Needham to banish Shelton from the property. The man was an unrepentant menace.

You should banish yourself *from the property. Lord Shelton did nothing untoward this morning other than be exceedingly helpful and proper.*

Stacia hated the accusation. He *had* behaved like a gentleman.

And that is why you're so miffed. You were expecting him to importune you or carry you off to the border.

No, actually, I wasn't. You forget that I heard his brutal assessment of me three nights ago. You forget—

Stacia pulled a face when she realized she was arguing with her own mind and scratched softly on the door before opening it.

The room was black—so black that somebody must have covered the windows because not even a sliver of light was showing.

"My lady?" she asked, hesitating on the threshold.

"Don't *shout* so, Martin." Stacia didn't immediately recognize the croaky husk of a voice as Lady Addiscombe's. "I have a dreadful migraine."

"I am so sor—"

"Do not speak."

Stacia closed her mouth.

"I want an ice compress brought up every two hours. And I want it delivered without *any noise.*"

Stacia almost said *yes, my lady*, but caught herself at the last second. Instead, she closed the door without making a sound and immediately headed toward the kitchen.

She entered the warm, noisy room and skidding to a halt when she saw Lady Needham seated at the roughhewn oak table, drinking tea with the housekeeper, Mrs. Nutter, and the cook, Mrs. Barton.

"I'm sorry to interrupt, my lady."

"It is no interruption, Miss Martin. I am finished here." Lady Needham gave her a sunny smile and pushed to her feet with a groan. "Neither of these ladies needs direction to keep things running smoothly, but they both humor me and discuss the menu every week."

Both women laughed, clearly at ease with their mistress.

"Did you need something, Miss Martin?" Lady Needham asked.

"The countess has a migraine and requires an ice compress." She turned to Mrs. Nutter. "She asked that on be delivered every two hours. I will wait for the first one."

Mrs. Nutter nodded and hurried off.

"This is unfortunate," Lady Needham said, and then cocked her head. "Has my mother had one of these lately?"

"Not since I've come to work for her."

"You should be aware that her migraines often last for days. Other than the compresses, what she really needs is complete quiet, darkness, and rest."

"I understand, my lady."

"There is no reason for you to wait, Miss Martin. A servant can bring the compresses to my mother—and Mrs. Nutter will make sure she gets them regularly."

"Er, I really do feel that I should bring it myself, my lady."

Lady Needham gave a dismissive flick of her hand. "Nonsense. I'll see to her myself. I have years of experience with my mother's migraines." She smiled. "Why don't you take the day for yourself while she is bedbound and does not need you?"

Stacia shoved down the excitement that bubbled up inside her at the other woman's words. "I couldn't—"

"Yes, you can. Needham is guiding a big party over to the pond. Our groundskeeper has assured him that it is frozen enough to bear even his great weight. You must go and have fun. I insist."

"But—"

"If my mother asks for you, I will tell her that I have co-opted your services for the day. But she won't ask for you. These episodes are quite debilitating, and it often takes her a week or more before she is ready to leave her room."

A *week*? Stacia's heart leapt at the other woman's words. She was an awful, awful person.

"I'm afraid I don't have any skates." Stacia said. "I have only ever been one time before."

Lady Needham chuckled. "My husband purchased enough skates to equip the entire neighborhood. Needham is from the north, Miss Martin. He believes that skating is a mandatory activity at Christmas. Go. You deserve to have a bit of entertainment." She gave Stacia a mock stern look. "That is an order from your hostess."

Stacia laughed. "Very well, then. I shall go."

Lady Needham wagged a finger at her. "And you must have fun."

"Yes. I promise to have fun."

Chapter 8

Skating?" Andrew repeated. He'd been eating a late breakfast when his cousin found him.

"Yes, it is an activity one does in winter—especially around Christmas. A person straps on a—"

"Very droll, Sylvester."

"Needham has a pavilion complete with braziers, a feast, and plenty of warm blankets for those who want to come and watch—like Hyacinth and Lady Shaftsbury."

"The duchess does not skate?"

"Oh, she does, but I forbade it."

Andrew raised his eyebrows. "That must have been an interesting conversation."

"I must admit I was reduced to playing the lord and master and issuing a ducal command."

Andrew laughed. "I'm sorry I missed that."

"Come with me. Even if you don't skate, you can keep the ladies company."

"I'm sure they would both adore that," he said with a roll of his eyes. "But yes," he added when Sylvester gave him a pained look. "I will come."

"Excellent! Go fetch your things. We are leaving soon."

A large group had assembled in the great hall by the time Andrew had returned with his coat and hat. He joined Chatham and his duchess, who were standing off to one side. "Where the devil did all these people come from?" he asked as he pulled on his gloves.

"Some are new arrivals, but many are neighbors," Chatham said.

The majority of the people milling about were between the ages of twelve and twenty.

Andrew suddenly felt ancient. "Have other, er, adults been invited to this house party?"

The duke laughed at his plaintive tone.

The duchess turned to him and did something she rarely did, which was to address him directly. "There will be even more young people meeting us at the pond. You have been brought along to chaperone."

Andrew gave a startled snort. "I must admit that is a first for me."

The duke gave his wife an affectionate look and said, "My wife is teasing you, Drew."

"Ah." Andrew saw no hint of anything playful in either her unnerving eyes or her expressionless face.

His attention was snagged by a solitary figure standing at the far edge of the group. Yet again, Miss Martin was conspicuous for being alone.

Several carriages rolled up and Chatham turned to him. "Hyacinth and I will be riding over in one of the carriages."

"Is it far?"

Her Grace rolled her eyes. "No, but Chatham will not allow me to walk. The carriages are just for the invalids."

Sylvester grinned at his wife's sour expression. "We will see you there."

"Abandoning me already," Andrew muttered as the two left.

The large, boisterous group set off, Lord Needham leading the way.

Evidently the skating pond was only a ten-minute walk from Wych House. Although the sun was out, the wind was biting, and the big group moved swiftly.

Miss Martin, with her far shorter stride, soon fell behind the crowd.

When she did, Andrew dropped back to walk beside her.

***

Stacia was hunched over and walking at a full trot to keep up when she saw booted feet fall in beside hers.

She looked up to find Lord Shelton smiling down at her. "How is your patient?"

"Patient?" she repeated stupidly, her heart pounding.

"The dog."

"Oh. Yes, well, Mr. Higgins believes he will be fine after a week of rest."

"That is good news."

"Yes, it is." She bit her lower lip.

"What is wrong?" he asked.

"Why do you ask?"

"Because you made this expression"—he caught his lower lip with his teeth and pulled a mournful face.

She caught her laugh just in time. "I did not."

"Did so."

She just shook her head and tried to suppress her smile. Of course she failed.

"So, what is wrong?"

"Have you ever been told that you were pertinacious?"

"I don't know. Is that another word for handsome?" He grinned.

This time she couldn't hold back her laugh. "There is nothing wrong, I am just concerned about what will happen to the little dog."

"Lady Addiscombe does not need a lapdog."

Stacia snorted at the thought of her rigid employer even allowing such an unprepossessing little mutt into her townhouse. "She is *not* fond of dogs. Or cats. Or birds." *Or people.*

"How astonishing," he said, not bothering to hide his sarcasm.

Stacia didn't respond to his comment, already feeling guilty over her disloyal words.

"If he is a good ratter, maybe Higgins will keep him," the marquess suggested.

"I asked and they don't need him. There are four terriers already, not to mention all the other dogs."

"Hmm. Maybe you could try and find his owner?"

"He is terribly thin. I think he has been on his own for quite some time."

"Still, it could not hurt to put the word out in the village. Perhaps at the post office and the Weasel," he said, using the locals' name for the small pub.

"Oh. I had not thought of that."

"You have not spent much time in the country."

"No, hardly any. But how did you guess?"

"If you had, you would know that post offices and pubs are the two social hubs in village life."

"What about the church?"

He made a scoffing sound. "There is no gossip and ale at church, Miss Martin."

She snorted.

"Do you want me to do it for you?"

"Er, that is very kind of you." Indeed, suspiciously kind. "But I will do it myself after skating."

He lifted an eyebrow. "You have a day of leisure?"

"Lady Addiscombe has a migraine."

Lord Shelton grimaced. "I would not wish those on anyone. Not even the countess."

"You are familiar with them?"

"Unfortunately."

When he did not offer anything more, Stacia said, "Lady Needham said they are quite awful and often last for days."

"They are and they can," he said grimly.

The walked in silence.

Stacia had no idea why he was beside her. Guilt, perhaps?

Just then they crested a slight rise that overlooked the pond. Beside it was a giant blue and white striped pavilion.

"My goodness!" Stacia said.

"It looks like something out of a medieval tale," Shelton said. "One almost expects a fool wearing motley to come cartwheeling out."

Stacia was delighted by the enchanting scene. There were huge copper braziers filled with glowing coals, a dozen tables with fluttering white cloths held down with yards and yards of ribbon, bunting, and greenery, and the centerpiece on each table was an enormous silver bowl heaped with nuts, sweets, and oranges.

"Ooh, oranges," she said before she could stop herself.

"Would you like one?" he asked.

"Perhaps in a little while," she said, not wishing to appear greedy.

Chairs and benches abounded and there were warm-looking lap rugs in piles.

"What say you, Miss Martin? Shall we skate?"

Stacia turned from the magical scene to the man beside her, who was equally magical, his golden hair glinting under the pale winter sun and his eyes so bright and beautiful they were like pieces of a summer sky.

"You don't need to keep me company, my lord."

"I don't have to do anything I don't wish to do," he retorted. "I am asking because I want to."

"Because you feel guilty."

"I am not proud of what I said the other night, Miss Martin. But I would not burden myself with a tedious companion to make amends. I am not that self-sacrificing." He cocked his head. "Can you not forgive my cruel, ignorant, and idiotic comment? If you truly cannot, then I promise to go away and leave you in peace."

Her heart lurched unpleasantly at the thought of him leaving. "Fine. I forgive you. But you don't need to flirt with me, my lord—you never have before."

"Before?"

She shook her head in amazement. "You truly do not remember, do you?"

"If you are asking if I recall meeting you before this house party"—she nodded—"then my answer is *no*. I take it that is not the truth?" Before she could answer he gestured to one of the many benches. "Come, let us sit. We are attracting notice just standing around."

Stacia willed herself to say *no, thank you*. Instead, she nodded and meekly allowed him to lead her to a seat.

"I will fetch us skates," he said, heading off before she could tell him that she could get her own skates.

All around her people were hurriedly donning their skates. A nearby trio of children tottered excitedly toward the ice. They could not have been more than nine or ten and she couldn't help smiling when one took a tumble and pulled the other two down with her. All three laughed and scrabbled about clumsily as they struggled to get up again.

A shadow passed over her and Lord Shelton dropped to his haunches in front of her. "Here, let me put them on for you."

"I can—"

"I am sure you can," he said, removing his gloves and tossing them aside before deftly unbuckling the straps without even looking.

His hands, she noticed—not for the first time—somehow managed to be beautifully elegant and yet powerfully, distractingly, masculine.

And they were reaching for her.

"Give me your foot," he ordered.

91

Stacia glanced around at his scandalous command, to see who was watching. But everyone was too busy either donning skates—or helping others put them on—or making their way to the ice. Nobody was paying them any attention.

She clamped her jaws tight to keep a fatuous smile from taking control of her face and extended her booted foot.

She was impressed that he had chosen exactly the right size. But then why would that surprise her? The man probably knew women's bodies better than they did.

"What is it?" he asked.

"What is what?" she asked coolly.

"You were smiling and then suddenly you looked as if somebody had just broken your favorite toy."

"I am not a child, Lord Shelton. I don't *have* toys."

His eyes swept over her in a bold way that stole her breath. "No. You are not a child."

Stacia's heart stuttered and she could only be grateful that she was seated.

"You are not going to answer me, are you?" he asked, closing the last buckle and holding out his hand for her other foot.

"No."

He laughed, squeezed her ankle, and then strapped on the skate before sitting beside her, his big body pressing against hers although she could see he still had at least three inches of bench on his far side.

So, she thought, *this is what it was like to be flirted with and pursued by an expert.*

It was…intoxicating.

Don't become too accustomed to it, the wry voice in her head warned. *He will lose interest quickly enough as soon as somebody prettier comes along.*

For once, Stacia refused to allow the voice to dampen her pleasure. Why not enjoy the moment?

"You seem to be very comfortable with skates," she observed.

"I grew up in Yorkshire," he said, pulling on his gloves. "We had frozen ponds every year."

"I am not very good," she warned him. "You might want to find somebody more your—"

"Nonsense." He stood and held out a hand. When Stacia hesitated, he smiled down at her. "Come, come, Miss Martin. It is Christmastime."

Whatever that had to do with anything.

But Stacia heaved a sigh and grabbed his hand, wobbling badly as they trudged across the frozen ground.

There were at least thirty skaters already on the ice, mostly gliding together in twosomes and threesomes.

"Hold on to my arm until you feel comfortable," he said when her ankles buckled, and her feet felt like they might slide out from under her.

She clung to him as he slowly pushed away from the shore.

"Not too fast," she warned.

He slowed his speed until all the other skaters were flying by.

"Don't lift your feet," he told her after a moment. "Just shift your weight from leg to leg. Here, watch." He lifted her hand from his arm and twined their fingers before skating ahead a foot or so to demonstrate, his movements smooth, his skates never leaving the ice.

Stacia tried it for a moment, lurching from side to side.

"Try to bring your feet a bit closer together—yes, that's good. There, see? Much better."

Stacia laughed. "I'm doing it!" She risked a glance up from her feet to find him skating backward. "Oh! You are so good at this!" she cried enviously.

He merely smiled, skating slowly and casting periodic glances behind him. "Chatham and I used to skate every winter." His blue eyes were distant, and a fond smile curved his lips. "This is the first time I have been on the ice in years." His gaze suddenly sharpened and his smile faded. He gracefully swung around until they were skating side by side.

"Where have we met before?" he asked after a moment.

"London and then Bath. Not one place, my lord, but at least a few dozen times."

"I'm sorry," he said after a long moment, the habitually amused glitter in his blue eyes nowhere to be seen.

His regret was worse than his ignorance had been. Why hadn't she just kept her mouth shut? When would she learn?

"When did we meet in London?"

93

"Four years ago."

He nodded. "And I know when we must have met in Bath because I've only been once in the past twenty years." He gave her a wry look. "I didn't go voluntarily. I was in such hot water with dunners that I felt like a hunted fox. I went to Bath to..." he paused and skated for a moment, as if searching for the right words.

"Hide?" she suggested.

Rather than be peeved, he laughed. "I was going to say *lick my wounds* but the word *hide* serves just as well. Regardless of my intentions, I'd scarcely been at my Great Aunt Lydia's house for five minutes when there was an announcement in the newspaper. Naturally, she asked me to escort her to the Pump Room and I could hardly say *no*. And when the invitations started flooding in—" he broke off and shrugged at the memory. After a moment he said, "My great aunt has no children and never married. Suffice it to say that I could scarcely deny her the small pleasure of escorting her about Bath, despite the fact that it had not been part of my plans."

Stacia recalled his visit with crystal clarity. He *had* looked rather haggard, although a haggard Lord Shelton had merely looked even more romantic, mysterious, and gorgeous.

"So, I saw you then, did I?" he asked.

"I was a companion to a friend of your aunt's, a woman named Lady—"

"Lady Hamilton!" he said, giving her a look of triumph. "Now I remember where I have seen you. You used to take her nasty little dog for walks."

Stacia told herself not to feel pleased that he'd successfully dredged his memory.

He snapped his fingers. "Lord, what was that ill-tempered creature's name?"

"Mr. Bunch-and-Stuff."

Lord Shelton laughed. "That is right! What a horrid little dog."

"He was," she agreed. He'd been a fat, whiny pug prone to nipping, and he had once peed on her shoe while she'd had him out on a walk. "I cannot believe you recall the dog."

"I remember him because he bit me once—years ago, on an earlier visit. And he pis—er, urinated on my best pair of boots."

Stacia laughed. "I'm sorry," she said at his reproachful look. "He did the same to me."

"Vile beast. I'm amazed that you didn't secretly throttle him."

"You mustn't speak ill of the dead, my lord. Mr. Bunch-and-Stuff passed on to his Eternal Reward shortly after your visit. And before you ask, *no*, I did not have a hand in that." She paused and then added, "Although I must admit the notion occurred to me more than a few times."

He laughed. "Lord, he must have been ancient."

"Just shy of twenty."

"No! Impossible."

"Lady Hamilton was adamant on the matter." She had also been broken hearted when the ill-tempered little dog had died.

They skated in companionable silence and Stacia realized she was gliding smoothly, no longer huffing along like a frantic calf after its mother.

"I recall my great aunt writing to tell me that Lady Hamilton had died," Shelton said after a moment. "Is that when you took a position with Lady Addiscombe?"

Stacia thought about the job she'd briefly held after Lady Hamilton and pushed the unpleasant memory away. "I had a small gap in employment between Lady Hamilton and the countess." That was not a lie, but neither was it the unpleasant truth.

"Kathryn said the previous Viscount Clayton was your father?"

"Yes."

"Where is your family seat?"

"Devon, but we never lived there." At his enquiring look, she explained. "My grandfather was…improvident."

Shelton nodded and Stacia saw not only comprehension on his face, but something that looked very much like guilt.

***

The last thing Andrew wanted to do was talk about improvident landlords, but he'd been the one to broach the subject. Besides, he was curious about her and how she'd gone from life as a gentlewoman to slaving for a shrew like the Countess of Addiscombe.

"Was your father forced to sell?" he asked after a moment.

"The property is entailed and so he leased it to a wealthy shipbuilder and his family who have occupied it for most of my lifetime. We kept small lodgings in London, near the museum. My father was a scholar."

"Ah. Probably why I didn't know him."

95

"You are not bookish?" she asked.

"Lord, no! Brains have never been my strong suit. Our tutor was fond of saying I had a great deal of vacant room in the old bone box."

She gasped. "What an extremely unkind thing to say to a child!"

"Perhaps, but that does not make it less true," he assured her. "I was a dreadful student from the beginning." That was an understatement, but it was far too mortifying to confess that he'd not learned to read until he'd been eight. "I couldn't wait to leave school and escape into the army. My uncle—Chatham's father— exercised his ducal influence and so I was able to join even though I was only fifteen."

"Fifteen! That seems very young."

"It was. But it also turned out to be a very good place for me."

"How long did you serve?"

"Almost eight years."

"A long time."

That was one way to put it. Andrew changed the subject. "How about you? How many Seasons did you spend in London?"

She laughed and Andrew happened to be looking at her when she did so. It transformed her from moderately attractive to startlingly pretty. "What is so amusing?" he asked.

"Just that you asked about London Seasons right after I asked you how many years you'd been in the army."

Andrew smiled. "Yes, I suppose that speaks to a rather telling mental connection. So, how many?"

"Just the one."

"And did you—"

"Shelton!" Kathryn skated up alongside them, twin blonde women on her far side and a trio of dark-haired young women trailing in her wake. Andrew bit back a groan.

"Kathryn, how delightful," he said flatly, wanting to strangle her for interrupting what had been a pleasurable *tête-à-tête*.

Her green eyes twinkled maliciously. "My neighbors desperately wish to make your acquaintance. I told them it would be anticlimactic—that you were better enjoyed from afar—but they insisted."

"Kathryn!" the blondes exclaimed in horrified unison.

Andrew turned to Miss Martin. "Let us move off to the side as we are impeding traffic."

She nodded, an anxious notch forming between her large brown eyes.

"Do you remember how to stop?" he asked. "You just push your toes slowly together," he said before she could answer.

"Push my toes together," she muttered, watching her feet. A smile slowly spread over her face as they came to a halt.

Andrew waited until they'd fully halted and Miss Martin had released his arm before turning to Kathryn and her friends. He recognized their eager, adoring looks and suppressed a sigh, his mask already sliding into place. "And who are these delightful young ladies?" he asked, smiling from face to face.

The twins giggled immoderately, and Kathryn gave Andrew a wry smile. "Miss Lowery and Miss Susannah Lowery are our neighbors—Sir Thomas and Lady Lowery's daughters—and these ladies," she gracefully slid aside and gestured to the other three, "are their cousins who are visiting. Miss Moore, Miss Arabella Moore, and Miss Coraline Moore." Her smile grew. "All of them begged me to introduce them to the most notorious rake in England."

Her last words were drowned out by the protests of the five young women, who were clearly mortified.

"We did *not* say that, my lord," one of the twins insisted—he'd already forgotten which was which.

Andrew gave the flustered young women a reassuring smile. "I recognize Lady Kathryn's words when I hear them. I am charmed to meet all of you." *Now skate away*, he wanted to add.

Unfortunately, rather than move off, more young people drifted up.

Bloody hell.

Lord Bellamy, the two lads he'd brought with him—whose names Andrew had already forgotten—and Bellamy's little blonde familiar, Miss Lucy, skated up.

"I say, Miss Martin," Bellamy said, "Kathryn says Lord Clayton—er, the former viscount—was your father. Hornsby here is from Devon—right next to your family's seat."

"I'm afraid it has been many years since my family occupied Clayton Abbey," Miss Martin said.

"Your c-c-cousin has recently moved b-b-back," Hornsby, informed her. "He cut down the rose garden and built a Greek folly," he added, apropos of nothing.

"Oh. I did not realize—"

"How are you finding our little corner of Hampshire, my lord?" one of the twins asked Andrew, forcing him to turn away from Miss Martin.

"I am enjoying myself very much." *Or at least I had been, up until a few minutes ago.* He turned to the three silent cousins, who were watching him with wide-eyed curiosity. "Of course I am even more pleased to be here now," he felt compelled to add.

The twins giggled—they were gigglers, that much was apparent—while the far more sensible cousins merely blushed and smiled at his ham-fisted flirtation. Lord. When had exchanging mindless pleasantries become such drudgery? He had obviously been mired in the country too long.

"Are you ladies visiting for long?" he asked the cousins, hoping to stem the giggling.

"Until the beginning of the year," the eldest said.

"And then we are all going to London," the youngest piped up. "It will be our first time."

Andrew smiled at her innocent enthusiasm. "Coming out, are you?"

The girl—Caroline or Catherine or something with a C—laughed. "I'm not old enough, sir. But Emma and Daph will be launched." She pulled a face, her freckled nose wrinkling. "Sounds rather like joining the navy."

Andrew laughed. "What will you do while they are attending balls and the like?"

"Lessons," she said glumly, but then brightened. "Although Miss Brambly has promised that we will visit the Tower and the British Museum."

He opened his mouth, but one of the twins decided her young cousin had been the center of attention long enough. "Our Papa says the Thames is frozen and there might be a frost fair if this cold weather continues. He has promised to take us to London, too."

This news caught the young males' attention. "I hadn't heard that," Bellamy said, and then fixed the Lowery girl with a look of mild scorn. "Are you sure you got it right, Twin?"

Both girls scowled at his form of address.

"It's true, Bellamy," his other mate—not Hornsby— said before either of the twins could lash into the young viscount. "I heard Lord Needham mention it at breakfast."

"We must go," Bellamy immediately said.

"The only place you're going is back to school," Kathryn taunted.

Bickering commenced.

The twins gave the arguing siblings disdainful looks, and one said to Andrew, "You probably think we are terribly rustic, my lord." She fluttered what were, he had to admit, impressive eyelashes.

"Er, why would you believe that?" Andrew asked, not telling her what he really thought, which was that they all seemed terribly, terribly young.

"Because we are so excited about a frost fair. You must have gone to dozens."

He opened his mouth.

Lord Bellamy gave a loud guffaw. "What a pea goose you are, Twin!" The viscount gave the girl a look of amused contempt. "He can't have been to more than one, can he?"

The other twin bristled on her sister's behalf. "Whyever not?" she shot back, her sophisticated disdain of only a moment earlier nowhere in sight as she squared up against the young lord.

Bellamy opened his mouth, but one of the cousins—the truly beautiful one—said, "Because the Thames hasn't frozen enough since 1789. And the time before that was in the 1740s."

Bellamy nodded approvingly at the cousin and gave the twin a derisive sneer. "*That's* why, Twin. Shelton ain't *that* old," he added, giving Andrew a look that clearly said, *girls!*

"Thank you, Bellamy," Andrew said dryly.

The young lord blinked in confusion as his mates jeered at him, but Kathryn gave her brother an approving nod and said, "Well done, Doddy."

The viscount's pale cheeks darkened when he realized just how his comment had sounded. "Oh, I didn't mean—"

One of the Lowery sisters discarded what little sophistication that remained, looked down her nose at the blushing lad, and said, "Your oafish comment is merely more proof that little boys should be seen and not heard."

Her salvo managed to get under the skin of not just one, but all three young gentlemen.

Andrew sighed as a battle of the sexes flared to life and the argument blazed.

He turned to Miss Martin to suggest they slip away while the others were brawling but found himself facing an empty space.

He frowned and glanced around him. But he saw no sign of her long gray coat—noticeable for its dowdy functionality, especially among this group, many of whom sported festive reds, greens, and blues.

"Excuse me," he murmured to nobody in particular—not that any of the others heard him—and left the ice, trudging toward the pavilion, thinking perhaps she had gone to enjoy an orange and some hot chocolate.

He saw Sylvester and the duchess and a few dozen older guests, but no Miss Martin.

Well. Where the devil had she darted off to in such a hurry?

Chapter 9

Stacia set her skates back with the others, cast a look of yearning at the braziers and mountains of food under the big tent, but then forced herself to head back to Wych House.

She nodded at a trio of younger people heading toward the pond, their fine clothing proclaiming they were yet more of the visitors who'd been pouring into Wych House over the last few days, rather than the humbler village denizens.

Skating with Lord Shelton had been…fun. And fun was something she'd not had in longer than she wanted to admit. She felt a stab of resentment that he'd been so quick to leave her company, but she was not exactly surprised. The Lowery twins and their cousins—especially the divine Arabella—were exactly the sort of beautiful girls who'd attracted Shelton's attention in the past.

Well, what had she expected? His taste in company would not have suddenly changed merely because he had apologized to her.

His apology—which had been unexpected—had blunted her anger toward him, but it had done nothing to soothe her injured pride. It would be a long time, if ever, before she forgot either his dismissive words to Lady Kathryn or the fact that he recalled Mr. Bunch-and-Stuff and not Stacia.

She made her way back to her chambers without encountering any of the guests. Thanks to Lady Needham, she had a full afternoon off and didn't intend to waste the opportunity.

She took the smaller of her two valises from the dressing room. Inside it were the tools of her second, almost more lucrative, trade. When Lady Addiscombe had told her that they would be coming to a big house party Stacia had splurged some of her small savings to purchase more of the expensive gold leaf that she employed in her paintings. She had produced some additional fans, reasoning that if she did not sell them in the little village of Little Sissingdon then she could offer them to the modiste in Bath who usually bought her wares.

This close to Christmas—and with so many wealthy guests at Wych House—surely somebody would buy the fans. In any event, it was worth the effort.

After she'd paid a visit to the village dress shop, she could post notices about the little dog.

Stacia removed all the fans, hesitated, and then put two back, the one with the poem by Mary Chandler, *To Mrs. Moor, A Poem on Friendship*, and the other—the best thing she had ever done and could not bring herself to part with—which had a lovely illuminated 'H' and several lines from Shakespeare's Sonnet 29.

Last night in the drawing room Lord Needham had mentioned there was to be a secret gift giving once the rest of the houseguests had all arrived. Evidently there would be a name drawing and people would not know who their secret St. Nicholas was. *Anyone*—that included servants, amazingly—who wished to join only needed to drop a slip of paper with their name on it into the big crystal bowl in the drawing room and names would be chosen and distributed with enough time before Christmas that people could secure gifts.

Lady Addiscombe had said it was foolish and that the servants, whom she'd complained were already cheeky, would only become worse if Needham continued to treat them as if they were equals.

"They might be *his* equals," she had proclaimed loudly to another of the guests—the sweet, rather vague, Baroness Mixon—"but they most certainly are not *mine*."

Not for the first time had Stacia wanted to disappear into a crack at something the older woman had said.

She chewed her lip for a moment and then sat down at the small desk in her sitting room, took out a sheet of paper, and neatly tore off a corner before writing her name. Just because her employer did not wish to join the gift giving did not mean Stacia could not.

Of course she would not tell the countess that.

And so, before Stacia went to the village, she made a stop in the drawing room and dropped her name into the bowl.

***

Without Miss Martin to entertain him Andrew found the skating party rather flat.

He was going to return to Wych House when he realized his right glove—from his favorite pair—had a tear in it. It wasn't too bad now, but if he left it the glove would be irreparable.

Little Sissingdon was too small to have a glover, but he'd seen a clothing shop. Perhaps somebody there could repair it.

Rather than go back for Drake he decided to walk the short distance. He passed clusters of people heading toward the pond. Needham, true to form, appeared to have invited the entire town. Or county, even.

It would be very easy to envy Needham, and not just because he was wealthy. The man was also an excellent steward of Wych House *and* the surrounding area. It had been a fortunate day for the denizens of the area when he'd decided to put roots down here.

Unlike Andrew's own people.

He grimaced at the thought, shame heating his face at how long he had pursued his revenge at the cost of his family estate.

Andrew knew he had no choice but to take a wife, and a wealthy one, at that. If he was serious about restoring Rosewood, he would need far more money than his stud farm or inheritance would provide.

But the thought of marrying a woman for her money was simply too depressing to think about right now. He would have plenty of time to contemplate it after Christmas, when he joined Chatham in London for yet another Season.

Yes, later. He could think about that later.

Little Sissingdon was bustling with pre-Christmas business, not just the shops, but there seemed to be some sort of activity on the village green that involved a great deal of hammering and shouting.

Andrew paused to watch for a moment. "What is this for?" he asked a man who was prying the lid off an enormous crate.

"The Christmas fete." The older man's eyes slid over Andrew's person, assessing him. "Lord Needham bought a brand-new tent." He gestured to the crate which held familiar blue-striped canvas. Andrew smiled at the sight of the pavilion. The man really did have his finger in everything.

"Any idea where I can get a glove mended?" he asked, holding up his hand to exhibit the rip.

"Aye, that be a fine one—don't want Mr. Oliver on that. He be the cobbler," the man explained. "Go to Mrs. Johnson—she who owns the dress shop. Mostly she has finery for women, but Mary Finley works for her. Right clever with a needle."

"Thank you," Andrew said, and then turned toward the dress shop.

Only to see the door open and Miss Martin come strolling out.

Interesting.

Andrew was about to hail her when a man approached her—Captain Walker, Crewe's son—and the two commenced talking.

He dropped his half-raised hand and watched as they turned and headed across the street to a tea shop.

Andrew stared for a moment, his mind strangely…frozen.

He blinked rapidly and shook himself. So, what if she had left skating with him to come and meet Walker?

Andrew was nothing to her; she could do whatever she pleased. With whomever she pleased.

If she preferred Walker to him, what of it?

It took him a moment to identify the emotion he was feeling as rejection.

He firmly put Miss Martin from his mind and strode toward the dress shop.

A bell tinkled when he opened the door and he was immediately assaulted by an almost oppressive blast of floral perfume—more than one sort of flower, if his nostrils served him correctly—and the hum of feminine chatter. Which stopped abruptly when heads turned toward him.

Andrew smiled and shut the door behind him.

One of the women, an attractive dark-haired female who was probably a few years his senior, hurried toward him.

"I am Mrs. Johnson, proprietress. How may I serve you today, sir?" she asked, her sharp eyes sweeping his body appraisingly—not once, but twice.

"I was told you might have somebody who could repair my glove?" He held up his hand.

She leaned forward and took his hand in both of hers.

Andrew's lips twitched as she examined the glove with far more thoroughness than it required. After a long moment she looked up at him through her thick eyelashes. "Indeed, yes—I can have this repaired. We even carry a few sizes of men's gloves here—if you need something to wear in the interim."

"Thank you." He gently removed his hand from hers. "Yes, I will take another pair to wear home today if I can leave these."

"Of course, of course. Right this way."

And then Andrew startled himself by asking, "Was that Miss Martin I saw leaving a moment ago?"

A lightning-fast look of chagrin flickered across her face before a sly smile replaced it. "*Tut, tut!* You should know better than to pry into a lady's personal matters, sir."

"I should know that," he agreed, already regretting his question. "Perhaps you might show me the gloves you have available."

Mrs. Johnson suddenly leaned forward, pressing her rather spectacular bosom against his arm while beckoning him closer with one finger.

Andrew found himself leaning forward out of courtesy. "Yes?"

"It wasn't buying that Miss Martin was doing here today. It was selling."

"Is that so?" Andrew said. He suddenly recalled her sitting with her basket, needle, and colorful threads in the drawing room. Perhaps she sold her embroidery or cross stitching or whatever it was she worked on every evening.

"The lady paints," Mrs. Johnson said.

Andrew looked around the crowded little shop. "Er, you sell paintings?"

She gave an earthy chuckle, and his gaze naturally dropped to her quaking bosom. "Not paintings. *Fans.*"

"Indeed?" he said, not sure what else he could say.

"*Mmm*, very lovely ones."

Well, that was…interesting.

Andrew realized the shopkeeper was staring up at him, still pressed against him.

"Er, the gloves?" he reminded her.

She quickly hid her disappointment and escorted him to her small selection, leaving him when another customer pulled her away with a question.

The choice was easy because there was only one pair that fit. They were dark brown and he preferred black, but it was bloody cold, and a functional pair was better than no pair.

He took his purchase to the counter and waited while she finished another transaction. He noticed the discreet sign advertising alterations and repairs and thought about the missing buttons on his favorite doeskin breeches, and a few other articles of clothing that needed some mending. He knew Chatham's valet would gladly do the work, but he did not like imposing.

He took out his notecase and handed her the money for the gloves. "If I send over a few other items that need mending will your seamstress have time to do the work before—say, a week from now?"

"Certainly, she will."

"I will have a servant run them over."

"Or you could bring them by yourself. Later tonight."

Andrew paused in the act of reaching for the coins she slid across the counter. He raised an eyebrow. "You are open late, are you?" he asked, deliberately misunderstanding her.

"I live above the shop and can always be available for a few...favored customers."

She was an attractive woman. He knew he would enjoy an evening spent with her. And yet...

He smiled politely. "That is generous of you, but tomorrow is soon enough. No, you needn't wrap them," he said when she laid the gloves in tissue. "I will wear them out. Good day to you, ma'am." He nodded and left the shop, pausing outside to pull on the new gloves.

He could not resist glancing toward the tea shop. Miss Martin and Captain Walker were at a table in the window. He watched for a moment as the two smiled and talked, obviously at ease with each other.

Andrew had the strongest urge to foist his company on the pair and see if he, too, could coax something other than a scowl out of Miss Martin.

He snorted at the impulse. Could he really be so vain that when he came across a woman who did not fall all over him, he was miffed?

The door behind him opened and Mrs. Johnson stepped out.

"Did I forget something?" he asked.

"No. I just came out for a breath of fresh air." She paused, and then gave him a look so scorching that Andrew was amazed that his hair didn't combust. "And to enjoy the view."

He laughed, took her hand, and lifted it to his lips, briefly regretting that he was not in the frame of mind to engage in some light-hearted bed sport. "I wish you a happy Christmas, Mrs. Johnson."

She smiled wistfully. "You as well, my lord."

Ah. So, she knew who he was, then.

With a last glance at the tea shop Andrew turned and headed back to Wych House, leaving the two young lovers to their tryst.

***

"Thank you for agreeing to assist me in my time of need, Miss Martin," Captain Walker said.

Stacia smiled. "I am more than happy to help you with your gift selection, although I am sure you would do quite well on your own."

He pulled a face. "I might have, but it is nice to have another artist to consult about a gift for Lady Crewe."

Stacia had seen Aurelia Crewe's work when she had come upon the other woman sketching in an especially lovely and sunny window seat—which had been Stacia's destination.

Lady Crewe had noticed the sketchbook in Stacia's hand and the two had chatted for a full quarter of an hour, sharing their work with each other. Stacia had been awed by the other woman's skill.

"How does one get into reproducing illuminated manuscripts?" Captain Walker asked after they had ordered from the waiter.

"I don't actually do that," she said. "When my father was still alive, he had a large collection." Which her cousin had stolen, but she did not bring that up. "I sometimes made small repairs to his manuscripts."

"He must have trusted you a great deal to do so."

"He is the one who trained me, so he had to."

He chuckled. "Yes, I can see that."

"He stopped doing his own work when he developed a palsy in his dominant hand," she explained. "What I do now is paint for my own pleasure." She hesitated, and then decided to tell the truth. "I also paint fans which I sell."

"Ah, an entrepreneurial soul like me." He leaned across the table, his handsome face creasing in a smile. "Should we keep our grubby trade a secret lest we be tossed out of Wych House, Miss Martin?"

"Considering that Lord Needham is one of the wealthiest businessmen in Britain, I think you and I should be safe."

He chuckled. "You are probably right."

Stacia caught sight of a familiar figure standing outside the women's clothing shop. It was Lord Shelton, and he appeared to be staring right at the tea shop window, although he did nothing to acknowledge them.

"You are friends with the Marquess of Shelton?" Captain Walker asked.

"No." That sounded too abrupt, so she said, "We are merely acquainted."

The owner of the dress shop came out on her front step and Shelton turned to her. Even from a distance Stacia could see the feline smile that curved the pretty shopkeeper's face.

She must have said something that made Shelton laugh. He took her hand, bowed extravagantly over it, and then turned and strode away.

Mrs. Johnson watched him until he was out of sight and then her shoulders slumped with dejection and she disappeared back into her shop.

What was that all about? Why had he been in a women's dress shop?

You know why...

The waiter arrived with their tea and Stacia tore her thoughts away from Shelton and the voluptuous shopkeeper and turned them back to her attractive companion.

Stacia enjoyed her tea and the shopping expedition with the captain. He was charming, witty, and she did not think she was flattering herself that he had some interest in her.

And yet all she could think about was Shelton and his interaction with Mrs. Johnson.

The thought of him taking a lover depressed her.

He had spent time skating with her because he had felt guilty. There was no more to it than that.

Doubtless he had forgotten her name all over again.

And yet, when Stacia returned to Wych House a few hours later she found a handkerchief with the initials A.W.D. sitting outside her door. Carefully wrapped up inside the fine white linen were two oranges.

Chapter 10

What sort of monster doesn't finish a floating island?"

Stacia looked up from her needlework at the sound of Lord Shelton's voice. Out of habit, she glanced around the drawing room before remembering that her employer was still in the grip of her migraine.

"What sort of gentleman teases a woman about her eating habits?" Stacia retorted, secretly pleased that he had noticed her at all. And then disgusted with herself for the thought.

Lord Shelton ignored her question and sat down on the settee next to her. Her heart thudded faster as he swept her seated body with a lingering look that made the room several degrees hotter. "You cannot be slimming as you are already far too slender."

"Is that your way of telling me I am scrawny, my lord?"

He laughed, the rich, low sound bringing to mind honey and hot summer days. "You are like a hedgehog, Miss Martin."

"So, scrawny *and* prickly. I can see why you are famed for your charm."

Again, he laughed, appearing delighted.

Stacia snipped the end of her thread and rooted through her basket to find the cornflower blue she needed for the next flower, more grateful than ever to have her needlework to cling to. "Thank you for the oranges, my lord." She risked a look up at him.

"Oranges?" he repeated, wearing an expression of wide-eyed innocence that nobody except a very young child would find convincing.

"They are my favorite treat," she said, ignoring his evasion.

"What sort of person likes fruit more than floating islands?"

"A monstrous one—I thought we had already established that?"

He smiled and held her gaze for a long moment during which Stacia found it impossible to breathe or look away. She knew she should offer to return his handkerchief, but the words would not come.

He gestured to her tambor, angling his head to better see it. "That is very pretty." He leaned closer and squinted, bringing the faint, mingled scent of soap, cologne, and port with him. "Is that a 'J'?"

"Yes," she said, threading her needle. Or at least attempting to. Could a man's scent actually intoxicate a woman?

"It looks like one of those, er—whosy whatsits."

Stacia laughed. "You really were not jesting about your scholastic aptitude, were you?"

Rather than be offended, he grinned. "*Inaptitude* would be more appropriate. What are those fancy letters called?"

"Illuminated."

"Ah, that's right. Monkish things, weren't they?"

"Many were." Stacia finally got the thread in the eye and began on the flower. She had smelled men's cologne in the past—often—but nothing had ever smelled like Lord Shelton. Not just clean and crisp, but…like desire. That was it. He smelled like desire in human form.

I am such a besotted idiot.

Stacia wished he would go away. At the same time, she reveled in his attention. Urges she could not identify bubbled up inside her—the desire to grab him and do…what?

Was this how gamblers felt when they saw a pack of cards?

He leaned closer, the heat from his body blazing along her side. "Where did you sneak off to this afternoon, Miss Martin?"

"I didn't *sneak*, my lord."

"One minute you were there; the next you were gone."

"I had some matters to attend to."

"It was cruel of you to abandon me with the infantry."

Stacia couldn't help smiling. "*Infantry*? I believe the Misses Lowery are nineteen, my lord."

"That is an infant from where I am standing. Besides, all that giggling makes them seem far younger."

Stacia thought so, too. The twins were beautiful but appeared to be interested in nothing other than clothing, balls, and boys.

"I would not have expected excessive giggling to be much of an impediment if the woman in question was beautiful enough."

He raised his eyebrows, his gaze suddenly uncomfortably piercing, as if he could see the jealous monster that lived inside her. "It depends on *what*, Miss Martin."

"I b-beg your pardon?"

"You said an *impediment*. An impediment to *what*? Marriage? A game of Whist?" His lips pulled up on one side. "Fleshly pleasures?"

Fleshly pleasures.

Stacia opened her mouth, but all that came out was, "Uh."

Mercifully, Lord Needham entered the noisy drawing room and rescued her from uttering anything else.

He came to a halt in the center of the room and the chatter instantly died away. "Tonight, we are choosing names for the secret gift giving. This is a tradition from my own family." He smiled faintly. "As many of you know, my father John Needham was an iron monger long before he was a lord. He was a man of the people who adored Christmastime and felt strongly that his employees and servants should be included in the revelry. To that end, he instituted a modern version of Saturnalia."

"Saturnalia?" Lord Bellamy repeated. Based on the curious expressions on most of the other guests he was not alone in never having heard of the celebration. Stacia, the daughter of an antiquarian, at least knew the essentials of the Roman bacchanal which turned the social order on its head.

"From the Roman celebration of Saturn," Lord Needham explained. "I have chosen a few of my favorite traditions to continue here at Wych House. In any event, the secret gift giving is open to any who wish to participate—you simply need to add your name to this bowl."

"What other sorts of events take place during Saturnalia?" Baroness Mixon asked, looking more animated than Stacia had yet seen her.

"We will have a treasure hunt—this is an event where the lord of the manor is supposed to share some of his wealth." Several people laughed. "On Christmas Eve we will have what many houses call a servant ball, but ours will have a slight…twist. Not only will it be a night for my employees and servants to enjoy themselves, but it is an event at which the masters wait on the servants."

The room erupted with excited chatter and Stacia saw Lord and Lady Needham exchange amused glances before he continued. "Naturally none of you are obliged to participate in that ball—or any of the other events, for that matter. There will be a second, more traditional, ball on Christmas Day. If you are interested in the gift giving, you need to put your name in now as Lady Kathryn has volunteered to assign the, er—what did you call it, my dear?" he asked his wife.

"Secret St. Nicholas," Lady Needham said.

Several people chuckled.

Lord Needham went to sit by his wife and people resumed their activities—all the newcomers and even some of the neighbor guests approaching the table where Lady Kathryn sat.

Lord Shelton was watching the young people jostle to add their names, an amused look on his face.

"Is your name already in the bowl, my lord?" Stacia said, relieved to find her voice and brain had resumed functioning.

He laughed. "No, it is not."

She lifted an eyebrow. "You are too grand a personage to participate in festivities including servants?"

He pursed his lips and fixed her with a look of dry amusement. "Hedgehog," he whispered.

And then he pushed to his feet and headed for the table with the bowl.

***

Andrew waited until the last of the youngsters had cleared off before taking one of the small pieces of paper and scribbling his own name. Before he could drop it into the bowl Kathryn's hand shot out and snatched it from his fingers.

She unfolded it, read his name, and snorted.

"What is so amusing?" he asked, although he could guess.

"You have the worst handwriting I have ever seen."

"So…that makes me the best at the worst handwriting. I enjoy being the best." He gave her his smug smile—the one Sylvester always said made a person want to punch him.

She rolled her eyes and then crumpled up the chit and tossed it aside.

"What? I'm not allowed to play?"

"I already added your name earlier," she said, smirking up at him.

Andrew couldn't help laughing. "You really are a fiend, aren't you?"

"I'm sorry I interrupted your *tête-à-tête* with Miss Martin at the pond today."

Andrew scowled and glanced around. "Perhaps you could shout that a bit louder? People in the back of the drawing room might not have heard."

She made a dismissive gesture with one hand. "Nobody is paying attention to us."

Andrew crossed his arms and leaned his hip against the table, his body, not coincidentally, between Kathryn and the settee where the subject of their conversation was sitting. Alone. "You will do her no favors if my name is coupled with hers, Kathryn."

Kathryn only smiled. "She is not your usual sort of flirtation, is she?"

Andrew felt the not unfamiliar urge to throttle her. "You know nothing about my flirtations, usual or otherwise."

"I will get to see them firsthand when we go to London."

Andrew ignored her, watching with growing displeasure as an especially handsome young man approached Miss Martin. He said something and she smiled up at him—blindingly—and then set aside her needlework and took his hand when he extended it.

"Who the devil is that?" he demanded before he could stop himself.

Kathryn followed his gaze. "That's Dixon. He's one of Needham's secretaries. Surely you remember? You were introduced the day we arrived."

"Of course I remember him," Andrew snapped. But he didn't. "I just didn't see his face," he lied.

"He is Viscount Cowper's youngest son," Kathryn said, staring at him strangely.

"I know that," he said testily. "I went to school with one of his brothers."

"Yes, you said that when you met him."

Dixon led Miss Martin to a large pair of doors disguised by murals of some battle or other and pushed one of the doors aside, exposing a pianoforte. Miss Martin said something that made Dixon laugh. She then opened the bench and sorted through some sheets of music.

Dixon shoved the other door open and turned to the assembled guests. "Lady Needham has suggested an impromptu dance and Miss Martin has agreed to provide some music."

Andrew winced at the cheer that went up.

"I'll just need some help moving furniture and rolling up this carpet."

A dozen volunteers rushed to help.

Andrew didn't think it was quite fair that Dixon had tapped Miss Martin to play and not take part in the dancing. Every young woman Andrew had ever met could bang out at least a few tunes on the piano. Surely somebody else could—

"Has anyone else noticed?"

He turned to Kathryn. "Pardon?"

"That you forget things—and people."

Andrew was accustomed to Kathryn's constant needling—he even enjoyed her sharp wit and found it amusing to bicker with her like an adolescent boy on occasion—but this subject was not one he was willing to banter about.

He leashed his fury before leaning closer to her, lowering his voice so that only she would be able to hear him. "You know, Kathryn, this propensity of yours to pry and meddle and share your unwanted opinion freely might be amusing in a child, but it is offensive and obnoxious in an adult. And it will quickly gain you a reputation as an interfering busybody." He'd started off speaking coolly and ended up almost snarling the last words.

Annoyed with himself he pushed away from the table, boiling with anger, and some other emotion he did not want to look at too closely.

Suddenly, the room was chokingly claustrophobic, and Andrew could not get away fast enough.

Chapter 11

Hyacinth's long, sinuous body rippled beneath Sylvester's as he pumped his hips.

"Harder," his wife ordered, her eyes black pools of lust as she stared up at him.

He slammed into her savagely enough to shake the frame of the huge four-poster bed.

And again.

And again.

"Is that the best you can do?" she taunted, the words gasped out between punishing thrusts. Her lips curled into a rare smile, this one almost evil. "Fuck me like you hate me, Sylvester."

He gave a bark of laughter and instantly ceased his thrusting, sliding a hand around her throat and squeezing—not too terribly hard, but enough to cut off her air. "You will take what I give you and be grateful for it, witch."

The vixen rolled her eyes at him, her pale, freckled skin darkening the longer she went without a breath.

Even after half a year of marriage a great deal about his wife was still a delectable mystery to Sylvester. But the one thing he knew for sure was that she *never* gave in first. His choices at that moment were to either kill her or fuck her as she'd demanded.

Sylvester smirked down at her; he would give her what she wanted. This time.

He quickly released her, withdrew from her body, and flipped her over, earning a startled squawk in the process.

"Up," he ordered, raising her hips off the bed while pushing her shoulders down, holding the back of her neck and pressing her head against the mattress. "Stay," he ordered, giving her slender neck one last squeeze before dragging his fingers down the vulnerable knobs of her spine.

He rose up high on his knees and stared down the creamy length of her bowed body. *Fuck.* Was there any sight more beautiful?

If there was, it was the next one.

Sylvester spread her buttocks and caressed down her cleft, sliding a finger into her wet, swollen cunt and pumping in and out of her tight sheath hard enough to force a grunt out of her. She canted her hips, and he smiled at her silent begging, adding a finger and fucking her hard while his other hand slid around her thickened waist. He caressed her rounded stomach, his balls clenching with primitive pride at the evidence of the child he had put inside her.

Sylvester gritted his teeth against a dangerous swell of desire and reluctantly released her belly, quickly locating her engorged nub and working two powerful, back-to-back orgasms from her body.

"Sylvester...please," she begged breathlessly when he thumbed the throbbing bundle of nerves, preparing to work her toward pleasure a third time.

He gave a mocking laugh. "Oh, *now* you are begging and not commanding?"

She whimpered.

"Once more," he ordered.

***

Hy knew it was never a good idea to taunt her husband—at least not unless he was tightly bound hand and foot and she had a whip in her hand—but it was simply too tempting to bring out the streak of sensual cruelty that he usually kept under such tight control.

"Once more," he barked, and then used his thumb in a way that *demanded* an orgasm from her exhausted body.

Hy gave in to the inevitable, too-intense wave of pleasure that crashed over her.

She had barely begun to convulse around his fingers when they disappeared, and he slammed his thick hard length so deeply she saw stars behind her eyelids. He remained motionless, keeping her stretched and almost uncomfortably full as she came undone.

Only when her climax ebbed did he move inside her, slow, deep thrusts that plumbed her so deeply that pleasure and pain met. He slid his hand into her hair and wrapped it around his fist, twisting her head to the side until she could see him looming over her, his eyes black with lust, his tightly clenched jaw making the savage scar on his cheek even more livid.

He drove into her *hard* and Hy whimpered, her eyes fluttering shut.

"Eyes on me," he snapped, his gaze burning into her when she could manage to lift her heavy lids. "Is this what you wanted?" he asked, his thrusts punishing, the words squeezed out between clenched teeth, the muscles of his torso hard, rippling, and glistening from his exertion.

He was utterly, completely—almost painfully—magnificent.

And he was *hers*. All. Hers. When would that stop amazing her? How had homely, gangly, awkward Hyacinth Bellamy managed to attract such a man?

"I…love…you," Hy panted the words between the brutal slamming.

He groaned, drove himself deep, and then his entire body stiffened as he filled her with liquid heat.

A moment later his big body collapsed over hers.

"Oh, Hyacinth. You undo me," he whispered, and then toppled them both to the side.

A short time later...

Sylvester carded his fingers through his wife's damp hair as she rested her head on his chest and toyed with his navel.

"It is odd that you are not ticklish at all," she said, not for the first time, her low voice vibrating through his body.

Sylvester smiled as she lightly glossed her fingers over his sides, down his thigh, seeking some part of him that would reduce him to a giggling heap. *She* was extremely ticklish; amusingly so. When he was feeling especially cruel— usually after she had driven him to it—he tickled her just to see his normally serious wife laugh uncontrollably. She claimed it was a worse punishment than a beating. His smile grew into a grin; it had been foolish of her to give him such a weapon.

"Katie is unhappy."

The smile slid from his lips. He had thought the same thing more than a few times but had not mentioned it because he had been so preoccupied with Andrew and their reconciliation.

He'd lived in the same house with Kathryn for months but did not know his young sister-in-law very well. Even so, he'd seen something he recognized in her eyes: desperation. It was an expression he'd seen in Andrew's eyes countless times over the years. Only recently had his cousin lost some of that haunted look. He had begun to hope that Andrew had left his pain and rage in the past.

But then earlier tonight, in the drawing room—right before Andrew had stormed out—he'd seen such a look of angry despair on his cousin's face that it had left him breathless. He had been about to run after him, to see if he could help. But he knew Andrew would not appreciate him prying. Sylvester would wait until tomorrow to check on him.

He turned his thoughts back to his wife, who was probably waiting for an answer. "Kathryn was not this way the last time you saw her—in the spring?" he asked.

She shook her head, her silky hair stroking his chest. "No. This is new."

He heard the anguish in her voice and knew she must indeed be worried because she so rarely exhibited any emotion—at least not outside of sex, the only time she seemed to loosen her tight control.

"Have you tried asking her if something is wrong?" he asked, even though he could guess her answer.

"No. At least not in so many words."

He smiled. "You might need to be direct with her, darling."

She made a thoughtful humming sound, which was her non-confrontational way of saying *no*.

"Phoebe said our mother is insisting that Katie return to Bath with her after Christmas."

His fingers stilled in her hair. "She will not allow her to have a Season?"

"She says Katie may have her come out next year and that *she* will come to London to oversee her launch."

He resumed his stroking. "Do you doubt that will happen?"

She shrugged. "I don't know."

Sometimes understanding what Hyacinth wanted was difficult. Sylvester decided to take his own advice from a few moments earlier and be direct.

"What do you think would be best for your sister?"

It took Hyacinth a good five minutes before she answered. His wife was not given to impulsive words or actions.

"My mother has always been critical of Katie—at least, she was critical of the way she *used* to be, which was something of a hoyden. I suppose it is possible she might no longer carp at her now that she is always so neat, tidy, and without a hair out of place, but…"

"But?"

"But all the evidence suggests my mother will simply find some other reason to criticize her."

He smiled at her wording, albeit a bit sadly. Sylvester's own mother was an unnatural bitch incapable of showing love—not even to her own children. He had been fortunate as a child not to spend much time around her as she had always avoided him and his brother as if they were carriers of the plague. Hyacinth, he knew, had not been so lucky with her own mother.

"Kathryn need not go to Bath," he said.

She rolled away slowly and then pushed up onto her elbow to look at him, a slight furrow between her glorious eyes. "But under the law she must obey her parents for the next three or so years."

He shrugged. "There are ways around that."

"What do you mean?"

He smiled and traced the sharp line of her jaw with one finger, awed as he often was by her stark beauty. "Being a duke doesn't just mean that I get to wear a funny hat and moth-eaten fur robes on occasion."

"You mean you would bring an action against her?"

"It would never come to that. There are other ways of applying pressure. The first and easiest method would be to simply talk to Needham."

"You think he would threaten to curtail my mother's allowance to gain her compliance?"

"I think he is no great admirer of the Countess of Addiscombe," he said dryly.

She nodded slowly, her gaze vague. Gradually, the tension drained out of her. After a moment, she looked into his eyes. "Will you see to that—if it becomes necessary?"

Sylvester slid a hand behind her neck and brought her close enough to kiss her gently, stroking her cheek with his thumb as he held her gaze, staring into her ridiculously beautiful eyes. Sylvester could count on the fingers of one hand the number of times his wife had asked him for anything, and it was only twice. She had wanted her friend Charles to live closer and she had asked for a comfortable pasture for her broken-down old nag, Thunder.

"Of course I will do that, Hyacinth," he said. *I would do anything you asked of me, my love. Anything.*

He kept that last sentiment to himself, knowing it would only embarrass her.

"Thank you, Sylvester."

"It is my pleasure."

Her eyelids suddenly lowered, and her hand slid beneath the sheet that was barely covering his spent cock. "How may I show my gratitude?"

Sylvester opened his mouth to confess that pleasing her was reward enough, but then her hand closed around his prick. He hissed in a breath as she stroked him with skilled, slightly roughened fingers.

"Were you about to say something?" she asked, her head lowering over him and her hot, wet tongue licking up his quickly stiffening shaft.

He groaned. "I was going to order you to thank your husband properly."

"Why do I think that is not what you were going to say?" she teased, tormenting the head of his cock with teasing flicks of her tongue.

He cupped the back of her head and lightly, but firmly, pressed down. "Less chatter and more gratitude."

She gave a soft, snorting laugh and then swallowed him deeply.

And those were the last words spoken for a long, long time.

Chapter 12

Lady Needham's *impromptu dance* did not end until almost two o'clock.

As a result of her late-night Stacia overslept the following morning, which meant she had no time for her usual walk and scarcely a moment to run down to the stables and check on the dog, whom she had named Terrance.

Mr. Higgins and Gerald had both laughed at the name, the older man calling it rather fine for such a little scrap. She supposed it was, but poor Terrence had so little that perhaps a grand name would give him something to aspire to.

As she made her way from the stables to her employer's chambers, she tried not to think about the night before. When Lord Shelton had suddenly left—in a huff, if she had read his posture correctly—she had at first been glad. After all, if she was playing the piano, she could hardly dance. And it would have been agonizing to watch him partner one pretty girl after another, all of them far more attractive than her.

But then Mr. Dixon had done something quite lovely and kind for Stacia, a mere companion—no better than a servant, really—and arranged for all the piano players, even himself, to play a few songs.

"It would be unfair to chain you to the piano all night, Miss Martin," he had teased.

So then she had been deeply annoyed that Lord Shelton had gone. Not that she could have been sure he would ask *her* to dance. But she thought he might have. If only to try and make up for the cruel comment he'd made in the conservatory that night.

But he did not return. As things turned out, she had rather a lovely time anyway and danced almost every dance, even once with the Duke of Chatham, who—despite his intimidating mien—was actually witty and charming

Almost as much as his cousin.

Stop thinking about him.

Stacia tried to obey, but it was a hopeless proposition.

And by the time she was outside her employer's room she was busily parsing their brief interaction in the drawing room last night, for at least the dozenth time, looking for deeper meaning. *What* deeper meaning, she did not know.

Over and over again her thoughts were snagged by the phrase *fleshly pleasures.* Who said that sort of thing out loud?

She firmly wrenched her attention to the woman who employed her and raised her hand to the door to scratch.

Before she could do so, the door open and Ackers hurried out.

"Oh! Miss Martin," she exclaimed. "I almost ran you over."

An agonized groan came from the darkness behind her and Ackers grimaced, noiselessly closed the door, and then took Stacia's arm and led her halfway down the corridor before stopping.

"Lady Addiscombe still suffers from her migraine?" Stacia guessed.

"She is in agony, poor, unhappy thing."

"What can I do to help?"

"She doesn't want anyone fussing over her, I'll give her that." Ackers laughed. "Far easier to get along with when she's sick than at any other time. I've finally convinced her to take some laudanum so I daresay she'll sleep most of the day, just waking long enough to eat a bit of gruel."

"And you're sure there is nothing I can do?"

"You should grab this little bit o' freedom with both hands, Miss Martin." She gave a toothy grin. "You can bet that I'm enjoying the extra time to myself and catching up on my sleep. She won't ask for you—I can almost guarantee that. Go on and enjoy yourself."

"You are too kind, Miss Ackers. If you need me to relieve you at any time, please let me know."

"I will, dear."

Stacia hesitated and then asked, "Er, did you put your name into the secret gift giving bowl?"

Ackers grinned. "Would anyone in their right mind miss a chance to get a gift from a toff?"

Stacia laughed. "I wonder when they will tell us whose name we drew."

"I got mine this morning." She leaned close and loudly whispered, "I drew Mrs. Barton."

"Oh. I wonder why I haven't been given mine?"

"When you go down for breakfast, you should ask Mr. Davis or Mrs. Nutter," Miss Ackers said.

"I will go right now," Stacia said, eager to see who she'd drawn.

Although she was even more curious to know who had drawn *her* name.

***

Andrew was still regretting his angry attack on Kathryn the following day. Not because he worried that he had hurt her feelings—the girl had the hide of a bull— but because he'd exposed his own insecurities, which would only be more ammunition in her hands.

He had considered returning to the drawing room after his snit, if for no other reason than to turn pages for Miss Martin while she slaved over the piano, but it had all seemed like too much bloody bother.

Instead, he had gone to bed. It had been such an appallingly early hour that he'd expected to wake up after a few hours and be up half the night. He had slept all the way through until dawn, but it had been a restless sort of sleep and he did not feel particularly restored. Something niggled at him in the back of his mind— something just out of reach.

It had still niggled when he'd gone on his morning ride, his usual serenity nowhere to be found.

As for Kathryn? Well, she could say whatever she bloody well pleased. If she took digs at him again—which she would, given the rise she'd got out of him last night—he would just ignore her.

There. Problem settled.

Andrew had also given some thought to Miss Martin during his frosty ride. It bothered him more than he liked to admit that he had wanted to go back to the drawing room to keep her company. He never did such things. He never even *thought* such things.

More alarming than his desire to be around her was the fact that he would have returned if only he could have been sure that he would have been allowed to turn her music. But that is not what would have happened. Instead, it would have been just like any other ball or assembly he'd ever attended, and he would have been coerced to dance. Unlike a London ball, he could not have escaped and would have found himself dancing every damned set.

It was best that he had stayed away from her. It was true that he would probably have to marry, and the last sort of wife he needed was a woman even poorer than he was.

And why the hell was he entertaining thoughts of Miss Martin and marriage in the same sentence?

Miss Martin was a complication he did not need in his life. He would avoid her for the duration of the holiday. If Kathryn had noticed his interest in her, that meant others had, too. Given his reputation—and her employer's hatred of him—his attention would not help her in any way.

Having at least addressed both matters, he was far less disgruntled—although nowhere near gruntled, if that was even a word—when he returned from his ride.

He had just finished washing, shaving, and was getting dressed when there was a knock on the door and Sylvester poked his head into Andrew's room.

"Ah, my valet has arrived. Did I ring for you?" Andrew mocked.

"I was hoping I'd catch you before you went down for breakfast."

"Why is it that those words have begun to strike fear into me?" Andrew asked as he finished tying his cravat.

"I wanted to talk to you last night, but you disappeared right before the impromptu dance." His brow furrowed. "Are you unwell?"

"I am fine." Christ. Could he do nothing that went unnoticed? "You wanted to talk to me?" he asked, changing the subject.

"Will you go to the village with me this afternoon?"

Andrew narrowed his gaze. "Why?"

"There is a Christmas fete and, after that, a dance and—"

"No."

Sylvester laughed. "At least you gave it some serious thought."

"I don't want to go to a village dance, Sylvester."

"Are you going to make me beg, cousin?"

"That actually sounds appealing."

Sylvester gave him a pained look.

"Why is this important to you?" Andrew asked.

"Because I have been sent on a mission."

There was only one person on earth who gave his cousin marching orders.

"How come *you* are the one who is married and yet I end up having to obey your wife?"

"It is all part and parcel of belonging to a family."

Andrew sighed. "Tell me what we have been ordered to do."

"Lady Needham has requested that her family take part in the village festivities. We don't need to stay long, but Needham needs to open the dance, so we should stay for at least the first few sets."

Andrew opened his mouth.

124

"Like it or not, you are now part of the Bellamy family, Drew."

Andrew closed his mouth.

The duke continued. "This Christmas festival is the highlight of the year for a good many people, not just from Little Sissingdon, but for miles around. Needham said there are some equestrian events which need judges—don't worry, you won't be roped into that; I have already volunteered—and there are booths filled with handicrafts and food."

Andrew pondered this fresh hell.

"Think of your attendance today as your Christmas gift to me," Chatham said. "And yes, before you ask—Kathryn is coming," he added, easily reading Andrew's mind. "Don't worry, I won't let her torment you. At least not much."

Andrew snorted. "If Kathryn is going that means we will be child minding, doesn't it?"

"All of the younger crowd will be going along," the duke conceded.

"And we are to spend all afternoon and evening there?"

"The dance begins unfashionably early. It is more of a family affair than a typical assembly."

Yes, it sounded like hell. "I'll wager young Bellamy and his mates are going under duress."

"Very much so—his sisters have applied thumbscrews."

Andrew's mind raced as he scrambled for a believable excuse. He could find none. "Fine," he said. "I will go."

Sylvester smiled in a way that said he knew all along that would be Andrew's answer.

***

Stacia found the great hall brimming with activity when she descended the grand staircase.

"Are you coming with us Miss Martin?" Lady Kathryn shouted.

"Lord, Kat," Viscount Bellamy said, scowling at his sister, "perhaps you could screech a bit farther away from my ear next time."

"Yes. I am coming," Stacia said. "At least for a little while."

"You will enjoy the Christmas market," Lady Kathryn assured her.

Lady Celsa and one of Lord Bellamy's school friends—Stacia could never keep their names straight—walked past, wrestling with a bulky burlap bag.

125

Lord Bellamy hefted another bag, or at least tried to, but it was almost as large as his slight frame. "Are you going to help me with this, Kat, or—"

"I will help you, my lord."

Stacia's body stiffened at the sound of Shelton's voice, and it was a struggle not to turn toward him, but Lady Kathryn's sharp eyes were resting on her, so Stacia pretended that pulling on her gloves was consuming all her attention.

"Bloody hell," Shelton muttered when he lifted the bag, his rude language making the younger men snicker. "What the devil is in here? Anvils?"

"Toys and such," Lord Bellamy said, and then turned to his friends. "Come along, you two. Help me fetch the rest."

"What do I do with this?" Shelton asked once the boys had gone. He had heaved the bag over his shoulder.

"The coaches are waiting outside," Kathryn said. "One of the footmen will direct you."

Shelton stalked toward the door, muttering under his breath.

"Are there more bags?" Stacia asked Lady Kathryn.

"Yes, there are. But wait—here is your name for the secret gift giving."

"Thank you," Stacia said, taking the piece of paper and quickly taking a peek. She smiled when she saw the name *Selina Shaftsbury* written in beautiful copper script. It would be a pleasure to choose a gift for such a kind, lovely person.

Stacia tucked the chit into her coat pocket and was about to go in the direction of Lord Bellamy and his friends when the young viscount appeared dragging a heavy bag.

Stacia hurried toward him and grasped the other corner, giving a slight grunt at the weight.

"Thanks," he said, gifting her with a smile that would be slaying young women all over London in a few years.

"My goodness," Stacia said as the two of them managed to lift the bag a few inches off the floor. "Where did all this come from?"

"Needham bought it all," he said in a strained voice.

Just then the viscount himself came down the steps. "Here, let me take that," he offered, striding toward them.

"I've got it," the younger man protested.

"You know you shouldn't be lifting such a heavy thing," Lady Kathryn chided. "And before you go outside you should be wearing your scarf and have your coat—"

"Leave off, Katie!" Lord Bellamy snapped, bright spots of red glowing on his pale cheeks as he stomped away.

Lady Kathryn looked amused rather than offended by her brother's anger.

Lord Needham picked up the bag without any visible effort. "Go bundle up in one of the carriages, Miss Martin. We lads can do the lifting and carting."

She nodded and followed behind him, pausing on the top step to survey the three grand coaches and two smaller vehicles lined up on the drive.

"Ride with me," Lady Kathryn said, appearing beside her and looping an arm through Stacia's before leading her toward the carriage that was last in line.

"Oh, thank you," Stacia said, once again shamed by the kindness being shown to her by people her employer wanted her to spy on.

Lord Shelton emerged from the carriage just as they approached, and Stacia's step stuttered when she met his brilliant blue gaze.

"I'm sorry. I didn't mean to drag you," Lady Kathryn said, misinterpreting the reason for Stacia's sudden clumsiness.

"I've just got two left feet," Stacia muttered, her face heating under Lord Shelton's knowing gaze.

Once they were settled in the carriage—just the three of them and one bag of toys—the silence quickly thickened until it felt awkward.

Stacia was racking her brain for something to say, but Lord Shelton beat her to it.

"Tell us a bit about this Christmas festival, Lady Kathryn."

"What would you like to know, *Lord Shelton*?"

The marquess smirked at the emphasis she put on his name. Stacia was once again impressed by the sophistication the younger woman exhibited. Most women giggled and blushed in Shelton's presence—a phenomenon she had had not only witnessed times beyond counting but had manifested herself on more than a few occasions.

"It is the highlight of winter for most people in the area. For hundreds of years, it has been the duty of the local lord to participate and contribute to the festivities." Her beautiful face turned hard. "My father's main contribution was to gut his tenant farms and neglect his people's basic needs, and my mother's was to treat them all like serfs. Fortunately for the hundreds of families in the area Lord

Needham isn't just leasing the Bellamy ancestral home, he has also taken the mantle of responsibility onto his shoulders."

There was a moment of almost ringing silence when she finished.

And then she smiled sweetly at Lord Shelton and said, "So, tell me about your estate, my lord. Rosewood, I believe it is called?"

Stacia's eyes slid from Lady Kathryn to Lord Shelton. Of the expressions she had expected to see on his face—annoyance, anger, and resignation—she had never expected to see grudging respect.

"I have been a less than impressive landlord, my lady." Shelton then turned to Stacia. "But a man can always change."

Chapter 13

Once Andrew had helped carry the monstrous bags of toys and gifts to the area designated for them, he glanced around at the bustling crowd, his eyes—without his permission—seeking out one small figure.

What about your resolution to avoid Miss Martin?

Bugger off.

His hectoring conscience retreated, likely to regroup.

"Here you are, Shelton!"

He turned at the sound of his nemesis's voice. "Lady Kathryn. How delightful."

"Oh, don't look so sour," Kathryn said, staring up at him with a dangerous glitter in her eyes that always made the hair on his neck stand up. "I just wanted to give you the name you drew."

"You mean for the drawing I did not enter?"

"Yes, that one." She flashed him a smug smile and then sauntered off toward the rows of colorful booths.

He unfolded the paper and snorted: *Eustacia Martin.*

For once, he could not be too angry with Kathryn for her meddling. He would enjoy buying a gift for the prickly young woman. And it was anonymous, so she never needed to know it came from him.

He repeated the name under his breath. "Eustacia." It was a serious name for a serious woman. He decided it fit her quite well.

Andrew folded the paper, tucked it into his pocket, and resumed his search for Miss Martin.

She was standing beside Lady Kathryn and the two were leaning down to examine some wares.

Oh, Kathryn. Just what are you up to now?

Andrew suspected he would soon find out.

Although it was frigid and the sky was an ominous gray, the atmosphere was festive, and it was difficult to remain annoyed that he'd been dragged into the affair when there were so many happy, smiling people milling about.

Not only that, but he now had a gift to buy. Several, actually, as he had not purchased anything yet. They were to assemble in Chatham's suite of rooms on

Christmas morning to have an intimate family celebration before joining the larger one in the main drawing room. That meant he needed to buy gifts for four people.

Lord. What would he buy for the duchess? That would be a challenge.

Andrew joined the throng of shoppers and meandered in the direction of Kathryn and Miss Martin. The first booth was selling honey, the jars sealed with wax and covered with a bright square of cloth. Nanny Dougal—the terror of the nursery at Chatham Park for more than fifty years—had often made honey toast for Andrew and Chatham when they'd been little. Suddenly he had the strongest yearning to taste it again.

He glanced up at the old man sitting behind the table. "I'll take two of these," he said, deciding that he should probably bring a jar back to Chatham, where Nanny had recently celebrated her ninety-second birthday and still scolded Andrew whenever she saw him.

Once the jars were wrapped in paper and tied with thick twine that formed a handle Andrew moved along. He bypassed the next two tables, one selling seeds, and one offering an assortment of farming implements.

The next table was heaped with feminine fripperies, and two women sat behind it. One of them was the owner of the dress shop. He remembered her, of course, but could not recall her name.

Andrew thought about the piece of paper in his pocket and paused, his gaze flickering over the profusion of items on the table.

He smiled at the women. "Hello, ladies."

"Good afternoon, Lord Shelton. If I had known you were going to visit our humble little fete I would have brought along your gloves." The shopkeeper gave him the same lascivious smile.

"Lord Shelton," the younger woman breathed, gazing up at him with adoration.

Andrew's smile became strained. "I am looking for a gift. For a lady," he added stupidly.

"What a lucky lady," the older woman said, giving him another good once-over in case he'd missed the first one.

Andrew met her gaze, no longer amused by her blatant lures.

After a moment, she blushed and became a bit flustered. "Er, a gift," she said, not quite subdued, but no longer looking at him as if she would mate him and then eat him.

She gestured to the goods on the table—hair combs, ribbons, and the like. "These are some of my most popular items, although of course I have more in my shop. I might steer you in the right direction if you gave me a hint of who the gift is for?" She gave him a hopeful look. "Perhaps a sister? A mother?"

Andrew couldn't help laughing at her persistence. "I noticed that Lady Kathryn and her companion lingered at your table. What were they looking at?"

She looked mildly disappointed by the question, but, like the practical businesswoman she was, quickly pivoted and gestured to a fan that was open on a stand. "Lady Kathryn was very taken with this."

Andrew had seen many fans in his day—probably thousands—but this one was unique. There were a few lines of elegant copperplate—a poem, it seemed—the first letter of which was an intricate O with dozens of butterflies seeming to emerge from the center of it.

"It is an illuminated letter," he mumbled.

"Indeed, it is. I have only ever seen one text with such work and this fan seems—to my admittedly untutored eye—to be every bit as good."

"It is exquisite." He looked up. "Is this what Miss Martin sold you?"

She gave a dramatic sigh. "Surely you cannot expect a businesswoman to reveal her sources?"

Andrew took that as a *yes*.

She unfurled another fan, exposing a field of wildflowers so realistic that Andrew swore a floral scent tickled his nostrils.

The next one displayed a field of deer. And the last had a portrait of a beautiful woman who was holding a fan.

Andrew gave a huff of amazement when he saw that the fan in the painting had another, even tinier, painting on it.

He glanced at the price, which was tastefully written on a card. They were expensive—far too expensive to sell in a village shop, he would have thought—but there was no denying they were worth the price.

"Which one did Lady Kathryn favor?" he asked.

"The flowers."

Andrew nodded, his gaze again drawn to the one with the woman with the fan. It was stunning. He could hardly buy Miss Martin a fan that she had painted herself, but he needed something for the duchess. Andrew chuckled to himself at the thought of giving her such a feminine gift. It was easier to imagine his cousin's wife wielding a broadsword than a pretty fan, but she would be in London for the Season. And she would have to make her curtsy before the queen. So…why not?

"I will take the flowers and the woman with the fan."

"Excellent! Shall I wrap them up in pretty paper for you?"

Andrew nodded. For some reason, another face popped into his head—the little blonde girl, Needham's daughter, Lucy. The industrialist was wealthy enough to buy her whatever she wanted, but it was Christmas, and Andrew was a guest in her father's house.

"I will take the butterfly one as well."

The shopkeeper didn't bother to hide her glee. "I might close early today."

He laughed.

Her gaze darted to something behind him and Andrew turned to find Neeham.

"Welcome, my lord," the shopkeeper said, suddenly proper.

Evidently the viscount did not put up with any flirting. Good for Needham.

"Hello, Mrs. Johnson, Miss Finley," Needham said politely.

Johnson! That was the name.

Needham grinned when he saw the honey Andrew was holding. "I see you are getting into the spirit of things, Shelton."

Andrew gave an embarrassed chuckle as the other man's sharp gaze moved to the fan Mrs. Johnson was wrapping and his eyebrows rose. "Something for a special lady?" he teased, but then his eyes widened when they landed on the unfurled fans. "That butterfly fan—did you just buy it?"

"I did." Andrew hesitated and then added, "I hope you don't mind, but I bought it for your daughter."

Needham's face creased in an expression of surprised pleasure. "That is remarkably handsome of you, Shelton." He hesitated, an almost sheepish expression taking possession of his harsh features.

"Is something wrong?" Andrew asked.

"No, no. It's just that my wife has a rather interesting effect on butterflies."

"Indeed, she does," Mrs. Johnson chimed in. "Why, I recall when she was just a little girl at the church fete we have every summer. She must have had a dozen of the creatures on her!"

Miss Finley nodded. "I wish they were so attracted to me."

"It is true," Needham said at Andrew's skeptical look. "They love her. If there is one in the area, it will find her."

"Then you should have the fan," Andrew said. "I will take the last one for your daughter. It has deer on it."

"Lucy will love that. She is wild for creatures of all sorts."

Andrew nodded. "I've seen her with the little red squirrel." The beast had scared the hell out of him when it had thrust its rat-like face out of Lucy's hair one evening in the drawing room.

"She dotes on Silas," the viscount agreed.

Andrew turned to Mrs. Johnson. "I will take the deer and give his lordship the butterflies."

"My wife will love it." Needham looked delighted. Who would have believed that a businessman who struck terror into the hearts of grown men all over Britain with his hard-nosed bargaining could look so giddy at the thought of a fan?

Andrew felt an unexpected pang of envy. What he was envious of, he was not quite sure.

***

Stacia lightly caressed a delicate silver ring in the shape of a rose. It had been a long, long time since she had coveted something so much. And an even longer time since she had made such an indulgent purchase.

Unfortunately, it was simply too expensive. Besides, she wasn't at the fete to buy *herself* a gift. She'd purchased a jar of honey for Miss Ackers so all she needed was a gift for Lady Shaftsbury. And Stacia had already decided on a gift for her.

"I know you like him."

Stacia looked up from the ring at the sound of Lady Kathryn's voice. "I beg your pardon?"

The beautiful redhead smiled, her eyes brimming with mischief. "You heard me."

Stacia returned the ring to its velvet box, unease unfurling in her belly. "I heard you, but I don't know what you mean."

"Lord Shelton. You like him. Not just *like* him, but—"

Stacia took the younger woman's arm and pulled her away from the small cluster of shoppers at the jewelry table before demanding in a low, unamused voice, "What are you talking about, Lady Kathryn?"

"Shelton. I can see how you feel about him."

133

"Don't be ridiculous." But heat surged up Stacia's neck and she knew her face was betraying her.

Lady Kathryn leaned closer. "I believe he is not indifferent to you, either."

Stacia felt a stab of anger at the beautiful young woman's taunting. "You are talking rubbish! And it is—it is unkind."

It was Lady Kathryn's turn to look bewildered. "Unkind? But why would—"

"Just look at me. And then look at *him*," Stacia hissed.

They both turned to where Lord Shelton and Viscount Needham were standing in front of a booth selling cheeses. The men were laughing, as were the farmer and his wife.

Actually, Stacia amended, the farmer was laughing, but the wife—a woman who was at least in her sixth decade—was gazing at Shelton with a poleaxed expression on her weathered face.

The same look that Stacia must have been wearing lately if Lady Kathryn's accusation was anything to go by.

Stacia wanted to curl up and die. How many other people had noticed her infatuation?

"So what if he is attractive?" Lady Kathryn asked, apparently the only female between seventeen and seventy immune to the gorgeous lord. "Just because he is handsome does not mean he cannot be attracted to you."

Stacia considered confessing to the other woman that she had overheard Lord Shelton's description of her. But that was simply too painful to admit. Instead, she said, "Handsome? He is perfect."

"Perfect?" Kathryn laughed. "I've lived in the same house with Shelton for months and I assure you that he is *not* perfect. He is a man with flaws, just like any other." Something bitter flickered in her gaze but was quickly gone. "What do you think of my sister Selina?"

Stacia blinked at the odd change of subject. "Er—"

"She is beautiful, isn't she?"

"Very." Indeed, Stacia had never seen a more beautiful woman.

"In fact, one might call her *perfect*."

Stacia had to agree. Lady Shaftsbury was so lovely that it was hard to take one's eyes off her whenever she was near.

"I would agree that she looks perfect," Stacia said, unclear as to where the other woman was going with this.

"And her husband—what about him?"

"Erm, Lord Shaftsbury is a very handsome—"

"I am not asking about his appearance. My sister married a blind man, Miss Martin."

"Yes. But what—"

"Doesn't it strike you as ironic that one of the most beautiful women in England married a man who neither knows, nor cares, what his wife looks like?"

Well, when she put it like *that.*

"That is interesting," Stacia conceded. "But I'm not sure I take your point. They are obviously in love, so it doesn't matter that he cannot see her and doesn't—"

"He loves her. And he has never seen her."

Stacia considered the other woman's words before answering. "You're saying that he loves her despite her beauty."

Lady Kathryn nodded. "He loves *her.* Not her face—her eyes, her nose. But *her.*" She gave Stacia a speaking look. "Selina told me that the only reason she became friends with Shelton last Season was because he understood what it meant to be so attractive that people only ever noticed her appearance."

Stacia tried to feel sorry for the beautiful marchioness, but—

"You don't think somebody that lovely should have the right to expect more than adulation," Lady Kathryn said, guessing her thoughts with disturbing accuracy.

Stacia looked away from Shelton to the woman in front of her. Lady Kathryn Bellamy might not be the vision of golden perfection her sister was, but she was an extremely beautiful woman. Was she speaking from personal experience?

"I will admit that I find it difficult to empathize," Stacia said.

Humor glinted in Lady Kathryn's stunning green eyes. "At least you are honest. But back to Shelton. I've watched him for months. Not because I am attracted to him, but because I find him interesting. Despite his reputation as an inveterate rake, I can tell you that he has looked nothing but bored—albeit skillfully hidden by a mask of charm—in the company of every woman I've seen him around. The only times I've seen him exhibit even a spark of interest have been the few times I've seen him talking to you. Like yesterday, when we were skating. I don't know what the two of you were discussing—and I'm not asking," she hastily assured Stacia, "but whatever it was made him come alive."

Stacia stared at her for a long moment. "Why are you saying all this to me?"

"Because I know you have been...*interested* in Lord Shelton for a long time."

"How could you possibly know that?" Stacia demanded, her face yet again blazingly hot.

"Earlier this year I stayed with my aunt who lives just outside Norwich in a small village called Westwick." She gave Stacia a curious look. "Have you heard of it?"

"No. Should I have?"

"One of my aunt's neighbors was a woman named Mrs. Leary."

Stacia gave an irritated shrug. "Should I know her?"

"Her maiden name was Creighton."

"Oh." Stacia could not think of anything else to say.

"Mrs. Leary is now happily—no, I would say *very* happily married—to a gentleman farmer."

"Happily? I'd heard—"

"I know what you heard because everyone else heard it, too. Her husband is a delightful, handsome man who is very much in love with his wife." Her expression turned sly. "He is of Irish descent and has that attractive combination of almost black hair and dark blue eyes. Interestingly, Sarah's little boy is an exact miniature of his papa." She hesitated and added, "With his jet-black hair and dark blue eyes."

Sarah was fair—almost as fair as Shelton. Was Lady Kathryn saying the child *was not* Lord Shelton's? And *happily* married? Was she claiming that Sarah had been in love with some obscure rural farmer and yet conducting an affair with another man? It made no sense.

"I still do not see what this has to—"

"I knew you were my mother's companion from her letters to me."

"Yes?" Stacia prodded yet again when Lady Kathryn paused.

"Your name came up in conversation—I forget how—and Mrs. Leary said she remembered you quite clearly. She said you'd not only gone to school together but had come out the same Season." Lady Kathryn paused. "She mentioned how mad all the girls were for Lord Shelton. How you all hated her for attracting his attention."

Stacia knew what she was driving at and did not bother to deny it. Instead, she shrugged and said, "That was the case for dozens of women, not just our group of wallflowers."

"Perhaps. But dozens of young ladies are not here. *You* are here, Miss Martin."

"I'm not sure why you are rubbing my nose in my unfortunate infatuation from *four years ago*. None of that makes any difference because *he* is not interested in *me*." She scowled as Lady Kathryn just regarded her calmly. "And even if he were, it would likely be the same sort of interest that destroyed Sarah Creighton's life."

"Did it?"

Stacia gave an exasperated sigh. "Why don't you tell me—plainly—what you are trying to say."

Before Lady Kathryn could reply, Lucy Needham nudged up between them, her eyes sparkling. "Look what I bought for Papa," she said, unwrapping a brown paper package to expose a wicked-looking blade with a hilt made out of an animal horn.

Stacia and Kathryn exchanged amused glances.

"I'm sure he will love it," Kathryn said.

Lucy pulled her lips between her teeth, glanced around, and then unwrapped a second, smaller package. "I had this made for Doddy."

This was a tiny squirrel that looked remarkably like the little rodent Stacia had seen riding on the girl's shoulder.

Lady Kathryn stared, chewing her lip.

"It is a beautiful fob," Stacia said when Lady Kathryn remained quiet. "And very lifelike."

"It is a seal, too," Lucy said, turning the little animal over to demonstrate an exquisite carving of a tree.

"A wych elm," Kathryn murmured, and then looked up from the distinctive Bellamy family device to the young girl and gave a slightly strained smile. "Doddy will love it, Lucy. Perhaps he will write more letters if he can use such a wonderful seal."

Lucy's grin was ear-to-ear. "Now I just need to find a gift for Phoebe, and I will be done with my shopping. But I don't know what she would like. I made her two handkerchiefs with her initials and a butterfly on each." She glanced at Kathryn. "But then I saw the ones you made for her. Phoebe said you did them when you were younger than I am now." Lucy pulled a face. "They are perfect! Mine look like I embroidered them with my feet."

"I'm sure she will love them," Kathryn said.

"Your work is so beautiful, and yet the duchess says you no longer do needlework?"

"No, I don't," Kathryn said abruptly. But then she smiled. "If you want to see some truly amusing embroidery you should look at Hyacinth's few attempts. Although I'm not sure where you would find one."

"Phoebe has one from her!" Lucy said. "In fact, she has one from each of you, all framed—so I have seen her work." She lowered her voice, as if the Duchess of Chatham might be lurking. "I thought it was a dog, but Phoebe said it was supposed to be a horse."

Lady Kathryn laughed. "That sounds about right."

Lucy's eyes suddenly lit up at something behind them. Stacia knew it would be Lord Bellamy even before she turned to look.

She couldn't blame the girl for being smitten with him. He was the male equivalent of his beautiful sister Selina. He would look like an angel come to earth if not for his broad grin and the two ridiculously huge cream cakes he held.

"Doddy!" Lucy squealed. "I will never be able to eat all that."

"I'll help you, Luce," Lord Bellamy promised.

They watched as Lucy laughingly took one of the cakes and the two wandered off, side-by-side, chattering away.

"I hope you won't tell my mother about my brother's friendship with Lucy."

Stacia gave Lady Kathryn a guilty look. "Er—"

"I am not angry," Lady Kathryn said before Stacia could conceive of something to say. "My mother has always tried to use us to spy on each other. It is a delicate balancing act of giving her just enough information to keep her satisfied but not enough to get anyone in trouble."

Stacia stared, horrified. Lady Addiscombe pitted her children against each other?

"You look surprised, Miss Martin. You forget that we were all subjected to her power for years." Lady Kathryn chuckled, but there was little humor in it. "Unlike you, however, none of us could quit."

138

Chapter 14

The snow held off until almost six, which was when the booths closed for the day and the village Christmas ball commenced.

Andrew had never heard of a dance beginning so early.

Their small party reassembled in the brand-new church hall and occupied a large table on the periphery of the dance floor.

Andrew found himself seated between Kathryn and one of Bellamy's school mates.

"Needham had this hall built last summer," Kathryn told Andrew, not that he had asked. He had begun to assume that anything that was new in the area was thanks to the generous viscount.

"The old church hall burned down more than fifteen years ago. For most of my life the village dances have been held on the second floor of the pub," Kathryn went on, her tone leaving no doubt of her opinion on the subject.

Andrew's gaze slid toward the dance floor, where Miss Martin was currently partnered with Dixon for a country dance. The man seemed to linger around her.

Whatever Dixon was saying to her was enough to have her smiling and laughing.

Andrew felt an unaccustomed—and unwanted—stab of envy. Or perhaps jealousy. He could never recall which was which. But he *did* know that both emotions were inappropriate in this situation. He had no right to want Miss Martin's smiles for himself. Thanks to more than a decade of pursuing nothing except revenge, he was the owner of a dilapidated estate and a nascent stud operation. He had nothing to offer Miss Martin. Well, nothing other than an awful reputation.

He would come into his inheritance next year. He did not know the exact amount—he had never bothered to talk to Sylvester's man of business, who managed his investments—but suspected it was barely enough to make some repairs at Rosewood.

There was no getting around the fact that he needed to marry an heiress. He wanted somebody not too terribly young—somebody who could be sensible because he could not offer love. No, never that. He had no desire to experience such a crushing emotion all over again.

It would be a practical arrangement. A true marriage of convenience. Her money would help restore his estate and he would give her status and children, one of whom would hopefully be a better steward than Andrew had ever been.

So, no. Miss Martin was not for him, no matter how much he appeared to be drawn to her.

Andrew watched with increasing displeasure as Miss Martin danced the next set with Needham's other secretary, a tall, dark-haired man who looked like he'd just stepped out of a Gothic novel.

Dennehy. That was his name. He was exactly the sort of brooding looking man that women seemed to find attractive.

Miss Martin was smiling up at him and laughing at something he'd said. Dennehy smiled—a faintly villainous smirk—his eyes heavily lidded as he stared down at her, a different expression slowly taking possession of his features.

Andrew recognized the look on the other man's face instantly because he'd felt the exact same thing himself. Dennehy had just realized how attractive his dance partner was. Oh, she looked pretty enough in general, but when she laughed or smiled? Then she truly came alive.

He didn't know Dennehy's background, but marriage to the daughter of a viscount—even one as impoverished and lacking in connections as Miss Martin— would certainly be a step up socially.

An image of Dennehy and Miss Martin doing something other than dancing— Dennehy's much larger body covering Miss Martin's delicate, far-smaller one— flickered through his mind,

Andrew gritted his teeth against the image. He did not like it. Not. At. All.

"Are you…growling?"

His head whipped around at the sound of Kathryn's voice. "Don't be ridiculous. I was clearing my throat."

"She would look at you the same way if you didn't constantly refer to her as a *drab little dab of a woman*."

Andrew didn't bother to pretend that he didn't know who she meant. "*Constantly?* I only said it once." *And I deeply regret it.*

He leaned back in his chair, putting some distance between himself and Kathryn's far-too-knowing gaze. But his irritation got the better of him and he leaned toward her and snarled, "It is *none* of your business who I look at or how I look at them."

"I have made you my business, Shelton."

Andrew felt a stab of genuine alarm at her words. "What the devil does that mean?" he asked, using a low, menacing tone of voice that had sent his soldiers scuttling to obey.

But the woman beside him only smiled. "I am determined to wipe that miserable, sulky expression from your godlike features."

Godlike was something he'd heard many times. But sulky? "I am not sul—"

"Oh, yes you are."

"What makes you think—"

"I overheard Hy and Chatham discussing you a few weeks ago."

"You *overheard* them? Eavesdropping is a nasty, craven, and detestable habit."

"My, my—how fierce you are! *Rawrrr.*" She clawed the air.

Andrew couldn't help laughing. "You are ridiculous."

"Do you want to hear what they said, or are you too *noble*?"

Andrew's hands itched to yank Kathryn over his knee and administer the spanking she so desperately deserved. Instead, he sneered and said, "Just get on with it."

"They said you were nothing like your normal self—not arrogant, obnoxious, or even indiscriminately amorous, as far as Chatham could discern."

Why did hearing that irritate him? Why should he care if his cousin and his wife had noticed that he'd not gone tomcatting while living in their house?

The fact that he was bothered, bothered him even more.

And it was all Kathryn's fault.

He retorted, rather lamely, "Little girls like you should not be privy to such information."

Rather than be offended or annoyed—as any normal adolescent would be—her smirk grew into a smile that was truly terrifying. "I know what you need, *Drew.*"

"Oh, do you?" Andrew heard himself taunt. *Christ! Are you mad?* some far wiser part of his brain demanded. *Do not poke her!*

Kathryn nodded. "Yes, I certainly do."

"And what is that, *Katie*?" Andrew asked, evidently unable to control his own mouth.

"You need a wife. And I am going to find you one."

He sputtered wordlessly and shook his head. "Why you—you impudent saucebox! Just who the hell do you think you are?" he demanded, not caring about his language or the barely leashed fury in his voice.

"Don't act so perplexed. It is our wager."

"Wager?" he repeated blankly.

"Don't you remember when I said that I would never marry, and you laughed at me?"

Andrew continued to stare in open mouthed incomprehension.

"You don't remember," she accused, looking peeved.

"No, I don't remember," he was happy to retort. "I daresay whatever you are babbling about is a product of your demented imagination as I sincerely doubt that I would wager about—"

"You. Did." Her quiet voice was unexpectedly menacing, and a shiver of dread rippled down his spine.

Andrew had been knee-deep in dead bodies, he'd charged into guns that all but promised death, and he'd stared his own mortality in the face a dozen or more times.

And yet Lady Kathryn Bellamy, a mere chit, somehow managed to put the fear of God into him.

It is because she fears nothing.

Andrew suddenly knew that was the truth. Kathryn was reckless, careless, and—quite frankly—half-mad. She reminded Andrew of the stories he'd heard about Richard Barry—the infamous Lord Hellgate. Andrew had been an adolescent when Hellgate had been in his prime, but he remembered well enough the tales he'd heard at Eton about how the young lord had arrived at school with an unprecedented £1,000 at his disposal. Barrymore's money had run through his fingers like water. His antics increasingly extreme until he had died at the tender age of three-and-twenty.

While Andrew doubted Lady Kathryn would eat a live tomcat, which had been one of Barrymore's more shocking wagers, he could see from the desperate glitter in her eyes that there were few self-imposed limits on her behavior.

Do. Not. Provoke. Her, a voice in his head commanded.

"Why don't you go talk to her instead of yearning from afar?" the object of his terrified ruminations demanded. "Ask her to dance. That *is* why we are here."

For once, Andrew refused to be drawn by her baiting.

"What? Is the big, brave war hero afraid to ask a *downtrodden dab of*—"

"Would you please keep your voice down," Andrew hissed.

"Nobody can hear me." She laughed, a warm throaty laugh that should have been appealing, but instead reminded him of how he'd felt when he'd heard artillery that was miles closer than it should have been.

"Is this revenge, Kathryn?"

"Revenge?" Her eyebrows shot up and she looked genuinely confused. "For what?"

"For abducting your sister?"

Kathryn scoffed. "Selina can take care of herself. If she wanted a pound of flesh, trust me, she would take it."

Andrew did not doubt that for a moment.

She leaned forward. "I know all about Sarah Creighton."

"What do you think you know?" Andrew asked, after a few seconds of slack-jawed shock. He *knew* that he should shut his mouth. But, once again, he could not seem to stop himself.

"You know what I know."

"Why don't you tell me, anyhow?"

She laughed.

Andrew struggled for patience.

"Oh dear," she said.

"What?"

"Look." She gestured to where Dixon was helping Miss Martin into her coat. "It seems that you missed what is often called a golden opportunity, Shelton."

Andrew wanted to say something clever and flip, but as he watched Dixon lay his hand on Miss Martin's lower back and guide her out of the church hall, he was forced to accept that Kathryn, for all her youth and inexperience was in this instance painfully correct.

He should have asked Miss Martin to dance.

Chapter 15

A treasure hunt?" Andrew repeated, and then raised a forkful of ham to his mouth.

"Yes, haven't you heard of one before?" Lady Crewe poured more tea into her cup and then dipped another piece of dry toast.

After a night filled with a great deal of tossing and turning and very little sleep Andrew had awakened hours after dawn. When he had finally made his way to the stables, he'd found them crawling with guests and servants. So instead of taking his morning ride he had decided to come to breakfast early, hoping to beat the crowd.

Instead, he had found the oldest Bellamy sibling reading a newspaper and eating sops.

"Er, a treasure hunt? What's that?" he asked, recalling that she had asked him a question. He wondered if the woman was ill. Why else would somebody eat something as tasteless as plain toast and watery tea?

"There are clues and whoever figures them out first will get the treasure."

"What's the treasure?"

She took a tiny sip of tea and then paled slightly.

"Are you unwell, my lady?"

She gave a small shake of her head, her lips pursed tightly, as if she might shoot the cat if she opened her mouth.

Andrew watched her surreptitiously while finishing his second helping of coddled eggs.

After several minutes a faint pink tinged her cheeks and she gave an audible sigh of relief and then took a swallow of tea.

"Nobody knows what it is," she said, setting down her cup with a sigh.

Andrew paused, his fork halfway to his mouth. "I beg your pardon?"

"The treasure. It is a secret."

"Ah."

"Lord Needham has provided it, and my sister Phoebe says it is something spectacular."

"How interesting," Andrew murmured. Unless the treasure was a large valise stuffed with £50 notes it sounded like a waste of time.

"It starts in less than an hour," she said.

"I see." The way she was looking at him made Andrew wonder if he had food on his face.

"Are you going to play, my lord?"

He glanced out the massive arched windows that flooded the breakfast room with light even on a gloomy day. Large drops of sludgy sleet slapped almost angrily against the panes. One of the huge wych elms for which the house was named whipped wildly back and forth in the wind.

"It looks a bit cold outside to be playing games," he observed.

"Are you afraid of a little rain, my lord?" Her lips curved up at the corners, making her look even lovelier than she already did. All the Bellamy women were beautiful—even the duchess, in her own terrifying way.

"Rain? It looks more like sleet to me." He pulled his gaze from the slate gray sky back to his breakfast companion. "As for participating in this *treasure hunt*, I hadn't—"

The door opened and Kathryn, Lucy, Lady Celsa, and a young woman Andrew had never seen before burst into the room, their coats, mittens, and pink cheeks proclaiming that they'd been out in the brisk weather.

"Ah, there you two are Shelton," Kathryn said. "Come along, we are forming teams."

"Teams?" Andrew repeated.

"For the treasure hunt!" Lucy said, bouncing up and down on the balls of her feet.

Kathryn turned to her sister. "Lia, your husband is teamed up with Linny and Lord Jevington. Miss Gordon is with Mr. Dennehy and Mr. Dixon—"

"Wait," Lady Crewe interrupted. "Dixon and Dennehy are on the same team? They are Needham's secretaries. Surely that gives them an unfair advantage?"

"They have assured me that Needham invented the clues himself," Kathryn said, and then turned back to her list. "Captain Walker is on a team with Doddy and—"

"Me!" Lucy chirped.

"That's right," Kathryn agreed. "So, Lia, why don't you—"

"I agreed to partner with Mr. Leeland and Chatham last night," Lady Crewe said.

Kathryn's forehead puckered. "Mr. Leeland?"

"He is one of Papa's friends," Lucy explained.

"Good, then you are sorted." Kathryn turned to Andrew. "What about you?"

Andrew frowned. "What about me?"

"Are you finished eating?" She looked at his plate, which was indeed empty of all but a few scraps.

"Er—"

"Good. You can be on my team." She gave him a sweet smile that Andrew did not for a minute believe. "I will wait until you finish." She dropped down into the chair across from him, laced her fingers together, set her chin on them, and stared at him.

Lady Crewe laughed.

Andrew sighed and tossed his napkin onto the table. "I guess I am finished. But first I must fetch my coat and hat."

Kathryn sprang up from her chair. "Excellent! This will be fun, my lord."

Andrew suspected it would be torture. "Who else is on our team?"

"It is a surprise!"

Why did her smile make Andrew feel like a fox with a pack of hounds on its trail?

***

"Her ladyship has asked not to be disturbed this morning," Ackers said when Stacia showed up at her employer's chambers after receiving no summons for a third morning in a row.

"She *still* suffers from her migraine?"

"Thankfully she is past that. But the pain took a great deal out of her and she is exhausted and sleeping."

"I see." Stacia chewed her lip, both elated to be free but worried that she was not doing what she was supposed to be doing. "Do you know when she might want me?"

"I have no idea." The older woman cast a worried glance at the countess's door.

"What is it?"

"This is a very unhappy family."

"Did something happen?"

Ackers hesitated and then said, "The countess was sitting up this morning. She even took a little tea and toast. And then her youngest daughter paid her a visit."

Stacia's eyebrows rose. "It is unusual for her ladyship to invite company so early."

"Lady Kathryn wasn't invited."

"I see." The countess did not care for unexpected guests.

"They argued. It became…heated."

Stacia was ashamed to be so eager to gossip about her employer, but could not help herself from saying, "Oh?"

Ackers inched closer. "My lady wants her daughter to return to Bath after the holiday is over. Lady Kathryn refused—loudly. She said something to the effect that the last time she'd obeyed her mother she had lived to regret it. Her ladyship…wept."

Stacia's eyes almost rolled out of her head at the image of the countess actually *crying*.

"It sounded as though something happened to Lady Kathryn when she was staying with the countess's sister this past summer."

"*Something?* What do you mean?"

Ackers shrugged. "I couldn't hear that part. They stopped shouting at that point." After a moment, the maid shook herself. "In any case, the countess has returned to her bed and will not need you today. You should look upon it as an extended holiday." The older woman gave Stacia a conspiratorial smile. "I heard talk at breakfast this morning that there is to be a treasure hunt. Evidently Lord Needham has supplied a valuable prize for the winner. Why don't you play?"

Mr. Dixon had told her about the treasure hunt last night when he'd escorted her home from the village dance.

Stacia had taken a liking to the handsome, kindly man. She appreciated that he seemed to be going out of his way to make her feel welcome at Wych House. She suspected that at least part of his kindness had to do with the way the countess treated her, but there was no denying the fact that he had danced *twice* with her last night and only one other time, with one of the Lowery twins.

Not only that, but he had been attentive during their dance, not flitting off to dance attendance on anyone else—no matter how attractive—like Lord Shelton had done at the skating pond.

Why are you thinking about him?

Stacia gritted her teeth. Dixon, like Captain Walker, was exceedingly attractive, attentive, and eligible. Why could she never enjoy a man's company without Lord Shelton weaseling his way into her head?

"Go and play, Miss Martin," Ackers said, pulling Stacia from her thoughts.

Stacia smiled. "I will."

***

When Andrew arrived in the foyer twenty minutes later, it was to find only Kathryn and Miss Martin waiting.

Andrew gave Kathryn a hard look, but she merely smiled.

"Where is everyone else?" he asked, glancing around the cavernous, chilly entry hall.

"Everyone else has already collected their clues and begun playing. Our team is you, me, and Miss Martin," Kathryn said, smiling from Andrew to Miss Martin.

Why was he not surprised?

Miss Martin, however, *was* surprised. And it wasn't a pleasant one, if her faint scowl was anything to go by.

Andrew had hoped they'd got past her hatred of him yesterday. Now he wondered if they'd really had that conversation on the ice, or if he had merely dreamed it.

"So," Kathryn said, either not noticing the other woman's sour expression, or not caring. "Here is our first clue." She unfolded a piece of parchment. Andrew stepped closer to read it and, after a moment, so did Miss Martin.

We possess four legs, but no feet. When you are weary, we can offer your body, and your soul, relief.

He looked up. "Chairs? Benches?"

"That could be anywhere," Miss Martin said, giving him a scornful look. "And neither of those things do anything for one's soul."

Andrew couldn't help grinning at her scathing answer. "Good point." He winked at her and was amused when her face darkened, and her scowl deepened.

"I agree with Shelton," Kathryn said.

Andrew did a doubletake at this unprecedented event.

"Benches in the chapel," Kathryn explained, her grin genuine—not the world-weary expression he was accustomed to seeing on her face. She grabbed Miss

148

Martin's hand. "Come, let us hurry. This was an easy clue; the others will already have collected the next one."

When they entered the ancient chapel a footman waited in the narthex, seated at a table with a silver bowl containing folded pieces of paper.

"Are we the last ones, Charles?" Kathryn demanded.

"No, my lady. I've got two left."

She clucked her tongue and glared at Andrew. "Thanks to your foot dragging we are the second-to-last group."

"Luckily for you, I am worth the wait, darling," he shot back.

She gave a justifiably scornful laugh and unfolded the next clue. *Not bockety but not steady. Home to many but not for people.*

Miss Martin's forehead furrowed. "Bockety?"

Andrew chuckled. "It is an Irish term and means unstable."

"How did you know that?" she asked, her tone oddly accusatory.

"I had Irish soldiers under my command. Why? Where did you think I'd heard it?"

"I'm sure I don't know," she retorted.

"You thought I heard it somewhere naughty, didn't you, Miss Martin?" *Like a brothel.*

She pursed her lips.

Andrew snorted and then turned to Kathryn, who was regarding them with an irritating smirk.

Andrew bared his teeth at the interfering minx. She just laughed.

"The stables."

Andrew and Kathryn broke off their staring competition at the sound of Miss Martin's words.

"The next clue is in the stables," she explained. "Home to many but not people, so horses. And not, er, bockety, so—"

"Stable." He smiled at her. "Well done, Miss Martin!"

She started to smile but caught her lower lip just in time.

Andrew decided he was beginning to enjoy himself.

***

Stacia decided to enjoy herself, regardless of Lord Shelton's presence.

She would not be fooled by his attentiveness—not after skating with him. She would remind herself often that he was only flirting with her because there was nobody else other than Lady Kathryn available, and he squabbled with her as if she were his younger sibling.

She purposely fell behind Lady Kathryn and the handsome lord as they headed toward the stables. He looked as lovely from behind as he did from any other direction. Broad shoulders garbed in a caped great coat, a tall beaver hat, breeches and riding boots.

Stacia had dressed for the outdoors, as well, but even swathed in heavy wool with mittens and a bonnet she felt the bite of the icy rain.

"—Lady Kathryn!"

All three of them stopped and turned.

It was the maid Dora who'd called out, and she was squinting against the sleet.

"What are you doing out here without a coat or hat, Dora?" Lady Kathryn demanded.

"Er—" Dora's gaze flickered from Lady Kathryn to Stacia and then back, something about her expression…off. "Lady Addiscombe sent me to fetch you."

"Her ladyship is up and about?" Stacia asked before Lady Kathryn could answer. "Perhaps I should—"

"No. It sounds as if she wants me," Lady Kathryn said. "You continue playing," she ordered, shoving the clues into Stacia's hands. "I will see what my mother wants and rejoin you. Come along, Dora. You will catch your death of cold out here."

Stacia watched until they disappeared and then turned to find Lord Shelton waiting for her, a sardonic smirk on his face.

"I'm sure—" she broke off and bit her lip.

"What are you sure about?"

"Nothing."

His smirk grew, and it irked her into speaking. "I am sure you have better things to do than play this game. You needn't stay," she said primly, and then headed toward the stables, not looking to see if he was coming or not.

"I am enjoying myself," he said, catching up to her easily with his long strides. When she didn't answer, he said, "How is your little dog faring?"

"He is fine." That sounded abrupt and rude, so she relented and added, "He has been up and about, there is no keeping him lying down. But Mr. Higgins keeps him in a stall, so at least he cannot put too much strain on the injury."

"He looked to be a sturdy little beast. I daresay he will heal quickly."

"I, er, spoke to the post mistress and also the innkeeper about him. Thank you for that suggestion."

"I am pleased to be of use."

Stacia pursed her lips as she studied his face for mockery. But he looked innocent. Almost suspiciously so.

There were several stable lads and grooms hovering about the entrance to the stables, all of them looking amused—no doubt at the foolishness of the treasure hunt—and one of them called out to Lord Shelton when they approached. "Going riding, my lord? Shall I saddle Drake for you?"

"Not today, Gerald. Today I am hunting treasure."

The men chuckled, their gazes sliding to Stacia in a way that made her face heat.

"Here is your next clue, my lord," Gerald said.

Lord Shelton took the piece of paper and handed it to Stacia. "Has everyone else already come and gone?"

"No, you are the first, my lord."

"The first?" Lord Shelton turned to Stacia. "You are a very good partner, indeed, Miss Martin."

She ignored the joyful leaping in her chest and moved past the clutch of servants, eager to be out from under their curious eyes.

Once they'd gone inside the building a few feet, she stopped and unfolded the clue.

Lord Shelton leaned closer to read, the action bringing a subtle whiff of cologne, leather, and wool with him.

Stacia filled her lungs and held the scent inside her. How could a person smell so good? *How?*

"*I have many arms but no legs,*" he read aloud. After a moment, he looked up. "What do you think?"

Stacia shook her head and repeated the clue, "*I have many arms but no legs.*"

Voices drifted in from outside and Stacia heard the Duke of Chatham say, "Are we the first?"

Before anyone could answer Lord Shelton called out, "Not hardly, Sylvester."

The duke's laughter preceded him inside. He did a doubletake when he saw Stacia standing beside Lord Shelton but smiled politely. "Hello, Miss Martin." His smile turned into a grin when he faced his cousin. "Fancy seeing you here, Drew."

Drew. What a perfectly lovely nickname.

"I wouldn't be here if not for Miss Martin," Lord Shelton said. "She is the brains of our operation."

Stacia tried not to preen.

"I'm fortunate to have two clever partners." The duke gestured to Lady Crewe and Mr. Leeland.

Lady Crewe, who was holding the clue, narrowed her eyes when she saw Stacia and Lord Shelton. "Don't say anything, Mr. Leeland! Spies are listening."

Everyone chuckled.

"Come, Miss Martin, I know when I am not wanted," Lord Shelton said, lightly setting a hand on Stacia's back and guiding her out of the stables just as two more groups arrived.

"Don't tell me we are last!" Lord Bellamy demanded of the groom with the clues.

Lord Shelton leaned close and hissed in her ear, "Let's sneak away while they are all chattering."

"Do you know where we are going next?" she asked.

"Yes."

They hurried off unnoticed as the new arrivals engaged in some good-natured ribbing.

"Where is the next clue?" Stacia asked as she took two steps to every one of his and still could barely keep pace.

He grinned at her. "You will see."

***

"Tell me, my lord," Miss Martin ordered as she trotted to keep up with Andrew.

"The armory."

152

Minerva Spencer & S.M. LaViolette

She frowned as if recalling the clue, and then her eyes widened, and she gave him a look of grudging respect. "How clever of you."

Andrew raised his eyebrows in mock amazement. "*Me,* clever? Why, thank you, Miss Martin!"

She pursed her lips primly at his teasing. Andrew was amused by her reaction. He suspected Miss Martin had no clue how alluring the expression was. How it drew attention to that full lower lip of hers.

"How are you enjoying the house party so far, Miss Martin?" he asked when it was clear that she would not break the silence.

Her eyes narrowed. "Why?"

"That was not a trap, Miss Martin, just a question."

"The Bellamy family is very welcoming and kind."

"Most of them are," he agreed.

Miss Martin opened her mouth, but then closed it without asking him what he meant. Her expression changed to one that was almost…curious.

"Go ahead and ask whatever you are thinking," he said, already able to guess her question.

"I was just wondering why you've come to the house of a woman you abducted."

"You do not pull your punches, do you. No—no, I will answer," he added when she began to make sounds of retracting her question. "My cousin asked me to come, as did his wife. They made the argument that our families are now joined so there should be no ill feelings. I had apologized to Lady Shaftsbury before—in a letter as she did not wish to receive me in person at the time—but I felt I owed her a face-to-face apology."

She nodded.

"What about you?" he asked.

"Me? I am here because my employer is here."

"Your family must be missing you."

"There is nobody else."

The way the muscles in her face tightened told him the subject was a sore one and Andrew decided not to pursue it.

153

Instead, he stopped in a wide, paneled corridor and glanced around. "The door is here…somewhere," he murmured, pushing on the scrolling and trying to recall where the catch was hidden.

"A hidden door?"

He smiled at the excitement in her voice. "Yes. The idea was to keep the armory a secret from any enemies."

"How do you know about the door?"

"Lord Needham took Chatham and me on a tour and delighted in showing us Wych House's many, many secrets." The tip of his tongue poked out and his brow furrowed in concentration as he continued to feel the panel. "I could swear it was— ah!" He pushed a carved acorn and there was a dull *click* and the panel swung inward.

Miss Martin peered into the gloom. "It looks as if somebody lighted the sconces, but it is still rather dark."

"Allow me to go first." He stepped onto the small landing and cast a glance down the wide stone stairs. "Yes, it is lighted all the way down."

"Should I shut this panel?" she asked.

"You'd better leave it open. There is a mechanism on this side to open it, but it will take some doing to find it. Hold onto this rope railing while you descend." The stairs had a very gentle curve, one that would not impede moving weaponry up and down and were wide enough for four men to walk abreast.

When they reached the bottom the massive iron-strapped door was already propped open and there was a table on the far side of the room, complete with a candelabra and large bowl, although no footman was seated beside it. "We're obviously in the right place."

"Look at those." She pointed to the suits of armor that ran along one wall as they crossed the vast, low-ceilinged room. "This is an impressive collection."

"They actually belong to Needham, not Addiscombe," Andrew said. "His father collected them. You might have heard of him—Iron Mad Needham?"

"He was responsible for inventing some sort of gun, wasn't he?"

"Something like that, yes. He gave the patent to the Crown."

"That is why he received his title, is it not?"

Andrew chuckled. "Yes, but it is not done to say it so baldly."

"Oh, I didn't mean—"

"I am only teasing you."

154

She scowled up at him, faint candlelight casting a warm glow over her features.

"Don't you like to be teased, Miss Martin?"

Andrew knew he shouldn't, but the way she was staring up at him…

He reached down and lightly caressed the gentle curve of her jaw with the back of his fingers.

Her lips parted and she drew in a ragged breath. "What are—"

Boisterous voices and the clattering of feet on stairs made them both jolt.

"We had better collect the clue," Miss Martin said, hurrying over to the bowl. She took out a piece of paper just as a small crowd of people poured into the room.

Andrew sighed. Thank God the others had come along when they did. What on earth could he have been thinking?

Chapter 16

Stacia hurried up the stairs, her heart still pounding. Had Shelton been about to kiss her? He *had!* She just knew he had.

"Miss Martin—where are you going?" Lord Shelton called out when they reached the top of the stairs and Stacia began hurrying down the corridor.

She stopped and reluctantly turned back to him.

"Where is the clue?" he asked.

She opened her fist and wordlessly revealed the crumpled paper.

He took it, smoothed it out, and read the words aloud. *"The only place where today comes before yesterday."*

"The only place where today comes before yesterday," she repeated, the intriguing clue pulling her thoughts from what had almost happened.

"Any ideas?" he asked after a moment.

They looked up at the same time and Stacia hastily lowered her eyes. "I don't know." Beneath her breath, she murmured, *"Today comes before yesterday. Today comes before yesterday. Today comes—"* she broke off and her head whipped up. Again, she met his gaze, but this time she gave him a triumphant smile. "I have it." She glanced around at the corridor and frowned. "I am disoriented. Which way to the library?"

"Just a moment," he said, "I can hear them all coming up the stairs." He strode over to the secret panel and shut it with a firm *click* and then grinned at her. "There, that will buy us a few extra minutes while they bumble and search for the latch."

"Isn't that rather...dirty?"

He set a hand lightly on her shoulder. "You know what they say?"

"No, what do they say?" she asked, trying not to think about the feel of his big, warm hand.

"All is fair in love and treasure hunting, Miss Martin."

"Funny, I've never heard that," she said wryly.

The others had obviously reached the small landing and were thumping on the door. Muffled voices barely penetrated the wooden panel. *"Hello? Let us out!"*

"Are you sure about this?" she asked, glancing dubiously at the panel, which was now vibrating with the fury of their pounding.

Lord Shelton laughed. "Don't worry about them; they will figure it out soon enough."

Stacia bit back her disappointment when he removed his hand and strode down the corridor.

When they reached the library a few minutes later it was to find it already occupied. But instead of another team, it was the maid from earlier, Dora.

She gave them a startled look. "Oh! I beg your pardon. I was just leaving."

"Were you looking for me?" Stacia asked. "Does Lady Addiscombe need me?"

"No, no, not at all, Miss. Er, I'm sorry, I was looking for somebody else." She dropped a curtsey and hurried toward the door.

Lord Shelton lifted an eyebrow. "That was…"

"Odd," she said. "I wonder if I should go—"

"Lady Addiscombe would send for you if she wanted you. Besides, the woman cannot deprive me of *both* my partners."

Stacia warmed at his words. It almost sounded as if he wanted her to stay.

He stared at her. "Well?"

"Well?" she repeated blankly.

"Where is it? The clue," he gently reminded her.

"Oh. In the dictionary."

His gaze went vague for a few seconds before sharpening. He grinned. "What a clever clogs you are!"

"Thank you," Stacia said.

He laughed at her lofty tone. "Chatham keeps his volume—which is massive—on a stand. I daresay Needham does the same," Shelton said, turning in a circle to survey the cavernous room. "Ah, that looks like it might be it." They hurried toward where the maid had been standing.

Stacia opened it to the word *today*, where a folded piece of paper was tucked. "There is only one clue," she said, looking up at Shelton. "Where are the rest for the other groups?"

He shrugged and took the paper from her. "That is not our problem."

Stacia snorted. "You are horrible!"

"I know," he said, sounding unconcerned. *"The only safe place for some religious treasures."*

Stacia puzzled over the clue, the only sound in the room the ticking of an enormous longcase clock. "Treasures are kept in a safe. Surely Lord Needham is not going to leave his safe open?"

Shelton barked a laugh. "I wouldn't think so."

"But where else do you keep treasures?" She frowned. "Jewelry caskets?"

But Lord Shelton was staring fixedly at the scrap of paper and didn't seem to hear her.

"My lord?" she urged after a moment.

"I know this one." He gave her a fierce, triumphant grin. "Come, let's go before the others arrive." He took her hand and pulled her toward the door.

"But what about the clue? Shouldn't we leave it?"

"No."

"That is *wrong*, my lord."

"*Mmm-hmm*," he said, and then opened the door a crack, peeked out. "The coast is clear! Make haste, Miss Martin! Make haste!"

Stacia laughed as he all but dragged her down the corridor.

***

Andrew could not recall when he'd last enjoyed a game so much.

"Where are we going?" Miss Martin asked in a breathless voice as they hurried toward the oldest part of the house.

"To the Wych House priest hole." He led her up a narrow flight of stairs and down a gloomy, unadorned servant hallway.

"Oooh! I didn't know there was a priest hole here. Ah, religious treasure! How clever. They are supposed to be impossible to find."

"They are, indeed, and this one is no different. Come, let's hurry before anyone else gets here." The door on the landing led to a broad, elegant corridor that was empty except for the maid from earlier, Dora, who was absently flicking a marble bust with a feather duster.

How odd that the woman was here when she'd just left the library.

He exchanged looks with Miss Martin and she shrugged. "Perhaps she is in charge of distributing the clues," she whispered, her warm breath on his throat causing a pleasurable tightening in his belly.

"If so, she is doing a poor job," he whispered back.

158

"Maybe we should tell her that she didn't leave enough clues in the library?"

He clucked his tongue. "Oh, Miss Martin! Where is your cutthroat impulse? Do you want this treasure, or not?"

A mischievous smile illuminated her usually serious features. Really, the woman was adorable when she smiled and should do so more often. "All is fair in love and treasure hunting?" she asked.

"That's the spirit!" he said, holding her sparkling gaze for a moment before turning to the wall. "Now, where is that catch?"

"*Another* secret stairwell?" she asked, coming to stand close beside him, the faint smell of soap and lavender teasing his nostrils.

"This panel is not a secret, although it is very well-hidden," he muttered. "Here it is," he pushed on the upper corner of a panel and exposed a small room. There were shelves filled with bedding, a bucket, a mop, and other housekeeping supplies.

"It is a linen closet," Miss Martin said, sounding so disappointed that Andrew chuckled. "This wouldn't have been difficult for priest hunters to find at all."

"Oh, ye of little faith," he teased, and then began shoving aside piles of sheets until he found the lever and pushed it into its slot. "How is this for well-hidden?" he asked, and then pulled the edge of the shelving toward him. It did not move willingly, but like an especially heavy, grudging door. Andrew kept pulling until there was a two-foot opening.

"There is nothing but a wall behind it," she said, yet again sounding disappointed. "What now?"

Andrew slid his hand to the far edge of the panel, to where there was a gap where two sections of wall met.

He tucked the fingers of both hands into the gap. "This slides open, but it takes…a…bit…of…*effort*." He pulled until an extremely slim aperture appeared.

She peered through the opening but hung back. "It's very dark."

"I'll go first," he said, amused by her reluctance to enter. The stairs were so narrow that his shoulders almost brushed the walls.

"It is warm in here," she said, her hushed voice coming from right behind him.

"The staircase runs alongside a chimney stack, which is how they managed to conceal it. From outside, it looks like there are six chimneys. If a person watched long enough, they would notice that smoke only came out of five."

"Clever," she murmured.

He stopped on the top step which served as a landing. There was one candle in a plain wall sconce to cast some light.

"I cannot believe they would put a clue up here," Miss Martin said as Andrew felt for the lever that would unlatch the door.

"I can. Needham is as proud of this priest hole as if he'd built it with his own hands. Evidently it is the second largest one in Britain. At least as far as people know." He slid his hand over the door again, but slower this time. "Needham is having three secret rooms constructed in the house he is having built. They are to be a surprise gift for his wife."

Miss Martin gave a delighted laugh.

"You would like that?" he guessed.

"Who would not?"

Andrew smiled. "There is speculation among the people who study this sort of thing that many hideaways still remain undiscover—ah, there you are," he muttered, depressing the metal latch and then grunting as he slid back the thick slab of wood to expose another narrow opening, this one so small that he had to turn sideways and crouch to get through it.

Once he was in the attic he turned, chuckling when he saw that she came through the space with ease. "It is a door made especially for you," he teased.

"Very droll." She looked around at the vast space. "I thought priest holes were supposed to be tiny. This is massive."

"Seventeen feet by twelve, or so Needham boasted."

"There is even a fireplace," she said, gazing toward the far end of the room, where all the comforts of a guest suite were arrayed—including a bed—the furnishings simple but elegant. "How on earth did they get everything up here through that narrow entry?"

"Much of the original furnishings had rotted away so Needham had carpenters build new pieces here. He said everything here is an exact replica."

"It seems rather ornate for a priest."

He laughed. "Indeed, whoever hid here must have enjoyed his creature comforts." He gestured toward the fire. "With that blaze going they must have been expecting visitors." Andrew had to stay toward the center of the room as the rest sloped from ceiling to floor as in most attics.

"What is all this?" Miss Martin asked, looking around at the piles of blankets, cushions, food hampers, a case of wine, corked clay jugs, and two ancient-looking trunks.

"I don't know," Andrew admitted. "And where is the next clue?"

"Perhaps on that table?" She pointed to a small console table on the other side of the fireplace.

Andrew took a step toward it but stopped and pivoted when he heard the distinctive sound of the heavy wooden slab sliding shut.

He hesitated only a moment before shouting, "Wait!" and breaking into a run, a sick feeling blossoming in his belly as the gap between the door and thick timber frame disappeared.

"We are inside!" he shouted, skidding to a stop and pounding on the door.

There was no handle or knob on the inside of the door, nothing but a smooth wooden panel. A *thick* wooden panel.

Miss Martin joined him, and they battered the wood together.

"Hello! *Hello!*" she yelled, hysteria coloring her voice. "You've locked us in! Please, let us out!"

Andrew stepped back, but she kept pounding.

He stared at the door. *No. This could not be happening.*

Miss Martin stopped and turned. Her wide eyes fixed on him, horror spreading across her face.

"*You!*" she shouted.

Andrew bristled. "Me, what?"

She flung her arms out. "You planned all this, didn't you?"

Andrew stared at her in disbelief.

And then he laughed.

Chapter 17

Kathryn

"Miss Martin does not feel well and did not want to risk passing her cold to any of us," Katie said when Phoebe asked why their mother's companion was not in the drawing room before dinner. "And mother is not here because she still suffers from her migraine," she added.

Phoebe frowned. "I will go and check on them both."

"No, you needn't," Katie said hurriedly, before her sister could heave herself to her feet. "Mama's maid said she does not want to be disturbed. And Miss Martin looked so ill that I sent Dora to sit with her."

"That was very thoughtful of you," Phoebe said, smiling at her.

Katie returned her smile with one that was rather forced. If only her sister knew…

"Do you think I should send for Doctor Murray?" Phoebe asked.

"I already offered. Miss Martin was most emphatic that we do not."

"Very well. So, we are down three for dinner, then."

"Who is the third?" Katie asked, although she knew that, too.

"Shelton left a note saying he was going to see a horse and would probably be away a few days," the Duke of Chatham said, a perplexed frown on his face. "He mentioned nothing about going to see a horse this morning. It is most unusual for him to leave without saying anything."

"He left my aunt's house with my sister and never said anything," Hy observed with a faint twist of her lips.

The duke smiled, but it looked a bit strained.

Before he could speak, Hy said in a low voice, "I'm sorry, Chatham. I should not have said that. It was…insensitive."

Katie's eyebrows shot up. She loved her sister, but Hy was not exactly known for her sensitivity.

The duke said something to his wife that was too quiet for Katie to hear, and her sister chuckled. "I will remind you of that later…Your Grace."

That was another new thing about Hy—her laughter. Katie could count on one hand the number of times she'd heard her older sister laugh before she married the duke.

Of course, there hadn't been much for Hy to laugh about growing up. Their mother wasn't warm toward any of her children, but she loathed Hy and never bothered to hide it.

After what had occurred at Aunt Agnes's house this past summer, Katie suspected that she had taken Hy's place as her mother's most loathed child.

Regardless of how much the countess disliked her, she was still insistent that Katie accompany her to Bath after Christmas rather than go to London.

"You will not continue to live in the same house as that—that *cad* Shelton. You will just have to wait for your Season until next year, when I can offer you proper chaperonage. After what occurred at my sister's house it is clear nobody else can manage you. So, I will be forced to do so."

The argument that followed had not been pleasant. Neither had it resolved anything. But Katie was not done fighting for her future, and she had several other weapons remaining in her arsenal. By hook or by crook she would not be going to Bath.

Her mother just didn't know that yet.

Without the countess to dampen the atmosphere at the dinner table the meal seemed to fly by and conversation was lively.

Afterward they retired to the drawing room, as usual. Katie had no heart for games—at least not the sorts that were played with rules—but she could not absent herself without drawing notice.

No, it would be unwise to attract attention after what she had done to Shelton and Miss Martin…

Katie's lips curled into a smile as she imagined the scene in the priest hole right about now. It was too bad she could not be a fly on the wall.

She had not yet decided whether to release the pair from their prison tomorrow while everyone else was out gathering greenery—which would mean that nobody would find out that Shelton and Miss Martin had gone missing—or if she should keep them sequestered for so long that Shelton's hand would be forced, and he would have to propose.

But that, she decided, was too cruel, even for Shelton.

Besides, there was Miss Martin to consider.

Not that it wasn't perfectly clear to her that the other woman burned for Shelton. Katie knew Miss Martin's besotted expression well because she had felt the exact same emotion briefly, last spring.

Despite Miss Martin's obvious desire for the marquess, it was entirely possible that she would refuse Shelton's gentlemanly offer of marriage. She was a proud woman, and Shelton had trampled on her pride in the past.

Even so, the woman was doubtless in seventh heaven at the moment, imprisoned with the man of her dreams.

As for Shelton? Although the ridiculously handsome marquess had denied it, he was intrigued by Stacia Martin. Katie had been around him for months and he'd never once noticed a woman the way he'd done with Miss Martin.

Poor Shelton was an unhappy, lonely man who'd been clinging to his love for a dead woman for more than a decade. He would vehemently disagree that Katie was doing this for his benefit, but one day he would thank her.

Katie should probably let them out after one night. That way the two of them could either take advantage of the opportunity she had offered them, or they could ignore the gift she'd given them, go their own two ways, and live miserable lives.

"Katie?"

She looked up from her thoughts to find Selina beside her. "Yes?"

"I'm going to partner Phoebe against Hy and Chatham. Shaftsbury cannot play cards as we haven't yet figured out a way to do that yet. But he enjoys chess a great deal and we've brought his set along, so—"

"I would love to play your husband a game," Katie lied.

"I've been telling him how clever you are, and he is prepared, so you needn't be kind to him."

Katie gave her sister a weak smile. Chess. Was there anything she hated more in the world?

Well, yes. Two things, actually. Plying a needle and Lord Jasper Raine.

What use were any of them?

She could not earn money with chess as her sister Hy had done with cards.

And needlework was either a drudge's job or a pastime for sleekly contented matrons to occupy their hands in between bearing heirs for their husbands or taking lovers.

As for Lord Raine...

Her mouth twisted into an unpleasant smile.

Raine's only purpose was as a walking, talking warning to women about the duplicity of man.

Ten minutes later Katie was seated across from Selina's gorgeous husband, in the middle of a game she could win at any time. But if she did, she would just be forced to play another, so she allowed her mind to wander and once again it returned to Shelton and Miss Martin.

Had she done the wrong thing? No doubt most people would answer an emphatic *yes* to that. Viewed objectively, she was risking two peoples' reputations. Or at least Miss Martin's, as Shelton's reputation was in such tatters nothing could make it worse.

As much as she teased and taunted Andrew, she had come to like him a great deal. If somebody didn't do something—that somebody being her, apparently—then he would likely go to London this Season and marry an heiress he didn't love, or even like, to save his estate.

Katie could not allow him to sacrifice himself that way. Even though he probably deserved it.

"I sense you are restless, Lady Kathryn," Lord Shaftsbury said, staring at her with eyes that seemed to look into her soul. "You could have had me in checkmate once already."

It was actually more like three times, but who was counting?

Katie shrugged, remembered he could not see the dismissive gesture, and said, "I hate chess."

His distractingly pretty lips parted in surprise and then he barked a laugh, the skin at the corners of his sightless gray eyes crinkling in a way that caused a fluttering in her belly. He really was extremely handsome—not to mention charming and so...*happy* that it was difficult to feel glum in his presence. Selina said he'd been as cross as a crab when she'd first met him. It was hard to imagine.

"We do not need to play," he said, pitching his voice so only the two of them could hear it.

"Oh, yes we do."

"Why?"

"Because my siblings will want to know why I'm not playing if I don't."

"Your sister said you are very good at the game. The best in your family."

"I am."

"And yet you sound unhappy about your skill. We can always just sit here in silence." He paused and then added with a sly twist of those sensual lips. "Or we could talk."

"Talk?"

He smiled.

"Talk about what?" she said after a moment.

He shrugged his powerful shoulders. "Whatever you like."

Katie wanted to ask what it had been like to be trapped in a carriage for days with his dying wife, but she doubted that was a subject he would appreciate.

Instead, she said, "I will have my first Season next year."

"Yes, your sister mentioned that."

"I daresay you've had many."

He laughed. "Why? Because I am old?"

He *was* old. At least compared to Katie's seven-and-ten years.

Before she could come up with a polite response he said, "Are you looking forward to it?"

"It will be something to do."

His eyebrows arched. "I cannot help thinking that you do not sound very excited."

Katie knew he was waiting for an explanation, but she had nothing to offer. She didn't know why she felt such a crushing sense of…ennui.

Oh, yes you do.

"I'm not terribly excited," she admitted. "I never would have believed that I'd miss being crowded at Queen's Bower and wearing gowns that had passed through four sisters before they became mine. But sometimes I wish—" she bit her lip, horrified by the burning behind her eyes.

"What do you wish?"

"I wish we had never left," she said, her voice barely a whisper. Where in the world had that come from? Katie swallowed hard, as if that would suppress the emotions suddenly threatening to overwhelm her.

"It is normal that you would miss such closeness," he said gently.

Rather than go away, the urge to cry built so quickly she had to tilt her head back. Why did she feel such a powerful compulsion to throw herself onto this kind man's broad chest and weep and weep and weep?

What was wrong with her?

"If London is not to your liking, then I hope you will come and stay with Selina and me," he said. "We will only remain in town for a month. Long enough for Selina to be presented and then we will go home."

It was a nice offer, but the last thing Katie wanted was to bear close witness to yet another joyously happy marriage. Or be a burden. Selina and Shaftsbury spent most of their time together—not just because he needed Selina, but because they were so deeply in love. Although Hy and Chatham were equally in love, they each led busy, independent lives and Katie's presence did not interfere with their lives.

"That is very kind of you, my lord, but I suppose I will give London a chance."

"I think you might enjoy yourself more than you expect."

Katie would be stunned if that were true. Wisely, she kept that bitter prediction to herself.

Instead, she said, "I daresay you are right. Shall we finish this game? I believe it was your move."

Chapter 18

Andrew glared daggers at the door, as if it might slide open if he stared long and hard enough.

"I am sorry, my lord."

He turned and faced his unwilling companion.

Miss Martin's lips were tightly pursed, and her cheeks were stained with dark red splotches.

"What are you apologizing for?" he asked.

"It was unkind of me to say that you had arranged all this."

Andrew opened his mouth to tell her it did not matter, but she was not finished.

"It was also foolish. After all, what could I possibly have to offer that would cause a man to lure me into such an indiscretion?"

He barked an unamused laugh at her backhanded apology. "According to my detractors I don't need a reason."

Andrew turned away from her and strode down the length of the room.

He flipped open the lids on the hampers; both were filled to the brim with food, enough to last several days. Beside the fireplace was a coal scuttle with ample fuel for a protracted blaze.

In addition to the food, blankets, and furniture, there was off to the side a rather modern-looking three-fold screen with a close stool tucked behind it.

Whoever had staged this had certainly thought of everything.

Andrew heard the scuff of a shoe and turned to find Miss Martin staring at the bed, her arms wrapped around her body, as if she were cold.

He scooped up more coal and tossed it onto the fire.

They might as well make themselves comfortable, because he suspected they would be there a while.

***

Stacia felt like a toad.

Even an idiot could see that Lord Shelton had been appalled when the door had slid shut, locking them both in.

Instead of snapping at her when she'd accused him of masterminding the episode, he'd merely looked resigned. And very weary.

And then she had compounded her bad behavior with her insulting apology.

Apologize. And be sincere, this time.

She wrapped her arms around herself, suddenly feeling chilled to the bone, although not by the weather.

Shelton was building up the fire, his back to her.

Stacia chewed her lip, unable to look away from the bed. It was simple in construction, almost monastic, the bedding a soft white cloud.

And there was only *one.*

She swallowed and briefly closed her eyes, as if that could contain the emotions that were swirling inside her—fear, joy, excitement, anxiety and more—the sensations pulling her in a dozen directions, like the tug of conflicting waves striking a beach. The resulting undercurrents created a vortex that threatened to overwhelm her, just like the lethal drag of an undertow.

I get to spend time with Lord Shelton! I do not need to share him with anyone else!

Mine! Mine! Mine!

Stacia could not help smiling at the thought of having him all to herself.

Lady Addiscombe will sack you and you will be cast so far beyond the pale you will never get another position.

The thought was not nearly as frightening as it should be. After all, Lord Needham had given his word to help her, hadn't he?

He might feel differently after this...

He might. But Stacia did not think a man who brought his illegitimate daughter—and her mother—to live under the same roof as his new wife cared overly much about social conventions.

If her reputation was going to be compromised—ruined—then she might as well enjoy herself in the meantime.

Why was that thought so liberating?

Because you are trapped in a room with the man of your dreams.

Stacia smiled.

And he is trapped with you, not exactly a dream woman for any man.

Drab little dab of a woman.

Her smile faded, as did the delight and giddiness she'd been feeling.

This disaster was not his fault and yet he would pay for it. Of course he could probably weather such a scandal as he had in the past—

Stacia blinked, seized by the thought.

Lady Kathryn's story about Sarah Creighton—now Leary—came back to her.

Surely something like this is not what had happened to Shelton and Sarah?

No. That would be too strange.

Wouldn't it?

"Come, Miss Martin—sit close to the fire."

"Thank you," she murmured, and perched on the edge of the lovely, if threadbare, settee.

Apologize. And this time, make it genuine.

"My lord?"

"Yes, Miss Martin?" he asked, his expression vague but…amused?

What did he find amusing? This situation?

What does it matter? Apologize.

"Are you hungry?" he asked.

"No, thank you."

"Something to drink?" He uncorked one jug, sniffed and frowned before turning to the second. This time, he sniffed and smiled.

"What is in them?" she asked.

"Lemonade or ale. Which would you like?"

She thought for a moment. "Neither."

"There is tea?"

Stacia shook her head. "No, thank you."

"I will make something for you," he said.

"What?"

"Something my batman used to make for me. It is half ale and half lemonade. He called it *lemon beer.*"

"That sounds…" It sounded disgusting, but that was rude. "Er, intriguing."

"It is refreshing." He poured the mixture and then handed her the glass.

"Thank you," she said, looking dubiously at the pale brown liquid for a moment before taking a small sip. It was not terrible.

"Well?" he asked.

"It is interesting."

"Do you want a glass of just lemonade?"

"No, I will drink a little more of this."

He filled a second glass with ale, took a deep pull, and gave a sigh of contentment.

At least one of them was content.

Apologize.

"I'm sorry."

Even in the dim light of the attic his eyes were a shockingly bright blue. He smiled. "You already apologized."

"That was for the first thing I said. Now I am apologizing for insulting you again."

He laughed, the skin at the corners of his eyes crinkling attractively. "You are forgiven—for any and all infractions you might have committed."

"You are not angry with me?"

"I am not." His gaze turned pensive. "You know what this means, don't you?"

"Yes," she said grimly. "I know what this means."

"Well, you needn't look so joyous about it."

"Why should I be joyous about being ruined?" she demanded.

"I was not talking about being *ruined*. I was talking about being my wife." The muscles in his face tightened until he looked just as gorgeous as ever, but stern and intimidating instead of his usual laughing and teasing self.

"Er, wife?" she repeated.

His jaws flexed, but he didn't speak.

"Why?" she blurted.

"You mean why would I marry you when I didn't marry Sarah Creighton?"

That was exactly what Stacia meant, but she hardly wanted to admit it.

Still, she was desperate for the truth.

Tell him what you know.

Shelton gave a mocking laugh. "Don't hold back for fear of hurting my feelings, Miss Martin. You haven't done in the past," he added with a wry smile.

There was the invitation Stacia had been hoping for.

"Lady Kathryn met Miss Creighton—now Mrs. Leary—and she told me that things are not what they seem."

"Kathryn met Sarah?" he repeated after a moment.

"Yes."

"When was this?"

"This past spring. Her aunt lives near Mrs. Leary."

He gave a huff of laughter. "So that is what she has been on about."

"I beg your pardon?" Stacia asked.

"I cannot believe Kathryn has not said anything about this until now. Who would have guessed she had such self-restraint? Obviously, I have been underestimating her."

Stacia did not know what to say.

"So, what did she tell you, Miss Martin?"

"That Mrs. Leary seemed very happy and not like a woman who'd been forced to marry a provincial nobody against her will." She cleared her throat and then forced herself to say, "She said that Mrs. Leary's child looks a great deal like her husband."

He inhaled deeply, the action expanding his already impressive chest. He held his breath for a long moment and then exhaled, staring at something she could not see. The past, perhaps.

When he did not speak, Stacia said, "Kathryn hinted strongly that she knows the truth of what happened between you and Sarah."

"That is not my secret to tell. However, I fear you will never get past this until I speak of it." He smiled coolly, the expression for once not reaching his eyes. "I do not wish to commence our lives together with such a... misunderstanding between us."

"I have not said I will marry you," Stacia quickly reminded him.

"Duly noted," he said. "I am sure I can depend on your discretion."

"I would keep anything you told me in the strictest confidence." She gave him a reproachful look. "Men are not the only ones who can behave honorably."

He smiled faintly. "No, of course not. Then I will tell you the truth about what really happened with Sarah, and why I never offered her the protection of my name." He paused and then added with a stern, uncompromising look, "And then you will understand why you will not have the same lucky escape from marriage that *she* did."

Chapter 19

I will go right to the heart of the matter," Andrew said. "Sarah's father, Sir Jonathan, wanted me to marry his daughter."

Miss Martin nodded, but didn't speak.

"He offered to pay off my sizeable debts, but that was not what piqued my interest. Sir Jonathan also possesses a third share in a valuable stud. The stallion in question is magnificent and, quite frankly, beyond price. I was sorely tempted." He smiled at her thinning lips. "You are thinking it is mercenary to contemplate marriage for stud rights?"

"Mercenary, not to mention slightly ironic."

Andrew's jaw sagged and he gave a startled laugh. "What a naughty thing to say! I highly approve of such comments, by the way."

Her cheeks flooded with color. "It *is* mercenary, but that isn't unusual among our class, is it?" she asked, evidently choosing to ignore his teasing. "Her father wanted you for your connections and the possibility that his daughter would be a duchess, so I suppose it would have been a good bargain on both sides."

"For me it would have been. And for Sir Jonathan and his wife and their family." He gave her a sardonic look. "It would have been an excellent bargain for everyone but Sarah."

Stacia frowned. "Why wouldn't—"

"Because Sarah was already in love with another man, but he was somebody her father did not approve of: a humble farmer."

"Mr. Leary," she said.

"Just so. In the weeks that I courted her I was increasingly aware that she was less than enthusiastic about my pursuit." He smirked at her. "Other than you, Miss Martin, I've met very few women who have, er, spurned my attentions. I know it sounds arrogant, but—"

"It might be arrogant, but it is also the truth. I saw it with my own eyes." Her look of irritated disgust told Andrew just how she felt about that. "So," she went on, "that is how you knew she was in love with somebody else? Because she didn't want you?"

"I guessed her interest might lie somewhere else, but I wasn't sure until she told me so."

Miss Martin's eyebrows arched. "It is difficult to imagine initiating such a conversation."

Andrew chuckled. "Fear is a great motivator."

"Fear?"

"Yes. Fear that I might actually propose."

"And would you have?"

It was Andrew's turn to raise his eyebrows.

***

Stacia bit her lip. "I'm sorry, that was rather—"

He waved aside her apology. "Honestly? I am not sure what I would have done. Sarah is a charming, interesting woman, so it would not have been a hardship. It would have made my cousin very happy, which might have convinced him to release my inheritance a few years early. And then there was the added incentive of King's Falcon—the stud," he explained at her querying look. "She said her father would not sanction the match with her farmer because of his hope that I would marry her. I confessed that I had no interest marrying a woman who was in love with another man." A pained look flickered briefly across his handsome face, but he shrugged it aside and said, "When I gave her my word that I would not propose—and that I'd find a subtle way to discourage her father's interest—she told me something else, something that made her situation dire, indeed."

"She was with ch-child." Her stammering irked her, and she cleared her throat and said more firmly, "It was the farmer's child."

"Not only that, but she was several months along. Even if her father did find another candidate to replace me, her condition was soon going to become obvious." He gave her a wry smile. "And then she asked me for a favor. Can you guess what it was?"

"She asked you to help her make sure that nobody else would marry her—to destroy her reputation. And so you sacrificed *your* reputation so she could marry the man she loved." Stacia chewed the inside of her cheek as she remembered the disgust she'd subjected him to. "I'm sorry, my lord."

He gave a bark of laughter. "Oh, don't make me a hero, Miss Martin. I am fairly certain that her father would have relented about her choice of husband when he discovered the truth. I did not save her, I just put an end to her father's plans sooner rather than later."

Stacia shook her head. "It is far more likely that he would have found a man willing to marry her and accept another man's child. How valuable is Sir Jonathan's stud right?"

He blinked. "Er—"

175

"I know you said it was *priceless* but humor me and put a price on it."

He looked thoughtful for a moment and then said, "A conservative estimate is five thousand pounds, but it might be as high as a hundred thousand."

"*A hundred thousand pounds!* For a horse!"

"Not for the horse; for the stud fees and for any colts. He's a young stallion and has already produced two Ascot winners, and he has years ahead of him."

Stacia was flabbergasted by the astronomical sum and had to force herself to return to her point. "And you don't think the promise of even ten thousand pounds would tempt plenty of unscrupulous men with titles and little else other than debts to their name?"

"Perhaps."

"Instead of leaving her future happiness to chance, you, a war hero"—Stacia held up her hand when he shook his head and opened his mouth, likely to demur. "No, do not try and gainsay that. You *are* a war hero and you made yourself an object of contempt to decent people all to help a woman you barely knew."

He laughed. "*An object of contempt.* You should be a novelist, Miss Martin. You have a way with words."

"Do you deny that you've been treated badly in Society?"

"Oh, sometimes by the highest of sticklers." He gave a dismissive wave, as if the calumny of his peers was nothing. "But it did not bother me. Besides, helping Sarah was not my only—or even strongest—motivation." The amusement bled from his face.

"Dare I ask what that was?"

His jaw flexed. "I did it because I knew it would infuriate Chatham."

Stacia had no response to that. What did it even mean?

He pushed to his feet and turned to the fire, jabbing at it with the poker.

Stacia stared at his broad back and the tense set of his shoulders. She wanted to know more—who wouldn't—but she had already pushed enough on this subject. And he was right: it had not been his secret to share and yet Lady Kathryn and Stacia had essentially forced his confession. Or at least he'd believed that he needed to tell her the truth as they would soon be married.

She wanted to tell him that her reputation among the *ton* was not important enough to merit a sacrifice on his part like marriage. But that was a lie. As a woman who worked for a living, her reputation was of paramount importance.

However, as difficult as such a scandal would make her life, she still had no intention of marrying him.

He would press her on the subject—she had grown up with aristocratic men and knew their code of honor—but she would resist him.

Sure you will.

Stacia chose to ignore the taunt. Instead, she changed the subject. "How long do you think we will be here?" Once she'd given life to the words another thought struck her, one that should have been her first question. "And *why* are we here? It must be an accident."

He hung up the poker and slowly turned to her. "An accident?" he repeated, clearly befuddled.

Stacia felt like an idiot. "I don't mean that all *this*"—she gestured to the food and blankets—"is an accident, I just wonder if somebody else was setting up a—a—"

"Seduction?" he suggested, looking amused by her sputtering.

"Yes. What if we just bumbled up here and then somebody saw the open door and closed it without thinking?"

"Who?"

"I don't know. A servant?"

He cocked his head at her.

"I know, I know—that sounds thin."

"*Very* thin. Transparent, in fact." He finished his ale and then lifted the jug in her direction.

She shook her head. "No, thank you.

He poured another glass, took a drink, and said, "It was Lady Kathryn."

"*Lady Kathryn!* Why on earth would you think this is her doing?"

He turned toward the fire, which was now blazing, and red and gold light danced over his perfect features.

"You must have a reason for thinking that," she prodded.

"I *know* it is her. I made a wager with her."

"You made a wager that she could lock us in a priest's hole?" she shrieked.

He winced. "Of course not."

"Then *what*, pray?"

177

"Evidently—and I only have her word for this as I do not recall any of it—she once told me she would never marry. I, er, *allegedly*, laughed at her and told her that she would marry before I did." He shrugged. "To her way of thinking, we made a wager."

"That's—that's…" She shook her head. "What in the world is wrong with the two of you? Are you both *twelve*?"

His jaws clenched. "As I've already said, I have no recollection of the conversation."

"But you believe she did this?"

"Yes. Although why she has suddenly decided to take action *now*, I do not know." His blue gaze flickered around the room, as if there might be reasons lurking in the dark corners. "I am joining Chatham at his house in London and she could have tormented me all Season long—which is a pastime she enjoys—so, why *now*? And why—" He broke off as his eyes settled on Stacia and slowly narrowed. He cocked his head, opened his mouth, and then closed it, still staring.

Stacia just *knew* what he'd been about to ask: why had Lady Kathryn chosen *her*.

Oh God. What if he guessed the truth?

***

Miss Martin was suddenly as silent as the grave. Andrew suspected she was fuming over the fact that his idiocy had led to her downfall: marriage to *him*. He could not blame her; he would not want to marry him, either. Even without the pall of Sarah's ruin hanging over his head, he was no bargain. At least not to a woman who saw through his appearance to the less than impressive man beneath.

She was right. What had he been thinking about to wager about such a matter with Kathryn? He knew how suggestible and unpredictable—no, *volatile*—the girl could be.

To be perfectly honest, he sometimes enjoyed her wild, somewhat unhinged, behavior a great deal. He suspected she was exactly what his younger sister would have been like if his mother and the infant she'd been carrying hadn't died in that carriage accident.

As often as Andrew complained about Kathryn, he had to admit she'd made his life more amusing since moving back to Chatham Park.

The last months had been…difficult. Not because of anything Sylvester had said or done. Not even because of Sylvester's mother, who was certainly a brutal bitch and strove to make everyone around her suffer.

No, it was none of that.

It sounded like madness to articulate it, but without Sylvester to hate, Andrew had been forced to focus on himself for the first time in eleven years. What he had seen—a rootless, irresponsible clod with nothing but shame to show for over a decade of living—had horrified him. And depressed him.

"I daresay I was simply convenient," Miss Martin suddenly said.

"*Hmm?*"

"I said that Lady Kathryn chose me because I am the only unmarried female staying at the house over the age of one-and-twenty." She gave a stiff huff of laughter.

Andrew studied her bowed head; *he* knew why Kathryn had chosen Miss Martin. And it wasn't because she was the only choice, either. The youngest Bellamy sister might be green when it came to life and love, but she had recognized Andrew's interest in Miss Martin like a falcon spotting an unfortunate rodent that had popped its head out of a hole.

His memory might be shoddy, but it worked well enough to recall at least some of Kathryn's mocking comments from the past few months. Every time he'd been forced to attend some function or other with Sylvester, Hyacinth, and Kathryn— and there had been far, far too many for his liking—Kathryn had taunted him about the matchmaking mamas who threw their daughters at him even though he was poor, disgraced, and an unlikely candidate for the dukedom now that Chatham had a pregnant wife.

It was lamentable but true that a great many women didn't seem to care what Andrew had done or how poor his prospects were; they simply could not resist a handsome face.

While it was undeniable that he had used Selina Bellamy last Season to get back at Sylvester—believing his cousin was in love with her—he really had empathized with the beautiful woman, who had understood more than anyone he'd ever met how tedious it was to be so physically appealing to members of the opposite sex that people lost their wits.

It had been a bloody relief to spend time with a woman who knew exactly how tiresome, not to mention insulting, such attention felt. As if Andrew's shell was all there was to him. Once his looks were gone—and he would grow old and wrinkly just like anyone else, provided he didn't die first—did that mean there was nothing left of him that was of any interest?

Selina also knew how complaining about her beauty would only irritate those around her. It hadn't surprised him at all that she had eventually fallen in love with a man who had no idea what she looked like. A man who'd fallen in love with *her* rather than her appearance.

Andrew had tried to explain the problem to Sylvester years ago—long before they had fallen out over Mariah—and his cousin had scoffed. "Poor, poor, Drew! So popular with the ladies that they flock to him like pigeons."

"And that's what you'd like—to be swarmed by pigeons?" he had retorted.

But his cousin had only laughed.

Selina, Kathryn, Hyacinth—and now Miss Martin—were among the very few women not fooled by his face. All four had seen past his appearance to the wreck of a man beneath.

Miss Martin was staring at him, waiting for his response.

"Kathryn chose you because you hate me and that gives her no end of amusement," he said, only partly lying.

"I do not hate you."

"Fine, not *hate*, but dislike. Certainly, you are not swayed by my looks." He shrugged, uninterested in parsing the finer points of exactly *how* she despised him. "Unfortunately for you, Lady Kathryn has chosen a husband for you whom she believes you cannot respect." He gave an unamused bark of laughter. "Have you displeased her in some way to earn such treatment?" Andrew did not wait for an answer. "Disregard that question. It doesn't matter why she engineered this. It irritates me to spend time discussing the willful chit. We are left to deal with the repercussions." Which meant marriage, but he wasn't going to bring that up again, not after the look of loathing she'd given him the first time he'd mentioned it. There would be ample time to discuss the subject later, when Kathryn decided to release them.

"You never answered my question about how long she will leave us here?" Miss Martin asked quietly.

He shrugged. "Your guess is as good as mine."

"What is in those trunks?" she asked.

He stood and opened the lid on the first one. "Toiletries, candles, and—" Andrew dropped to his haunches and opened a very familiar red leather case. He laughed. The *nerve* of the girl!

"What is it?" Miss Martin asked.

"My spectacles."

"You wear glasses?"

He cut her a sideways look. "Yes."

"I have never seen you wear them."

"And you shan't today, either." Andrew turned back to the trunk and pawed through the rest of the contents.

"You choose not to wear them because you are vain."

He ignored the comment, only looking up when she laughed. Yet again he was taken by how different she appeared with a genuine smile rather than the prim pursing of lips that usually passed for a smile. "I'm so pleased you find my visual deficiency amusing."

"I am not laughing because you need to wear them. I am laughing because your vanity won't allow you to."

Andrew closed the trunk before moving to the second one, which held a folding chessboard, spillikins, several packs of cards, a faro board, and a half dozen books.

"What is in that one?"

"Games and books." He looked up and smiled grimly. "You asked how long I think she will keep us here? I'm guessing the answer to that is exactly as long as she likes."

Three hours later...

Stacia eased the fourth-to-last stick from the pile without disturbing the other three, and then quickly picked up the remaining ones.

"Congratulations. You won. Again," Lord Shelton said sourly. "May we play something else, now?"

She grinned. "Are you pouting, my lord?"

He snorted.

The winner got to choose the next game and Stacia had won five games in a row. First they had played three games of chess and now two games of spillikins.

"You choose the next game," she said, putting the sticks back into the fancy lacquer case.

"No, no, you won, so you choose. Those are the rules we agreed on. I am no shirker."

He was definitely sulking, and Stacia knew she should not find it so adorable, but...how could she not? This big, strong, gorgeous man was pouting like a toddler because she had beaten him five times running. Stacia wasn't a great chess player—

or even a very good one—but Lord Shelton was truly abysmal. He made one headlong, ill-conceived move after the other, losing pieces left and right to no effect.

He was slightly better at spillikins, but still too impatient.

"Do you want to do something else, my lord?"

He suddenly looked alert. "Like what?"

For some reason, Stacia's face heated. "I don't know. Take a nap?"

"A nap?" His handsome face screwed up into an expression of horror, as if she'd suggested they plait each other's hair. "Just how old do you think I am that I'd need a nap in the middle of the day?"

Stacia pulled her lips between her teeth, struggling not to laugh.

"Oh, that amuses you, does it?"

"Since you've brought it up, how old are you?"

"How old do you think I am?" he shot back.

She tilted her head to the side and pretended to study him. Stacia knew how old he was, of course—she knew almost all there was to know about the man. At least all the public information that had been bandied about. Now was her chance to get her own back for that *drab little dab* comment.

"Not much over forty," she said after a long moment, during which time his frown had deepened.

His eyebrows nearly launched off his forehead. "*Forty?*"

Stacia was biting her tongue so hard it was almost bleeding. "Nine-and-thirty?" she asked in a choked voice.

"I am *four*-and-thirty," he said frostily. "How old are you?"

"It is rude to ask a lady her age."

"Perhaps that's the case when the lady is older. But you cannot be much more than twenty."

"So, what is next," she asked, ignoring his fishing.

"I don't care," he said petulantly.

"Do you want to read for a while?" She knew the answer to that question even before she'd asked. After all, she'd watched him that first evening in the drawing room, when he'd held a book as if he had never held one before, not turning a page the entire time.

He glanced at the stack of books he'd removed from the trunk and scowled. "No, thank you."

Yet again, Stacia had to smother a laugh. Lady Kathryn—if that is truly who'd done this—had included four gothic novels from the Minerva Press and two books that Stacia had already read and adored: *Sense and Sensibility* and *Emma*, both written by "a Lady."

"Have you read any of these books?" she asked, already knowing the answer.

He scoffed. "No."

"And yet you are already condemning them."

"They are *romantic* novels—melodramas."

Stacia smiled.

"Why are you smiling like that?"

"I get to decide what we do next, and I choose to read *Emma*. Out loud."

"Just one minute! That is not a game."

"I already asked you what you wanted to do, and you said it was my choice."

He bared his teeth.

"Don't worry; I have an excellent reading voice, honed by years of reading aloud to my employers."

Lord Shelton groaned and flung himself back in his chair, resting his forearm over his eyes like a damsel in distress. "Go on, then. Commence the torture."

"At least you are approaching this with an open mind," she said dryly.

He dropped his arm and crossed both over his chest, his expression that of a martyr being lashed to a bundle of kindling.

Struggling not to laugh, she picked up the handsome red leather tooled edition, turned to Volume I, Chapter I, and began reading.

Stacia had been reading for less than a minute and had just uttered the line, *"How was she to bear the change?—It was true that her friend was going only half a mile from them—"*

"Good lord!" Lord Shelton shouted. "Is this entire book about this annoying chit?"

Stacia held up the book so he could read the gold embossed title.

He muttered something that did not sound complimentary. "If Weston knows what is good for him, he will pack up his new wife and move to the Outer Hebrides."

Stacia laughed.

He dropped his head against the chair back. "Go ahead. I won't interrupt again."

But over the next forty-five minutes Shelton interrupted no fewer than eleven times.

"Mr. Elton was the very person fixed on by Emma for driving the young farmer out of Harriet's head. She thought it would be an excellent match—"

Shelton suddenly leapt up from his chair and darted toward her. "God save me from matchmaking women." He plucked the book from Stacia's hands before she knew what he was doing and shoved it under a pile of extra blankets. "No, more. Please, I beg of you, Miss Martin, I cannot endure another word, or I will run amok. No. More."

Stacia laughed. "Are you perhaps not exaggerating a little?"

"Absolutely not. I am underaggerating."

"That's not a word."

"It should be."

"As you capitulated, I suppose that means that I won again?"

"Yes, yes. You won again. Anything to end the agony." His gaze flickered over the now scattered books, games, and cards. "How about Piquet?" he suggested with a hopeful look.

"I am dreadful at it."

"Excellent!" he rubbed his hands together and reached for the cards.

"It is still my choice," she said in a sing-song tone that she knew was annoying.

He growled but dropped the cards. "Well?"

"Let's play Dictionary."

His forehead wrinkled. "How does one play with a dictionary? Does one kick it? Throw it?"

"You don't know how to—" Stacia noticed the slight twitch of his lips. "You are teasing me."

"Yes, I am. I'm not utterly uncouth. I've heard of the game although I've never actually played it." He frowned. "When people played it at school there were always more than two."

"It is easy enough to play with two. One person writes down the real definition and then makes up two false ones to confuse the person guessing. If the person guessing selects the correct one, they get a point. If not, then the person who wrote the definitions gets the point."

He heaved the sigh of a man who'd been pushed almost beyond endurance. "Very well. Who goes first?"

"You may guess first—so I will write the definitions."

Stacia chose a page in the dictionary at random and then closed her eyes and pointed at the page. She opened her eyes, lifted her finger, and said, "The word is *indumentum.*"

***

Forty-five minutes later...

"You won. *Again!*" Lord Shelton seethed.

Not only had Stacia won, but the score had been 10 to 2. Lord Shelton's invented definitions had been some of the worst she had ever heard. Also some of the most hilarious.

For the word *plaud* his two invented definitions had been: *a burr in a horse's tail* and *a horse that is very slow.* When he'd had the word *maugre* he'd made up: *the holes in stirrup leather* and *a breed of pony used in the mountains of Portugal.* It had gone on and on. Every single definition he'd invented had had something to do with horses.

"May I have those?" Stacia asked, gesturing to the pile of papers that held his scribbled definitions.

He scooped them up and was about to hand them over but then frowned suspiciously and pulled his hand back. "Why do you want them?"

"I thought I might save them."

"For what?"

"I just w-w-wanted to—to—" Once she started laughing, she could not stop. Tears streaked down her cheeks, and she tipped onto her side on the settee.

Shelton's face appeared above hers, his big body caging her. "I think you are mocking me, Miss Martin."

Stacia rolled her head from side to side. "No—n-no," she gasped in between snorts and chuckles.

185

"You found my definitions lacking, did you?"

She was laughing too hard to speak, so she shook her head again.

"You are a fibber." His eyes narrowed and then his gaze moved to her mouth. His nostrils flared slightly and then he looked up again, his pupils suddenly huge and black.

Stacia's laughter turned to ragged breathing, her heart thudding loudly, each beat distinct and powerful.

"You look like an entirely different person when you smile and laugh, Miss Martin."

"Everybody does," she said in a breathless voice.

"True. But everybody doesn't look as bewitching as you do."

A whimper slipped from her parted lips.

"I'm going to kiss you. If you don't want me to, now would be the time to say *no*."

Stacia did not move, breathe, or make a sound—nothing that could be construed as *no*. Instead, she prayed more fervently than she had ever prayed in her life. *Kiss me. Please, please, please...*

Lord Shelton's handsome face flexed into an expression of pleased astonishment. And then his mouth lowered over hers.

Chapter 20

Andrew had been resisting the urge to kiss Miss Martin for the past three hours.

Hell, it had actually been far longer than that. He'd wanted to taste those pouty lips that rarely smiled and only opened to issue sharp aggressive words—at least around Andrew—since the morning he'd seen her cradling the injured, bloody mutt in her lap, heedless of the damage being done to what he suspected was one of her very few dresses.

Watching her win games today—and listening to her read that asinine novel—had allowed him to observe her when she didn't have all her spines up. She looked far younger and less bitter when she was occupied with something other than throwing barbed comments Andrew's way. She looked like a young woman who'd been hurt thanks to an oaf's callous behavior. Not just the idiocy that had flowed from his mouth in the conservatory that night, but also the fact that he'd evidently been around her dozens of times and did not recall her. He knew his memory left much to be desired, but what she'd told him had chilled him. Could he really be so…oblivious?

But he had her in his arms now, and he intended to make up for at least some of his neglect.

The first thing he realized was that this woman had never been kissed before. She met his mouth with the sort of tight-lipped peck one would offer one's grandmother.

Virgin! Virgin! Virgin! a warning voice shrieked in his head.

Andrew had known that all along. He didn't care; she was going to be his wife. She was his to kiss. His to touch.

His to take.

Wild and utterly unanticipated lust roared through his body at the thought, his arousal so intense he actually felt dizzy.

When had he last been so hard? He'd not taken a lover for months—not since before he'd abducted Lady Selina. In truth, it had been a chore to fuck for longer than he liked to remember. The only reason he'd had sex at all had been to annoy Sylvester by parading whores around his London house last Season.

But this? This was no chore. Not at all.

She made a slight noise but remained pliant as he cupped the satiny skin of her jaw, gently positioning her for his invasion.

Rather than simply thrust between her lips, he feathered kisses, learning the shape of her prim upper lip and lush, pouty lower one. He sipped at her, nipped gently, and then kissed the same spot, soothing and licking and caressing.

Her body softened; the tension that had kept her rigid replaced by something else. Something...eager.

Only when she began pressing back against him did he slick his tongue over the swell of her lower lip.

She stiffened, turning into a plank once more.

"*Shhh*," he murmured, lightly flicking her with the tip of his tongue. "Let me in."

Astonishingly, not only did she tilt her head to give him better access, but she rubbed her body against his and moaned softly.

Prickly, judgmental Miss Martin had a fire burning inside her.

Andrew smiled to himself as he pulled back enough to meet her eyes. "Let's get more comfortable."

When she nodded, he slid an arm beneath her legs and lifted them up to join the rest of her body on the settee before lying down alongside her. "Much better." He slid an arm beneath the soft curve of her waist and pulled her closer, their torsos pressed tightly together as he kissed her. She responded quickly, an eager participant, her clumsy efforts not just endearing, but stunningly arousing.

He was hard—achingly hard. It had been so long—so very long—since he'd buried himself in a woman's tight heat.

This is not the time for that, Andrew.

No, it most certainly wasn't. Andrew didn't need his prodding, nagging conscience to tell him that; he had no intention of taking matters that far.

Instead, he reveled in her innocent discovery of kissing, rediscovering it for himself along the way. He must have kissed lovers over the years after Mariah, but he honestly could not recall the last time. Nor could he recall it being so damned erotic.

Miss Martin was an intelligent, sensual woman and she took to kissing like a proverbial duck to water.

The first time she shyly slicked her tongue into his mouth Andrew's hips bucked, thrusting his erection into the cradle of her tightly clenched thighs.

Yet again she stiffened in his arms.

He pulled back just enough that he could see her face without it being blurry—something that was worryingly difficult to do. Her eyes were wide, the pupils slick black pools of desire. But there was unease in them, as well. "You needn't worry, sweetheart. We are only kissing…touching. Our clothing will stay on." *Unfortunately.* He brushed a stray lock of hair off her temple. "What is it?" he asked when she just stared.

Her eyes darted from his eyes to his mouth and then back again. "This is—this is wrong."

Andrew cocked an eyebrow. "Wrong? But…why?"

***

Stacia goggled. "Why?"

"Yes. Why is it wrong to enjoy kissing each other?"

She sputtered. "Because…Well, just *because!*"

He laughed and this time Stacia was close enough to his gorgeous face—mere inches away—that she could see his eyes were comprised of a hundred shades of blue and how the dark gold of his ridiculously long lashes was the same color as the flecks of night beard poking through his sun-kissed skin.

Truly, it was not fair.

"Haven't you ever sneaked away with a boy at a ball—ducking behind a potted plant or hiding in some ridiculous recreation of a Grecian temple—and kissed?"

"No! Of course not."

"Pity," he murmured, his unearthly blue gaze flickering over her face before landing on her mouth. He smiled lazily as he slid his thumb over her lower lip.

Stacia hissed in a breath, but did not pull away.

"You have a beautiful, alluring mouth. So sweet, for all the sharp words that come out of it." The corner of his own beautiful, alluring mouth pulled up higher on one side. "Oh, Miss Martin! The things I have imagined doing with your mouth."

Stacia sucked in a shocked breath.

His eyes rose to meet hers and he grinned, the boyish expression breathtaking. "Was that a shockingly vulgar thing to say?"

Shocking? Definitely. If it was vulgar, then so was Stacia because his words had caused a pulsing in her sex that was so intense she itched to shove her hand between her thighs and rub.

She did nothing of the sort.

When she merely gaped at him like a stunned fish he gave her one last wistful look and gracefully rose to his feet before helping her until she was once again sitting upright.

Stacia had a sudden, mad impulse to grab his coat and yank him back down.

She resisted it.

He lowered to his haunches in front of her, smoothing back strands of her hair that had escaped. "Are you hungry?"

She nodded, not because she wanted to eat, but because anything was better than staring into his knowing gaze. Had she believed being ignored by him was uncomfortable?

Being the focus of his attention might just be enough to break her. Because what would happen when they got out of this room, and he looked through her once more?

It would destroy her. That is what would happen.

Chapter 21

Stacia wasn't hungry in the least. But eating was better than thinking about what had just happened. Not that she *wasn't* thinking about being kissed by him.

About *kissing* him.

But at least shoving food into her mouth gave her an excuse not to speak. Much.

"Are you sure you don't want more of this cheese?" he asked, gesturing to the quarter wheel that took up a sizeable portion of one of the baskets.

Stacia shook her head, her cheeks doubtless bulging like a squirrel's as she masticated.

He wrapped up the cheese and put it back into the hamper, digging around for a moment before coming out with another wax-cloth wrapped bundle. "Let's see what we have here," he murmured, unwrapping the package.

Stacia swallowed, contemplated stuffing the last of her bread into her mouth, but then froze when he lifted up the bundle so she could see it.

"Oh, dear," he said, pulling a face.

Stacia brightened. "Fruitcake!"

"You say that as if it is a good thing."

"I adore fruitcake."

He muttered something beneath his breath as he set down the cake.

"What was that, my lord?"

"Oh, nothing, Miss Martin," he said, holding a knife over the cake. "Here?"

"A little more, please."

He made a gagging noise but did as she bade him.

Stacia watched greedily and said, "More for me."

He grunted and handed her the plate.

"Thank you." She admired the luscious cake for a few seconds before using her fork to cleave off a piece. It was dense and studded with more nuts and candied fruit than she had ever seen, the cake glistening moistly. Stacia briefly closed her eyes as she allowed the morsel to rest on her tongue before chewing. The tang of citrus and spices she associated with Christmastime exploded in her mouth.

"*Mmm,*" she hummed, opening her eyes.

Lord Shelton was staring at her, his lips slightly parted, his eyes a darker shade of blue than they'd been a moment earlier. In fact, they looked similar to the shade they'd been when he'd had her laid out on the settee, pressing *that* against her belly.

Suddenly, it was almost impossible to swallow. She lifted the glass of lemonade, choked down a mouthful, and then looked up and held the plate toward him. "Are you sure?"

"I would much rather watch you eat it, Miss Martin."

Stacia could just imagine how red-faced she was. The last thing she wanted to do was compound her hideousness with bulging cheeks. "I cannot eat with you staring at me."

"Why not?"

"Just…because."

"Oh, *because.* One of your favorite reasons I have noticed." He leaned back in the big wingchair, steepled his fingers beneath his chin, and his eyes narrowed. "How about we play another game while you eat?"

"But it's still my—"

"I know, I know," he rudely interrupted. "It is still your turn to choose as you've thrashed me mercilessly all afternoon long. But right now, you are busy indulging. So, let me have a chance, *hmm?*"

"How can I play and eat?"

"Easily. This game is called, Tell me Two things you Like and one thing you Dislike."

"You just made that up."

He shrugged his broad shoulders, his gaze suddenly intense.

"I shan't be able to eat as I'll be talking." Stacia's breathing quickened under his stare.

He raised his eyebrows.

Stacia wanted to know about him—anything, no matter how minor and insignificant. But what would *he* ask about her? Not that she had that many interesting things to hide.

Don't be such a coward.

"Fine," she said.

"Good. You go first," he said.

"It is your game. *You* go first."

He smiled. "Very well. I like cheese and horses and I *loathe* the name Sebastian."

Stacia had just taken a bite and choked, her eyes watering as she tried to swallow and laugh at the same time.

He pushed her glass of lemonade toward her.

"That was not fair," she said hoarsely after she'd taken a sip.

He grinned. "But it is true."

"Why do you dislike the name Sebastian. It is a very nice name."

"I said *loathe* and it is a horrid name. It is your turn."

Stacia could see he was adamant, so she took another bite of cake, chewed leisurely, and considered what she would say.

***

Andrew decided it was time to open a bottle of wine.

"Take your time," he told her a bit sarcastically as she was certainly showing no signs of haste. He looked at the various bottles, trying to decide which of the excellent vintages would not be utterly destroyed by pairing it with fruitcake. The fourth bottle he lifted from the case was a sherry he knew to be dry. Not exactly his drink of preference, but it would go well with the sickly candied cake she was eating.

He fetched another glass, this one smaller—Kathryn had included a truly impressive selection of glassware—and poured it half-full.

"Here, this should go well with your cake." He pulled a face as he handed her the glass. "Rather, it will be the least wrecked by being paired with *fruitcake*."

She gave the contents of the glass a delicate sniff before taking a tiny sip. "Thank you."

Andrew opened a bottle of madeira for himself and then sat back in his chair. "Well?"

"I like dogs and fruit cake and I dislike animal traps."

He snorted. "Tell me something I don't know."

"What? Like you did?"

"Fair enough." He cast his gaze ceilingward, deciding what he should share and just how much he could push her. He lowered his eyes to hers a moment later. "I like the feel of cool linen against my bare skin on a hot summer day—"

She choked and set her plate and fork down with a clatter.

Andrew refilled her lemonade and waited until she'd drained fully half the glass and stopped coughing before asking, "Are you all right, Miss Martin?"

She nodded, her eyes watering as she gave a last cough.

"Shall I go on?"

She opened her mouth, closed it, and then nodded.

"I like the game of billiards—because it is one of the few I can actually win," he added. He paused, considering his next words carefully. "And I hate that I don't recall meeting you before."

She had a forkful of cake halfway to her mouth but lowered it untouched to her plate. Her gaze held his for a long moment before she nodded, more to herself than to him.

She took a sip of her sherry and then said, "Cerulean blue is my favorite color, and I like reading more than playing cards." Her jaw flexed. "And I hate that I never got to say goodbye to my father."

***

Lord Shelton's gaze was filled with so much sympathy that Stacia's eyes burned, and she looked away. "Your turn."

"I like your needlework from the other night—embroidery?"

She looked up at the question in his voice and nodded.

"And I like seeing my cousin so happy in his new marriage."

Stacia smiled. She, too, was charmed by how obviously the Duke and Duchess of Chatham loved each other.

"And I hate that I wasted so many years trying to hurt him." He held her gaze for a long moment before breaking away and reaching for the bottle of sherry. When he gestured toward her glass, Stacia saw that it was almost empty. When had that happened?

"Oh, come, Miss Martin," he said when she hesitated. "We are trapped here for God knows how long. Live a little."

Stacia wasn't sure that becoming tipsy on sherry—something she'd done once before in school, to ill effect—was *living*, but she nodded.

The answers seemed to come easier as she worked her way through the second glass.

They both liked plays more than operas. Unlike Stacia, his lordship liked the country better than town, but they both preferred London to Bath.

Her favorite season was summer, his winter. He liked the color green and waltzes.

"How can you possibly like a quadrille more than a waltz?" he demanded when she confessed her own preference.

"I just do." Stacia reached for her glass, hesitating when she saw it was, yet again almost empty. She snatched it up, swallowed the remainder, and set it down a bit too firmly.

When she looked up, he was watching and waiting, a faint line between his eyes. "Why do you not like waltzing?"

Stacia scowled. "Because everyone I've ever waltzed with—apart from our dancing master at school—was awful." She did not have the courage—liquid induced or otherwise—to confess she'd had fewer than a half-dozen partners.

Rather than give her a pitying look, which she would have *hated*, he said, "I have noticed that a great many men haul their partners around about as skillfully as they do their horses."

"How like a man to compare women and horses."

"*Tut, tut* Miss Martin—you did not listen. I just compared ham fisted dancers with ham fisted equestrians." He stood up and held out a hand.

Stacia just stared. "What?"

He wiggled his fingers. "Come. I will show you how to waltz properly."

"But…"

"But?"

"There's no music."

He reached down and took her hand, gently lifting her to her feet. "I will provide the music." He led her across to the center of the room, his large hand warm, the skin slightly rough.

Stacia felt like a doll as he positioned her, taking her hand and setting it on his shoulder before taking her by the waist. She swallowed as she stared at the top button of his coat, feeling even smaller than she normally did.

"Look at me, Miss Martin."

She craned her neck until it felt like it would snap. But looking at him so closely was worth the pain.

He stared down at her, his gaze intense and utterly focused on her—just plain Stacia Martin—and then he began to hum. After a few bars, he led her into the familiar steps of the dance.

Except...it was an entirely different animal. Even Monseigneur Renault had not been so smooth, so graceful, so exquisite.

As Stacia glided around the floor with him she experienced an almost crippling feeling of loss.

Because never, ever again would she be able to waltz—or even dance—without thinking about this moment. About *him*.

"Why do you look so grim?" he asked, and then suddenly spun her in a circle, her feet leaving the ground for a moment before he set her down as gently as a priceless vase.

His impulsive yet graceful action surprised a high-pitched laugh from her. "That was like flying," she said, feeling foolish once the words left her mouth.

He grinned down at her, still humming as he twirled her again and again, until she was dizzy, both from the spinning and the sheer joy of dancing.

"Stop," she said, breathless. The room continued turning even after he'd obeyed her. "I can't keep up," she explained.

"Put your feet on mine. Go on."

"But I'll crush your toes."

"*Pfft!* A feather like you? You won't. Trust me."

"Your boots—I'll ruin—"

"Hush and do as I say."

Still hesitant, she set first one foot and then the other, on the toes of his boots.

"Good girl," he murmured, and then resumed his humming and dancing, his steps just as smooth as they'd been before, even with her weight.

"I feel like a doll," she said, yet again laughing.

Stacia's breasts brushed against his chest when he turned, his body by necessity far closer than before. She hissed in a breath, her face heating when she met his unsmiling gaze.

"You are very good at this," she accused, breathy and giddy.

He nodded slowly, unsmilingly, his eyes turning a navy blue.

Stacia realized a moment later that he was no longer humming. She wanted to look away but was captivated.

"Well?" he asked after they'd made another turn in silence.

"Well?" she said, her voice a rusty echo.

196

"Do you still dislike the waltz?"

She shook her head. "No."

Stacia did not know they'd quit moving until his hand lifted from her waist and he cupped her cheek.

She raised up on her toes, her eyes fluttering shut, her lips parted.

But instead of an intoxicating kiss like earlier, his lips pressed chastely against hers and disappeared.

Stacia opened her eyes to find him regarding her with a look she could not decipher. "You should get some rest, Miss Martin. The hour is late."

It took her a moment to remember that she was still standing on his toes, and she clambered off him. Her eyes slid toward the bed.

"You take the bed. There are plenty of blankets and the settee will be fine for me."

She opened her mouth to point out that he was much taller and would never fit on the sofa.

"Take the bed," he repeated firmly, turning on his heel and ending the conversation.

Chapter 22

Andrew shifted yet again on the torture contraption of a settee, the ancient wood creaking beneath his weight. He picked up his watch and squinted at it in the low light from the fire. It was only ten after one—scarcely a quarter of an hour since the last time he'd checked.

He bit back a groan. *Christ.* He'd never get any sleep. He'd been tossing and turning since eleven o'clock, when he'd had the presence of mind to send Miss Martin to bed before he did something he knew he'd be less than proud of later.

When he closed his eyes, he saw her face tilted toward him like a flower, laughing and joyous at something so simple as a waltz. The sight had been like a kick in the jewels. How had he ever thought her a grim little dab, or whatever idiotic description it was that had tripped off his tongue?

He'd merely seen a tiny female garbed in grays and browns and had dismissed her.

For years.

Andrew flopped onto his side and tried to pull his legs up onto the settee, but his tight pantaloons—and his current tumescence—made the action unpleasant. He ran a hand over the hard ridge of his arousal, touching himself too lightly to do anything but tease and torment. He had removed his coat, waistcoat, and boots, but had prudently kept on his shirt and pantaloons. It would have been too easy to take the edge off his desire if he'd been naked, which is how he preferred to sleep.

He rolled onto his back, grunting at the way the sofa sagged beneath him, pushing his spine in ways that woke up old injuries.

"My lord?"

Andrew made a thoroughly unmanly sound and sat up so quickly that his head spun. It took a moment for his blurred vision to focus on the figure of Miss Martin wrapped in a blanket, standing at the end of the settee.

"What are you doing up?" he demanded.

"It is impossible to sleep with all your thrashing about."

He slumped onto his back, grimacing at the discomfort. "So sorry to inconvenience you."

"You take the bed. I will take the—"

"I'm not taking the bed and putting you on this torture rack."

"I am a foot shorter than you; it would not be nearly so bad."

"No."

The room was silent but for the slight settling of the old timbers.

"Then we can share the bed," she said quietly.

Andrew sat up—all of him. "What?"

"You are clothed, as am I. And if—if—"

She appeared to be stuck, like a clock with a broken gear. "If?" he prodded.

"If you give me your word to behave, then I believe we can both enjoy a comfortable rest."

"Behave, *hmm*? I have never heard that word before. What does it mean?"

"Very droll, my lord."

"I'm not sure I'm capable of behaving, Miss Martin."

She heaved a sigh. Even though it was dark, he could imagine her tightly pursed lips.

"But I will try," he said after a moment, and then stood up with a groan.

"Was it very bad?" she asked as they walked toward the bed.

"Awful. Left side or right side?"

"Oh. Er, I don't know. Do you have a preference?"

"The left."

They changed sides.

Andrew gave a sigh of pleasure when he sat on the mattress. It was soft—perhaps too soft—but it was leagues better than the settee. Once he was fully reclined and covered, he turned to her. It was too dark for him to see anything but an outline.

"You can get in any time, Miss Martin."

She barely depressed the mattress when she laid on the bed. Andrew felt something brush against his shoulder and then the bed shook as she jerked away.

"Lord Shelton!"

"Yes?" he asked mildly.

"You are not on your half."

"My left shoulder is hanging off the mattress. If I move over any further, I will fall off the bed."

She muttered something and again the bed shifted. This time, no part of her touched any part of him. A pity.

Andrew laced his fingers behind his head and stared up into the darkness overhead. Beside him, Miss Martin vibrated with tension. He frowned and turned to her. "Are you sure you will be able to slee—"

"I am fine." The words sounded as if they'd been forced between clenched teeth.

He grinned. "You don't sound fine. You sound—"

"I will be far more likely to sleep if you stop talking."

He laughed. Not for the first time did the strangeness of the situation strike him. What could Kathryn have been thinking to organize such a stunt? She had done something similar at Chatham—locking the two of them together inside the armory, although not with the forethought and planning she'd employed this time. Thankfully they had only been sequestered for five or six hours and his cousin and the duchess had known it wasn't Andrew's fault, although he'd felt like an idiot for falling into her snare.

He had felt marginally better when she'd employed a similar trick on Fowler, trapping the two of them in one of Chatham's hunting boxes, an episode that had lasted most of the night, far longer than his own incarceration with the vixen.

Lord only knew why she did such things. He smiled ruefully. It certainly kept life…exciting.

"My lord?"

He turned toward the motionless lump beside him. "I thought you were trying to sleep?"

"I am awake *now*."

He chuckled at her accusatory tone and turned onto his side. "What did you want?"

The bedding shifted slightly, and he saw her small form propped up on an elbow, mirroring his pose.

"I cannot sleep."

"Probably all that fruitcake you ate."

"More likely that sherry."

"You seemed to like the taste of it."

"My father used to drink it."

"Tell me about him."

There was a long silence, and then, "Why?"

"Because I would like to know. Unless it is too painful to talk about him."

Again she was quiet. This time for so long that he thought she might have fallen asleep. "It was only the two of us for a long time. He was a very fond parent, but…absentminded."

Andrew thought she sounded affectionate more than exasperated. "Your mother died when you were young?"

"I was eight."

"My parents died when I was four."

"*Both* at once?"

"Yes. A carriage accident."

"I am sorry."

"I hardly remember them as I rarely saw them. I'm sure it was far worse for you at eight. You would remember more—have more to grieve."

She did not confirm or deny his words. Instead, she said, "The Duke of Chatham's father took you in after your parents' death?"

"Yes. I was raised with his two sons, Nicholas and Sylvester. Sylvester—that's Chatham—was only a few years older, but Nick was an intimidating fourteen when I came to Chatham Park."

"The duke's older brother died?"

"Yes. Nick died in a hunting accident while Sylvester was in a field hospital recuperating from the injury to his face. I was given leave to accompany him home—he was still in a bad way and unable to travel alone—but afterward I was to return." Andrew's thoughts touched dangerously on the particulars of that trip and he shied away. "But you have changed the subject. We were talking about your father."

"There is not much to say. That sounds bad," she quickly added. "What I meant is that he had a solitary nature and lived a quiet, scholarly existence."

"What did he study?"

"Illuminated manuscripts."

Andrew thought of the fans he had purchased—of the absolutely exquisite detail and how long it must have taken her to master such an art. Had she learned to paint to please him? To make him notice her?

He did not ask.

Instead, he said, "He was absentminded and yet you had a Season, so he must have lived in the real world to some degree."

"My aunt—on my mother's side—reminded him of his duty. As it was, I didn't end up going until I was twenty. Almost on the shelf."

Andrew wished like hell that he could recall meeting her. "We, er, never danced?"

"No."

He wanted to tell her that she was better off not having attracted his notice, that he had been too busy nursing his hatred and looking for ways to harm Chatham to care about anyone he met at the balls and parties he haunted. But the argument would sound too self-serving.

"When did your father die?"

"A few weeks before the end of the Season. He died in his sleep. We—I—there was no hint or clue that his heart was weak, so it was completely unexpected."

"I'm sorry, Miss Martin."

"Thank you."

"And your cousin inherited the title?"

"He inherited everything." Pain and anger colored her voice. "He even—"

"Yes?"

"He even took my father's personal possessions—his books, his few pieces of jewelry, not just the Clayton signet."

"Was there no provision for you?"

"My father's will was old, made when he reached his majority and he never thought to change it. There is a little money that was part of my mother's settlement, but it is not enough."

"I cannot believe he threw you out. What a scoundrel. I beg your pardon for my blunt words, but there is no excuse for that."

"He was…angry."

"That is no reason to toss a woman out on the street. What about your aunt—you mentioned your mother's sister?"

"Er, she was angry, too."

"What, pray, happened to make them both so angry that they would abandon a—how old were you?"

202

"I had just turned one-and-twenty."

"What happened to make them abandon a young woman barely of legal age?"

"I think I have already shared enough, my lord."

"You are going to be my wife, Miss Martin—" he broke off with an irritated huff. "What is your Christian name?"

"We do not yet know that will be necessary, my lord. It is poss—"

He gave an unamused laugh. "You are lying in a bed with me, alone, in the middle of the night. There is no getting out of this, ma'am. My name is Andrew, so you might as well—*Eustacia!* That is it!" He felt foolish, not to mention disturbed. How had he almost forgotten her name when he had so recently learned it?

"Ugh. Nobody calls me that, my lord."

Andrew shook off his unease. "Tell me what you prefer or I will call you Eustacia."

"Stacia."

"Stacia." He liked the sound of that a great deal more than Eustacia, which called to mind a strict governess, the sort of woman who'd rap your knuckles at the slightest infraction. Of course there was a certain appeal to that, as well...

"I do not wish to share all the details of my life. At least not without some reciprocation," she added.

"Good Lord! I told you about Sarah—was that not reciprocation enough?"

"It was a start," she said primly, shifting and sending another tantalizing whiff of something floral to tease his nostrils.

Roses. She smelled like roses.

"I propose we exchange information the tried-and-true way," she said.

"Which is?"

"Question or Command."

Andrew gave a startled laugh. What in the world had come over the prim and proper Miss Martin?

***

What in the world had come over her?

Stacia was stunned at the words that had come out of her mouth. Who would have guessed that something as simple as darkness could make her so bold?

"I accept," Lord Shelton said before Stacia could retract her words. "I will go first—"

"It is *my* suggestion, so I will go first."

He made a low growling sound, but said, "Go on then, ask."

"You have to choose before I—"

"Question."

Stacia suspected he would be even less eager to play if she started off with the questions she really wanted to ask.

Build up slowly, lull him into a false sense of security. Pry around the edges. Be subtle.

Then…pounce.

"If you have no intention of remarrying as you mentioned earlier, then why were you going to London for the Season?"

He sighed. "I might have misrepresented myself to Kathryn."

"What do you mean?"

"I mean that my thoughts about marriage have recently changed."

Stacia stared into the darkness as she assessed his words. Did he mean—

"It is my turn," he said.

"But wait—"

"I answered your question."

Stacia sputtered.

"Question or Command?" he asked, implacable.

"Command."

Stacia felt him jolt and couldn't help smirking. *There! You don't know everything, after all. Do you?*

"I beg your pardon?" he asked.

He is giving you a chance to retract your foolish choice.

"You heard me, my lord."

"Kiss me."

This time it was *her* body jolting. "That is not fair."

He laughed—which she deserved. "You were the one who chose *command*. Kiss me. And make it a good one," he added. "Not the sort I give my Great Aunt Lydia. I am ready," he said a moment later, when she'd remained frozen.

Stop stalling. You know you want to.

Of course she did, but…

"Shall I come closer, or—"

"I can do it," she snapped, shoving forward, only realizing he was far closer than she'd thought when her chest bumped against his and her knee struck something…hard.

"*Ooof.* Careful, darling. Don't break your betrothed before we are even married."

She swallowed at the *darling*—not to mention his threat of marriage—even though she'd heard him call half-a-hundred girls by pet names as he'd outrageously flirted.

She reached out a hand.

"*Ow!*" he bellowed when her finger poked something soft and wet. "That was my *eye.*"

"I'm sorry!" Stacia caught her lower lip with her teeth. "Are you—did I hurt you?"

"Yes."

"I'm *sorry.*"

He grumbled and she felt his arm move as he likely rubbed the offended organ. "I am still waiting for my kiss."

She couldn't help smiling at his petulant tone. She reached for him again, her hand a bit lower, and swallowed when her fingers skimmed fine linen, the body beneath it warm and hard.

He grunted, this time a more approving sound.

Stacia took a deep breath, leaned forward, and kissed his…chin.

He snorted. "I meant my—"

"I *know* what you meant." She inched closer, until her hand was pressed between their bodies, and adjusted her aim. This time, she encountered soft, full lips.

He groaned and she felt the tension in his big body, as if he struggled against something.

Stacia kissed him once, twice, and then softly, gently, did as he had done earlier and nipped his lower lip.

"Bloody hell!" he muttered explosively.

Stacia scooted back away from him as quickly as a startled shrimp in a rock pool, not stopping until her bottom hung over the edge of the bed.

"My turn," he said.

Why did that sound so threatening?

***

Miss Martin was damned lucky that Andrew hadn't grabbed her. How could a kiss that innocent—like the brush of a feather—get him so hard?

Your cock was already hard.

That was true. Her kiss just made it *hurt*.

Her voice, with a bit of a quaver now, came at him in the darkness. "Question or command?"

Andrew briefly considered saying *command*, but suspected hers wouldn't be nearly so pleasurable as his. He suspected he'd find himself putting his tongue on a frozen pump handle, or whatever the equivalent would be in their comfortable prison.

"Question," he said.

The silence told him that he'd surprised her.

She cleared her throat and asked the question he expected. "Why did you want to hurt your cousin?"

Andrew rolled onto his back and closed his eyes—as if that would make what he had to confess better, somehow—and said, "I hated him for marrying the woman I loved."

After an eternity, she said, "Oh."

"Question or command?" he asked.

"C-command."

His lips curled into a slow smile. Well, well, well. "Touch me for an entire minute."

"*What?*"

"You heard me."

"That seems…extreme."

Andrew gave a delighted laugh. Oh, Miss Martin! Life with her sharp tongue would never be boring. "Are you trying to renege, Stacia?"

He heard a gulping sound. "No. B-but how will I know when a minute is up?"

"I might not be the smartest of men but even I can count to sixty," he said dryly. He waited rather than taunt her again, enjoying the tightening in his groin at the prospect of her small hands touching him. Andrew fully suspected that she would thwart his desire by concentrating on his elbow or the heel of his foot, but he didn't care.

Her touch, when it came, was even lighter than her kiss had been. It wasn't his elbow—or his heel—but his chest. The muscles jumped beneath her hand, and she gasped. Andrew caught her wrist before she could jerk away, his physical reaction and instincts accurate, even in the dark.

And even though so much else about him was now less than sharp.

He placed her hand back over his heart. "Don't stop, Stacia."

Chapter 23

Stacia marveled at the sheer size of him. The body beneath her palm radiated heat and power, the thudding beneath the hard slab of muscle strong and…fast.

She swallowed repeatedly, as if that would rid her of the jittery feeling that threatened to overtake her. If she had not known exactly what he would say, she had known it would be naughty.

You are in command; touch him.

Stacia obeyed and her hand moved. Something hard grazed her palm. She circled back around to feel it again.

A low, predatory rumble vibrated beneath her hand as she caressed the tiny bump again. And then again, frowning. What was—

And—her hand froze.

A nipple!

His nipple!

Why was she so stunned by that? She knew men had nipples. But the reality of feeling one was…

"Stacia." His voice was gruff and needy, and his chest lifted beneath her hand, pressing his erect nipple into her palm.

She felt dizzy. And then remembered to breathe and sucked in a noisy lungful of air.

She caressed him again, desperately hungry for that sound he had made.

This time, it was even better. He didn't rumble; he *purred*.

And then he took her wrist again, lifted her hand, and slid it beneath the linen onto the hot silk of bare skin.

"My lo—"

"Andrew." He moved her hand, which had gone rigid with shock, over the bare, erect nipple. He groaned. "S'good," he slurred, and then moved her palm over to its mate, which was every bit as hard.

Stacia only realized that he had released her wrist when she found herself being lifted.

She squeaked and tried to balance with the hand that had been happily stroking his chest. But he didn't let her fall. Instead, he positioned her over his hips, her knees spreading and pushing the hem of her petticoat up her calves.

"Even better," he growled, his hands seemingly everywhere all at once, until she found herself pressed against him, torso to torso, as he held her head and angled her for a deep, penetrating kiss that sent pleasure arrowing directly to her nether regions.

He released her lips, leaving her both breathless and desperate for more while he trailed kisses across her cheek and then nibbled on her ear.

A giggle slipped from between her parted lips.

He chuckled and the sound was evil. "Ticklish ears? Fascinating." He nuzzled his nose inside her ear and snuffled, the sound shockingly loud.

Stacia laughed again and tried to squirm away. Something wet slid over the edge of her ear and she shrieked and pulled back.

He laughed, his body shaking beneath hers, his hands around her waist, keeping her pressed against him.

Stacia pushed a finger in her ear and wiggled it around. "You *licked* me!"

"I did," he agreed, sounding pleased and unabashed, his thumbs rubbing circles over the thin skin of her ribs, the action making her squirm.

Stacia shifted her hips and ground against something hard.

He groaned. "Stacia."

"I'm sorry. Did I hurt you?"

"No," he said, and then rolled both their bodies to the side. "I cheated," he said, caressing her cheek with one hand, finding strands of hair in the darkness and tucking them behind her ear.

"What do you mean?"

"My minute was up a while ago."

Stacia closed her eyes and pressed her cheek into his palm, wishing he had gone on cheating.

What was wrong with her to think such brazen thoughts? It had to be the darkness; it was far too easy to forget herself—to forget who *he* was—in the dark.

You want this. The darkness only gives you an excuse to act on your desire.

She felt him move and then the soft pressure of lips on the tip of her nose. "This is a dangerous game we are playing," he murmured in the darkness. "Get some sleep, sweetheart," he said, reaching over her to pull the blankets up over her.

Disappointment, as sharp as any dagger, sliced through her and she forced herself to say, "Good night, my lord," before rolling onto her other side and staring into the darkness, listening to Lord Shelton's breathing as it far too quickly turned deep and regular.

Stacia envied him; she would never sleep. This had easily been the most exciting night of her life.

And the most unbelievable.

Stacia felt inside her ear, smiling foolishly when she imagined a dampness remained from his playful, silly behavior.

Unwanted memories of all those ballrooms, when she had watched the man beside her glide about with female after female, assaulted her brain. She had always known he was an accomplished flirt. Hadn't she watched him charm every woman he had given even a moment of his time? Making them laugh as he had just done with her?

Stacia chewed her lip, her stomach boiling like a witch's cauldron. She could marry him. He was determined to do what he felt was *the right thing*.

It warmed her heart that he was not a heartless cad.

You wouldn't have cared if he had *been as bad as he's been painted; you would* still *want to marry him.*

That was true, but it didn't mean she wasn't pleased to be wrong about his character.

He might be innocent—or even noble—when it comes to Sarah Creighton, but what about Lady Shaftsbury?

Stacia did not know what had ensued between Shelton and the beautiful marchioness, but she would not be so quick to judge him as she had been in the past. Besides, if Lady Shaftsbury and her family had forgiven him—all except Lady Addiscombe—who was she to bear a grudge?

She believed that he was determined to marry her. Stacia suspected that beneath his light, teasing manner was a will of iron. Something told her that Andrew Derrick would not be swayed from his purpose once he had made up his mind.

The thought of being such a man's wife made her shiver with excitement, desire, and—could there even be a twinge of hope in her breast?

It is easy to be hopeful when it is only the two of you in this attic. But what happens when you leave? What happens when you find yourself in a ton ballroom with a husband who plies his irresistible charm on every other woman? Women more beautiful and seductive than you could ever be.

Stacia swallowed down the lump in her throat, or at least she tried to, but it refused to budge. *Just because he insists on marriage does not mean I have to agree.*

You will never be able to deny him. Don't lie to yourself.

Could she say *no* to him?

She did not know.

***

Stacia shifted. Or at least she tried to, but something heavy and burning hot was draped over her back and shoulder and hip. She opened her eyes, but no light came from the window that overlooked the gardens.

She blinked, confused.

And then her memory of the night before came back to her. There was no window because she was in the priest hole.

With Lord Shelton.

Lord Shelton, who was currently molded more closely to her body than any blanket had ever been.

Stacia's heart pounded so hard she could hear the actual *thud, whoosh. Thud, whoosh. Thud, whoosh.*

His chest rose and fell slowly and deeply, pressing hard muscle against her shoulder blades. His arm was tight around her ribcage and brushing the undersides of her uncorseted breasts.

One heavy thigh was slung over hers, the slight, but constant tension in the powerful limb keeping her tucked snugly against him.

And there was something else. Something…hard pressed against her lower back.

Her entire body tensed when she realized just what it was.

Calm down, she told herself. *And quit panting like an exhausted foxhound.*

Stacia had to tell herself that several times before she finally listened.

You might as well enjoy this while he is deeply asleep.

She chewed her lip, struck by the logic of the suggestion. Rather than wake him, as she should, she allowed herself a moment to just…*feel.*

Curiosity, truly her besetting sin, made her push her bottom toward him slightly. Surely, he could not be as long and—

He moaned softly and his arm snugged around her, like a snake squeezing its prey, pulling her even closer, until his *membrum virile* slotted between the cheeks of her bottom, the iron hard ridge thrusting against a part of her that nothing had ever rubbed against before.

211

She opened her mouth but still couldn't seem to draw in enough air.

Dear God, he was…monstrous!

Like the coward she was, Stacia slowly, painstakingly, tried to inch away, but he mumbled something and then rolled his hips, *grinding* his arousal against her. A low rumble of pleasure vibrated from his body to hers, and then he did it *again,* the hard prominence grazing her skin even through two layers of muslin and the soft doeskin of his breeches.

"My lord?" Stacia whispered, barely able to hear her voice over the pounding of her heart.

His hips fell into a lazy rhythm.

"*My lord!*" she yelped.

The big body behind her jolted and stiffened—all of it, this time, not just the fascinating part—and his arm briefly tightened before releasing her, as if it was a struggle to do so.

"Miss Martin." His voice was gravelly with sleep. He cleared his throat. "I beg your pardon." He lifted his arm and thigh and rolled off her.

Stacia remained on her side, turned away and clinging to the mattress as it shifted, his weight threatening to roll her body his way.

The bed shifted yet again and was followed by the soft thuds of feet hitting the floor. A moment later she was no longer in danger of rolling toward him.

The old plank flooring squeaked as he shuffled across it and—

Thwack!

"Bloody hell!"

Stacia had to bite her lip to smother a laugh. "Are you hurt, my lord?"

He merely grunted. Somebody woke up grumpy.

Deciding it was safe to look, she turned over and propped her head on her hand, squinting in the direction of the sitting area, where there were sounds of the grate being moved and coals being stirred.

All was darkness until slowly, a faint red glow spread over his crouching figure. He threw more kindling and fuel onto the fire, poked it until it blazed, and then stood. His body stood out in sharp relief against the light from the fire, the thin linen of his shirt doing nothing to conceal the magnificent chest and shoulders beneath it.

Stacia could not look away.

He reached down and took something—his watch, she supposed—off the table and lifted it close to his face before dropping his arm and heaving a sigh.

And then he casually raised his other hand and rubbed his groin.

Stacia's face heated; he was touching what had been pressed against her.

Before she had time to examine the thought, he took the black cast iron kettle off the triangle in the hearth and made his way toward the screened wash basin.

Stacia heard the sound of water splashing—what sounded like a great deal of it—and bit her lip when she realized what it was.

She rolled onto her back, mortified, lifting her hands to her hot cheeks. After a moment, she swung her feet off the bed and took the opportunity to slip her loosened stays over her chemise and pull the laces tight before donning her gown. Once she was decently covered, she made her way to the trunk that held a brush, comb, and several other toiletries.

By the time Lord Shelton emerged from behind the screen Stacia had re-plaited her hair and pinned it up, which gave her a feeling of control, no matter how illusory.

Shelton held the kettle in one hand and there was a towel draped over his shoulder. "Good morning," he said. He had not yet put on his coats and cravat, but his shirt was now tucked in. "I half-filled the basin with very hot water and there is cool water in the canister beneath the wash table, you'll find a dipper in it. Soap leaves beside the basin and fresh bath linen in the wicker basket. If you leave your wash water, I will empty it for you when you are finished."

"Empty it where?" she asked.

"There is an empty cannister for used wash water." His lips twisted. "Our captor thought of everything."

Stacia had to agree. She lifted a hand and pointed to her own jaw. "You have a bit of soap here."

He raised the corner of the towel and wiped his jaw. "Better?"

She gave an abrupt nod, her face heating at the oddly domestic exchange, and hurried past him.

When she came out from behind the screen a short time later it was to find the candles lighted and the tea pot steaming on the coffee table, bread, ham, butter, and preserves along with what looked to be a small jug of milk and a sugar bowl.

"Ah, you are just in time. How do you like your tea?"

"Black, please. Not too strong. What time is it?"

"Just after seven. Did you sleep well?" he asked, handing her a cup and saucer.

Stacia thought about his body pressed against hers, hastily shoved the memory away, and said in an admirably cool voice, "Yes, thank you. Er, you?"

"I had a delicious sleep, thank you."

Her eyes jumped to his face. He was smiling broadly, clearly aware of what she'd felt digging into her lower back and utterly unashamed of himself.

Men!

He sipped his tea, gave a happy sigh, and then hooked one muscular leg over the arm of his chair and slumped into an utterly masculine sprawl.

She swallowed at the sight of his leather-clad thigh, feeling the echoes of its weight and firmness pressed against her, almost as if her body had a memory all its own.

Again, she banished the disturbing memory. "Do you think Lady Kathryn will let us out today?"

"It is impossible to say what she will do." He rubbed the heel of his free hand over his thigh and winced slightly.

"I do not understand how she could be so wild after growing up with such a strict mother."

"I think that might be exactly *why* she is so wild," he said dryly. A notch appeared between his blond brows. "Although I have the feeling, from some comments the duchess has made, that Kathryn was not like this before spending time with her aunt."

Stacia thought back to what Ackers had told her—about the heated conversation between the countess and her daughter which had referenced that visit—and suspected he was right.

"So," he said, staring across at her with an unreadable look on his face. "How will we occupy ourselves today…Stacia?"

Chapter 24

Selina

L ady Selina Shaftsbury studied her youngest sister from beneath her lashes. Katie was eating breakfast—or at least playing with her food—and repeatedly glancing at the huge longcase clock in the corner that ticked as loudly as a hammer pounding an anvil.

Indecision twisted her sister's beautiful face as she glanced at the clock and then looked out the window. The world was blanketed in blinding white snow, a delightful surprise that had been waiting for them when they'd awoken that morning.

Katie's lips twisted in an odd smile and then she turned her attention back to her breakfast and shoved her eggs to the other side of her plate.

Something was amiss with her youngest sister; she was not the same girl she'd been ten months ago.

Still, Selina was hardly the same, either, so perhaps the changes in Katie were not necessarily bad.

A large warm hand covered hers and Selina turned to the reason for her own transformation. Caius was smiling at her in a way that always made her feel like he could *see* her, even though she knew her husband scarcely saw more than dark shapes.

"Yes, my lord?" she asked him pertly, employing a tone and form of address that would surely remind him of last night, when she had purposely been naughty.

His wicked grin told her their minds were running as closely as two adjoining plots of land. "I have decided that I will go with you, Selina."

Her eyes widened in pleased surprise and she leaned closer—close enough that the others at the table—could not hear her words. "Thank you, Caius."

"You realize, of course, that you will have to make sure I don't end up arse over teakettle in a snow drift, *hmm*?"

"I would never allow that to happen," she said, her exaggerated tone suggesting the exact opposite of her words.

He gave a bark of laughter that drew every eye at the table. "Minx. I have a few things I must go through with Wilson, first," he said, referring to the clever young man who served as part secretary, part companion, and part friend. "And then I will meet you in the great hall." He leaned toward her and, with the unerring ability he sometimes exhibited when it came to kissing, planted a peck on her cheek.

Selina gestured for the footman to accompany her husband as Caius got to his feet. "If you will all excuse me," he said to the table at large.

"Will you join us today, sir?" Doddy piped up.

Caius smiled in Doddy's general direction. "I wouldn't miss it." He turned to Selina. "I will see you soon, darling."

Once he'd gone, Selina's siblings all turned her way.

"*Darling,*" Katie repeated, smirking.

Doddy made exaggerated kissing noises.

"Hush," Selina murmured. Her face, she knew, would be bright pink.

Phoebe grinned widely and Aurelia gave Selina such a lovely, affectionate smile that it made her eyes prickle.

She dropped her gaze to her plate before she began blubbering with happiness. Being around her siblings—and their new families—was utterly delightful. She had not realized how much she'd missed her siblings until seeing their dear faces again.

And then Selina remembered their mother, whom she had not visited in days, and grimaced.

First the countess had been laid low with a migraine and now, according to Katie, she had a cold.

Selina laid aside her napkin before looking up. "I will go and check on mother."

"I've already been to her chambers," Katie said. "She asked not to be disturbed."

Selina exchanged glances with Phoebe—who had always borne the brunt of her mother's myriad illnesses over the years—and her younger sister gave a slight shrug, her joyful expression of a moment earlier gone, a look of resignation taking its place.

"If she does not want to be disturbed, I would not go," Phoebe said.

Selina nodded, guilt following on the heels of relief, and promised herself that she would visit her mother tomorrow. The day after, at the latest.

"I want to talk about your court gown, Lina," Phoebe said. "I *do* wish I could be presented with the three of you."

Hy, who was sitting across from Selina, immediately threw down her napkin, shoved back her chair with a loud *scritch,* and stood. "I have to go and do…something."

"Hy! I wanted to hear about your gown, too!" Phoebe called after her.

"Katie can tell you all about it. She is the one who went through all the bother of picking materials and such," Hy threw over her shoulder.

"It is true," Katie said, looking amused. "Hy wanted no part of it and told me to choose everything. I can describe it all in detail if you like."

Hy strode from the room in the mannish way that had not changed even though she was now garbed in the highest kick of elegance as befitted her elevated station.

"I chose the gown she is wearing right now, too," Katie said.

Selina thought their youngest sister had chosen well. Hy's gown this morning was a dark green wool that made her unusual eyes, her one claim to beauty, glitter like precious stones. The severe cut of the dress flattered her tall, slender form.

The Duke of Chatham watched his wife leave with an intensity that made Selina blush yet again. Who would have ever believed her reserved, mysterious sister—who had never looked at a man as far as Selina could recall—would not only attract England's most sought-after bachelor, but bewitch him utterly in the process?

It was never easy to read Hy's cool, controlled features, but Selina thought her sister might be almost as bewitched as her husband.

When Selina turned away from the duke, she realized that Katie had, somehow, slipped around her and out of the room without her noticing

***

Katie leaned against the wall and stared broodingly at the wall panel that hid the door to the linen closet.

By the time she had been old enough to explore Wych House her family had, due to financial exigency, been forced to move into Queen's Bower. For years and years Katie had listened to her older sisters whisper about the secrets of their ancestral home, much of which had been falling down and far too dangerous to explore.

Phoebe's new husband had worked a miracle in less than a year. Even now, in the dead of winter skilled craftsmen brought in from as far away as Sweden worked to restore the rooms known as the Queen's Suite. It had been secretly built by Katie's Catholic ancestors for a monarch who never had never come. Not for Elizabeth, but for Mary, the ill-fated Queen of the Scots.

Katie felt a certain sympathy for the long dead monarch, who had been betrayed by not just one man, but by many in the course of her tumultuous life.

217

Men and betrayal, Katie firmly believed, went together like guns and bullets.

"My lady?"

She looked up from her thoughts to find Dora waiting.

"Are you going to release them?" the maid asked, when Katie only stared.

"What does Ackers say about my mother?"

The countess had refused to admit Katie when she'd called that morning. Yet another lie she'd told her siblings at the breakfast table.

"Her ladyship remains in bed." Dora cleared her throat. "Er, she believes she has caught the same cold Miss Martin suffers from."

Katie laughed and then felt a twinge of guilt for mocking her mother's imaginary cold. She quickly shoved her guilt aside. Her mother deserved to be mocked. And more.

Dora went on, "Miss Ackers says her ladyship will not be up today and she doubts she'll be up and about tomorrow, either."

Well, then.

Katie pushed off the wall. "Return to Miss Martin's room and continue your vigil."

Dora's eyes bulged. "Kat! You're not going to release them?"."

Katie smiled at her childhood friend's slip. She and Dora were only a year apart and had been as thick as thieves back when Katie's family had been every bit as poor as Dora's—if not poorer—and living in the small dower house called Queen's Bower. Now, Katie's sisters had all married wealthy men, nobody lived at Queen's Bower, and everything was different. Everything.

"There is enough food, water, and fuel for another night?" she asked Dora.

"Aye, my lady—for several. But…are you sure about this?"

Katie cast a glance at the window at the end of the corridor. The snow was still falling and there had to be close to eight inches already.

"I'm sure. Everyone will assume that Lord Shelton will have difficulty getting back to Wych House in this weather. As for Miss Martin, she is still too weak to leave her bed. That is the story if anyone asks," she said firmly.

"Yes, my lady."

Katie left the maid behind her and made her way to her own chambers. She was looking forward to gathering greenery this afternoon, regardless of the snow.

Captain Walker, Lord Crewe's son, was an extremely handsome man had had been attentive to her on more than one occasion.

And then there was the added bonus that Katie's mother hated the illegitimate man.

Perhaps Katie and the captain might steal a few moments alone together this afternoon and find themselves under some mistletoe.

Smiling at the thought, Katie hurried to join her family, the couple in the priest hole forgotten.

Chapter 25

Andrew stared down at his pile of counters. Although...could a person really call three counters a *pile?*

"This is fun," Stacia chirped as she scraped all her winnings toward her.

They had divided up a bag of cobnuts from the food trunk. She now possessed all of them except three.

"I don't believe that you've never played this before," Andrew said, pulling the nutcracker out of the trunk and putting one of his counters out of its misery. He offered her the nut—which she took with a triumphant grin—before cracking the second one and tossing it into his mouth.

"Do you play cards a great deal?" she asked.

He smirked at her not so gentle jibe as he chewed and stared, amused when her cheeks darkened under his silent scrutiny.

"I wish you would not look at me in that odious way," she finally blurted.

"What way is that?" he asked, cracking his last nut.

She waved aside the proffered nutmeat. "You know how," she accused, and then gave him a demonstration of what she meant.

Andrew laughed at the exaggeratedly villainous face she pulled. "My, that *is* odious."

She scowled, or tried to, but the smile tugging at her lips made it difficult.

Stacia sighed. "She is not going to release us today, is she?"

Andrew glanced at his watch and saw that it was past noon. "I doubt it."

"What if—what if nobody comes?" she asked, a look of genuine fear taking possession of her features. "What if nobody knows? What if are left here to starve? To die—"

Andrew leaned over and took her hand. "Somebody will come."

"How do you know that?"

"Because Kathryn might be reckless, but she isn't homicidal."

"What if something happens to her and she can't—"

"I can get us out, Stacia."

She blinked. "You—you can? You mean you know where there is a latch?"

"No. I mean I can use what little we have"—he gestured to the heavy fire tools hanging from their cast-iron rack— "and hack the door open. You needn't worry— I will not allow you to perish here."

"So why haven't you opened it?"

Andrew smiled, even though he knew it was inappropriate—not to mention probably the same smug expression she had just called *odious*. "I have a few reasons. First, because it will cause a great deal of destruction and racket. Not to mention that I am not looking forward to wrecking Needham's pride and joy. Second, we've already been in here a day so it's not as if we can be in any more trouble if we wait. Which leads me to the most important reason"—he gently squeezed her hand— "I am in no hurry because I am enjoying myself far more in here with you than I would be out there with everyone else."

***

Stacia could not have been more surprised if he had just declared his undying love for her.

Well, that wasn't quite true, she amended, but she was flabbergasted all the same.

"You are?" she could not resist saying.

"Yes, Stacia. I am."

Why did her staid name sound so sensual on his tongue?

Because he could make the word dishrag *sound alluring.*

"Why is it so hard to accept that I am enjoying myself here with you?" he asked.

"Because…"

"Ah, yes. Your favorite reason: because."

Irked by his teasing, she said, "*Because* you have never even noticed me before. Why are you doing so now? Is it—is it just because I am convenient?" Stacia immediately wished she could take her questions back.

He inhaled deeply, and a new expression flitted across his gorgeous features: indecision.

Lord Andrew Shelton was many things—arrogant, insouciant, flirtatious, cavalier, dismissive, charming, amusing, mocking—but Stacia had never seen anything less than absolute assurance on his face.

His hand, which was still holding hers, began to slide away, but Stacia held on.

Both his eyebrows raised at her brazen action, but he did not pull away. Instead, his lips, which she now knew were soft and outrageously skilled, curled up at the corners.

"*Hmmm*, I don't know…" he drawled, his tone once again teasing. "You want answers for free? I am tempted to demand we play another round of Questions or Com—"

"You asked me yesterday what I did that made my aunt and cousin angry with me. It was because I rejected an offer of marriage. That is why *they* rejected me. They said I had made my own bed, and that I could sleep in it."

Stacia was pitifully grateful when he did not look particularly surprised, as if the thought of a man offering to marry her was not so outside the realm of possibility.

"Who was it?" he asked, no longer teasing.

She shrugged and pulled her hand away, disappointed when he let her go. "What difference does that make?"

"I need to know who I have to keep my eye on when I take you to London."

She snorted. "I never said I would marry you," she reminded him. "Furthermore, when and if I marry, I would not be the sort of woman to engage in dalliances."

Rather than look offended at her rejection, he gave her a boyish grin. "Tell me who it is, anyhow. It will stop me from eyeing every man with suspicion."

"You are being absurd, my lord. Besides, if anyone had a reason to *eye everyone with suspicion* it would be your w-wife." Stacia wanted to kick herself for stumbling over the word.

"Oh?" he said, wearing an innocent expression he had no right to, she was sure. "What do you mean?"

"You know what I mean. I daresay the ballrooms of the *ton* are littered with your—your—"

"Are you trying to say the word *lovers*?"

"You know exactly what I mean," she snapped.

"You are adorable when you scowl." He pulled a face—which she assumed was supposed to be her—and Stacia couldn't help laughing. "There," he said. "That is better. Now, be a good girl and tell me who you rejected."

"I don't see why I should."

"Because I am tenacious."

She could believe it. Well, what difference did it make if he knew? "The Earl of Townshend."

His eyes went vague for a moment before they widened. "Not the one who breathes through—"

"He has to breathe through his mouth because he has terrible allergies," Stacia said icily.

"Ah."

Stacia snatched a cobnut off the table. If he laughed, she would throw it at him.

But instead of laughing he said, "The Earls of Townshend are wealthy—unless this latest one has managed to fritter it all away."

"No, he does not gamble. Or place wagers of any sort."

"He sounds boring."

He was, but Stacia was hardly going to admit that. "You find virtue boring, do you?"

"O-ho! He is *virtuous,* is he? And *yes*, to answer your question. Virtue is boring." One of his eyebrows lifted and his nostrils flared slightly. "At least most of the time." He swept her person with a boldly appreciative gaze that made her skin prickle.

Before she could stop herself, she threw the cobnut.

He slapped a hand over one eye and moaned. "Good Lord! I think you put my eye out!"

"I didn't mean to actually hit you!' Stacia knocked into the table in her haste to get to him, sending cobnuts flying. "Here, let me take a look." She bent low in front of him. "Show me, my lor—"

Stacia squeaked when her feet left the ground, and she suddenly found herself cradled tightly in his arms.

He grinned down at her—*both* eyes sparkling and undamaged.

Stacia glared up at him. "You *liar!* That was not fair."

"No, it wasn't," he agreed. She squirmed, but his arms locked around her more tightly. "Oh no you don't. You are a prisoner and here at my leisure." His gaze dropped to her mouth. "The cost of freedom is a kiss."

She thrashed—or tried to—but his hold, as gentle as it was, was unbreakable. "Do you often have to resort to threats for kisses?"

"Never, and it has quite unmanned me. You see the lengths to which I'm willing to go for you, Stacia?"

She lowered her eyelids at his words, as if she could hide her greedy desire from him. "One kiss and you will release me?"

"Yes. But it must be a real one. No grandmotherly pecks."

Who was she trying to fool? They both knew she wanted to kiss him.

He shifted his hold, until their lips were barely an inch apart. Stacia, seized by bold lunacy, flicked his lower lip with the tip of her tongue, as he had done to her.

He groaned and his arms tightened. "More."

Stacia stared in wonder as his pupils swelled until the black almost swallowed the blazing blue. His lips parted when she pressed her mouth to his and she allowed herself to taste him, tentative at first, but bolder as he purred beneath her.

Yesterday the thought of putting her tongue into another person's mouth would have revolted her. Now, Stacia could not get enough, plundering him as aggressively as Sir Francis Drake invading Cadiz.

By the time they pulled apart, they were both breathing hard. His lips were slick and red, his expression unsmiling and sensual. "I am glad you did not accept Townshend, Stacia. You would have been wasted on him." He lightly caressed her jaw, his gaze flickering across her face and lingering on her mouth before returning to her eyes.

And then he set her upright, until her bottom rested on one thigh, and his arms fell away.

For one mad moment she considered crawling up his chest the way she'd seen Lord Bellamy's red squirrel climb up Lucy's arm to nestle against her neck.

Fortunately, reason intervened before she could make an utter fool of herself and she forced herself to stand and walk on wobbly legs back to her own seat, sending cobnuts skittering across the attic floor as she went.

Stacia told herself that she deserved a medal for getting up and walking away from him.

But all she got for her self-control was an almost suffocating wave of yearning when she sat down across from him, recalling how much lovelier the view of his face had been from inches rather than feet.

She was actually debating throwing pride to the wind and launching herself across the table and demanding some forfeits of her own, when he said, "I owe you honesty in return."

Stacia frowned at his grim tone.

224

"I told you that my older cousin, Nicholas, died while Chatham and I were in the army?"

She nodded.

"Nicholas was betrothed to a woman whose father had been a great friend of the late duke. The two men had arranged the marriage when Mariah was in her cradle and Nick just a lad. When Nick died, they decided to pass Mariah along to Sylvester." He gave a bitter laugh. "Men who wouldn't loan out their horse had no problem trading away their children." His lips twisted into an unhappy smile. "Chatham sold his commission and returned to England. You've seen Chatham's scar—it's...Well, it is savage even now, but eleven years ago, when it was fresh, it was—in all honesty—terrifying. Not just what it did to his face, but the pain he must have suffered—" Shelton broke off as he engaged in some sort of internal struggle.

After a few moments, he continued. "I came home on leave to attend my cousin's wedding." He sighed. "I will not beat about the bush. Mariah and I fell in love. I'd met her before, of course, but I'd been a boy when I went off to war and she was my age, so she'd been a girl." He smiled, his gaze fond but vague. "The last time I saw her before going away we bickered like siblings when her parents brought her to spend Christmas at Chatham. She followed Sylvester and me around like a shadow, all coltish legs and scraped knees and wild beauty. But a child." He paused, his eyes moving from Stacia to something over her shoulder—perhaps the past—as he thought. "And suddenly, when I returned, she was a woman. The most beautiful, vibrant, desirable woman I had ever seen."

Stacia was grateful he was not looking at her at that moment because she was incapable of hiding her pain and jealousy at his words. Shame at experiencing such an unpleasant emotion about a dead woman did not lessen the feeling. Especially because she now knew the truth: the Duke of Chatham's former wife might be dead, but Andrew Derrick was still deeply in love with her.

***

Andrew had regretted letting Stacia go after she had paid her forfeit. He had immediately missed her soft warm body which somehow managed to arouse and yet comfort him at the same time.

But now that he was getting to the ugly heart of his confession—for that is what it was—he was relieved that he did not have to face her shrewd gaze from mere inches away, no matter how much comfort he might have derived from holding her.

And no matter how willingly she had wanted to give herself to him.

Because Stacia's desire for him had been painfully clear. Andrew could have taken her then and there and she would have come to him most willingly. But she was a woman who could not even kiss without guilt. She would hate herself after they'd laid together.

And she would hate him, too.

No, it was better to tell her the truth about the man she thought she wanted so badly.

The revolting, sordid truth.

Andrew had never talked about that time of his life with anyone, not even during these past months while he'd lived with Sylvester. He and his cousin had talked for hours—about the war, about their experiences and the aftermath—but they had wisely avoided the subject of Mariah, choosing to focus on their future friendship rather than their past enmity.

Recalling the details of the ancient, painful tale brought Mariah back in ways he'd never expected. For years all he had felt was an aching sense of loss that she wasn't beside him, like the stories he'd heard men tell when they had lost a limb.

Only now that he was forcing himself to articulate the details of that brief time did he realize the appalling truth: he could barely remember her.

Not what her laugh sounded like.

Not her voice when she told him she loved him.

Not how it had felt when he'd been inside her.

And, worst of all, he could not even recall her face.

When had he forgotten those things? *How* could he forget?

He willed himself to remember so hard that beads of sweat broke out on his brow.

But when he tried to imagine Mariah, he saw a different face, heard a different laugh, and saw brown eyes, instead of blue.

Andrew looked up to find Stacia waiting, patient but pensive.

"We fell in love." He held her gaze, forcing himself to meet the judgment in her eyes.

But there was none.

"You aren't disgusted with me for falling in love with my best friend's—no, my *brother*'s—betrothed?"

"It is not my place to—"

"I want to know your thoughts."

Her throat flexed as she swallowed. "I am not sure it is possible to talk oneself out of love, no matter how hopeless or wrong or destructive the emotion might prove to be."

Andrew was usually not the most of observant of men, but he was arrested by the intense pain in her eyes. A shocking insight followed immediately on the heels of that observation. Stacia Martin had been in love. Deeply in love. And, if her expression was anything to go by, heartbreakingly.

She could not mean her mouth-breathing earl, could she? That made no sense. If she loved Townshend, then why would she have refused him?

No. There was someone else. Somebody ineligible? Perhaps even someone who had died?

"You speak from experience," he said. It was not a question, and she did not respond.

Andrew burned to know, but her eyes hadn't just shuttered, there might as well have been stone walls and a deep moat around her.

She had not *been* in love. She was protecting herself because she was *still* in love.

Disappointment stabbed him—startlingly sharp. How could he, of all people, marry a woman who loved somebody else?

"Finish your story," she said, so cool and distant that Andrew wondered if he had imagined her brief, raw-eyed desperation.

"Mariah begged her father to let her out of the betrothal, but he was adamant. So I went to him." He grimaced at the memory. "That...did not go well. He spoke to Chatham, who was slowly taking up his duties but hardly up to his pre-injury strength, and Chatham came to me. I had no pride; I begged him. He insisted the marriage was a matter of honor to his father and to Mariah's family. But that was not all—or even most—of the reason. You see," he said, his lips twisting at the memory, "Chatham was in love with her as well. It was inconceivable to him that Mariah might prefer me. He was the duke, and I was the younger cousin with nothing but a rundown northern estate, beholden to him for my money and his ward in the matter of my inheritance. I had always idolized him—worshipped everything about him—and neither of us could accommodate the sudden change in our positions. That *I* could demand something that was supposed to be *his*." He gave an unhappy laugh. "When he did not capitulate, Mariah went to him and *begged* him to release her. Still, he would not relent. Rather than give in to our pleading—and unbeknownst to Mariah and me—he changed the wedding plans. Instead of a grand ceremony in St. George's, he acquired a special license, and they married three days after we had confronted him with the truth."

Andrew stood and poked at the fire. He stared at the sparks for a long moment, willing his blasted memory to give him even a glimpse of Mariah's face.

He saw…nothing.

Andrew slammed the poker onto the hook and spun to face her. "One more day and we would have been on our way to the Scottish border."

An expression of unease had settled on her face.

Andrew was glad. He didn't want what came next to be an utter shock to her.

"Chatham believed that was the end of it. But I made sure that it was merely the beginning of my revenge. You see, Mariah didn't just hate him, she feared him."

Her eyes widened. "He was cruel to her?"

"Sylvester never lifted a hand to her. He is not a violent man. It was something else she feared." Andrew shoved a hand through his hair and stared at the ceiling. Just how did a man say such things to an innocent—a virgin?

You never had any trouble telling them to Mariah.

He dropped his hand and forced himself to meet her gaze. "I told Mariah that Sylvester had unnatural appetites in the bedchamber."

Her lips parted in shock.

"She went to him filled with terror and loathing. Not only for that, but—and I regret having to admit this—Mariah could not see past Chatham's scar. I could have helped her overcome her revulsion at his appearance. But rather than tell her about my cousin's honor and decency, I encouraged her disgust. She cried when Chatham came to her on their wedding night and he vowed not to touch her until she welcomed him into her. Instead, she came to my bed. Night after night."

Andrew stared at her, waiting for the loathing he expected.

But it never came. Instead, he saw a mingling of sadness and pity.

Rather than feel gratitude, he was even more determined to make her *see* what a revolting cad and scoundrel he really was. "But that is not all. Mariah was already with child on her wedding day. We were careless and it was inevitable we were caught. Rather than show remorse, we taunted him with the fact that Mariah had already been pregnant when they married." He loosened his clenched jaws. "So, in that regard, Mariah and I had won. Or so we believed. My cousin banished me that very night. I did not go willingly. Sylvester had me dragged to his coach while Mariah watched, sobbing. And that was the last I saw of her. She died in childbed seven months later. I hated him for keeping me from her and for more than eleven years I made that hatred the center of my life."

Andrew felt exhausted, but also relieved that somebody other than Chatham knew of his infamy. He forced himself to meet her gaze. "That is how I carried on until this past summer, when I almost destroyed Lady Shaftsbury's life in pursuit of my revenge." He lifted his hands. "And there you have it."

She eyed him warily. "Your cousin has forgiven you?"

"Yes," he said shortly. "As little as I deserve it."

"And you have forgiven him?"

Andrew lifted an eyebrow. "You astonish me, Miss Martin. Do you think he has done something unforgiveable? She was his legal wife, after all."

"Forgiveness isn't about right and wrong, my lord. It is something you give *regardless* of right and wrong."

Had he forgiven Chatham? He thought so, at least mostly. Although he did on occasion experience a twinge of unarticulated resentment, like a pebble in one's boot.

"For the most part," he said when he saw she was waiting.

"And what about you, my lord?"

"Me?"

"Have you forgiven yourself?"

He opened his mouth to deny he felt any guilt, but that would be a lie.

Mariah had been pregnant with his child. And while she might have died from her pregnancy, regardless of the father, there was no denying that months of struggle and strife had left her fragile and weakened even before he had been banished. What had her life been like, alone with Chatham? She would have suffered horribly; he knew that instinctively. Not that his cousin would have been cruel to her, but she would have missed Andrew just as much—nay, more probably—than he'd missed her. After all, Andrew had had the War to keep him busy. What had Mariah had except her marriage to a man she hated?

If Andrew had stepped aside—if he had not poisoned her mind against his cousin—would Mariah have, in time, looked past his scars to see the man beneath?

You know she would have. She was not a cruel woman. Not until you made her that way.

Andrew met Miss Martin's shrewd, not unsympathetic gaze, and realized she was right. He *had* blamed himself.

And he still did.

A Very Bellamy Christmas

Chapter 26

*I*gnorance is bliss, people were fond of saying. Stacia hadn't really agreed with that maxim until now.

To her eternal shame, it wasn't the sordid details of his past that she hated learning. No, it was the fact that the man she had been in love with for four long years had loved another woman so deeply. That he *still* loved her.

His story had not destroyed her tenacious, inexplicable attachment to him, nor even given it much of a battering. After all, Stacia had wanted him even when she had believed that he'd impregnated Sarah and heartlessly abandoned her.

His tale had, however, given her a headache and her belly roiled with too much conflicting, confusing emotion.

"I am going to examine the door," Lord Shelton said, getting up and leaving without waiting for an answer.

A wave of exhaustion rolled over her. A few moments of rest and some time to ponder what she'd just learned; that was what she needed.

She went to the bed, which she had made after rising, and unbuttoned her ankle boots before lying down.

It felt… heavenly. Just a few minutes of rest…

The next time Stacia opened her eyes again, she could feel that time had passed—not because of any change in light, but because of a heaviness in her body that said she had not moved for some time.

She yawned, pushed up on her elbows, and looked toward the seating area. Lord Shelton was sprawled in the chair she thought of as his, all four candles in the candelabrum burning on the table at his elbow.

And he was reading. Or at least he was holding a book, she amended, her lips twitching into a smile.

And then it all came back to her—the reason she had needed to close her eyes and stop thinking.

What he'd done to his cousin had been awful. But then…what he had done for Sarah had been noble, regardless of his claim to the contrary.

Don't forget Lady Shaftsbury.

Stacia scowled. Fine. He had done one wretched thing, one ignoble thing, and one self-sacrificing thing.

Those are only the things you know of…

Who am I to stand in judgment of him? she retorted.

You are determined to forgive him. Anything.

Stacia wanted to argue with that, but she could not lie to herself. At least not to that degree. Besides, it was not her place to concern herself with his character. Who was she to him?

His wife, if he has his way…

No.

It is what you want more than anything.

That wasn't true. What she wanted more than anything was his love.

But you will settle for possession…

Stacia swallowed. The thought of possessing him—even if it was only ever in name—was so intoxicating that she simply could not imagine it. She was terrified that she was not strong enough to resist him, that she would latch onto a future with him like a child reaching for something bright, not caring if what she wanted was as dangerous as a dancing flame.

She needed to keep in mind their past, his dismissal of her so many, many times. She needed to remember that he was still in love with somebody else. She needed—

Use your head all you want; it is your heart that will decide.

***

Andrew looked up and smiled when he heard Miss Martin's boots. "Are you refreshed? You should be."

"Have I slept long?"

"More than two hours."

"Goodness!"

He closed his book without bothering to mark the page and set it aside.

She stared at him, an odd smile curving her lips.

"What?" he asked. "Why are you—oh." He smiled wryly and removed his spectacles. "I'd forgotten."

"I like them," she said.

"You may borrow them any time you wish."

She smiled and shook her head. "I like them on *you*." Once the words were out her smile turned to an expression of chagrin.

"Do you indeed, Miss Martin?" he drawled.

As he had hoped, she scowled at his teasing. "Yes, as a matter of fact. They make you look clever."

He laughed. "The perfect disguise, then."

"What were you reading?" She'd tilted her head to read the spine, but the gilt had long ago been worn off by the hand of some happy reader, no doubt one of the Bellamy chits.

"It is called *The Perils of Lady Louisa*." As far as he could tell, the only peril in the book had been the purple language. Or perhaps the suppressed sexual tension that had rampaged through Lady Louisa's tightly corseted body every time the villain—hero?—had twirled his mustachios in her direction. All that twirling had made him wonder if he should grow facial hair. But then the only time he'd tried, his beard had looked patchy and piebald.

"Is it good?" she asked, a faint twist to her lips.

"Hmm?"

"The book?"

He smiled. "Riveting."

She laughed. "Why do I not believe you?"

He could have told her that he'd only managed to get through about six pages. He'd never had an easy time reading but was even more painfully plodding since injuring his head during the War. The spectacles helped, of course, but they did not stop the letters from performing their tricks and he could never read for more than a half hour without developing a devil of a headache. He knew not everyone was as dull-witted as he was because he'd made the mistake of once asking Sylvester about the moving letters. His cousin had been startled, and then had laughed, believing Andrew had been jesting. That had been the first and last time he'd mentioned *that*.

Before Andrew could answer her, her stomach growled.

She set a hand over her midriff, her face flooding with color. "Oh. Pardon me."

"Hungry?" he teased. "I cleaned the crockery earlier." He pointed to small collection of plates, cups, and glasses on a dish cloth. "If you set places then I will lay out a feast."

Her gaze slid to the dishes. "I should have done that."

That made him smile. "I might be useless in a kitchen, but I can certainly wash a dish."

"I suspect that is quite rare among the men of our class."

"Yet one more way in which I am a man among men."

Again, she laughed.

They worked in companionable silence, the little domestic space already familiar after barely a day.

She must have been thinking the same thing, because she said, "It is astonishing how quickly one becomes accustomed to a new set of circumstances."

"I agree. It was something I first noticed during my time in the army."

She gazed up at him curiously. "How do you mean?"

He dug to the bottom of the larger trunk and unearthed an entire pie. "Look at this."

"Ooh! What kind?"

He peeled off the layers of waxed cloth, the bottom of which had frozen onto the pan. "There is even ice in the bottom of the trunk," he snorted. "Our captor thought of everything." He pulled a corner free, sniffed, and then grinned as the spices hit him. "A meat pie with hints of nutmeg and cinnamon."

"I adore those. Our cook used to make those, but only at Christmas."

"Ours, too. Shall I warm it on the hearth for a bit?"

"Yes, please."

Once he'd positioned the pie so it would heat without scorching, he gestured to their beverage selection.

"Wine, ale, or lemonade?"

"Wine, please."

They helped themselves to bread, butter, cheese, and a bit of ham while they waited for the pie.

"This bread is getting hard," she said. "We will have to toast the rest of it."

"Luckily for you, cheese toast is my specialty. I was famous for it in the army."

"Impressive," she mocked. "Are there medals for that?"

He laughed. "A knighthood. By rights, you should be calling me Sir Andrew Cheese Toast."

She snorted and rolled her eyes. "Will you tell me about your time on the Continent?" When he hesitated, she said, "I know it is not done to talk to women about such matters, but I would like to know what it was like—but only if it does not disturb you."

The parts of the war that disturbed him were buried so deeply that Andrew himself never looked at them. There was a great deal to tell her that might not be suitable for polite company, but it would not leave her emotionally scarred.

"We moved often, occupying whatever was convenient: castles, churches, entire villages at times." Andrew told her about the wonders he had seen, the natural beauty of the land—no matter how scarred by war—and the monuments, buildings, and works of art that most people only ever read about.

Her questions were intelligent and informed, as one would expect from a scholar's daughter.

"People will tell you that war is hell—and there are parts of it that qualify for that description—but most of it is tedium and discomfort and uncertainty. And of course, in my cousin's case, there were times of horrific pain."

"And you were never injured?"

"Several times, but nothing to what Chatham suffered. He was fortunate he was not killed, although I doubt that he felt fortunate at the time." He saw that her glass was almost empty and clucked his tongue. "I've been maundering on for too long," he said, refilling both their glasses. "And I daresay our pie is ready."

He placed it on a cloth between them and handed her the knife, handle first. "You do the honors."

"How big?" she asked.

"Is it piggish to say a quarter?"

"It is almost Christmas; I think we are allowed to indulge."

They dug into their respective pieces—hers barely half the size she'd cut for Andrew—and silence reigned for several moments.

"This is good," she said after she'd enjoyed several mouthfuls.

"It is," he agreed. "Now, it is your turn."

"My turn?"

"Tell me about yourself—your life."

"But I have no experiences like yours."

"I am glad to hear it," he said dryly.

"I just meant that my life has not been very interesting."

235

"I'll be the judge of that. Tell me about school—how long did you go? Where? Did you like it?"

"I went to the same school my mother attended, a lovely old manor house that accommodated only forty girls."

"*Only* forty? That sounds like a great many girls for one house."

She laughed. "It could feel crowded and lacked privacy at times, and I occasionally yearned for the solitude of my father's house, but I loved the companionship. I am an only child, and my father often forgot my existence—not in a cruel way, but it made for a lonely life. I went to Mrs. Pritchard's Academy for four years, leaving at eighteen. After that I kept house for my father, until my aunt decided I should have a Season." She shrugged. "And you know the rest. My father died and my first position took me to Bath."

"You felt nothing for the young man who proposed to you—er, Townshend, was it?"

"I felt the sort of affection I imagine one feels for a brother."

"Obviously he felt otherwise."

"No, that was the problem. He did not ask me to marry him because he loved me. He asked me because he valued my expertise and knew I could be of help to him when it came to his collection. That was why I could not say *yes*, no matter how much easier it would have made my life in some ways."

Andrew took a sip of wine to wash down his mouthful of pie, wiped his mouth, and said, "Expertise?"

"Yes, with illuminated manuscripts. I had been helping my father restore them for years. On occasion I did work for others—Townshend was one—but my father kept me busy enough that did not often happen."

"You *restore* illuminated manuscripts?"

"I did, but it has been years." She cocked her head. "Why are you smiling like that?"

"Because I should have guessed your work was too good to be that of a dabbler."

Her lips parted in surprise. "But how do you know what my work looks like?"

"Mrs. Johnson let slip that you'd visited her shop to sell some fans."

"Oh. I wish she would not tell people about that."

"I suspect I am the only one she shared that information with."

She frowned at him. "Why would she tell you?"

236

"I can be very persuasive."

She snorted. "I can imagine. You saw the fans at the Christmas fete?"

"I not only saw them, I bought three."

"*Three!*"

Andrew found her expression of shy delight...delightful. "You have an extraordinary talent. Why are you working as a companion when you could be restoring priceless documents?"

"The paintings I do are good enough for fans and such—no," she said when he scoffed at her tepid description, "I am not denigrating my talent, my lord, but it is a far cry from the work done by experts. There are only a few people in the country—probably in the world—who would notice such differences, but they are the same ones who can afford the valuable manuscripts. They want the best, and I am not that."

"To my untutored eye your work is magnificent. By the by, you made Lord Needham a very happy man. Evidently his wife attracts butterflies, and your fan was the sort of gift he had been hoping for."

"I am so glad! She is a lovely woman. They are both very kind. Indeed, all the siblings and their spouses are delightful." She pulled a face. "Even Lady Kathryn, as much as it pains me to admit it."

"She *is* exceedingly likeable," he agreed. "It is part of her evil charm."

She laughed. "I think, despite some strong evidence to the contrary, that *evil* might be a bit strong."

Andrew was not so sure. "You are right about the siblings being charming," he said. "Even my cousin's wife has grown on me over the months I've lived at Chatham Park."

"Were you at loggerheads initially because you abducted her sister?"

"Kidnapping Selina did not help matters," he admitted dryly. "But Hyacinth was not fond of me even before that."

She gave him a querying look, but the duchess's masquerade was not Andrew story to share, no matter how much he might have liked to satisfy her curiosity.

"I do hope that Mr. Higgins is taking care of Terrence," she said after a moment.

Andrew blinked. "Er, Terrence?"

"That is what I've named the dog you helped me rescue."

"Terrence?"

"What is wrong with that name?"

"*Terrence?*"

"Why do you keep repeating it in that obnoxious way? Terrence is a fine name"

"Terrence *might* be a fine name—not that I am willing to concede that just yet—but it is still a name for a dog that spends its days in a lady's lap, drinking milk from a saucer, wearing a bow on its head."

She laughed. "How ridiculous. What would you call him?"

"He is clearly a survivor of more than a few battles and deserves a suitable moniker." He paused. "I think Scrapper fits him admirably."

"Scrapper? *Scrapper?* That is exactly the sort of name that will give a dog terrible ideas."

"Such as?"

"Such as wandering away from home and getting stuck in traps. Haunting neighborhood chicken coops and drawing the ire of farmers. Pushing over rubbish bins and—why are you laughing?"

"Because you are adorable."

Rather than look pleased, her mouth immediately screwed up as if she had just sucked a lemon. Ah, Miss Martin didn't care for compliments. Andrew would have to break her of that after they were married.

"In any case," Andrew said, "You don't have to worry about the dog as Mr. Higgins isn't the sort to neglect any animal under his care."

She looked pleased by his reassurance. "I'm sure you are right." She gestured to the wreckage of their luncheon. "We should return the pie to its ice. Do you think it will keep?"

"Surely until later today."

They busied themselves tidying up. All too soon they were finished with their chores and, once again, staring at each other.

"Do you—"

"Should we—"

They both laughed. "Ladies first," he said.

"Do you want to play a game?"

"I would rather get some exercise." Andrew wasn't accustomed to lolling about all day and it was making him restless.

"Exercise? What do you mean?"

Only with great effort was Andrew able to bite his tongue and rein in his first response.

Instead of scandalizing her and drawing her *sour lemon* look, and perhaps even getting a well-deserved slap, he said, "Waltz with me."

She gazed steadily at him for so long he expected a *no, thank you.*

But then Miss Martin surprised him yet again and said, "Very well."

Chapter 27

You know that you lose what few wits you have when you have your hands on him, the voice of reminded her.

Stacia did not care. Earlier she had told Lord Shelton that it was near enough to Christmas that he should indulge.

Well. *She* would indulge, too. If she did not, she suspected she would regret it for the rest of her life.

"Very well," Stacia said, getting to her feet.

Lord Shelton held out his arms and Stacia swallowed and took her position.

He stared down at her, his face unsmiling and his blue eyes glittering beneath lowered lids. Stacia wasn't just indulging herself, she was courting danger.

She did not care.

He did not bother to hum, and neither of them seemed to need it. Stacia kept pace with him easily.

He was so much taller than her that it should have been uncomfortable to look up at him—and it certainly should have been awkward gazing into his eyes without talking—and yet she had never felt more at ease with him. The sheer physicality of the dance—his moves more daring and demanding the longer they danced—would have made talking difficult in any case.

Only when she noticed the sheen of perspiration on his forehead did she realize her own skin was hot and damp, the air in the room more like a summer day than the end of December.

"Tired?" he asked her in a voice that was a little breathless.

"No," she lied, cocking an eyebrow. "You?"

He laughed. "No."

Now that Stacia had both the measure of the dance and also knew what it was like to have a superlative partner, she could read his body well enough to anticipate his moves.

Or so she'd believed.

Then he spun her into a turn and allowed the momentum to carry her into a twirl, only his fingers lightly holding hers.

Stacia laughed with delight as he smoothly captured her free hand and resumed the dance. "I have never done that!"

He smiled. "There are a number of other starting positions—would you like to try them?"

"Of course."

For the next half hour he demonstrated variations, some quite scandalous. But none quite so enjoyable as the one they adopted last, where Stacia's hands rested on his shoulders, near his neck, and both his hands were on her waist. Their rather significant height difference meant their bodies were close together, far too close for a *ton* ballroom.

"This is my favorite," he murmured, his eyes glinting down at her as he slowed their pace, their perfectly synchronized movements taking on a dangerously sensual feel when his leg brushed against the inside of her thigh as he turned her.

Stacia swallowed, her heart pounding and her breasts tightening.

His lips curled into one of his lazy, mischievous smiles and she just *knew* that *he* knew what she was feeling.

It was difficult to breathe, even though they were not moving fast. Indeed, they were moving so slowly they certainly would have attracted the wrong sort of attention on a normal dance floor.

The next time he turned her, he slid to a halt, and she found her back pressed up against the room's only door.

His eyes blazed down at her, hungry and hot, his smile of only seconds earlier nowhere in sight.

They stared, frozen. And then his grip on her waist loosened.

He was stepping away from her!

Stacia yanked him down while standing on her toes, all but thrusting herself at him.

His big body resisted only for a second before he groaned and took what she offered, seizing possession of her mouth with a carnality that robbed her of breath.

As she had with their waltzing, Stacia initially struggled to keep pace with him, his lips, tongue, and hands shattering what few wits she had.

And then his knee pressed against the juncture of her legs. With hardly a thought, she opened to him.

It was Stacia's turn to groan at the delicious friction.

"Yes," he murmured into her hair. His hands slid to her bottom and he lifted her until she was straddling his hard thigh.

The wantonness of her position should have left her red-faced with shame, but the jagged pulses of pleasure were too powerful to ignore—too delicious not to chase.

"That's right," he said, his voice gravelly and his breath hot on her ear as he rocked her hips with both his hands, moving her with ease until her body fell into the rhythm. "Just like that, Stacia." His hands slid beneath her thighs and he spread her wider, adjusting the angle of his leg until the sensation was unbearable and she clung to him, her fingers digging into his shoulders, her hips writhing and bucking.

She whimpered, struggling to get away from a pleasure that threatened to undo her. "I can't—"

"You can." Again, his hands urged, rocking her at the perfect speed and angle, until Stacia was unable to contain the explosion of sensory pleasure that shot from her sex up her spine.

Over and over the bliss rippled, her muscles stiffening and then going limp between each wave. She had just begun to float back down to earth when he slid a hand between his thigh and her sex, cupped her mound and used one finger to unerringly find the source of her pleasure.

The second explosion was less of a surprise than the first, but the muscles inside her stunned body clenched even harder.

Stacia was vaguely aware that Andrew had lifted her in both arms and was carrying her, the sounds of his boot heels drumming the insensibility from her and bringing her back sharply to reality.

"Oh, no you don't," he said when she tried to sit up. He kissed her ear and took her not to the settee or bed, but to his wingchair and then sat, with Stacia cradled in his lap. "Shh, shh," he murmured when she tried to cover her scalding face. "You did nothing wrong and everything right, darling." He covered every part of her face—at least anything that was visible between her splayed fingers—with kisses. "Leave guilt for other people, Stacia. For boring people."

She gave a watery laugh, suddenly noticing that her cheeks were wet.

"Here then," he said, gently pulling one of her hands away. "Why are you crying? Did I hurt you, sweetheart?"

"No," she snapped, or at least she tried to, but it came out as more of a snivel, which only angered her. "I am embarrassed—surely you can understand that?" This time she *did* manage to snap.

He shifted her and reached into his pocket, drawing out a handkerchief. "Here."

"Thank you," she muttered, her tone distinctly ungrateful.

Naturally, he laughed. And then kissed her. "Never be embarrassed of your sensuality, Stacia. I wish you could have seen what I did—a beautiful, erotic, magnificent woman taking what she wanted." He ignored her mortified groan and caught her hand, keeping her from covering her face again. He claimed her mouth, giving her a deep, drugging kiss that left her wrung out.

"There," he murmured when she sighed and went limp in his arms. "That is much better." He rocked her gently, kissing and murmuring.

Stacia did not recall ever feeling so cared for, so…cherished. And loved.

But it was an illusion, she was not so far gone as to not realize that.

Even so, she decided that for once, she would simply enjoy the moment rather than look toward the cold reality that would come afterward.

***

Andrew smiled when he saw that she'd fallen into a doze, her lips parted, breath coming in soft, even little puffs. He knew he should tuck her into bed and let her sleep. She would be mortified when she woke up in his arms. But he decided to please himself and keep her. What a delicious little armload of passion she was. Watching her orgasm not once, but twice, had been bloody erotic. He'd been a hair's breadth away from spending in his breeches. It was a good thing he hadn't. Not just for his pride, but these were the only pair he had.

As he studied her face, so much younger looking in repose, he remembered that he had promised himself not to touch her again after last night.

So much for that.

He wanted to touch her again. And again. All kinds of touches—especially the ones that would leave her with no choice but to marry him.

Andrew had no idea where this sudden desire for marriage—not just with anyone, but with *her*—had come from. It seemed insane to admit it, even in the privacy of his own head, but he felt like he *knew* her.

He snorted softly. According to Stacia, they had met dozens of times.

Andrew lightly traced the gently curve of her jaw. How could anyone forget this woman? True, she was small—tiny, in fact—but she was so self-assured and seemingly self-contained, two characteristics that were rare in any person, but especially in a young woman who'd been cast out into the world by the only family she had left.

It took true strength of character to reject an offer of marriage when the alternative was working for harridans like Lady Addiscombe.

Which made him recall their current predicament. Andrew grimaced when he thought about the countess's reaction once they finally got out of this attic.

"I could throttle you, Kathryn," he muttered.

If he managed to break the door open and get them out tonight—which was his intention—was there any story they could concoct to justify their absence?

Andrew snorted. Christ. What sort of story could they come up with to explain a two-day absence *for both of them*? There simply wasn't one.

Well, at the very least Stacia could sleep in her own bed before the circus commenced tomorrow morning. He glanced down at the woman who was as good as his wife and smiled. As much as he hated to admit it, Kathryn had chosen well for him. Never in a hundred years would he have imagined himself falling for a woman so much cleverer than him. Not that Mariah had been stupid, but they'd both been so young and in love that nothing else had mattered, certainly not mere practicalities. Would their marriage have been a happy one? Or would their physical passion have burnt out and left nothing but two people who had little in common?

Not that he had much in common with Miss Martin—other than he genuinely enjoyed being with her. Even getting drubbed in every damned game they'd played had been amusing. He liked watching her brain work far more than he cared about winning or losing. And he *loved* watching the joy that transformed her normally stern mien when she trounced him.

Andrew snorted. Sylvester would never believe that he had become besotted with a woman's mind.

Besotted. Is that what he was?

He wasn't sure that was accurate. Entranced might be better. He wanted her body—fiercely—but he wanted to see her blossom, not just for those rare moments when she forgot herself, but to bloom in a way he suspected would happen naturally when she was secure and had some stability and didn't need to fetch and carry for a demanding harpy.

Because you are so good at creating security and stability for those you care about.

He winced at that accusation, unable to deny it. Andrew Derrick and stability had long been strangers. But a man could change, especially if he had a reason to do so. Andrew already had at least two reasons: regaining his people's trust and his cousin's respect. Making Miss Martin happy would be a third.

What about your discovery from earlier that she is in love with somebody else? You said you would never marry a woman who loved somebody else.

Andrew frowned at the reminder. He would just have to ask her outright. Obviously, there must be some obstacle to her love or she would not be working as a companion. For all he knew, whoever had her heart might be dead.

In any case, her reputation would be shattered after this episode. She needed a man's protection. And it should be Andrew who offered it. She might not love him, but he knew when a woman wanted him sexually, and Miss Martin wanted him badly. What she felt for him was not love—perhaps it wasn't even liking—but it was an opportunity. If he was careful—also not his forte—he might be able to forge something more enduring from sexual attraction.

Unless she simply rejects your offer. She rejected a peer—and a wealthy one, at that—once before, after all.

Andrew scowled surprisingly disgruntled by the thought. It had scarcely been more than a day, but he had come to like the thought of being married to her.

She clearly does not feel the same way about marrying you—she has already rejected you at least twice.

He would have expected to feel considerable relief at the thought of escaping marriage and responsibility. Instead, he felt an almost howling emptiness at the thought of leaving Wych House in another week and never seeing Miss Eustacia Martin ever again.

Good God. When had that happened? More to the point, *what* had happened? It wasn't love he felt for her. It couldn't be. It felt nothing like the feelings he'd harbored for Mariah for so long.

If not love, then what? Lust, surely, but that—at least—was an emotion he knew inside and out. This was something different.

Something more.

Something confusing.

Something more than a little alarming.

***

Stacia blinked up into a pair of smiling blue eyes, her own face immediately forming an answering smile.

She shifted and felt something beneath her that was neither a chair nor a bed. Something warm and…hard.

Stacia was still lying in Lord Shelton's lap.

Memories of how she'd gotten there led to other memories. Of what she had done on one of his legs.

He chuckled softly. "I thought we already went over this?" he chided, reading her expression—likely one of mortification—correctly.

"How long did I sleep?" she asked, not wanting to think about her behavior.

"Not long—a half-hour."

"I should get up."

His arms tightened. "I will let you up when you promise me no more guilt or embarrassment."

"I cannot promise that."

"Why not?"

"Because—" She ground her teeth, choosing and discarding words, all of which sounded more embarrassing even in her own mind. "Just because."

"Not good enough."

"I can't help feeling embarrassed."

"Why?"

"*Why?*"

"Yes, *why?* And *just because* isn't good enough."

"Because of the way I just—just *used* you like that."

His smile was slow and wicked. "Would it make you feel better if I used you the same way?"

Stacia thought her eyes might roll out of her head. "*What?* No!"

He grinned. "I will leave the offer open."

She squirmed and this time, to her regret, he let her get away.

"Hungry?" he asked.

"Not really. You?"

"Not for food."

Stacia frowned.

"I apologize for that remark," he said.

"You don't look very apologetic." Indeed, his blue eyes glittered with poorly suppressed amusement.

"Would you like to play more *vingt-et-un?*"

Stacia eyed her cobnuts, which she had gathered up and put in a bowl, and the empty space on his side of the table. "You don't have any more counters."

"We don't have to play for cobnuts." He lifted one eyebrow.

"What do you mean?"

"There is other...currency."

"Such as?"

He shrugged. "Clothing."

"You cannot be serious."

"Deadly."

"Don't be ridiculous."

"If not clothing then you could extend me a loan."

"A cobnut loan," she said flatly.

"It is called *accepting vowels*."

"*Hmph*." Stacia stared at her bowl of cobnuts, her mind stuck on his first suggestion. She cleared her throat and then looked up to find him giving her the sort of knowing smirk that told her he knew exactly what she was thinking.

Well, who cared if he knew?

"How does one play with clothing as counters?"

Forty-five minutes later...

Stacia looked from her cards to his. And then looked at them again. And then she looked up at Lord Shelton—who was still *fully clothed*.

She shook her head. "I-I don't understand what I am doing wrong this time. I did so well before—with the cobnuts."

"Lady luck is fickle," he said, giving her a sympathetic look that she did not believe for an instant.

Stacia could not seem to catch her breath. Nor could she meet his gaze, which had gone from lazily amused to distinctly predatorial. She looked instead at the pile of garments beside her. And the shoes on the floor. Although he had allowed her to don her bonnet, gloves, pelisse, scarf, and cloak before they began playing, she was still down to her dress, petticoat, stays, stockings, and chemise. Six more items.

A thought struck her. "What about my g-garters?"

He grinned. "Those count."

"And my hair pins?" she asked, not caring that her face was flaming at having said *garters*. "Surely they count?"

"*Hmmm.*" He tapped his chin.

"Two pins equal one garment?" she asked hopefully.

He cut a glance at her hair.

Something told Stacia that he knew more about how many hairpins a woman needed than she did.

"Three pins equal a garment," he said.

Stacia exhaled raggedly. Surely her luck would turn by then. Earlier, when they had used cobnuts, she had beaten him every sing—

Her head whipped up. "You—you've *tricked* me!"

His eyebrows rose and his expression grew haughty. "Are you accusing me of cheating, Miss Martin?"

"No—of course not. I didn't mean—" And then she saw the slight curve of his lips and gave a huff of disgust. "You know exactly what I mean. You purposely lost earlier, didn't you?"

"Now you are calling me a Captain Sharp?" He gave her a hurt look.

"I cannot *believe* you!"

He grinned. "All is fair in love and cards."

"You are abominable. How far would you have allowed this to go? Until I was n-n—without any clothing." Her face was doubtless fiery at her inability to articulate a simple word.

Lord Shelton, naturally, looked delighted. "I would have stopped long before you were n-n—without any clothing."

She laughed before she could catch it. "You are a horrible man!"

"I am trying to be better," he said meekly.

"I don't believe that for a minute." Stacia threw her cards at him, and he laughed. "How could you be so sure of your skill? I might have had a run of luck, after all."

"True," he said, gathering up the cards and then tidying them into a stack before setting them on the table. He shrugged. "The trick is not caring if I won or lost."

"What do you mean?"

"I mean that as much as I wanted to see you *naked*, I would also enjoy taking off all my own clothing in front of you…Stacia." The laughter that had been brimming in his eyes was gone and the same hunger she had seen before replaced it.

The memory of her hand on his taut nipples and hard muscles slammed into her.

Stacia swallowed down the moisture that flooded her mouth.

"Come, Stacia…be brave. Life does not offer a person opportunities like this very often." He gestured to the room around them, as if she didn't know exactly what he meant.

"I—" the word came out a choked squeak. She cleared her throat. "I am not going to marry you just because Lady Kathryn forced our hand."

"So you have said. What I am suggesting is not marriage, Stacia. It is sensual pleasure."

If you don't take what he is offering, you will regret it every single day for the rest of your life, Stacia.

She would.

And yet… Stacia knew that she could not look at his naked body—and certainly not touch it—with the twin blue flames of his eyes burning into her.

Why do I want this so much?

Stacia suddenly, and vividly, imagined herself years from now, a faded specter of a woman who was still a companion, walking some ill-humored dog, and dreaming of her past, reliving the memory of these few days over and over again. Wishing there was more to remember…

She *wanted* this. Maybe she even needed it.

She risked a glance at him. "Nothing we do would mean more than what it is."

"If that is what you wish."

She *did* wish it.

Darkness, which had so emboldened her the night before, would hide what she so wanted to see, so there would be no point—

"A blindfold," she blurted.

His eyebrows arched. "Er, you want to wear a blindfold while I undress?"

Stacia snorted. "I want *you* to wear one."

Rather than look shocked or uneasy or anything a normal man would likely look, he appeared thrilled.

A Very Bellamy Christmas

"I would love to wear a blindfold while I strip for you, Miss Martin."

Chapter 28

Andrew knew he shouldn't tease her too much—she might change her mind, after all—but watching her blush was simply too precious to resist.

"We can use my cravat," he offered before she could come to her senses. Andrew pulled it off with a tug and offered her the wrinkled strip of linen. "Will you do the honors or shall I?"

"You do it."

He cocked his head, his amusement fading when he saw how tightly clenched her jaws were. "Are you sure you—"

"Just because I am nervous does not mean I am not sure," she shot back.

He nodded and reached up, quickly tying the strip over his eyes. When he was finished, he lowered his hands to his sides. "What next, Stacia?"

***

Stacia chewed her lower lip furiously as she stared at him, unable to believe this was happening. Because *this* sort of thing did not—had *never*—even come close to happening to staid, plain, practical Stacia Martin.

"T-take off your coats," she ordered.

His hands immediately went to the buttons of his clawhammer, his long, elegant fingers moving deftly.

Stacia wanted to tell him to go slower—that things were moving too fast—but he'd already moved on to the buttons on his waistcoat, which was a sober gray and white striped silk. Now that she thought about it, he did not dress like a dandy. All his clothing fit well, but he was not given to peacocking about in wasp-waisted evening coats or the ridiculously tight trousers many of the younger tulips of the *ton* had taken to wearing these past years. And she had never seen him in evening clothes that were anything but black and white, a stark combination which suited his blond good looks to perfection.

He tried to shrug out of the fitted coat but struggled. "Some help, please?"

"Oh, of course," she leapt up and stepped close enough to help him remove the sleeves of his coat.

"Thank you," he said as she peeled the fine wool off his arms.

The garments were still warm from the heat of his body. Yet again, she was exposed to the intoxicating scent of him and greedily filled her lungs.

Lord Shelton stood unmoving before her, the deep V of his badly wrinkled linen shirt exposing the mysterious terrain of his chest to her gaze.

She turned away and carefully laid his clothing over the back of the settee, her hands shaking so badly she dropped his waistcoat twice.

She smoothed a bit of dust from the expensive silk and something about the sight of her hand on the masculine garment brought the unreality of the situation thundering back to her.

Stacia had just helped Lord Shelton remove his coats.

She swallowed convulsively. *Am I really doing this?*

You can still stop.

She turned and looked at him.

He waited patiently, arms loose at his sides, one hip cocked, booted feet spread in a casual stance.

I will look like a coward if I stop.

The voice in her head had no response for that. What was worse? Looking like a coward or a strumpet?

The answer was easier than she would have expected.

"Sit down and remove your boots."

***

Andrew wondered if the lengthy pause after she'd helped to remove his coats was a sign that she was losing her courage.

Regardless of what it meant, he should put a stop to this. He was an experienced man who'd goaded a virgin into demanding that he strip. But if he called a halt to things right now, she would probably think it had something to do with her, rather than a gentlemanly impulse—albeit weak—to spare her tender sensibilities.

Liar. You just want to get naked in front of her.

Well, there was that too, he thought as he obeyed her command, sank into his chair, and speedily, if not exactly gracefully, wrenched off first one boot and then the other.

"St-stockings, too."

He bit back a grin as he pulled them off, tossed them aside, and then flexed his liberated toes.

He heard the sound of movement from across the room, the faint creak of the settee—was she sitting down? Or getting up? And then came the subtle squeak of one of the ancient floor planks, her footsteps so quiet that she must have shed her ankle boots. His lips twitched at the thought of those diminutive boots. Had he ever seen such a small pair before?

"Why are you smirking?" she asked, her voice coming from far nearer than he'd expected.

"Because I am happy."

"It does not embarrass you to remove your clothing in front of somebody you hardly know?"

He chuckled, not just at her question, but at just how *un*-embarrassed she would discover he was if she ever got around to demanding that he shed his leathers. "No."

"Stand up," she said, her tone sharp, as if his answer had annoyed her.

Andrew stood.

"Remove your breeches."

His eyebrows almost launched off his forehead at her unexpectedly bold command, but his hands were already in motion, nimbly flicking open the catches on his fall and giving a tug that pulled all the buttons out of their holes in one fell swoop.

And then he let the soft doeskin fall to the floor and kicked the garment to the side.

The air shifted around him, and he heard more floorboards creaking, farther away this time.

You should put a stop to this. It is up to—

"Your shirt."

He hesitated.

"Was that confusing, my lord?"

Andrew laughed. "No, Miss Martin." He grasped the hem of the garment, which was long enough to reach almost the bottom of his small clothes and pulled it over his head.

She gasped.

Andrew was arrogant, but he suspected it wasn't the sight of his tented smallclothes that had drawn her gasp.

No, it would be the hideous scars scattered about his person. Women seemed mesmerized by the mute evidence of violence. Perhaps because so much about war was a mystery to them. Or maybe just because the wounds were ugly.

Andrew dropped his shirt to the floor when she did not take it from him.

"What happened?" she asked, her voice coming from right in front of him.

"Sabers happened."

He could feel soft warm puffs of air against his chest; she was close.

"Touch me, Stacia," he said, his cock throbbing at the memory of her cool, smooth hands on his chest the night before and the pleasure they'd given him.

Andrew heard an amusing gulp and could see her expression of indecision in his mind's eye.

It was even odds whether she—

He hissed when she touched him, the muscles in his abdomen clenching. "Good God! Your hands are like ice."

She jerked her hands away.

"Here," Andrew said, holding up his own hands, which were on fire. "Put them between mine and I'll warm them. Do it," he added when she hesitated, pleased when she complied.

He chafed her hands between his. "Are you always this cold?"

"Are you always this warm?" she countered.

"I burn hot."

He rubbed in silence for a moment longer, until she felt, if not warm, then at least not chilled. "There," he said, releasing her. "You may proceed."

"You really don't mind?"

"I adore your hands on me."

"Even *here?*" She lightly grazed the largest of his scars, the place where the saber had gone all the way through him.

"Yes, even there, Stacia."

Her hand shook slightly at his admission, but she didn't pull away. Indeed, she became bolder, tracing the other wounds—one on his shoulder and the other close to his heart—but returning to the large, puckered strip of skin on his side.

"This must have hurt."

"It did." He did not tell her that he had almost died. That he had prayed for death at the time. Not because of the saber damage itself, but the putrefaction that set in afterward.

"I was very sick afterward," he said, sensing she was waiting for more. "The care I received at the time was...less than adequate. I might have become even sicker if my cousin had not come for me."

The conditions had been squalid, fetid, and nearly mortal. He had been in a tent with dozens of others, no beds, damned few blankets, and only one overworked nurse and doctor for all of them.

Andrew knew enough about wounds to know that he had been dying. And then Chatham had found him. His cousin rarely lost his temper, but that had been one of the few times.

Months afterward, when he had felt well enough—and grateful enough not to curse Sylvester for not allowing him to die—he'd had a ring made for his cousin, a thick Viking band that proclaimed his life now belonged to Sylvester.

Two years later, when he'd taken care of Sylvester after his cousin had been hit in the face by a piece of shrapnel that should have killed him, Sylvester had bought him an identical ring.

Sylvester had never removed his ring, not even during the years they'd been estranged.

Andrew absently rubbed his finger over the bare spot on his thumb. The indent from the ring was long gone. So was the ring, which he'd flung in Chatham's face eleven years ago when his cousin had refused to release Mariah.

"This looks like the worst one," she murmured, carefully caressing the wound, as if it might hurt.

"It is the worst scar, but..."

"But?" she prodded.

"I had my bell rung rather dreadfully once. I was passing too close to one of the big guns when it went off. It quite rattled my brain, and I was stone deaf for almost six weeks. I was terrified that I would never regain my hearing. *That* fear was worse than any saber cut."

"But it came back?"

"For the most part," not telling her about the headaches that had come back along with it. "But why am I talking about such a thing now?"

"Because I asked you."

"Surely we can make better use of our—*ah*!" He sucked in a breath as Stacia's palm left the scar and skimmed over one of his nipples.

She jerked her hand away at his gasp, but as he'd done last night, he caught her arm and held it in place. "That feels good." It felt bloody intoxicating and made him burn to throw her onto the bed and bury himself in her so deeply that it would be impossible to know where she began, and he ended.

Andrew was smart enough to keep those thoughts to himself. After all, she was already skittish, he didn't want to terrify her.

Her touch was tentative at first. Even so, he bit his tongue until he tasted blood, vibrating with need by the time she raised her other hand and caressed the neglected nipple.

A growl tore out of his chest when the soft, cool pads of her fingers lightly pinched the pebbled buds.

"Bloody hell," he ground out, reaching unerringly for her waist, holding her easily with one arm as he tore off the blindfold and stared down into eyes that were pools of black. He began to pluck the pins from her hair. "I want to feel it loose."

She did not stop him.

"It is as I thought," he murmured once it fell free.

"Wh-what?"

"It is so long it covers your bottom." He wrapped the thick rope around and around one hand and then tugged her head back. "Unless you tell me *no*, I'm going to carry you over to that bed and strip off all our clothing."

Her mouth opened and her eyes widened in shock.

But then she nodded. "No light," she added hastily.

Andrew growled. He would have liked to argue, but...

"Fine," he said. "But first I'm going to carry you to the bed, so I don't trip and fall in the darkness and embarrass myself."

***

Lord Shelton lowered Stacia onto the bed and met her gaze in the dim light while he stroked her hair. "If you let me leave the light on, I can do some wonderful things with this hair of yours."

Stacia blinked, momentarily distracted by his words. "Er, what?"

He grinned, his fingers quickly dividing the heavy mass in half. "Oh, so many uses. I could use it as a rope to tie your wrists to the bed and—"

"The lights, my lord," she yelped.

He laughed and then across the room so quickly that Stacia didn't even have time to consider his words before he snuffed the candles and plunged the room into near darkness, the only light the red glow of the fire.

A moment later the mattress dipped beside her and his voice rumbled close to her temple. "Change your mind?" He kissed the rim of her ear.

"No," she said, not needing so much as a second to reconsider.

"Good. May I undress you?"

She hissed in a breath and exhaled noisily. "Yes."

The mattress moved again as he left it.

Before she could ask where he was going, he took her ankle and set her foot on his thigh. Both his hands caressed up her calf slowly, his fingers warm as they untied her garter. He didn't immediately roll down her stocking. Instead, one hand massaged the indentation left by her garter while the other caressed the thin inner skin of her thigh.

"You need to breathe, sweetheart."

His amused voice broke her from her trance, making her aware of the burning in her lungs.

Shelton removed her other garter and stocking, gently lowered her leg, and then sat beside her. "We can stop any time you want—I won't think any less of you." His hand cupped her jaw and turned her face toward him. The faint light from the fireplace cast a warm glow over his profile but was not enough to see more than an outline.

He kissed her gently, a series of light, tender brushes of his lips until her body began to relax. "Tell me what you want, Stacia."

She closed her eyes and tilted her head back when he nudged her chin up and began kissing her bared throat.

"This," she whispered as his mouth moved lower, until his lips and nose brushed against the swells of her breasts. "I want this."

He dropped one last kiss before his hands closed around her waist. "Stand up for me, darling." He did most of the lifting, positioning her like a doll in front of him, his knees bracketing her legs as his hands moved on the buttons of her gown with an assurance that she didn't want to examine too closely.

"Arms up."

Stacia's body complied although her mind was frozen.

He raised the dress over her head and leaned to the side to lay it somewhere near the foot of the bed. Next, he reached for her laces and speedily loosened her stays before pushing them down to the floor. He found the tape securing her petticoat and tugged it loose. The garment joined her stays leaving her in nothing but her thin shift.

257

"On, or off?" he asked, his hands lightly caressing her hips.

Stacia took a deep breath, and before she could lose her courage, she reached for the hem and pulled the well-worn garment over her head.

His warm hands slid over her again, this time without anything between them. He groaned. "Silky," he muttered, and then pulled her closer, kissing the hard spot between her breasts as his hands moved up to cup a breast in each palm.

And then his mouth was on her nipple and Stacia thought her head would spin off her shoulders. Just when she could not bear a moment more, he moved to the other breast and commenced a second sensual assault.

"Yes," he hissed, which is when she noticed that she'd buried her hands in his hair and pulled him tighter. "Don't stop," he ordered when she began to release him.

He alternated teasing her nipples, suckling and licking.

And then he gave her a stinging nip.

She gasped, the sudden pain causing the muscles in her sex to clench almost as intensely as they'd done earlier, when she had lost control. Twice.

"Sorry, darling, did that hurt? Let me make it better." He kissed the offended nipple and then suckled it.

And then nipped her again, harder.

She cried out and he responded by lifting her by the waist and then setting her astride his thighs. "My lord, what are you—"

"Andrew," he chided, nipping and massaging and kissing until she was writhing and thrusting herself at him, all but begging for the mystifying pain that brought such pleasure in its wake.

He licked one of her breasts before lightly suckling the swollen, sensitive nipple. "Such pretty little tits you have been hiding beneath your gowns, Stacia."

She sucked in a breath at his crude words, shocked at the burst of arousal that slicked her thighs.

Thighs that were spread indecently wide.

She tried to pull her legs together, but he gave a low chuckle and, maintaining his torment of her breasts, lowered his hands to her legs and gently but firmly spread her wider. Her tendons stretched and the ache reminded her that this was a position no decent woman would ever find herself in.

Stacia could not even imagine the sight she must make.

That thought overcame the wicked pleasure she felt in her pose. When she increased her efforts to pull her legs together, he released her breast with a wet *pop* and his hands disappeared from her thighs, his powerful arms wrapping around her body as his night beard grazed the sensitive flesh of her breasts.

"Shall I stop?" he asked, his low voice sending vibrations through her chest that arrowed directly toward her widespread sex, compounding the distracting pulsing.

Stacia thought she might actually die if he stopped.

Thankfully, she didn't say that. Instead, she gave a slight shake of her head.

"You need to use your words, sweetheart."

She swallowed several times, shocked at how her mouth could be so flooded with moisture and yet her throat so dry. "I feel wicked." Those weren't the words she'd intended to say, but they were certainly the truth.

"*Mmm*," he murmured, shifting his embrace until the bulging muscles of his upper arms pushed her breasts together, trapping his face between them. "You certainly do," he said, and then sucked the side of her breast that rested against his mouth.

Stacia's head fell back, and she bit her lower lip to keep from moaning.

This time, when he resumed his attention to her nipples and his hands wended their way toward the apex of her thighs like twin serpents, she did nothing to stop him.

***

Andrew had known her sweet little body was lush—he'd felt her plump arse pressed against his cock that day he'd taken her up on Drake with him—but he'd had no clue as to the perfect pair of breasts she was hiding beneath her prim, high-necked gowns.

Andrew adored breasts—big ones, small ones, matching ones, ones that pointed in different directions—it didn't matter, he loved them all.

But he could not recall enjoying a pair of breasts quite as much as he was doing right now. They were soft and perfectly filled his palms, tipped by small sensitive nipples that he'd joyously sucked to nubbly points. He wanted to bite them even harder and had to restrain himself. Thus far he'd caused her only pleasurable pain and wanted to keep it that way.

He nuzzled and sucked and kissed while moving toward the treasure between her thighs with agonizing slowness, imagining how she looked in his mind's eye, the soft frills of her pussy spread, swollen, and slick, her body readying itself for his—

Andrew shook himself. Christ! Why had he ever agreed to this foolish darkness?

His fingers shook when he encountered the dampness at the crease where her thigh met her sex.

He squeezed his eyes shut as his body thrummed with need, until the evidence of his overheated desire slid down his aching shaft.

He only had to push down his drawers and move her an inch or two closer and he could sink into what would assuredly be a tight, virginal cunt.

He'd had only one virgin before—Mariah—the experience so long ago that he recalled very little other than her expressing discomfort but not wishing to stop.

And you didn't stop. You put a baby into her.

That thought was almost enough to kill his erection.

Tonight, he would give Stacia pleasure, not a child.

Andrew released the nipple he'd been tormenting and was amused by the small whimper of disappointment she made.

He proceeded slowly in case she wanted him to stop, stroking up and down her inner thighs, higher each time, until the sides of his fingers caressed the soft lips of her outer sex with each stroke.

Rather than stiffen or jerk away, she pulled his head down toward her chest.

Andrew smiled and went willingly, attaching himself to a nipple as eagerly as any nursing babe, sucking little gasps and moans out of her while he covered her mound with one hand, gently cupping her and letting her become accustomed to his touch on such a private part of her body.

When she pulled his head off one breast and guided his mouth to the other, he decided she was *accustomed* enough and slid his middle finger between her folds, groaning at the slick heat he encountered.

"So wet for me," he muttered against her taut nipple, and then suckled her even harder as he stroked the swollen petals of her sex, easily finding her engorged, eager nub and teasing her to the brink of climax, stopping just before she toppled over the edge.

She made an irritated little growling sound that was…adorable.

There was that word again.

Andrew chuckled against the erect nubbin in his mouth, unable to resist giving her a nip.

She hissed and jolted, her hips rolling in a way that gave her the friction she wanted.

Andrew kept just far enough away from her clitoris that she was forced to take what she needed from him. "Yes," he encouraged as she bucked her hips and ground herself against him.

When she began to shake and jerk with need, he took over and fingered an orgasm from her responsive body so quickly he was left starving for more.

It was all he could do to wait until the tremors had faded before lightly rubbing his slick thumb at the base of her throbbing sex organ—careful to avoid the too-sensitive peak—drawing out her climax and sending her crashing into a second orgasm.

She was still shaking when he lifted her off his knees and laid her out on the bed.

He stood beside the bed and stared down at her through a darkness so murky it was impossible to see anything but an outline of the lush little body laid out like an irresistible buffet.

Andrew pulled the tape on his drawers and pushed them down to the floor, his hard, leaking cock eagerly springing free.

And then, before she was fully back in possession of her faculties, he spread her legs and lowered himself between them.

***

Stacia jolted at the feeling of something unspeakably soft on her thigh.

She had barely been aware when Lord Shelton—*Andrew,* why avoid such an intimacy after what he had just done to her—had lifted her from her wanton pose over his hips and laid her out.

Now, feeling the heat of his broad shoulders pressing against her inner thighs, she pushed up onto her elbows.

"What are you doing?" she asked breathily.

"I am licking you," he said, his tone so normal he might have said, *I am going for a walk.*

"But…why?"

"Because you taste good."

"I *do?*"

"*Mmm-hmm,*" he murmured, the firm, wet swipe of his tongue running up the top of her thigh, through the crease and then continuing without pausing into her private curls.

She squawked. "My lord! What—"

"Andrew," he muttered, and then his tongue—slick, hot, and insistent— pushed between her nether lips.

Stacia was so shocked that she could only stare into the gloom—wide eyed and wide-mouthed—as he moaned and *burrowed* into her, shoulders shifting and nudging while he parted her with skilled, gentle fingers.

It was unbelievably, deliciously, wickedly *filthy.*

It was also the second-best thing she had ever felt—the first having occurred only moments before—and she was powerless to stop him.

His voice rumbled in the darkness. "If you had allowed me any light, I would make you watch what I do, Stacia."

Her jaw sagged lower.

"But it is like a coal mine in here. So, lie back, relax, and allow me to enjoy myself." He nudged her legs even wider and lowered his mouth until his tongue prodded at the opening to her body.

"Andrew!" she gasped.

"Hmm?" he murmured in between long, languorous licks, the tip of his tongue flicking into her with each stroke.

"This is—it's—"

His mouth lifted off her. "What is it?" he asked, his voice thick with desire, amusement, and curiosity.

Stacia didn't have the strength to tell him that what he was doing was wrong. How could she, when it felt so very right?

***

For one tense moment Andrew thought she might stop him. But when she flopped onto her back with a groan, he knew he'd won.

He grinned in triumph and threw himself into his pleasurable task, his plan for the next hour laid out in his mind as clearly as any military commander had ever conceived a battle strategy.

Her tiny little erection was too sensitive so soon after her orgasm, but there was plenty to keep him happily occupied until he could make her come again. He used his tongue to do what his cock was not allowed to and fucked her with leisurely precision, feasting on her sweet pussy until she forgot about how shocking all this was and her hips began to lift—her body's way of demanding more—only then did he move back to her clitoris, licking and gently sucking until she was grinding against him.

He opened his jaws wider and took as much of her cunt as he could fit into his mouth.

A moment later she cried out and lifted off the bed, body convulsing as she flooded his mouth with her bliss.

Andrew buried his tongue inside her to enjoy the echoes of her orgasm and then employed his thumb yet again to force one more climax from her body.

Only when her hands plucked at his hair to pull him off did he stop.

He prowled up her body and kissed her then, giving her a taste of herself. He could tell by her initial stiffening that she was scandalized, but then her tongue—shy and tentative—pushed into his mouth and he let her explore.

When she pulled away, he rolled them both onto their sides. "Do you like the taste of yourself?" he asked, amused when she gave another of her adorable gasps.

"Is that—" she broke off and Andrew could easily imagine her expression of mortification.

"Is it what, my adorable lover?" To his amusement, she pushed her face into the hollow of his throat—as if to hide even more than the darkness already afforded.

"Is that something everyone does?" she asked, her voice muffled against his skin.

He rolled onto his back and laughed. "If Kathryn ever lets us out of this attic you can ask the other guests that when we retire to the drawing room, it would be more entertaining than cards or spillikins."

She shoved him with a small hand. "You know what I mean—is it…normal marital activity?"

Andrew lazily stroked his cock—which was so wet with need that it felt as though he'd already ejaculated—and considered how to answer her question. "I am going to hazard a guess that it is not something Addiscombe—who strikes me as a selfish three pumps and done man if I ever saw one— ever did to his wife. If he had, perhaps she might not be such a miserable crone. What?" he asked when she made a mortified squeaking sound.

"That was an extremely vulgar assessment."

Andrew merely smiled.

"But I do like hearing the truth, for once," she added quietly.

He spread his legs just enough that he could reach his balls and tug on the tight skin of his sac.

"What are you doing down there?" she asked a moment later.

"Stroking myself."

She turned over so quickly the bed shook, he could see the vague outline of a dark shape looming over him, as if she had risen up on her knees. "You—that is, er..."

Andrew grinned lazily and waited to hear what she said next.

"Will you put the blindfold back on?"

Chapter 29

Lord Shelton laughed at Stacia's question but immediately said, "Of course."

He began to get up.

"I will fetch it," Stacia said. She slipped from the bed and felt around until she located her chemise and slipped it over her head before picking her way back to the seating area, searching until she found his neckcloth where he'd tossed it, and then hurried back to the bed and dropped the linen strip over the spot where his torso should be. "Here it is."

"Shall I—"

"Yes. You put it on." She threw the words over her shoulder while heading back to the fireplace. By the time she located the bowl of spills and lighted two of the candles a quick glance in the direction of the bed showed that he'd already tied on the blindfold and was lying on his back.

Her gaze jumped immediately to where his hand languidly moved up and down.

She sucked in a breath, her heart thundering at the shockingly erotic sight.

His head rolled toward her when she approached the bed, his lips wearing the lazy, sensual smile she'd seen in dozens of ballrooms as he'd charmed hundreds of women—a look that had filled her with so much yearning that she could still feel it.

"Well?" he asked.

"Well?" she echoed.

"Shall I pleasure myself, or do you want to do it for me?"

"*Me?*"

He laughed and she marveled as the muscles in his chest and belly flexed. He used the hand not stroking himself to caress his belly, his broad palm sliding slowly up the ridged muscle to the slab of his breast. He gave a low purr of pleasure when he dragged his fingers over an erect nipple.

Stacia watched all of it in open-mouthed wonder.

"Are you still there?" he asked, amusement coloring his husky voice.

She nodded dumbly, recalled he could not see her and said, "Yes. You are—" She bit her tongue before the word *magnificent* slipped out.

"Without shame?" he suggested, his grin sinful.

"Yes," she said, and then gave a choked laugh.

He laughed with her, his hands not ceasing their mesmerizing motions.

Stacia wanted to touch him so badly her clenched hands ached with the effort of not reaching for him. But she was, at the end of the day, a coward. "I w-will watch." She was so embarrassed she could hardly force the words out.

If he was disappointed, he gave no sign of it, merely nodding and leaving her to enjoy the sight of his body and what he was doing to it.

Stacia had never seen a penis in full, er, bloom. It was far larger than one was given to believe based on the classical statues. The rest of him, however, was as beautiful as any marble depiction of masculinity she had ever seen. Of course none of the statues had borne scars on their perfectly chiseled torsos, but that only made him more beautiful in her opinion.

"Do you like watching me, Stacia?"

"Yes." She pulled her rapt gaze from his stroking fist and moved slowly up the artistry of his abdomen and chest, fascinated to note that he was now sheened in perspiration. His face was a mask of raw sensuality, his full, shapely lips slack.

"You were magnificent earlier—giving your pleasure up to me so perfectly—it is a miracle I did not humiliate myself and spend all over myself." He smiled faintly. "And yet that is exactly what I am about to do in any case." His breathing grew rougher and his strokes quickened. "Touch me while I come for you, Stacia."

Her hand was moving before the request had left his mouth. She wished she were close enough to claim his lips, but the way he was shaking told her he was about to experience what she had enjoyed—*four* times today—and so she slid a hand up his thigh, not close enough to interrupt his motions, but close enough to lightly brush the shadowed bulge between his splayed thighs.

It was happening too quickly—it would all be over too fast.

"Not yet." Stacia spoke the words without realizing it.

His hand instantly stopped. "No?" he asked in a strained voice.

She swallowed. "No."

Rather than look annoyed—which was how she had felt when he had teased her earlier—he smiled. "You are a cruel mistress," he murmured. "Would you like me to beg?"

Her jaw dropped, her breathing so rough she could hear it. "Yes."

His nostrils flared. "Please let me stroke myself, Stacia."

Stacia swore the room rocked around her at his plea. Yet again she gaped like a landed fish before collecting scrambled wits.

"You may. But s-slowly."

The muscles in his abdomen and chest tensed as he stroked himself all the way from crown to root, his hips lifting off the bed as he thrust, his erection appearing obscenely huge.

"Again," she commanded.

He repeated his caress, but only as much as she allowed him.

Power and desire warred inside her, the eroticism of having such a body at her control...intoxicating.

Stacia tormented him as long as she could bear it—until they were both tense with need—and then said, "M-make yourself—" her voice broke. "Do it," she ordered gruffly, her tongue refusing to form the naughty words he'd used earlier.

He did not hesitate to comply, his hips pumping savagely, his slick length slamming into his fist. It took scarcely a half dozen thrusts before his muscles grew taut beneath his sheened skin. He reached out blindly with his free hand and when Stacia grasped it his hips rose off the bed, and she watched in wonder as his release came. Jet after jet after jet, crisscrossing as far as his chest, his grip on her hand crushing as each wave rolled through his big body.

His back arched until every striation and sinew must be visible. And then, suddenly, he sagged into a boneless heap, still gasping for breath as he reached up and flicked the blindfold from his head, glanced down at himself, and then used the expensive linen to wipe up his chest and belly.

He tossed the cloth aside when he was finished and offered her a heavy-eyed smile, looking as contented as a sleek cat lounging in a patch of warm sunshine. "*Mmm*, I liked having you watch me."

Her face scalded under his sated gaze.

"Now I have embarrassed you," he said as she disentangled their laced fingers.

"No, I just need—"

He caught her wrist when she would have slid off the bed. "Come and lie with me—it is late, and I am no danger to your virtue in this condition." He grinned sleepily. "Not for some time, at least."

"But...the candles?"

"Let them burn." He released her long enough to pull the blankets from beneath their bodies and cover them. And then he wrapped an arm around her waist and pulled her to him, once again holding her with his front to her back. "There.

Just like that." He yawned. "I should have asked if you needed anything—food? Something to drink?"

"No," she said faintly, her belly churning at the thought of trying to choke anything down at this point.

"*Mmmm*," he rumbled, pulling her tighter and molding his body to hers. "Are you traumatized?"

She gave a startled laugh. "What?"

"Have you ever seen a naked, aroused man?"

"When would I have had a chance to see such a thing?" she demanded in a high, unnatural voice.

Predictably, he chuckled. "You mean you've never been locked into a priest hole with a strange man at any of the house parties you've attended? I thought it was all the rage."

"I once saw the bare backside of my friend's brother when I was visiting her during the summer," she blurted.

"Oh?" he said, sounding slightly more awake. "And how was that experience?"

She snorted. "How do you think it was? I screamed and ran."

His big body shook with mirth as he kissed her temple, ear, and neck. "Poor Stacia. How old were you?"

"Six-and-ten. He was younger and we were fortunate that he and his mates were more mortified than we were." She paused and then couldn't help asking, "When did you first see a woman without clothing?"

He made a thoughtful humming sound. "I must have been fourteen. It was certainly before I turned fifteen because that is when the old duke finally gave in to my nagging and bought me a commission."

"That is so young!"

He shrugged.

"What happened?" she asked.

"What happened?" he repeated blankly.

"Yes. Where was she when you saw her?"

"Beneath me in bed."

Stacia gasped and then twisted in his arms.

"What are you doing? I was comfortable," he complained petulantly when she turned until she could see his face, their bodies no longer touching.

"You were with a woman when you were only *fourteen*?"

"Yes."

"Who—who was it?"

He lifted one eyebrow at her.

"I just meant, was it—it wasn't a servant, was it?"

An expression of distaste flickered across his face. "What do you take me for? The sort of cad who foists himself on powerless women?"

"No. Of course not," she said. "I am sorry if I implied that. It is just that we once engaged a maid who'd been molested by her employer—a man I saw dozens of times during my London Season. Nobody would hire her because he had so blackened her name. My father believed her rather than her employer. He said some aristocratic men thought that everyone who lived in their home belonged to them— like their dogs and horses."

"Your father was right. But my uncle would have beaten his sons—or me—if we'd ever been inclined to such behavior."

"So…then who was the woman?"

He grinned at her. "So curious! Why is that?"

"I told you about my first time," she retorted, even though she knew it was hardly the same.

But it seemed her argument convinced him, because he said, "It was the old duke's mistress."

Her jaw dropped. "But—but—"

"You sound like hen. *Bock! Bock!*"

She ignored his teasing, so many questions roiling inside her head it was hard to know what to ask first. "How old was she? And why would she do such a thing?"

"I have no idea how old she was. As to the why? I can only assume the duke had irked her in some way." He smirked. "Or she simply could not resist my male beauty."

"You were a child!"

"I was an ignorant, horny young lad." He grinned. "And when I returned to school, I was a very well-respected, not-quite-so-ignorant, swaggering lothario."

"Shame on you! I thought a gentleman did not share such details."

"I was a callow youth. Besides, it wasn't me who let it slip but Sylvester."

"You must have told him."

"Er, not exactly."

"What do you mean?"

"I mean he was there, too."

Stacia stared in openmouthed shock—a state this man reduced her to far too frequently.

For the first time ever, Lord Shelton looked embarrassed. "I probably should not have shared that. I beg your par—"

"Is that something people do often?"

"Er—"

Stacia shoved his chest, not that he budged so much as an inch. "Oh, just answer my question! Nobody ever tells women this sort of thing and I am four-and-twenty."

"Four-and-twenty?" he repeated, his eyebrows raised.

"What?" she demanded.

"Nothing."

Stacia wanted to ask him what that look was for, but she wanted an answer to her previous question more. "If you can experience such a thing at fourteen, certainly I am old enough to simply hear about it?"

"Well," he said drawing the word out while regarding her with a wary look. "Young men are—how should I put this?" He seemed to be asking the question of himself. "They do not last long."

Stacia frowned, trying to put his meaning together and save herself from appearing more of an ignorant dunce than she was.

"They ejaculate quickly." He paused. "Er, do you know what ejac—"

"Of course, I know what that means!" Although only because of the context.

"A young man goes off far too quickly to ensure his partner's pleasure. *Two* young men, however, might manage to get the job, er, done."

Comprehension, along with—at least—the fiftieth blush of the last few days, came to her.

It would be extremely difficult to look the Duke of Chatham in the eye the next time she saw him.

Stacia frowned as a thought came to her. "Do two women ever lie with one man?"

His eyes widened slightly. "Er—"

"Never mind," she hastily said, not wanting to allow that picture purchase in her mind.

"It does seem rather unjust that young ladies get no education on such matters," he said after a moment, absently reaching out and smoothing a lock of hair behind her ear. His gaze sharpened on her and his hand slid around her waist and settled on her lower back. "I will answer any questions you have about sexual matters—just ask."

"I have none," she lied.

He smiled. "That offer will remain open. Now, come here," he said, gently but inexorably pulling her closer. "Rest your head on my arm," he said when it was clear she didn't know quite what to do with herself. "And slide your upper leg between my thighs. Go on," he urged when she gawked—yet another expression she'd worn more often than she liked.

She did as he bade her and he lowered his leg over hers, fitting them together yet again, but more like forks than spoons. Stacia shifted slightly and finally put her upper arm around his body.

"*Mmmm.* Good. Comfortable?" he asked.

"Your arm hardly makes a soft pillow."

He chuckled and shifted until her head rested on his shoulder. "Better?"

She burrowed in a bit more before giving a satisfied grunt.

"Good night, Stacia."

"Good night…Andrew."

Stacia was amazed at how quickly he fell asleep, his breathing deep and even within what felt like seconds. How could he possibly sleep after what had just happened?

Because it is nothing special to him. Not like it was for you.

The thought was all the more painful because she knew it was true. How many lovers had he had? How many times had he done these things with another woman?

This is not love, Stacia.

She didn't think it was. At least not on his side. It was just lust.

Stacia squeezed her eyes shut, as if that would stimulate thought. No, *lust* didn't sound right, either.

Whatever it is, it is not enough to sustain a marriage.

She stared up at the slanted ceiling, her vision suddenly hot and blurry. Her mind was like a tangle of embroidery silks. She could not think clearly while she was so intimately…enmeshed with his body. She would wait until he was dozing deeply and then carefully disengage herself from him.

Yes. That is what she would do. And then she would be able to think.

Stacia wiped her eyes and then closed them and commenced to wait.

Within seconds, she surrendered to sleep.

Chapter 30

Earlier that same evening, two floors below...
Kathryn

Katie found herself seated between the Earl of Crewe and the Duke of Chatham at dinner that night. Although she had lived in the duke's house for months, she could not claim to know him. Nor was she very comfortable in his presence.

Especially not since she'd locked his cousin in the priest hole.

Lord Crewe, who was also scarred, handsome, and extremely intimidating, caused the same fluttering in her belly that all her sisters' husbands seemed to do. Not because of anything inappropriate they said or did, but because Katie now knew what these men did with her sisters in their respective bedchambers.

Had what her mother shouted at her several mornings earlier really been true? Was sexual intercourse all these men had wanted from any of them? Were they only married because her sisters had denied them pre-marital favors? Could that really be the only difference between Katie and—

"You are not eating your dessert, Lady Kathryn. Are you not hungry?"

She looked up at the sound of the Duke of Chatham's quiet voice, his cool gaze causing the same disorganization of thoughts it usually did. "Er, no. I think I ate too many cakes earlier when we were decorating."

Katie couldn't help noticing that his own baked custard had barely been touched. "You d-didn't care for yours?"

He ignored her question. "Her Grace went to check on Piquet just before dinner."

Katie's mind spun at the sudden change in subject. "Er, is he injured?" Piquet was the name her sister had given to the massive dun gelding the duke had given her several months earlier. The animal was, in Katie's opinion, brutishly ugly and ill-tempered—he'd snapped at Katie on more than one occasion—but Hy loved the beast.

Again, the duke ignored her question. "Can you guess what the duchess saw in the stables?"

"Um, horses?" Katie gave him a cheeky grin, but it died a quick death at the frosty look in his eyes.

Footmen appeared behind their chairs and the duke nodded, as did Katie.

Chatham continued to stare at her through narrowed eyes as the servants collected their mostly untouched desserts. "Your sister and I wish to speak to you after dinner."

She swallowed. "Er—"

Lord Crewe's voice came from her other side, sparing her from the duke's icy gaze. "Aurelia tells me that you are an exceptional chess player, Lady Kathryn."

Katie latched onto Lord Crewe's question like the lifeline it was, wrenching her gaze away from Chatham and turning to her newest brother-in-law.

"I have been told I am," she said with a forced smile. "Do you like to play?"

"I do. Perhaps you will honor me with a game?"

She forced a bright smile. "Of course."

He leaned closer, the action bringing his scarred but handsome face and single, magnificent eye close enough for her to see the shards of blue that comprised his iris. He dropped his voice and said, "I never again want to play cards against Chatham and Her Grace. The last time I was mauled that badly I lost an eye."

His words startled a laugh out of her. "Yes, they are…savagely skilled."

He grinned, suddenly looking boyish. "I could not have worded it better myself."

Phoebe, seated at the foot of the table, stood. "Ladies, shall we retire to the drawing room? I believe there is still a great deal of decorating left to do."

Katie breathed a sigh of relief at the prospect of escaping Chatham's brooding presence and began to stand when Lord Needham's voice cut across the murmur of voices.

"We gentlemen will forgo our nightly ritual of port and cigars to assist you, my dear."

So much for Katie's chances of escape.

Beside her, Chatham opened his mouth.

Katie hastily turned to Lord Crewe, who was in the middle of saying something to Mrs. Leeland and grabbed his arm. "Let us have a game right now! Before we are dragooned into decorating, my lord."

Crewe blinked at her likely demented expression and said, "Of course." He excused himself to Mrs. Leeland before allowing Katie to drag him off.

She chattered brainlessly all the way to the drawing room and while she set up the board, her gaze flickering to where Hy and Chatham stood, both regarding her in a way that promised no quarter.

An hour later—in the middle of her third game—her sister had obviously waited long enough.

Hy leaned over and hissed in her ear, "I want a word with you once you are finished with this game, Kathryn."

Kathryn.

Katie swallowed at the sound of her full name. She wanted to ignore Hy, but something about becoming a duchess had transformed her erstwhile unassuming sibling into somebody who was slightly…terrifying.

"As soon as I am finished."

Hy jerked a nod and strode away.

As much as she would have liked to draw the game out—preferably until after Christmas—she had already taken both of Crewe's bishops, knights, and one rook. She'd had at least three opportunities to take his queen, but that would have made an already boring game unbearable.

Crewe heaved a heavy sigh—obviously realizing the futility of his current position—and set his king on its side. His single eye slid up to meet hers and he wore a rueful smile. He was virile, charming, and handsome and it was easy to see why Aurelia was so infatuated with him. Regardless of his woeful lack of chess acumen.

"Aurelia beats me quite soundly, but never as badly as this," the earl said.

Katie suspected her sister—no mean player herself—probably had mercy on her attractive spouse.

"Will you play me next?" Doddy asked the earl. Her little brother had been hovering around the famous naturalist almost as much as he'd been dogging Lord Shaftsbury, who'd evidently been a famous Corinthian prior to losing his vision.

Crewe raised a brow at Katie. "If your sister is finished with me?"

"I will relinquish the chair, my lord."

He looked relieved.

She stood and saw Hy waiting for her only a few feet away, her husband right beside her. It was a sign of their displeasure that both of them had given up thrashing all comers at cards in order to buttonhole Kathryn.

"The Jewel Room," Hy murmured.

Hy and the duke walked on either side of her—as if fearing Katie would try to run—on the short distance to the cozy sitting room that was, inexplicably, called *the Jewel Room.*

275

"I have always wondered why this is called the Jewel Room," Katie said when Chatham had shut the door. "Do you know why, Hy?"

Hy ignored her conversational ploy. "What have you done with Shelton and Miss Martin?"

Katie swallowed as she looked up several inches into Hy's crystalline green eyes. They never looked exactly *warm,* but she could not recall a time when they'd appeared so very frosty.

She briefly considered pretending ignorance, but a quick glance at the duke convinced her otherwise.

"They are both safe and sound."

Hy's normally unreadable face shifted into an expression of profound shock, and she seemed at a loss for words.

Katie hurried on, "I was going to let them out tomorrow morning—before anyone was up and about. That way nobody would be the wiser that Miss Martin hadn't really been ill and Shelton hadn't really gone to see a horse."

Hy's jaw had sagged as she listened to Katie's babbling. "When Chatham told me what he thought, I did not believe him." She took a step closer to Katie, anger rolling off her long, thin frame. "What is *wrong* with you?"

Katie quailed at the disgust in her sister's gaze.

The duke set his hand on his wife's arm. "Hyacinth," he murmured, drawing Hy's rigid body against his.

"I did it for *them,*" Katie protested, grimacing as she noticed that her reasoning—when spoken aloud—sounded less than convincing. "For their own good," she added lamely.

"You destroyed both their reputations for their own good?" the duke repeated in a tone of cool disgust that was even more cutting than her sister's anger.

Katie flung up her hands. "Were you not listening? I told you that nobody will ever—"

"Even if what you say is true—and I am not yet willing to believe that—*they* will know, Katie," her sister said. "Can you imagine how Miss Martin will have worried these past few days? And Shelton has only just begun to be somebody I might want to claim as family."

The duke cut his wife a startled look at her admission, but Hy wasn't finished. "What do you think this will do to him? To both of them?"

"They both like each other—a great deal. This is the only way either of them would have acted on their attraction. I merely gave them a—a push."

276

Her sister and the duke looked at her as if she'd suddenly sprouted a second head.

Desperate for understanding, she turned to the duke. "Do you know why Shelton ran off with Miss Creighton and then abandoned her?"

The duke's pale cheeks darkened with displeasure. "That is hardly—"

"Because Sarah Creighton *begged* him to."

Was it satisfying to see their thunderstruck expressions? Yes, it was. And yet somehow, Katie suspected their surprise would not help when it came to digging herself out of the hole she'd made.

A few minutes later, after she had related the details surrounding Sarah's confession, her assessment was borne out.

The duke had briefly looked delighted to hear about Shelton's innocence, but the moment did not last. Instead, he now fixed her with a look of such cool disappointment that Katie wanted to crawl under the settee. "As relieved as I am to hear my cousin is not guilty of that particular crime, it was not your place to make decisions for them. Regardless of whether their disappearance goes unnoticed or not, you might very well have taken away their choices when it comes to marriage."

When he put it like that...

"Er..." Katie could not think of a word in her defense.

"Now. Where are they?" the duke demanded.

Chapter 31

Andrew was having a lovely dream. It was nothing specific, just a sense of comfort and rightness. He also felt strangely…light, as if a pallet of bricks had been lifted off his chest.

Odd, that. Because not until that moment had he even noticed how heavy his heart had felt.

He opened his eyes and was temporarily disoriented. First, by the strange bed and slanted roof he could see above him.

And then by the small body that so tightly knitted to his.

Stacia.

He smiled just thinking the name and glanced down at the head burrowed into his chest. Her breathing was that of a person in deep sleep.

And she felt utterly delicious.

Unfortunately, he needed to use the chamber pot.

He also needed to begin working on the attic door, even though he hated the thought of damaging it. But…needs must.

Andrew kissed her head and carefully extricated himself from her tight embrace. He covered her with the blanket, turned toward the screen, and then almost leapt out of his skin when he saw a man in the wingchair he had begun to think of as his.

Chatham.

After a quick glance at the door—which was open—he searched for his drawers in the tangle of clothing on the floor, slipped into them, and went behind the screen to take care of business before washing his hands and face in cold water and facing his cousin.

The duke looked up at him without speaking, his expression weary in the light of the guttering candle.

Andrew dressed without speaking, donning everything except his cravat and boots. He shoved the former in his pocket and picked up the latter before walking quietly toward the door.

Rather than stand in the suffocating stairwell, he descended to the corridor below. The instant he stepped outside the linen closet he saw he was not alone. The duchess waited, arms crossed over her chest, her expression as unreadable as ever. When she pushed off the wall and strode toward the secret stairwell he shook his head.

"She is sleeping." He pulled out his watch. It was far earlier than he thought—barely two o'clock. "I will wake her shortly."

The duchess looked as if she wanted to argue, but gave an abrupt nod as the duke joined her.

Andrew bent to pull on his boot and asked his cousin, "How did you find us?"

"Kathryn told us."

Andrew's eyebrows shot up.

"Not voluntarily," the duke added.

"I assume the house has been in an uproar searching for us? Or did they assume we headed for the border?"

"Neither. Nobody even knew you were missing."

Andrew paused in the act of pulling on his second boot. "But...*how?*"

"Kathryn is devious, I must give her that." Sylvester chuckled, received a look of disbelief from his wife, and then quickly smothered his amusement and said, "She made it seem that you'd gone to look at a horse somewhere and that Miss Martin was bedridden with a terrible cold."

"And nobody noticed or bothered to check on her?" His gaze slid to the duchess. "Not even her employer?"

"My mother is a hypochondriac and feared catching whatever had forced Miss Martin to take to her bed."

"So... nobody knows but you two?"

They both nodded.

Andrew gave a sharp bark of laughter. "Now there is an outcome I never anticipated."

Chatham frowned at him and Andrew could read the question in his cousin's eyes as clearly as if Sylvester had shouted it at him.

"It is not what you think," he said quietly, holding his cousin's gaze.

The duke's jaw worked—as if he wanted to ask something. After a moment, he gave an abrupt nod. "I hope so," was all he said.

"She will not marry me," Andrew said. "And I will not force her to."

Chatham inhaled until Andrew thought his chest might explode and then nodded grimly. "She is of age—four-and-twenty, Kathryn said"—Andrew nodded—"then the choice is her own." He glanced at his wife who nodded without hesitation.

279

"The choice is hers," she repeated firmly. "What of her family?"

"She has a maternal aunt who appears to have disowned her and, then there is a cousin who inherited her father's title and property." Andrew scowled as he thought about the man who'd essentially thrown Stacia out on her arse. "The reason she works is because of him. There is nobody else."

After a moment the duchess said, "Everyone except us is in bed. If you go and wake her, I will escort her back to her chambers. It will raise far fewer questions than if she is seen with either of you at this hour."

Andrew knew that was true, and yet it was hard to make himself agree. "Very well. Give me a quarter of an hour?"

The duke and duchess nodded.

And then Andrew turned and made the short journey back up the stairs.

***

"Sweetheart?"

Stacia smiled. She loved it when Andrew called her that. She snuggled deeper under the delightfully warm blankets, reaching for the big warm body she'd just been pressed against.

And frowned when she encountered nothing but bedding. "Andrew?" she murmured, unwilling to wake from her happy dream.

Gentle fingers carded her hair off her forehead and soft lips pressed far too briefly against hers. "Stacia, love. You need to wake up."

"Just a little longer," she said, grabbing his hand and tugging him closer.

His low chuckle warmed her. "I would love to crawl in beside you, but the door is open, and we must make haste to return you to your chambers while we have the opportunity."

Stacia's eyes flew open, and she scrambled upright, her head swiveling toward the attic door, which was indeed open. "You opened it!"

"Not exactly." Andrew stood and the mattress shifted dramatically with the loss of his weight.

Stacia squinted up at him. "You are dressed. How long have—"

"Not long." He gestured to the foot of the bed. "Your clothing is all there—a bit wrinkled, I'm afraid, but that cannot be helped. I found several hairpins and put them near the wash basin along with the brush and comb from the trunk. There is already hot water waiting for you in the basin. We have enough time for a quick cup of tea before we go."

Stacia swallowed at his crisp tone and hurried to comply, realizing that Andrew must have lighted some candles while she'd slept because she had no trouble making her way to the screened area.

Her mind whirled while she washed her face, brushed and re-plaited her hair, and then dressed in everything except her boots, which must still be by the settee, where she'd shucked them so she could prowl around Andrew's body quietly.

Stacia shoved the memory aside as she stepped outside the screen.

Andrew was already seated and setting out cups and saucers. He smiled up at her when she took a seat on the settee.

"Good news," he said.

"Oh?" she asked, bending over to slip on her boots and button them.

"Our captor managed to keep our disappearance secret."

Stacia's eyes widened. "*What*? How?"

He handed her a cup and saucer. "Drink your tea while I tell you what happened.

Stacia listened in stunned silence as Andrew explained her *illness* and his sudden trip to…somewhere.

"Nobody else guessed?" she asked.

He took a sip of tea. "Only Sylvester and the duchess and that's because they saw Drake in his stall."

"So that means the servants know."

"Only the stable lads—which is who Kathryn bribed to move Drake from his stall whenever Higgins did his inspection. Oh, and the maid, Dora."

Stacia gave him a mocking look.

"What?" he asked.

"I keep forgetting that most people of our class have no idea what goes on below stairs," she said dryly.

"Are you saying the entire staff knows?"

"I am guessing all but the uppermost servants. If Davis or Mrs. Nutter had known they would have told their employer."

He nodded slowly and pursed his lips. "I see." He cocked his head at her. "I don't suppose you would change your mind about marrying me?"

"My reputation is intact. There is no reason to marry." She set down her cup and saucer with a clatter.

"Your reputation is not the only reason I asked, Stacia."

She stared at him, trying to see beyond his beautiful eyes and charming smile to the man inside the body. But he was as polished and charming as ever.

He was lying—being a gentleman.

Stacia shook her head. "I cannot."

His eyebrows rose. "I suppose that is better than *I don't want to.*"

Stacia snorted. "Is there a young woman in England who doesn't *want* to marry you?"

"You, apparently."

She sighed. "You don't want this, my lord. And I do not want a husband who has been forced by circumstance—or conscience," she hurriedly added when he opened his mouth to argue.

He stared at his half-full teacup for a moment and then looked up, no longer smiling. "I have enjoyed my time with you more than any woman in over a decade. When I asked you to marry me, it was for *me*." He smiled, and it was…wistful. "You won't believe me because I don't recall meeting you before—not just once, but evidently dozens of times—and because, in your heart, you cannot forget how I described you that night in the conservatory."

Stacia wanted to deny it, but it was *part* of the reason she could not marry him, if not the most important part, which was far too humiliating for her to lay out for him.

"Is there anything I can do to convince you to change your mind?"

Tell me you love me.

"Do you hesitate because you have given your heart to another man?"

Stacia's head whipped up at his question.

"If that is the case, I will not bother you further," he said when she didn't immediately answer.

Here is your chance to put an end to this. Once and for all.

"I do not love another man," she said.

Was that relief on his face?

"Then I reiterate—is there anything I can do to change your mind?"

She tried to force out the word *no*, but it wouldn't come. It was too final—too painful—no matter how badly she needed to say it.

Coward that she was, she said, "Come find me in a year. If you still feel the same way, I will say *yes*."

"A year," he repeated.

She nodded.

"Are you saying that because you think I won't remember who you are in a year?"

Something about his glittering gaze was dangerous.

"No. I believe you will remember me this time." And she meant it. "I am saying you will feel differently once you have had time to consider the foolishness of your offer." And she meant that, too.

His jaw flexed, but he nodded, soundlessly set down his own cup and saucer, and stood. "We should not keep the duke and duchess waiting any longer."

Chapter 32

"—the ridiculousness of such an affair!"

Stacia was vaguely aware the countess had stopped speaking, but she wasn't quick enough to meet her employer's gaze. She opened her mouth, but the other woman was already glaring at her.

"Are your thoughts so important that you cannot listen to me, Martin?"

"I'm sorry, my lady. I just had a slight feeling of biliousness." It wasn't a complete lie.

The countess looked horrified and recoiled back against the fluffy cushions stacked behind her. "You assured Ackers you were over your putrid fever."

"I am, my lady. I'm just a bit…worn." Not a lie, either. "I am fine."

Lady Addiscombe lifted the cologne-soaked lace handkerchief to her nose and inhaled deeply, as if that would be enough to repel an influenza. "I wish to talk to you on the subject of Lord Bellamy and Needham's bastard."

Stacia flinched at the unkind word. "Yes, my lady?"

"You insist that Viscount Bellamy does not encourage the chit?"

"Nothing I've seen him do seems encouraging. Indeed," she lied boldly, "he barely pays her any attention and prefers to spend his time with his school friends."

Amazingly, Lady Addiscombe's lips curved into something that almost resembled a smile. "I am pleased with the connections my son has made. Jevington is the Duke of Linton's heir."

Stacia wasn't sure what to say about that. Luckily, the countess didn't require an answer.

Instead, she continued on her rant about Needham's servant ball, a function she had forbidden Stacia, Ackers, her footman Lionel, and coachman, George, from attending.

"I cannot believe Needham is requiring not only his wife, but my other daughters and their husbands, to wait on their own servants!"

Stacia entertained herself with the thought of Andrew waiting on Ackers or Lionel.

Or you.

Stacia smiled. *Or me.* Indeed, she would have greatly enjoyed—

"—will be retiring to my room and ringing for a tray. Martin? *Martin!*"

"I'm sorry, my lady." Stacia met her employer's gaze and took a wild guess. "I can bring your dinner, my lady. I'm sure all the other servants will be—"

"Of course you will bring my dinner! Did you not just hear what I said? I will not countenance my servants engaging in such idiocy."

"No, my lady."

And so it went.

An hour and a half later—after Stacia had unpicked a section of Lady Addiscombe's cross stitch that the countess had been especially displeased with and read the Society section of three newspapers paid for by Viscount Needham—"*It is the least he can do to better himself*"—and then wrapped the gifts Lady Addiscombe had bought for her six children, the countess sent her to the kitchen for yet another of the infernal possets that only Mrs. Nutter could make.

The scene in the kitchen was one of joyous chaos as servants hurried to finish chores before being dismissed from their labors to prepare for tonight's ball.

Even the staid butler, Davis, had let some of his reserve slip and was kissing Cook beneath a kissing bough somebody had hung directly over the entrance to the kitchen.

Dora, Lady Kathryn's accomplice, sidled up to Stacia. It was the first Stacia had seen the maid since the Duchess of Chatham had escorted her to her chambers two nights earlier.

"Are you comin' to the ball, Miss?" Dora asked, exhibiting no evidence of shame at having assisted Lady Kathryn.

"Unfortunately, not."

"Oh, Miss! Whyever not?" Before Stacia could contrive an answer Dora leaned close and whispered loudly, "Lady Kathryn will keep the countess occupied, Miss. You and Ackers deserve a bit o' fun. As for Lionel?" She made an appreciative growling sound. "Well, it would be a crime not to allow such a handsome man to dance."

Stacia couldn't help laughing. "I'm afraid you will have to do without the delectable Lionel."

"Surely you can all slip away for an hour?"

"I shall see," she said, knowing it would never happen. Even if Lady Kathryn managed to divert her employer's attention for long enough—doubtful, as the countess had told Ackers to deny her youngest daughter access to her chambers— Stacia's only ballgown, a grim gray thing suitable for a companion, was hardly the sort of *drab* garment she wanted to be seen in. It was fine for Bath functions, but she already knew she would look pitiful in any other company, even a ball for servants.

You danced well enough with his lordship in only a plain brown day dress...

Stacia wanted to slap the voice in her head, which had done nothing but chide and nag her since she'd left the priest hole. And before, too, now that she thought about it.

Shut up, she snapped viciously in her mind.

"Miss Martin?"

She looked at Dora. "Hmm?"

"If you don't have a gown there are ballgowns aplenty in the suite adjacent to Mrs. Ellen Kettering's rooms."

"Mrs. Kettering?" Stacia asked.

"Lord Needham's former mistress," Dora whispered.

"Ah, yes." Stacia had forgotten the woman's name, if not the shocking fact of her presence at Wych House. She frowned. "Why are there ballgowns?"

"Some are Mrs. Kettering's. She was a debutant in Edinburgh. Or mayhap Leeds." Dora shrugged, as if to say that all obscure northern cities were much of a muchness. "Wherever it was, she has dozens of fine gowns—a bit old-fashioned, but I found a lovely blue silk with a silver spangled over gown. *And* she says that we may keep them!" Dora did a quick dance step and flourish, as if imagining the dash she would cut.

"But that's not all," Dora went on. "Lady Needham found trunks in the attics—gowns from long ago—that we are all welcome to wear, although not keep as her ladyship says they are—er, I don't recall the words she used."

"Historical importance?"

Dora nodded. "Aye, something like that." She raised her hand to cover her mouth and shield her next words. "Oh, Miss! You should see the gown Cook found to wear!" Dora was too overcome with mirth to describe Mrs. Barton's dress.

"Perhaps I will go and look at the gowns later," she said again. Time was wasting and Lady Addiscombe would be displeased. "But right now I need to speak to Mrs. Nutter about a posset. Do you know where I might find her?"

Before Dora could answer her a footman—a towering man with sleepy blue eyes and shoulders so broad he could scarcely fit though the kitchen door—grabbed Dora by the waist and led her into a very boisterous facsimile of a waltz.

It took Stacia ten minutes to locate Mrs. Nutter and another fifteen before she was carrying the tightly corked jar of poultice and hurrying toward her mistress's chambers. She was imagining the raking she would get when an arm shot out from a recessed doorway and snagged her wrist.

She gave a squawk of surprise.

"*Here* you are," Andrew said, pulling her close. "I have been hunting for you for days and days!" he said, his tone accusatory.

"It has scarcely been two days," she couldn't help saying.

"It felt like weeks. Months."

Stacia couldn't help laughing. "The duchess thought it might be best if I spent the first day in my room—overcoming the last of my cold."

He grunted. "I fail to see the reason for that."

"I could scarcely go from death's door to playing spillikins in the drawing room."

He still did not look convinced, but dropped the matter, instead saying, "You were not at breakfast this morning."

"I always have a tray in my room."

He frowned. "Why?"

"Why does it matter?"

His frown deepened. She thought he might argue, but he seemed to think better of it. "I *know* you like early morning walks. Where were you this morning? Lord Bellamy, Lord So-and-So, and Sir Such-and-Such attacked me with snowballs on my morning ride."

She laughed. "I take it you mean Lords Hornsby and Jevington."

He gave a dismissive flick of the hand not still holding her. "Why have you stopped taking your morning walk, Stacia? Is it because of the weather? Or because of me?"

"It is because I have been *working*," she retorted, only partly telling the truth, which was that she did *not* want to encounter him while walking.

"*Hmmph.* I wanted to make sure you saved all your waltzes for me tonight." He gave her a teasingly brooding look. "I am quite looking forward to being your slave, Stacia. I will endeavor to behave and please you as I already know you can be a cruel mistress."

Stacia's face heated at his unsubtle reminder of that night.

He leaned forward and hissed in her ear, "Will you have me flogged and put in the stocks for the slightest infraction?"

She pursed her lips at his foolishness. "This is not ancient Rome, or even medieval Briton. Your person is quite safe from whips and chains."

He made a pouting moue. "Pity."

She forced herself to quit smiling—to quit hoping. "You will have to find somebody else to serve as I won't be there."

His eyebrows descended. "What?"

"Lady Addiscombe does not approve."

His scowl deepened. "Why the devil not? Needham isn't the only one to revive the old traditions. In the north there is even a King of Misrule who is permitted to order his master to do the most shocking things. Surely your taskmistress is planning to go and do her part? This is her husband's ancestral home, for all that she is a guest in it now. It is all in good fun."

"Exactly what has given you the impression that Lady Addiscombe is interested in *any* fun, good or otherwise?"

"Good God. You are serious!"

"Very."

He set his hands on her shoulders and pulled her closer. "You needn't keep working for her, Stacia. The woman is appalling—even her own children don't want to be around her. Hyacinth would be delighted to take you on as a companion."

"I know," Stacia said. "She mentioned it to me already."

"She looks intimidating but is actually quite kind. And if you don't want to work for her, I am sure she would help you find a position elsewhere. Unless you are willing to reconsider—"

"No." Stacia twitched her shoulders until he released her. She hated the injured look on his face, but she simply could not bear him touching her—or even standing near her—without wanting to fling herself into his arms and never let go. She forced a smile. "I appreciate your concern, but—"

"But you want me to mind my own affairs."

"Please."

He heaved a sigh and then stepped closer, closing the gap between them once again, regarding her with a warm look that made it hard to breathe. "Fine. You will not be there tonight. But surely she will allow you to go to the ball on Christmas Day? Surely *that* one will not offend the countess's sensibilities?"

She took a determined step away. "That is up to Lady Addiscombe." He looked so chagrined that she felt compelled to add, "I am not being purposely obtuse, my lord. If I ask her about it, it will only set her hackles up."

"*My lord?*" he said, and then shook his head sadly.

His expression of rejection was simply unbearable. "I have already kept her waiting too long," Stacia said sharply, her voice growing colder as her misery deepened. "I must *go.*"

He merely stared.

Stacia hurried away before she did something they would both regret.

Ackers was just leaving the countess's chambers when Stacia approached her ladyship's door. "Ah, there you are."

"Oh, dear. She sent you to look for me?" Stacia guessed.

"Yes. Lady Kathryn is with her." She paused before opening the door and pulled a face. "She's…in a mood."

When was she not?

Stacia nodded and they entered the apartment.

"Where have you *been?*" the countess shrieked.

"I'm sorry, my lady. I had difficulty locating Mrs. Nutter."

"No doubt she was behaving like a fool just like all the others." Lady Addiscombe gestured to the small, corked jug Stacia held. "Well, go ahead!"

Stacia removed the stopper, decanted a small amount, and re-corked the jug.

Lady Addiscombe scowled and took the water glass from Stacia, raising it to her lips.

Stacia's gaze slid to Lady Kathryn as the countess drank the posset.

The younger woman gave her a guilty smile.

Kathryn had come to Stacia's room the day after she'd been released from the priest hole and had apologized profusely while her older sister, the duchess, had looked on.

It had not been difficult to forgive the younger woman for the best two days of Stacia's life.

"Oh, do stop *looming*, Martin," the countess snapped.

"I'm sorry, my lady." Stacia went to sit in the chair beside Lady Kathryn.

"No, not there. Just—just *go*," Lady Addiscombe said. "My daughter has insisted she will remain with me. Despite my desires." She pressed her lips tightly together and glared at Lady Kathryn, who returned her look with a cool, almost challenging, one of her own.

The countess made a feral snarling sound and then, looking as if she would prefer to chew out her own tongue, turned to Stacia and spat, "I do not require the two of you cluttering up my bedchamber. Send Ackers away, too. I cannot bear her accusatory stare at being denied her night of *fun*. Tell her she may attend this idiot function until *eleven* o'clock." Her jaws worked hard, as if she were chewing gravel. "All of you may attend for a few hours."

Stacia heart leapt. "Thank you, my la—"

"Do not thank *me*." She fixed her daughter with a look of loathing. "Thank my interfering son-in-law. He has *insisted* that every servant—not only his own—be allowed to take part in his asinine function."

"Er, Lord Needham?"

"Who else?" the countess snapped. "Now *get out*, Martin!"

Stacia curtsied. "Yes, my lady."

"One more thing, Martin."

Stacia stopped, her hand on the door, and turned. "Yes, my lady?"

"I may have been forced to comply with Needham's demands, but you will be back here no later than midnight. If you are not, then you can find yourself another position. You may pass that along to the others."

"Yes, my lady."

Stacia shut the door and then looked left and right to make sure nobody was watching and did a little dance.

She would get to waltz with him! *And* order him around like a servant!

Just wait until she told Ackers.

The woman herself emerged from the stairwell as Stacia hurried toward it. "Ah, I was looking for you."

The maid rolled her eyes. "Lord. What does she want *now*?"

"She sent me to tell you that she does not want any of us until midnight. She is spending the day and evening with Lady Kathryn."

Ackers shook her head. "I can't make heads or tails of those two. You should have heard them going at it hammer and tongs earlier." A sly smile slid across the older woman's face. "And then Lord Needham popped in for no more than a minute." Ackers cackled. "Wasn't my lady fit to be tied after *that?*"

"There is more," Stacia said, bouncing on the balls of her feet. "We may go to the ball—but must be back by midnight."

Ackers's joyous shriek made Stacia jump. "This is all his lordship's doing! I just know it!"

"She admitted as much."

"Miss Martin!"

Stacia turned to find Dora hurrying toward her. "I was just going to look for you, Dora. Miss Ackers and I will need gowns." She grinned. "We are going to the ball. Could you tell me again where Mrs. Kettering's chambers are?"

"In the south wing, Miss. But I just put a gown on your bed."

"What?"

"Aye, Lady Needham sent it for you."

Stacia blinked. "She…did?"

The maid nodded excitedly. "She had her own maid alter it for you using the dress you gave to me."

Dora meant the gown from the day Stacia had found Terrence. Dora had removed all but a shadow of the stain, but it was still nothing Stacia could wear in Lady Addiscombe's presence. She had given it to the girl, who could probably use the fabric for something.

"Don't you want to see it?" Dora asked.

Stacia turned to Ackers, who waved her away. "You go along, Miss Martin. I need to hurry along to the south wing and see if there is anything left for me to wear!"

Dora grinned and took Stacia's hand, all but dragging her to her chambers. The gown that waited on her bed was like something out of a dream. It was a deep, vibrant pink that immediately made her think of lilies, the sort of color Stacia had never been allowed to wear during her Season, when she'd had to wear white, a color that made her look insipid.

"Isn't it beautiful, Miss?" Dora asked when Stacia wordlessly stroked the lustrous silk. "Lady Phoebe—er, that's Lady Needham—is dark haired just like you and she favors deeper colors. I'm sure it will look a treat on you."

"I wonder that she parted with such a beautiful gown."

"The master spoils her something fierce. She has a hundred gowns or more."

It was the most gorgeous dress Stacia had ever seen.

"I will come back in a few hours to help you dress, Miss," Dora said.

"But what about you?" Stacia protested. "You will need to get ready, as well."

"Several of us maids are going to get ready together, but you've nobody to help you."

"Well...if you do not mind?"

"Of course not!" She stared at something over Stacia's head.

"What is it?" Stacia asked, patting her hair, which was covered with a lace cap, as Lady Addiscombe required.

"Short hair is all the crack, Miss, and yours would have some lovely natural curls if there was not so much weight.

Stacia had often lamented the time it took to wash and dry such a mass of hair—especially when it was not an especially beautiful color. But...short?

She met Dora's hopeful gaze. "How short?"

"Short."

Stacia swallowed, suddenly aware of the weight bearing down on her neck. "You are sure?"

"Aye, I'm sure of it, Miss. You're such a tiny, dainty lady that all that hair is too much. Er, beggin' your pardon."

Stacia smiled. "Don't apologize. I appreciate your honest opinion."

"I cut everyone's hair. I will do a good job. I promise."

Stacia hesitated.

"I can do it right now if you like."

"Now?" Stacia repeated. She reached up and felt her hair again, as if to check that it was still there.

Dora nodded.

"Very well," she said after a moment. "Do it."

Thirty minutes later Stacia could not stop staring at her reflection. "Why, you've made me pretty, Dora!"

Dora laughed as she swept up the long tresses that littered the floor. "You were pretty all along, Miss Martin."

She kept stroking the brown curls, which looked glossier and far healthier. She felt at least a stone lighter, although of course that wasn't possible.

Dora's hand landed lightly on her shoulder and Stacia met her gaze in the mirror. "Did I cut it too short?"

Only then did Stacia realize that her eyes were glassy with tears. She shook her head vigorously, sending the curls dancing. "No, you did a wonderful, wonderful job." Stacia reached for her reticule, which was on the dressing table. "Here, let me—"

Dora set a hand over hers and Stacia looked up to find the normally smiling girl serious. "No. Let me do this for you. After what I helped Lady Kat do to you and his lordship...Well, I'm sorry, Miss. You're not angry?"

"No, I am not angry. But I really would like to pay you."

"The haircut is a gift. And now I must run! I will be back half-an-hour before the ball." She turned and was gone before Stacia could argue about the money.

She turned back to the mirror and smiled at her reflection. She looked...pretty.

She couldn't wait until Andrew saw her.

***

Several hours later Stacia found herself gazing at her reflection for the second time in one day. Her attention this time fixed on her bodice. "Are you sure this isn't too low?"

Dora laughed. "It's perfect, Miss. *You* look perfect."

Stacia wasn't so sure, but she had fussed enough. She turned to the other woman and made a shooing gesture. "You must hurry and dress, Dora. You've wasted all your time on me."

"I'll not be late. At least no later than I want to be. Thomas Gresham has been flirting with Lady Shaftsbury's maid." She scowled. "Tonight I will show him what he lost." And with that, she sailed from the room, chin high.

Stacia almost pitied the unsuspecting footman.

Lady Needham had also sent along a matching pink reticule and pink and cream burnt velvet shawl. She slipped the latter over her shoulders and then picked up her fan.

A flick of the wrist revealed her favorite lines from Shakespeare's Sonnet 29:

Haply I think on thee, and then my state,

Like to the lark at break of day arising

From sullen earth sings hymns at heaven's gate.

Stacia was rarely satisfied with her work, but this fan had been one of those times.

It truly filled her with hope to read the words and look upon the overlarge H in the word *haply*, glinting with gold gilt and exploding with spring flowers and, yes, a lark joyfully soaring.

She slipped the fan into the pretty beaded bag along with a card of pins and a handkerchief, stole a last glance at her marvelous new hair, and turned toward the door just as somebody knocked.

Dora must have forgotten something.

But when she opened it, it was Lady Needham in the corridor, looking magnificent in a teal blue silk gown with a gold lace overdress.

"Oh!" the other woman exclaimed, her gaze wide and admiring as it swept over Stacia's gown. "It is *perfect* on you! I knew it would be. And your hair looks delightful."

Stacia brushed her hands over the skirt. "Thank you for this. Thank you for all the many kindnesses you've shown me since my arrival. You are generosity itself."

"This gown always belonged to you," Lady Needham said. "I only returned it to its owner—so don't think of sending it back to me."

"Oh, I couldn't! It is too much—too—"

"Hush. It is a Christmas gift. Please," she added. "It would make me happy."

Stacia blinked back the tears that seemed so eager to fall today. "Thank you."

"It is my pleasure. Were you headed to the ballroom?"

"I was, even though it is early."

Lady Needham offered Stacia her arm. "We will be unfashionably early together," she said as Stacia closed the door and took her arm. "Needham says I am not allowed to carry trays or deliver drinks or do anything strenuous. Chatham and Shaftsbury insist that Hy and Selina are also barred from exertion."

Stacia knew all three women were increasing and could understand their husbands' concerns.

"What are you permitted to do?" she asked.

The viscountess laughed. "Nothing other than dance and flirt." She gestured toward her prominent midriff. "Although why he thinks a dance with me is a treat for his servants is anyone's guess."

Stacia thought the men would be lining up to dance with the viscountess, who was not only lovely but radiated happiness.

"Will you sit with me and my sisters and join us in running our husbands off their feet fetching lemonade and wraps and smelling salts—or whatever else we might contrive to keep them busy?"

Stacia laughed. "That sounds lovely."

When they reached the ballroom Lady Needham stopped abruptly and burst out laughing when she saw the evening's *butler* and two *footmen* hovering near the entrance.

Lord Needham announced the names of his guests in a ringing voice as they arrived while the Earl of Crewe and Duke of Chatham both collected a wider assortment of wraps than were ever seen at a *ton* function and transported them with pomp and ceremony to the cloak room.

Lady Needham looked from Crewe to Chatham, grinned, and said, "I have always wanted a matched pair of footmen."

The two handsome aristocrats—both with scarred faces—looked at each other and laughed. The duke grinned down at the tiny viscountess. "I seem to have forgotten my eye patch."

A throat cleared loudly somewhere behind Stacia.

"Duty calls," the duke said, hurrying to where Cook—clad in a seventeenth century confection of celestial blue, complete with a jeweled stomacher, huge headdress, and black patch beside her lips—stood tapping her foot in mock impatience.

"I think some of your servants require more training, Needham," the viscountess rebuked, smirking up at her towering spouse.

"May I take your wrap, Miss Martin?" Lord Crewe asked, looking very piratical in his evening blacks and matching eyepatch.

Stacia glanced down at the scrap of velvet, which at least marginally hid some of her rather shocking décolletage. "I believe I will retain it, er, Crewe," she said in a lofty tone, getting into the spirit of things.

The earl laughed and said in a confiding voice, "Why I never thought to have such a ball, I do not know. I think I shall have to have one next year. Not at Christmas, but perhaps during our annual harvest fete. Ah, back to work!" He turned toward a new arrival, one of the real footmen and his sweetheart.

Lady Needham had been joined by Lady Crewe and the two sisters had their heads together, so Stacia slipped into the ballroom unnoticed.

She gazed around at the magical scene. Holly and evergreen in profusion, with the addition of huge potted plants and masses of flowers from Lord Needham's hothouses, somehow combined to create a winter wonderland that also held a promise of spring.

"It is beautiful, is it not?"

Stacia turned and found Lady Shaftsbury beside her. As always when she was confronted with the stunning woman, she felt a bit tongue tied. "It is magical."

"Yes, that is exactly the word." Lady Shaftsbury took in Stacia's hair and gown. "I must say that *you* look magical, Miss Martin. I am delighted to see you so recovered. And your hair suits you marvelously."

Stacia looked for some sign that the other woman knew where she had really been, but the marchioness's beautiful face held nothing but genuine good will.

"Thank you, my lady." She self-consciously fingered her curls. "It feels lovely, but…conspicuous."

"I can imagine. Your hair must have reached past your waist."

"It did."

Lady Shaftsbury lightly touched her own elegant upswept hair, which was probably as long as Stacia's had been. "I would like to rid myself of some of this bothersome length, but Shaftsbury is enamored with it."

Her words reminded Stacia of Lord Shelton's erotic threat involving her hair and the bedposts and felt a pang of remorse that whatever he had meant would no longer be possible. Would he be disappointed?

Lady Shaftsbury leaned closer, pulling Stacia from her thoughts. "Incidentally, I am currently in search of a companion—more of a secretary, really—to assist me both in London and when we return to the country. I would be delighted if you considered the position."

Stacia gazed into the other woman's magnificent blue eyes—the only pair she'd seen to rival Shelton's—and experienced an almost overwhelming surge of gratitude.

"That is very kind. And—and I will certainly consider it if I leave her ladyship's employment."

The marchioness smiled, touched Stacia lightly on the arm, and then drifted across the room in her elegant sky-blue gown, looking so much like an angel it was hard to pull her gaze away.

Even though the ball had scarcely begun the small orchestra cued a country dance and the dance floor filled with an enthusiasm rarely witnessed in a London ballroom. No sophisticated ennui at this particular function.

Stacia was subtly scanning the room for Shelton, when a voice behind her said, "Are you free for this dance, Miss Martin?"

She turned to find Mr. Dennehy, Lord Needham's tall, dark, and mysterious secretary standing behind her. He looked dangerously handsome in his evening clothes, the exquisitely tailored garments making his whipcord lean form appear even taller.

"I would love to, Mr. Dennehy."

She had danced with him at the village fete, so she knew he was an exquisite, if not exactly comfortable, dance partner. His dark blue eyes regarded her almost somberly, the lush black eyelashes that fringed them the only soft thing about the man, who was all sharp angles, his thin shapely lips and high cheekbones giving him an almost starved look, although his body was far too substantial to explain her odd assessment.

"Are you enjoying your stay at Wych House, Miss Martin?" he asked, when the steps brought them close enough to talk.

"Very much so. Lord and Lady Needham have made me feel very welcome." She tilted her head. "I detect a slight accent, Mr. Dennehy."

His lips curved so slightly it would be a stretch to call it a smile. "I am originally from Dublin, but I have lived in England since I was a lad."

Stacia did not think he could be much older than she was, although his deportment and air of seriousness made him seem older.

"I understand that your coworker Mr. Dixon will soon be leaving," she said, when he appeared content to let her lead the conversation.

"Yes. The day after Boxing Day will be his last day."

"Will you be alone for long, or will Lord Needham engage another secretary?"

"It will just be me." After a moment, he added, "I've worked for his lordship for several years, but only during the summers, when I was not at university. Now I will work for him all the time."

"Where did you study?"

"Cambridge."

"So did my father! What college?"

"Trinity."

"That was his, too. He was a medieval scholar."

His lips twitched, closer to a smile, but still leagues away. "I studied mechanical arts. Which is often called the vulgar arts."

She laughed. "Because it is practical, and therefor vulgar?"

"Just so," he murmured, still unsmiling, although she thought she saw a glint of humor in his hooded eyes.

No sooner did Mr. Dennehy deposit her at the table where the Bellamy sisters had gathered than Mr. Dixon claimed her.

After that, she danced a set with the distinguished Mr. Davis.

Two hours later...

Stacia had danced every single dance, a first for her.

She was waltzing with Thomas—the strikingly handsome young footman Dora had accused of switching his affections—and laughing so hard at his description of his catastrophic first dance at a local assembly, that it was difficult to keep her feet as he led her smoothly and skillfully around the dance floor.

"It is easy to laugh now," he said when they'd both stopped chuckling, "but the poor lass whose frock I almost tore off still gives me the cut direct when I pass her on the street in Little Sissingdon."

"You dance divinely now. I would never have guessed that you were once such a menace on the dance floor," she assured him. "Who taught you to waltz?"

Thomas swirled her around in a flamboyant show of skill. "Thank you, Miss Martin. My mother taught me and my brothers. She was a governess before leaving service to marry my father. She taught a goodly number of the people here. Everyone wanted to learn when Lord Needham told us about this ball." He glanced around them at the crowded floor of dancers, most of whom had clearly newly discovered the waltz, and lowered his voice, "I know Dora helped you dress for the ball, Miss. Did she happen to, er, mention me?"

Stacia considered her answer a moment before admitting, "She said something about Lady Shaftsbury's maid."

Thomas grimaced. "I've only been on two walks with her—and one dance at the village Christmas fete—and all three times I could hardly say *no* to her without being rude. She's pretty but laughed at everything I said, even things I'd not meant to be funny."

"She is probably nervous around you."

He shrugged his broad shoulders. "Aye, maybe, but it's caused no end of trouble for me with Dora ever since." He lowered his voice so much that Stacia had to dance on her toes to hear him. "I drew Dora's name in the secret gift giving but I don't want to keep it a secret. I'm worried she might think my gift is from Charles." His worried blue gaze slid to where Dora was, quite shamelessly, flirting with another footman, also tall, blond, and handsome.

"I don't think there is any rule against letting her know it is from you," Stacia said.

"It's a claddagh ring," Thomas said.

"Pardon?"

"My mother is from Ireland and the ring belonged to *her* mother."

"What did you call it?"

"A claddagh ring. It has hands and a crowned heart on it."

"Oh, that sounds like a *fede* ring. It's a sort of promise ring," she explained at his questioning look.

"Aye, this is a ring a man gives to his girl. The way she wears it tells others if somebody has her heart." His cheeks flushed a dark red.

"I think you must certainly tell her it is from you," Stacia said. After a moment she added, "You might also tell Dora what you told me about Lady Shaftsbury's maid."

Thomas looked thoughtful at that advice and his gaze slid across the room yet again to the woman who obviously had his heart.

Stacia took the opportunity to look yet again for the man who held hers.

The ballroom was filled with aristocratic men and women mingling with servants—even Lord Bellamy's young friends were here dancing and waiting on giggling maids—but there was no sign of the man who had promised to be her slavishly devoted servant for an evening. Why had he waylaid her in the corridor if he was not going to be at the ball?

Stacia stayed at the ball beyond sense, beyond hope. She remained until ten minutes before midnight—which meant she had to all but run to return to her employer in time—and Lord Shelton never appeared.

Chapter 33

Y ou are still quite pale. You are not suffering a relapse, are you Martin?" the countess demanded the following morning, peering at Stacia through suspicious, squinty eyes. "Or is it reveling with rustics that has left you so hollow-eyed?"

"I feel fine," Stacia lied. She was exhausted. And miserable. She had tossed and turned in her bed until after eight o'clock, alternately shedding tears and cursing Shelton's name.

Obviously, he had better things to do.

Lady Addiscombe gestured to the bed tray across her lap. "You may take this, Martin." She aimed a dissatisfied moue at the nearly untouched coddled eggs. "I don't recall Cook being so heavy-handed with cream when I oversaw the house."

Stacia lifted the tray and was about to set it near the door and ring for a servant when her employer said, "No, Martin. I want you to take it down. You may bring me a poached egg and plain toast. Pray tell Cook that eggs do not need to *swim* in cream."

"Yes, my lady."

Stacia was amused to note the number of sleepy, heavy eyes in evidence when she reached the kitchen. So, she was not the only one who'd got too little sleep.

"I don't see how the swells do this night after night," Dora was saying to Sally, one of Cook's helpers.

"They can do it because they don't have to get up the next morning and set fires," groused Kitty, another maid, who was scarcely much larger than Stacia but had an amusingly booming voice.

"Any more complaining and I might have to advise the master against such entertainment in the future," Davis said, coolly surveying the larger than average collection of servants milling about.

Maids and footmen scattered in all directions like mice running from a cat.

Cook glared from the tray to Stacia. "Is something wrong with my food?"

"Her ladyship said it was delicious. It is just that she is feeling a little delicate this morning. She would like a plain poached egg on plain toast." Stacia smiled at the grim-faced woman. "I will wait and bring it up to her."

"Plain," the Cook snapped and then turned on her heel and stormed off.

Davis frowned and hastened after Mrs. Barton, probably to soothe her ruffled feathers.

"Would you like a cup of tea while you wait?" Mrs. Nutter said, gesturing to a steaming pot.

"Thank you." Stacia took the chair across from her and poured a cup while the housekeeper resumed drawing up a massive shopping list.

She sipped her tea and enjoyed a moment of relaxation, something she knew would be in short supply as Lady Addiscombe had announced that she was going to rejoin her family tonight at dinner to ensure their Christmas antics did not *get out of hand.*

The door opened and two maids entered burdened with empty breakfast trays that told Stacia Lady Addiscombe wasn't the only one having a lazy morning.

"—gone to Brighton, is what I heard," one of the maids said, carefully putting crockery from her tray into a basin of water where a scullery maid was washing dishes.

The other maid chortled. "Or to the village, I reckon. I was in Mrs. Johnson's shop the day he popped in to have one of his gloves re-stitched. She asked if he wanted to collect his gloves in person from her house later that evening."

The women laughed.

"She's always boastin' about the lovers she had when she lived in London," another maid chimed in.

The first girl nodded. "Aye, she casts eyes at the master whenever he is—" She stopped abruptly when Davis entered the room.

But it was too late, the intimidating butler had overheard.

He frowned at the gossiping maids, his face a mask of displeasure. "You will not speak disrespectfully of his lordship beneath his own roof, Grace Tilney!" His cold eyes swept over the other two. "If the three of you have nothing better to do than engage in idle chatter you can help Thomas and Anthony carry the rugs from the drawing room. I am sure you will do an excellent job beating them clean."

The girls fled.

Stacia remembered well the lush beauty of the shop owner. Mrs. Johnson was a gregarious and sensual woman, that much had been clear just from looking at her. She'd also been generous and kind to Stacia, offering to connect her with a friend in London who had a dress shop.

Is that where Shelton had gone last night?

Stacia could see how Mrs. Johnson would appeal to a man who was so sensual and experienced. Doubtless the dressmaker would happily invite him into her bed without engaging in such foolishness as darkness and blindfolds.

She was suddenly assaulted by a vivid image of the lush-bodied widow spread out on Andrew's lap the way Stacia had been, his lips teasing a bosom that was far more impressive than her own.

"Here you are, Miss."

Stacia jolted, pitifully relieved when the unsettling mental image dissolved. She stood and took the tray with shaking hands. "Thank you."

As she hurried back to her mistress, she pushed down the revulsion that threatened to overwhelm her. Surely Shelton would not go from begging Stacia to come to the ball straight to another woman's bed a few hours later?

Surely not?

By the time dinner was finished Stacia was a grim mass of nerves. She had spent the day—and twice during the meal—fetching and carrying for the countess, who was even more fitful and demanding than usual.

Several times she'd been on the brink of running out of the room screaming and throwing herself on the mercy of Lady Shaftsbury or Lady Needham. The only thing that kept her from accepting any of the kind offers of employment she had received was the knowledge that working for the Bellamy family would mean continued exposure to Lord Shelton in the years to come. Who knew, perhaps she would be forced to encounter him next Christmas with a wife beside him!

No. It was simply too miserable to be borne.

"Do you play whist, Miss Martin?"

Stacia looked up from the needlework in her lap—or Lady Addiscombe's rather—and smiled up at the tall, slender Duchess of Chatham, the most reserved of the Bellamy siblings. She opened her mouth to admit she was an indifferent player at best, but her employer—who had been sitting with her eyes closed, looking pained at the revelry occurring around them in the drawing room—where not one, but three kissing boughs had been hung—opened her eyes and turned a truly venomous gaze on her daughter.

"Martin is busy being of use—she has no time to squander on *cards*."

Rather than look hurt, offended, or *anything*, really, the duchess merely blinked and turned her calm gaze on her parent.

Lady Addiscombe glared up at her for a moment and then began to fuss with the shawl she was wearing. "Martin!" she snapped, as if Stacia were across the room rather than three feet away. "I am ready to retire to bed. You will attend me."

Stacia set aside her employer's mangled needlework, smiled at the duchess, and then helped the countess to her feet.

"Don't pull on me so!" Lady Addiscombe grumbled. "And bring my basket up with you. I will want to work on it in the morning." She cast a searing gaze at the revelers. "There will be no point leaving my room until well after tea, I am sure."

Stacia picked up both work baskets and hurried to open the door for Lady Addiscombe.

"You will no longer remain in the drawing room after dinner. I have realized— far too late—that leaving you with my children and their *friends* every evening was not worth the paltry bit of information you managed to gather." The countess cut Stacia a scathing look. "Do not think I have forgotten your refusal to support me on the matter of Shelton, Miss Martin." She sniffed. "Although I am pleased to see that somebody must have come to their senses and rid the house of the scourge."

Stacia opened the door to Lady Addiscombe's chambers without comment. She had heard nothing about Lord Shelton's whereabouts. And she did not have the courage to ask anyone.

By the time she was permitted to hand the fractious countess over to Ackers for the evening it was almost midnight and Stacia was utterly exhausted.

She had hoped that sleep would come to her quickly, but she tossed and turned for at least an hour before dropping into a restless doze, her mind filled with unwanted images of Lord Shelton and Mrs. Johnson.

The last thought Stacia had, just before surrendering to oblivion, was that she should have said *yes*.

***

Stacia woke a few hours after dawn on Christmas Day feeling scarcely more rested than when she had gone to bed. But a quick look out the window and the sparkling wonderland beyond, complete with a fresh blanket of snow sparkling with the pale lemon yellow of dawn, was enough to lift even her depressed spirits.

She dressed quickly and warmly and hurried to deposit her secret gift outside Lady Shaftsbury's door. Hopefully Stacia would get to see the beautiful, sweet lady employing her new fan at the dinner before the ball, which Lady Addiscombe was deigning to attend, although not the ball itself.

Stacia couldn't work up much regret for missing the event. Not with Shelton gone.

She shoved the beautiful man and his whereabouts from her thoughts and hurried down to the stables to see the dog.

Terrence had greeted her after her two days in the attic as if she had been gone for a decade.

Stacia had not been able to visit him yesterday, or the day before, either. If she didn't go to the stables now, she would once again be drawn tightly into the countess's orbit and have no time to visit later.

Mr. Higgins and two grooms were in the courtyard when she approached.

"Ah, come to check on the wee beastie, have you? But you're too late, Miss."

Stacia's jaw dropped. "He—he is *dead?*"

"Ach! No, lass," the stablemaster said with a grimace, patting her awkwardly on the shoulder. "I just meant that he's gone with his lordship."

"His lordship?" she repeated stupidly, her heart still pounding from her shock.

"Lord Shelton," one of the grooms said, earning a look from Higgins that caused the younger man to quickly turn back to his task sweeping off snow.

"Aye, Miss. Gerald be right—the mark-wiss did take the master's curricle and pair. The wee dog hopped in and when Lord Shelton put him out again, he ran behind the carriage." Higgins grinned. "The hound, that is, not Lord Shelton."

The two grooms chuckled and even Stacia smiled.

"But why would Terrence insist on going with Lord Shelton?"

"All the treats and bones is reason enough," the irrepressible groom piped up, risking his superior's chiding. But Higgins just chuckled and nodded, his eyes twinkling fondly.

"Lord Shelton has been bringing Terrence bones?" she asked.

"Between you and his lordship the little rogue is right spoiled. He learned to hide the bone you'd given him when his lordship came—and then did the same with you, Miss. A right clever little creature," he added, clearly admiring such canine enterprise.

"And his lordship left—with the dog," she hastily added. "Yesterday, you say?"

"Nay lass, the day before."

"The day of the dance," she repeated stupidly.

"Aye, left in the middle of the day—right after flying to the village and then flying back just as fast." He clucked his tongue. "I told him t'would snow, but he just gave one of his laughs. *I'm from the north, Higgins, where we know what real snow*

304

means." Higgins gave a sharp laugh and shook his head. "*Real snow!* As if I don't recall Scottish winters from when I was a wee'un and it was stacked higher than my heed."

Stacia couldn't help noticing that his accent seemed to have become more pronounced.

So, evidently, had the two grooms, who snickered.

Higgins shot them a warning look before turning back to Stacia. "Gone to London he has."

"London! What for?" she blurted before she could catch herself.

"Ha! A lad like his lordship? Likely needing a bit o—" he broke off when he recalled to whom he was speaking, cleared his throat, and then said rather lamely, "Don't rightly know why, Miss."

Stacia saw sympathy in his gaze and that was enough to make her skin burn in the chill morning air. "Thank you," she said shortly, and then strode back to the house.

He went to the village first but quickly returned. Had he gone to see Mrs. Johnson as the maids had suggested? Had she not been available, so he'd gone to London to satiate his carnal needs as Higgins had implied?

You told him no. What he does is no concern of yours, is it?

Stacia tried to convince herself that was true, but her heart was not fooled.

By the time she reached her room she wanted to crawl under the covers and—

"Miss!"

She turned to find Dora hurrying toward her, a steaming pitcher of water in her hands.

"Oh, I've already washed, Dora. But thank—"

"No, this isn't for you. But I *do* have something else." She slipped a hand into her apron pocket and came out with a small, gold-foil wrapped package.

Stacia looked from the gift to Dora. "Are you my secret St. Nicholas?"

"No, Miss. This is from"—she broke off, glanced around, and leaned close, sloshing water over both their shoes as she hissed, "Lord Shelton. He said to deliver it to you this morning if he wasn't here." She grimaced. "I was to leave it while you were sleeping, but I got, er, distracted, like." She grinned and thrust her free hand into Stacia's face, wiggling her fingers to display the ring she wore. "Thomas told me how you said to explain about Lady Shaftsbury's maid chasin' after him. He also said you told him that he needed to tell me the gift was from him." She chortled. "The daftie. If you'd not spoken to him, I might be betrothed to somebody else right now!"

"Betrothed? Oh, congratulations, Dora!"

"Thanks, Miss. He's a good lad—so pretty his lack of sense don't matter."

Stacia laughed. Down the hall a door opened, and Lord Crewe's valet poked his head out and scowled.

"Whoops!" Dora said, hurrying toward the other servant.

Stacia stared at the box in her hand and then opened the door to her room and set it carefully on the bed before stripping off her outer layers. And then she sat and held the pretty gold present, just looking at it, her mind in a tangle.

What did this gift mean? Was he her secret St. Nicholas? Or was this something else?

Stacia took a deep breath and struggled to calm her thoughts. After several moments she carefully unwrapped the gift, trying to save the pretty paper.

She gasped when she opened the box and saw not just the loveliest pair of cream kid leather opera gloves, but also a dozen hairpins with sparkling brilliants.

Tucked inside one of the gloves was a folded note.

She swallowed, set aside the box, and unfolded it.

Merry Christmas, Stacia. I am sorry I could not deliver this in person, but important business in London has called me away. The gloves are for you to wear to the ball—I do hope you will defy the countess and make an appearance—and it will give me wicked pleasure to know you are wearing something I bought for you on your delectable body, so close to your skin.

"Andrew," she muttered, blushing even though there was nobody to see.

As for the glittering hair pins, they were just a silly afterthought that appealed to my magpie-like sensibilities. Also, I suspect you are guilty of denying yourself such frivolous pleasures. And then there is the fact that they will come in handy as counters the next time we play a naughty card game.

Your servant (although you refused to allow me to show it!)

Andrew

Like a ninny, Stacia pressed the note against her heart. The gloves and pins were lovely—and he was right that she'd not bought herself anything pointless and pretty in years—but the note scrawled in his almost unreadable handwriting was the real gift.

He had not forgotten her, after all.

Chapter 34

Andrew would have been back at Wych House late on Christmas Eve if not for one of the job horses going lame.

And then, after he'd secured a new pair, one of wheels had developed a distinct wobble. That had meant Andrew had to stop and wait for the wheelwright to be rousted from his Christmas Eve dinner—with the promise of thrice his going rate for his efforts—to see to the curricle.

By the time the wheel was secured it was dark. That did not stop him from resuming his journey. But the heavy snow that began to cover the already slushy road when he was still six hours from Wych House forced him to seek shelter at an inn with damp sheets, watery ale, and weak coffee.

"What a miserable night *that* was," Andrew muttered to his companion the following morning. His sigh of disgust was accompanied by billowing clouds of steam as the curricle rolled slowly through the early morning chill.

Scrapper, who sat on the seat beside him when he wasn't sprawled out using Andrew's thigh as a pillow, turned at the sound of his voice and then scratched behind his ear with his hind leg.

Andrew frowned down at the mutt. "You better not have picked up fleas when you slinked down to the kitchen last night, my boy. And don't think I didn't notice the way you eyed that pretty little bitch dancing around the ostler's feet."

Scrapper gave him a look that said butter wouldn't melt in his mouth.

"Scattering offspring around the countryside is bad *ton*, sir."

The dog hoisted one hind leg and commenced polishing his jewels.

Andrew laughed. "That will put me in my place."

The inn had not only afforded an uncomfortable sleep, it had also given him far too much time for introspection—not his forte by a longshot. Or perhaps it had been just enough time to think and consider and ponder what he had rushed up to London to do. And why.

Did he feel a certain degree of guilt for having masturbated naked in front of an innocent? Yes, a little, although that was easily overcome by the erection that he sprouted every single time he relived the memory.

Was he displeased that she might feel tarnished by the experience? Yes, that was more of a consideration and far from humorous.

But those concerns were nothing to one very startling admission: he could hardly wait to see her tomorrow.

And the day after.

And…shockingly…ad infinitum.

She was prickly, snappish, and yet more addictive than anyone he had met.

Even Mariah?

The question had floored him. Not because Stacia could not compare to his long-dead lover, but because Andrew had never even thought to compare them.

The truth was that his memory of Mariah had grown as fly-specked and dulled as an ancient mirror.

As if thinking that thought had summoned her, the night before, as he had thrashed in the damp, unpleasant bedding, he had dreamed of Mariah for the first time in years. Or at least he had felt her presence in his dream, although he had no recollection of seeing her face. The dream had left an aftertaste of sorrow. Not passionate longing or aching desire, or even love. It had felt like the sort of regret he sometimes felt when he had parted with friends or family.

Was that what Mariah had come to say to his sleeping self? Had she come to take her leave? Was the only thing holding her Andrew's cracked and faded recollections of a love that had bloomed for less than two months more than a decade earlier?

Forty-one days they had lived under the same roof before he had been banished and fled to the Continent.

He had stayed in the army less than a year before coming home for good, his hatred for his cousin the only thing keeping him alive at that point.

Andrew wondered, as he rolled along in the frigid dawn, if his life the last decade had really been living?

He already knew the answer to that—the past months with his cousin had taught him how hollow his existence had become. It did not escape his sense of irony that the first woman he had wanted in over a decade had rejected him at least three times.

If she rejected him a fourth time, then Andrew would wait a year for her, as she bade him, demonstrating that his offer was not a product of availability and convenience, but a *choice*.

Yes, he would wait for her. A year or even more if need be. Waiting a year did not mean he could not enjoy her company in the meanwhile, did it? Although her living in Bath, with Lady Addiscombe in proximity, certainly militated against such a possibility.

Even if he could not see her, he would wait.

Perhaps then she would believe that his memory, admittedly shot full of holes, had a place that was exclusively, enduringly hers.

His mood lifted along with the dawn, and he was just beginning to believe he would make it in plenty of time to enjoy a lazy bath before the ball that evening when he rounded a corner and reined in so sharply the curricle skittered dangerously on the wet and slushy road.

"Bloody hell," he muttered as he calmed the horses, set the carriage brake, and hopped out to help a clearly harried coachman assist his passengers out of the window of an overturned carriage.

By the time Andrew had made a detour of *nine miles* to deliver the effusively grateful widow and her daughter to her brother's house—what she was doing travelling on Christmas Day was a story he never fully understood—it was once again past dark.

The number of carriages clogging the driveway when he finally guided his weary pair into the courtyard at Wych House told him the ball was in full swing.

A groom trotted out to take the horses' heads and Andrew hopped out, dislodging a sleepy, yawning Scrapper in the process.

He tossed the man a coin and hurried toward the house. "Oh," he said over his shoulder. "See that Scrapper is fed—and make sure he doesn't muscle his way into the house."

The groom laughed. "Aye, my lord. A juicy bone will win him over."

Andrew hurriedly gave himself a sponge bath, shaved, dressed in his evening kit, and then took a moment to study his reflection in the mirror.

He was hollow eyed from long days and miserable nights on the road, but he was clean, tidy, and as respectable as he ever looked.

Andrew glanced at his prize for a long moment and then shoved it into the nightstand drawer.

And then he took the small jewel pouch off his dressing table and dropped it into his pocket.

Now he was ready.

Chapter 35

The difference between this ball and the servant ball was…

Well, it was difficult to articulate, Stacia decided.

Many of the same people had attended both. The Bellamy sisters and their spouses, as well as their houseguests, for example. But the magical feeling of having stepped out of time, not to mention the utter lack of social convention—a duke and a scullery maid performing a country dance together and a duchess partnering a stable lad for a Scottish Reel for pity's sake!—was sorely lacking.

Also lacking was Lord Shelton.

Again.

The one thing that *wasn't* lacking, in a completely different sense of the word, was her employer's attendance.

Nobody could have been more dismayed than Stacia that Lady Addiscombe had decided to attend the ball after all. Even her youngest daughter's entreaties, and Stacia had overheard Lady Kathryn's pleading and not-so-subtle insinuations about the putrid influenzas one could contract in a crowded ballroom, were not enough to convince the countess to remain in her chambers.

Stacia really could not comprehend the woman. All day long the various Bellamy children had celebrated intimate Christmas gatherings with their new families and then assembled in the great hall for one big celebration and Lady Addiscombe had not attended even *one* of those functions.

Instead, she had sent Stacia to deliver her gifts—the exact same thing for all five daughters and her son: a book of self-improving sermons that Stacia had collected from the bookbinders several weeks before.

She had briefly opened one of the books, read a few pages, and slammed it shut, disgusted that any person could earn money from the sale of such sanctimonious claptrap.

Stacia, who'd grown up yearning for siblings and cousins and aunts and uncles, could not comprehend the countess's determination to ignore—if not outright alienate—every single one of her children.

Stacia suspected that the only reason she had come to the ball tonight was to cast a pall over the festivities.

Without Shelton in attendance, the countess focused her ire on Needham and Lucy, and, to a lesser extent, Captain Walker.

Although Lucy had only turned fourteen today—a Christmas birthday—her father had allowed her to attend the ball. There was nothing shocking in Lucy attending a country dance under her own father's roof, but Lady Addiscombe had been glaring at Needham as if he had invited naked courtesans to debauch the guests.

And when Lord Bellamy had solicited Lucy's hand for country dances, not the scandalous waltz, Lady Addiscombe had sounded like a goose being sacrificed for Christmas dinner.

She had looked around frantically, as if looking for somebody she could order to intervene. But all the Bellamy sisters had been dancing themselves.

Temporarily thwarted, Lady Addiscombe had watched the dancers in brooding silence, her mood boding ill for the rest of the evening.

The set was drawing to a close and Stacia had just begun to hope the older woman might have swallowed her wrath when she turned to Stacia and said, "I suppose you had no inkling of this—this *travesty*, Martin?"

"Travesty?" she repeated, her hope of avoiding a public raking dwindling to dust when she met her employer's enraged blue eyes.

Lady Addiscombe's lips drew into a thin, bloodless slash and she hissed, "If you think I believe that you knew nothing of my son's budding friendship with that—that—"

Stacia interrupted the other woman before she could give life to that ugly word. "It is an innocent infatuation on her part, my lady. Your son is merely being courteous to the daughter of his host."

"How *dare*—"

Just then Lady Lowell and Sir Thomas—parents to the giggling Lowell twins—drifted over with their daughters and three nieces

"Sir Thomas, Lady Lowell," the countess said, her tone grudging and her expression hardening as she turned to the younger women. "And the Misses Lowell." She offered up an exaggerated pause. "Unless, that is, either of you have recently married?" She smiled, the expression that of a cat toying with two mice.

But Sir Thomas was not to be outdone. He chuckled heartily. "I have not found anyone I'd be willing to give them to, my lady. Unlike some other, more unfortunate girls, there is no pressing need for them to sacrifice themselves to a man they do not love."

Stacia was amused to see a malicious glint in his gaze. The countess really did bring the worst out of people. She had chatted with Sir Thomas a half dozen times over the past ten days and he had been nothing but charming.

Lady Addiscombe's smile curdled at Sir Thomas's not-so-subtle dig.

Lady Lowell, the peacemaker of the couple, changed the subject by asking how the countess liked Bath.

That left Stacia with the five young women.

The twins ignored her, but one of their cousins—the sweet natured beauty who made her fair cousins look insipid by comparison—asked Stacia, "Is it true that Lord Shelton has gone away, Miss Martin?"

Before she could respond, one of the twins gave a tinkle of laughter that might have been pleasant if not for the spiteful sparkle in her blue eyes and said, "Poor Arabella! Are you hoping the third time will be the charm?"

Rather than look angry, Arabella cut Stacia a wry smile. "My cousins are referring to the fact that Lord Shelton forgot my name—"

"*Twice!*" one twin said gleefully.

Arabella cut her cousin an exasperated look. "Yes, that is true."

"And not just your name, he forgot that he'd even met you," the twin persisted, smirking. "While he most certainly remembered *me.*"

"He confused your names, Susannah," the elder of the Moore sisters pointed out.

Susannah scowled.

But before she could retort Miss Coraline, the youngest of the cousins, who had the smudged gloves and slightly disheveled look of a girl more comfortable on horseback than in a ballroom, fixed Susannah with a searing look and said, "Of course he remembered *you.* It would be difficult for anyone to forget such a silly pair of bookends."

Susannah's jaw dropped. "You—"

"Martin!" The countess bellowed loudly enough to silence the buzz of conversation around them.

Stacia turned. "Yes, my lady?"

The older woman's wide-eyed look of revulsion was fastened on something beyond Stacia's shoulder. "I need you to—"

"Good evening, ladies."

Stacia turned slowly and looked up almost a foot to meet Lord Shelton's warm gaze.

"Miss Martin," he murmured and then, as if it took effort, he turned to the countess. "Lady Addiscombe."

When the older woman merely stared in appalled silence, Shelton turned back to Stacia.

He held her gaze as if she were the only other person in the room. The delicate skin beneath his brilliant eyes was shadowed, as if from a lack of sleep, but he had never looked more beautiful to her. "I would be honored if you would partner me, if you are not otherwise engaged for this set." He gestured to the dance floor, which she saw was filling up for a quadrille.

"Martin!"

"Yes, my lady," Stacia said faintly, unable to turn away from Shelton.

"You put the wrong quizzing glass in my reticule. I want the silver chased one. You will have to fetch it from my room. Martin. *Martin!*"

Shelton's lips pulled into one of his truly wicked smiles and he raised an eyebrow as if to say *well?*

Beside her, Arabella cleared her throat. "I am not committed for this set. I will be glad to fetch it for you, my lady."

Stacia gave the girl a startled look.

Arabella flashed her a conspiratorial smile and then—to her surprise—mouthed *go*.

"Miss Martin?" Andrew offered Stacia his arm.

And she took it.

***

Andrew felt the Countess of Addiscombe's flaming gaze scorch his back and shoulders as he led Stacia onto the dance floor. "Did I get you in trouble my dearest Stacia?"

"I was already in trouble."

He laughed at her dry answer.

"Shelton!"

He turned at the sound of Kathryn's voice.

"Bloody hell," he muttered, and then demanded rudely, "What do you want?"

Undaunted, she waved him over. "Come join us."

He glanced at Kathryn's partner—Captain Walker—and then down at Stacia. "What say you? Should we trust the vixen enough to form a square with her in it?"

Stacia laughed and the action did lovely things to her snug, uncharacteristically low-cut bodice. "What possible mischief can she get up to in the middle of a crowded ballroom?"

He gave her a look of only partially mock horror. "Lord, Stacia! Do not tempt fate in such a reckless manner. Ah, look—reinforcements," he said as Chatham, the duchess, Needham, and Lucy joined them. "Needham will keep her in line," he murmured as their host and his daughter took the head position in the square, Chatham and the duchess opposite them, leaving them across from Kathryn and Walker.

He leaned down and whispered. "You look utterly delicious. Your hair is delightful and suits you perfectly. It pleases me to see you wearing my gloves and you are so lovely you make those brilliants look dull. And that gown..." He growled and his eyes burned into hers. "You are exquisite."

Predictably, his prickly Miss Martin scowled at him. "I am sure I look even better now that I am as red as a tomato."

Andrew laughed. "I missed you. Did you miss me?"

She pursed her lips, but her eyes sparkled in a way that said his words pleased her. "Where did you take Terrence?"

"Terrence? Oh you mean, Scrapper? It wasn't a case of me taking *him* so much as *him* deciding that he would not be left behind." He cocked his head. "Was that your way of asking me where I went?"

"No." She took the opportunity of the music beginning to ignore him.

Andrew grinned, turned, and bowed to the corner.

The duchess regarded him with a level look and dipped a curtsey so slight as to hardly qualify as one.

He turned back to Stacia, and they joined hands.

"I do not think your vaunted charm works on the Duchess of Chatham, my lord," Stacia taunted as they passed to the right of the Captain and Kathryn, the latter of whom simpered at Andrew.

The saucy, unrepentant minx.

"You don't think Hyacinth likes me?" he asked Stacia. "I had not noticed."

She laughed and moved into the ladies chain.

Kathryn said something to Stacia that made her blush and purse her lips.

"What did you say to her?" Andrew asked Kathryn when he took her hands.

She ignored his question. "Did you enjoy your Christmas gift, Shelton?"

Andrew raised an eyebrow.

"Haven't you guessed? I am your secret St. Nicholas."

Andrew shook his head at her. "If your gift is what I think it was, you are incorrigible and deserve to be beaten." He paused. "But it was also inspired."

She laughed triumphantly as she moved back to the center.

***

"She is a menace," Andrew said to Stacia when she returned to his side, and they joined hands.

Stacia didn't need to ask who he meant.

"Have I mentioned how delectable you look with that hair and gown?" he murmured as he took her hands, and they made the promenade.

Stacia pretended not to hear him but suspected that her face was too flushed to be explained by exertion.

He chuckled, eyeing her with such open, obvious affection that it was difficult to pay attention to the steps *and* engage in flirtation—an activity she had no experience with, unlike Andrew, whom she had watched charm beautiful women times beyond counting.

Beautiful. All of them. Except you...

The words lacked the power to crush and shame her, as they usually would.

Instead, they brought to mind something else entirely. For some inexplicable reason, Stacia's thoughts went to the scars on Shelton's body, the mute evidence of all the brutalization his body had endured.

But suddenly she thought about all the injuries that were *not* visible, especially the one that had frightened him the most.

He had called it having his *bell rung*. Stacia had no idea what one of the big guns sounded like, but she had read first-hand accounts of Waterloo and they had been horrifying.

Shelton had stood next to one of those weapons of destruction when it had fired. And it had taken his hearing.

True, it had returned, but had that been the only damage?

Random conversations from the past days came back to her in a rush.

315

Andrew had not recalled the names of Lord Bellamy's school friends—that was not so unusual as they were callow youths—nor had he seemed to remember Mr. Dixon.

But he had also forgotten Arabella Moore. Twice.

And she was beautiful.

Pieces of a puzzle that had niggled at her began to click into place, although many blank spots remained. Why did he remember some people, but not others?

"What are you thinking about?" Andrew asked when he next had an opportunity. "You have the oddest expression on your face."

"Nothing," she said, and forced a smile.

How often and how many people, places, and events did he forget?

She watched him laugh and smile and tease those around them—making even the duchess thaw—and her heart hurt to think of the pain and suffering his body and mind had endured.

Was Andrew even aware of the gaps in his memory? Had the damage really healed as he believed?

Or was he becoming worse?

"So serious," he teased as they engaged in the final chasse and ended up side-by-side. He smiled down at her and then tucked her arm under his, keeping her close, and headed not toward Lady Addiscombe, but in the opposite direction.

"Where are we going?"

"It is too cold to walk outside, but Needham has lighted the gallery for strolling."

She glanced anxiously in the countess's direction.

"Just a moment or two," he said. "Please, Stacia."

"Just for a moment." She suspected that the instant she returned to her employer's side she would be sent on another errand, one that would last the rest of the evening, if not the rest of the house party.

Couples strolled arm in arm up and down the magnificent gallery, whose marquetry flooring was as much a work of art of all those hanging on the walls.

Andrew did not speak until they were at the far end of the hall and then he paused in front of a life-sized portrait of a blond man with a neatly trimmed van dyke and an extravagant mustache. The long dead Bellamy was wearing a rather unfortunate frockcoat of mustard yellow with high red heels and a jeweled buckle the size of a teacup.

"He's quite the lad," Andrew said, laughing as he turned from the portrait to Stacia. He took her hands in both of his and her heart pounded at the warmth in his eyes. "You are very somber for a ball, Stacia. What thoughts are consuming you? Is it your employer and how I've landed you in hot—boiling, probably—water?" He clucked his tongue before she could answer. "You needn't suffer her ill humor, love. You know you have friends here—powerful ones like Chatham and Needham—and they will help you find a more pleasant mistress."

Stacia felt strangely disappointed in his words.

Why? Because you wanted him to offer marriage so you could reject him yet again? *You will need to wait a year to hear the words you now want. If you are fortunate, that is.*

"There is another alternative, of course," he said, his eyelids lowering slightly, his gloved fingers tightening around hers. "You could marry me and let me sweep you away to a life of moderate comfort in a ramshackle Yorkshire manor." His mouth twitched into a self-mocking smile. "I wish I could fib and say that I will one day make you a duchess, but that is a position I have never wanted. Not just because Chatham would first need to die, and I would dislike that terribly, but because I would make a dreadful duke." He raised a hand to her cheek, lightly skimming her jaw. "If you marry me, you will likely have to satisfy yourself with living out your days as plain Mrs. Andrew Derrick." He cocked his head. "What say you, Miss Martin? Will you throw in your lot with a man who will never be screamingly wealthy, whose ridiculous definitions will always ensure you win at Dictionary, and…" his smile grew wicked, "who will always agree to don a blindfold and perform naked whenever you desire."

Nobody was close enough to hear his naughty words, although she could tell by the way several of the couples were stealing glances and smirking that at least a few people suspected Andrew might be proposing.

"If you say *no* today, I will come ask again in a year, Stacia," he said, his serious tone bringing her gaze back to his. "But if you tell me to leave you alone forever—that you do not want me—then I will not trouble you again."

The stab of fear she felt at his words told her—even if she had not already decided—what she had to say. "I do not care about titles or ramshackle manors or stylish frocks. But I cannot marry a man who does not believe in fidelity."

His expression turned almost terrifyingly stern. "Is this a condition to you saying *yes,* Miss Martin?"

Stacia quailed slightly beneath his intimidating gaze. This was it—the moment that could change her life forever. The men of their class kept mistresses—or at least patronized brothels. Even her father, least aristocratic aristocrat she had ever known, had kept a mistress.

If you stand your ground on this matter, you might lose him. Not just for a year, but forever.

That might be true.

But if I do not remain firm . . .

No, it was too unbearable to contemplate a future in which he not only did not love her but gave himself to other women.

"Yes, my lord. That is precisely what I am saying."

He nodded slowly, his expression, for once, difficult to read. "My immediate reaction was to be offended by your question," he said. "But then I realize that I have earned it with my reckless, caddish behavior over the years. I believe in marital fidelity, Stacia—not just for men, but also for women." His nostrils flared slightly. "I will not share you. Ever."

She caught her hysterical laugh before it broke free. As if that was even a remote danger!

But she didn't say that. Instead, she reveled in the raw dominance—and yes, affection and desire, too—that blazed in his eyes. It was not love, but it was more than she had ever expected from the unobtainable Marquess of Shelton.

Was it enough?

That was a difficult question to answer. And she wasn't sure it was a fair question, either. Could people ever know what might be enough ten, twenty years hence?

One thing Stacia knew for a certainty was that she did not want to envision a future without Andrew in it.

And that, she decided, was answer enough.

"I will marry you, my lord."

A slow smile spread over his face, and he took her chin between his fingers, his eyes boring into hers. "You have made me a very, very, very happy man, Stacia. And a proud man. I vow that I will always put your comfort and needs before my own." He kissed her upturned lips.

Stacia told herself that what he offered—companionship and hopefully children—was far better than what he must have had in his youth with *the love of his life*. Passion burned out, after all.

Did it not?

Yes, this was better.

She was still trying to convince herself of that as they walked back toward the ballroom. Before they were even half-way there, the countess—trailed closely by the Duke and Duchess of Chatham—entered the hall.

"A word in the drawing room, Martin!" The countess didn't wait for an answer before storming toward a door and flinging it open before a hovering footman could sprint over to open it. "Leave us," she snapped—although it was unclear who the words were directed at: the servant, Shelton, or the duke and duchess.

Andrew turned to her. "You don't need to face her, Stacia. I will speak—"

"I need to do this."

He stared into her eyes for a moment and then nodded. "I know you feel as if you owe her service until she can find a replacement companion, but you do not. I will see there is somebody to accompany her back to Bath. Even if I must do it myself."

Stacia nodded, her head in a whirl.

He pressed her hand and then released her.

She took a deep breath and followed her employer.

Chapter 36

J ust what have you been doing while I have been ill, Miss Martin?" Lady Addiscombe demanded the moment Stacia shut the door, her voice almost scarily quiet.

Stacia swallowed several times to force down the ball of anxiety in her throat. "I—"

"You have *been* with him—do not lie—I can see it in the lecherous, possessive way he put his hands on you."

Stacia opened her mouth to say what, she did not know. But the countess was not interested in an answer.

"I knew about you when I engaged you, but I thought to give you a chance to redeem yourself—to rescue the shreds of your tattered reputation."

"I beg your pardon?" Stacia said, recoiling. "What are you talking about?"

"Do not affect that innocent façade with me. I saw the shameless way you threw yourself at Colonel Kelly when I took you to Baroness Lindsay's ball."

"He asked me to dance."

"Only after you thrust yourself at him."

Stacia gave a laugh of disbelief. "Actually, my lady—not that it is any of your affair—long before I ever *thrust* myself at the colonel, he asked me to marry him. Three times, I might add."

The countess scoffed. "A likely story!"

"Why would I lie about something like that?" she asked, truly curious as to the other woman's inner workings.

Lady Addiscombe ignored her question. "And I suppose that Shelton has offered you marriage, as well?" She gave a scornful laugh.

"Yes. And I accepted." It was petty of her, but she could not help enjoying the other woman's flabbergasted expression, which was quickly replaced by an ugly, insinuating look.

"You are with child, I suppose."

Stacia's jaws tightened. "You are insulting, and I refuse to answer."

Lady Addiscombe did not seem to even hear her. "You think Shelton is going to rescue you, but let me tell you what will happen, you stupid trollop."

Stacia gasped. "I ref—"

"You spread your legs for him, which is all he ever wanted. Now you are nothing to him. Even if what you are claiming is true and he were so desperate as to marry a dowdy, penniless spinster—which I find highly suspect—the truth is that Shelton is as deeply in debt as my idiot husband. His only chance at salvation was to inherit the dukedom." Her face turned even uglier, which Stacia had not believed possible. "Now that Chatham has married my unnatural daughter—yet another foolish whore who could not keep her legs closed—there will be a litter of children between Shelton and the title. The moment Chatham has an heir of his body he will drop Shelton like a hot coal. And then where will you be?"

Stacia opened her mouth to tell the other woman that the last thing she was hoping for was Shelton to inherit at the expense of a beloved cousin's death.

But the countess was not finished. "I will tell you where. You will be living on that decrepit estate Shelton has only held on to because of Chatham's generosity. Or perhaps the duke will stop supporting his debauched habits after he no longer needs him. Regardless, you will be poor and fortunate if you have so much as a scullery maid, so all your grand dreams of a title are for naught."

Stacia felt as if she had been punched. Repeatedly. She swallowed down her pain and fixed the other woman with a direct look. "As it happens, my lady, I accepted him because I love him, not because I want the hollow comfort of a title. Is that what happened to you? If so, I pity you. But do not suppose that everyone else is so mercenary."

The countess's eyes bulged "You *love* him?" she demanded, evidently not hearing the second part.

"Yes," she said, holding her ground no matter how much the older woman's scorn cut her. "I *love* him."

Lady Addiscombe's shapely lips twisted into a hideous snarl as she strode up to Stacia.

For a moment, she thought the countess might actually strike her and it took all the strength she had not to shrink away from the fury in the other woman's gaze.

"Do not think that I didn't hear your snide comment about my own situation. Yes, I married a man with feet of clay but not for a moment was I stupid enough to fancy myself *in love*. You pity me, do you, Martin? Funny that, because I feel the same way about you. I wonder how your love will endure when Shelton sets up his mistress almost in front of you or brings home some filthy disease. I wonder how much you will pity me then."

Stacia could scarcely comprehend the bile pouring from the other woman's mouth. "Why are you *saying* such horrid things to me? What can you gain from such hateful behavior?"

"I am trying to save you from my own fate, you stupid—"

"Enough!" a familiar voice roared from behind her.

Stacia spun around. Not only Andrew, but also the duke and duchess of Chatham stood in the opening where the screens to the music room had been pushed aside, their shocked faces proclaiming what they'd heard.

Andrew strode toward them, his eyes spitting fire at the countess as he slid his arm around Stacia.

She could not help it; she melted against the protection of his hard chest.

She also should have plugged her ears, as Lady Addiscombe was not yet finished.

"You!" she seethed. "I see you for what you are, Shelton. I am not some ignorant persuadable chit; do not waste your lies and *charm* on me."

"I would not waste even my spit on a harpy like you." Andrew ignored Lady Addiscombe's outraged squawk, raising his voice to talk over her. "You have no right to spew your venom at Stacia. You were in a position to help her and all you've done is denigrate and terrorize her. You are a *monster* and if you were not a woman, I would not wait for dawn to see you at twenty paces and make you answer for your cruelty. But my tolerance has its limits, and if you are even a shred as wise as you seem to think you are then you will get out of my sight before I forget that you are my cousin's mother-in-law."

Lady Addiscombe's face was as red as a boiled lobster as she turned to her daughter and the duke and flung a hand toward Andrew. "Are you going to *say* something or just stand there and allow this—this churl to threaten me with violence?"

It was unclear who the question was aimed at. The duke and duchess exchanged a brief glance before Her Grace stepped forward.

"I am proud in this moment that you have never wanted me to call you *mother*, my lady."

Lady Addiscombe gasped.

"If this were my house, I would have your baggage on the front steps already," the duchess continued, her quiet voice pure steel. "I am certain that my sister—your hostess—will feel likewise when she learns how you've spoken to my cousin and Miss Martin. But you are fortunate because Chatham's carriage will be ready and waiting to take you back to Bath in the morning. If you know what is good for you—and your future comfort—you will take his generous offer." She took a step closer to her mother, her eyes glittering coldly as she stared down at the older woman. "In case I have not made myself clear, you will never darken the doors of any of my homes as long as you draw breath."

The countess hissed. "You vile, unnatural—"

"If you finish that sentence, you will find yourself walking to Bath," the duke said coolly. He strode across the room. "I will escort you to your chambers, my lady, where you will remain until first light." He gestured to the door and—to Stacia's astonishment—Lady Addiscombe went, too shocked to do more than sputter.

When the door shut behind them, the duchess came toward them, her face as expressionless as ever, but her green eyes brighter than usual. "I am sorry for what you have endured at my mother's hands," the other woman said. "I was not able to save my siblings—or myself—from her poison, but I am grateful that you are no longer subject to her abuse." She inclined her head and left the room, the door closing silently behind her.

Andrew lifted her chin until she met his gaze. "I will never stop regretting that my attention exposed you to such a viper, Stacia."

"None of this was your fault. If not you, then something—or somebody—would have set her off eventually."

He rubbed her bare upper arms. "You are remarkably contained in the face of such viciousness."

"I am relieved that is how I appear. Inside I am—" Her voice, which had held firm all through the countess's attack, finally broke.

Strong arms enfolded her and drew her close. "My poor darling." Andrew stroked her back while she sobbed. She had been a companion—a servant, in truth—for almost four years and had suffered countless slights. But never had she been assaulted so baldly and brutally.

"It is all over now, sweetheart," he murmured, his gentle hands and words a balm on her wounded soul. He stood patiently and absorbed all her pain, comforting her with his body and words.

When she stopped trembling a short time later, she looked up at him. "I am better now."

He stared down at her with a wondering smile, his face so beautiful that it squeezed the breath from her lungs. "Why me, darling?"

She considered pretending that she didn't know what he meant, but what was the point? They were to be married, her love for him would slip out sooner rather than later. "Ah, you heard that part, did you?"

He nodded mutely.

"Why you?" she repeated. "Need you ask? You are"—she made a helpless gesture to encompass his magnificent face and body. "You are *you*. Surely having women falling in love with you in droves is something you are accustomed by now."

"And is that it? You love the body I inhabit?" he asked, his gaze no longer hopeful but...hollow.

"Of course that is not all I love, Andrew. I love the man who makes me laugh—at my own folly as well as his own. I love the man who went out of his way to help a bloody, injured mutt and a bloody, muddy woman who had only snapped and snarled at him. I love the man who helped a stranger marry her lover, even when he suffered for it. I love the man who would not take my virginity even when I all but offered it to him on a platter."

His mobile eyebrows leapt. "Damnation! I had not realized that was an option. I really *am* slow witted."

She rolled her eyes.

He became serious again. "I am honored you have chosen me. But there is one thing I want you to understand. I may have executed heroic deeds from time to time, but I am a man who is excoriated in decent society for what he has done—"

"Only because they have been told lies about Sarah—"

"And that is something they must continue to believe," he said firmly. "Just because she told Kathryn does not mean we are free to tell the world."

Stacia ground her teeth but could see by his expression that there would be no talking him around the matter.

"And forget about Sarah for a moment. You cannot deny that I abducted Lady Shaftsbury with the sole intention of using her against my cousin."

"No, I cannot deny that. And it was a cruel act. Are you ashamed of what you did to Lady Shaftsbury?"

"More than you will ever know."

"Then let that be an end to it, Andrew. Do people not deserve a second chance? Are we not allowed to get up once we have stumbled? You wronged her, it is true, but she also credits your actions with bringing her to the marquess—the love of her life."

"She is too kind-hearted."

"She *is* kind-hearted. But she is also right."

He took her hands in his. "You are forgetting what I did to the duke—to his first wife."

Stacia set her hands on his broad shoulders, suddenly realizing that for all his magnificent strength and brawn he was as vulnerable as anyone else. "We talked about this once before, Andrew. Everyone else has forgiven you—all the people who matter, at least. The only one who hasn't forgiven you is *you*. Please, isn't a decade long enough to punish yourself?"

***

Andrew stared in awe at this woman who loved him and argued so strenuously in his defense. He was not as sure as she seemed to be that he deserved forgiveness, but perhaps it was time to let go of the mistakes he had made and look toward the future. Certainly, it was not fair to Stacia to dwell so much in the past.

I love him, she had shouted, defying the harpy to her face. Would he ever forget the intense wave of wonder and joy he'd felt when he heard those words?

Andrew had done nothing to deserve such bounty, but he was going to seize this opportunity with both hands.

Stacia smiled up at him, her brown eyes so warm—so *trusting*—that his knees were momentarily weak with terror.

She loved him.

He lightly caressed her jaw. "I am the luckiest man in England, Stacia."

Her eyes became glassy. "Are you trying to make me blubber?"

Andrew laughed. And then suddenly recalled something and patted his chest, smiling when he felt the small bump beneath his lapel. "I almost forgot to give you your Christmas gift."

"But I am wearing my gifts."

He let his gaze drift over the brilliants that sparkled in her flattering new haircut and then down to the soft leather sheathing her arms. "Those were just trifles I bought in case I could not get your real gift sized in time."

"Sized?"

He reached into his coat and brought out a small leather pouch. "This is your real gift."

She caught her lower lip with her teeth and took the pouch.

Andrew watched her face as she fumbled with the drawstrings and then tipped the ring into her palm.

"Oh!" She gasped, her eyes wide as she gazed at the rose ring she had admired so much at the Christmas fete. After a long moment, she lifted her eyes to his. "But—this is…How did you know?"

He indulged in a bit of gloating before taking the ring and slipping it over her glove. It was a snug fit but would be perfect without the leather. "I cannot divulge my secrets."

She stared at the delicate rose on her finger, her lashes glinting.

"Happy Christmas, my darling Stacia. The first of many to come." He dropped a kiss on her soft lips. "I don't deserve you—*no,* I don't," he said, talking over her when she tried to demur. "But I swear on everything sacred that I will strive to."

She threw her arms around his neck, pulled him tightly against her small body, and then mumbled into his crushed cravat, "I didn't get you a gift, Andrew."

He loosened her grip and took her chin in his fingers, making her meet his gaze. "Don't you understand you wonderful, lovely, adorable woman? *You* are my gift, Stacia. The best Christmas gift I have ever received."

Chapter 37

Hyacinth

Hy finished giving a brutally honest retelling of the Countess of Addiscombe's behavior to her gawking siblings—even Doddy, whom she knew they had all been treating like a child for far too long—and looked from face to face, waiting for somebody to speak.

"I know this will sound horrid, but I am glad she will be gone in the morning," Phoebe said, her hand absently stroking her belly. "She made me ill—and she drove Needham to distraction. We have all given her chance after chance. I know it is unnatural of me to say such a thing about my own mother, but until she relents and changes her ways... Well, I do not want her poison infecting my own children."

"I agree," Selina said. "At least about sending her back to Bath. As to her relenting?" Selina shook her head. "I do not see that ever happening."

Hy never would have believed that her gentle sibling would utter such a harsh prognostication.

"Please tell me I will never have to go to her again," Katie said, the words aimed at Hy. "She has been threatening me with returning to Bath with her ever since I arrived at Wych House."

Phoebe, Selina, and Aurelia all spoke at once.

"Needham and I would love—"

"You are welcome at—"

"Crewe has already mentioned that—"

"Thank you—all of you!" Katie said, her eyes glassy as they slid from face to face, ending with Hy, her watery smile fading. "I would like to remain with you, Hy, if you and His Grace will have me after—after everything."

Hy couldn't help noticing that her youngest sister looked her age for the first time in months. Katie was just a girl still, no matter how much she tried to behave otherwise.

Doubtless she was recalling their discussion after Katie had confessed to locking Shelton and Miss Martin in the attic. It did not matter that the ending was a beneficial one for the pair; Hy was still horrified that her sister had done such a reckless thing.

She pushed the thought away for now, and said, "Chatham and I were hoping you would stay with us through the Season and beyond." It wasn't a lie. Sylvester had greatly enjoyed watching Katie terrorize Shelton and Fowler—yet again proving that her husband was twisted in more ways than one—and Hy appreciated anything that gave her husband that much pleasure. While Shelton would marry and move to his estate, Katie could still toy with Fowler. Even Hy had to admit she enjoyed watching such a huge man go about in terror of her little sister.

"As you all know," Aurelia said, her quiet voice drawing everyone's attention, "our mother told me I was no longer her daughter—that I was dead to her— months ago when I took the position in Scotland. While her opinion altered when I showed up married to Crewe, she expressed no remorse for her behavior and commenced to enumerate my husband's shortcomings and what I needed to do to overcome them." She gave an unamused laugh. "That was before she heard who Nora and Guustin were. She has not said a word to me since learning their identities. Crewe said, and I could not blame him, that if her treatment of Needham was any indication of what her approval looked like, he could live without it."

"She told me Caius was an embarrassment and should stay in the country when I went to London," Selina said, her beautiful face looking angrier than Hy had ever seen her.

"She told me I will be coming to Bath in the summer," said a quiet male voice.

All heads turned toward Doddy. Their brother had been so reserved that it had been easy to overlook him. But the anguish in his voice spoke louder than a shout.

"I will tell Needham, Doddy. You will never have to go," Phoebe said. "He will use the only persuasion the countess respects: money."

Doddy sighed, looking pained and old beyond his years. "Pheeb, I can't keep relying on your husband to solve my problems." He looked around at the rest of them, raising a staying hand before they could speak. "Or any of your husbands, either."

His blue eyes were more troubled than Hy had ever seen them, making her wonder what sort of experience he'd had at school. She had asked Sylvester about Eton, and he had confirmed every suspicion she'd had and more about the brutality that often occurred there.

"There is no shame in taking help from your family. Certainly not while you are not yet of age," Hy said, holding her brother's gaze. "We are your family and taking care of you is both our duty and our honor, Doddy. And one day, when you are old enough and have your own children, or if you are ever called upon to take care of ours, you will know I speak the truth."

Her sisters nodded.

But Doddy looked unconvinced. "All I have done is take, Hy." He gestured to the elegant, freshly decorated room around them. "Needham has poured a fortune into this house, and it is *all* going to benefit me. He pays for my schooling. He pays for the clothing on my back. He pays for *everything.*"

Phoebe struggled to her feet and went to sit beside their brother, draping an arm around his slumped shoulders. "At the risk of sounding vulgar, the money Needham is spending on both the house and your schooling is a proverbial drop in the bucket, Doddy. Would you have him stint you when it is something he can do with little cost to himself? And it is also something he does for *me.*"

Doddy nodded, but Hy could see it would take time—if ever—before he felt easy in accepting so much help. She thought it spoke well of his character.

"Your impulse is decent, Doddy," Selina said, speaking Hy's thoughts. "You aren't behaving like Mama and Papa, with your hand constantly extended."

"Which brings up a matter Hy, Selina, and I discussed the day of the skating party," Aurelia said, turning to Hy—as if suddenly *she* were the one to lead them. Was that a dubious benefit of rank?

Hy nodded to indicate she recalled their conversation.

"Crewe wishes to share the burden of supporting both our parents," Aurelia said.

"Shaftsbury has said the same," Selina agreed.

"As has Chatham," Hy said.

They all turned to Phoebe.

She sighed. "Needham expected your offers of help and is pleased to accept them. He suggested we all assemble after the guests have gone and discuss what is to be done about Papa." She grimaced. "He has repeatedly outstripped his allowance, which is shockingly generous. Mama, for all that she is impossible, at least is not profligate."

"Shaftsbury says that Father will never be brought into line as long as he is one of the Regent's set," Selina said.

"That is Chatham's opinion, as well," Hy said.

Phoebe nodded. "Then let us ponder possible solutions and discuss them before we leave for London."

"And before I leave for Eton," Doddy added, not looking especially happy.

"You do not have to go back," Selina said, giving their little brother—who looked to have lost weight and appeared even more fragile than ever—a concerned glance. "Shaftsbury and I would *love* to have you come live with us."

Doddy smiled. "I appreciate your kind offer. But I need to go back."

Privately, Hy agreed. Her brother was a peer and would one day wield political influence that would affect hundreds of dependents. A place like Eton might be brutal, but he would learn about his responsibilities there.

Phoebe patted Doddy's hand. "Well, now that all that is settled—"

"There is one more thing," Hy said.

The other five turned to her.

Hy cleared her throat. "Er, I suspect that we shall have a wedding to prepare for."

Phoebe's eyes bulged. "You think Miss Martin and Lord Shelton would agree to marry *here?*"

"Shelton has a special license."

"That is where he went?" Aurelia asked, looking amused.

Hy permitted herself a slight smile. "Chatham said he made miraculous time to get to London and back. He did not look like a man who wanted to wait when last I saw him."

"A wedding!" Phoebe breathed. "And with Wych Chapel just restored! Oh, but how will we ever manage a wedding *and* all these guests?"

Selina laughed. "Don't worry, Phoebe, you won't have to do it all yourself. We will all pitch in."

"It will be a pleasure," Aurelia said.

Hy wisely did not offer any assistance.

"Stacia has no father or mother to represent her interests," Katie said, the grim look in her eyes made Hy wonder, yet again, what had happened to make her little sister so pragmatic.

"Needham will do it," Phoebe immediately said.

When Selina and Aurelia looked prepared to protest, Hy threw her vote behind her younger sister. "I think that is an excellent idea, Phoebe. He is master here and the wedding will take place beneath his roof."

The others nodded.

"Who would have believed that any woman could bring Shelton up to scratch," Selina said, looking delighted.

"Chatham is still in a state of shock. *Pleased* shock but shock all the same. In my opinion, Shelton is the lucky one," Hy couldn't help adding.

Selina laughed. "You never did like him."

Hy had never told her sister about encountering Shelton at the various London gambling hells and how badly the handsome marquess had behaved. "I do not dislike him," she felt compelled to say.

Katie gave her a skeptical look.

But Hy was not lying. She was impressed that Shelton possessed the good sense to choose Miss Martin as his mate. Her husband's too-attractive cousin had been lost in self-indulgent debauchery—and the past—for far too long. Mariah, the woman both Sylvester and Shelton had been in love with was dead and gone. It was time to move on. Past time.

"I think she is perfect for him," Phoebe said, and then suddenly sat bolt upright. "Oh dear! I have quite forgotten it is Christmas and there is a ball in progress." She laughed. "And I am the hostess."

Hy had been hoping everyone might forget and they could all just retire to their chambers. But, accepting the new mantle that had been thrust upon her, she nodded at her sister and stood. "Let us rejoin the guests. There will be plenty of time to discuss wedding plans after we actually consult the bride and groom."

Chapter 38

Eight Days Later

Andrew was beginning to think his groomsman and his betrothed had eloped together.

He glanced at his watch and then at the doors to the narthex and then at the vicar—the Reverend...*Something!* Damn and blast, Andrew had forgotten the man's name already—but the clergyman merely smiled, seemingly unconcerned, his confident smile assuring Andrew that nothing was amiss.

He glanced at his watch and found only a few seconds had passed. He resisted the urge to hurl the useless thing across the nave and, instead, clasped his hands behind his back so he was not tempted to look at it again.

The moment he linked his fingers he felt the ring on his thumb and his mouth pulled into a smile, some of the tension draining from his body as he absently turned the metal circle round and round, lightly tracing the Norse symbols with the pads of his fingers.

His cousin had paid a visit to Andrew's chambers the evening before. "I have something for you," Sylvester had said, looking uncharacteristically uncomfortable while holding out his hand.

Andrew had given him a look of suspicion that had only been partly mocking. "It had better not be keys."

A few days before Sylvester had tried to make Andrew a wedding present of a house in London, his argument being that such a gift was really for him, rather than Andrew and Stacia.

Sylvester chuckled. "No, it is not a key. It is not a gift at all. It already belongs to you." He dropped something cool and metallic into his palm.

It was the ring his cousin had given him when Andrew had saved his life, a twin of the one Chatham had never taken off.

Andrew had felt an alarming moistness in his eyes when he'd slipped the heavy ring onto his thumb. "Thank you. I am glad to have it back."

"And I am glad to have my brother back," Chatham had replied.

"If you are trying to make me weep like a schoolgirl, you are not going to be successful," Andrew had warned, belying that promise when he'd needed to glare up at the ceiling for a full minute while his cousin had caught him in a rib-cracking embrace.

Andrew knew it wasn't the ring itself which settled his jittery nerves. It was the meaning behind it. And the man who'd given it to him.

And where the hell *was* that man now? Andrew glanced around the church yet again, jittery. He reached for his watch but stopped himself just in time.

He had no idea why he was so agitated. He had been fine that morning when he'd' woken up. Optimistic, even. Marriage had not been something he'd given serious thought to for as long as he could remember. The only reason he would have contemplated taking a wife was to manipulate Sylvester in his war of vengeance.

But now...

Now he was eager.

Indeed, waiting these past eight days had been agony. He constantly relived those nights in the priest hole and burned for her.

But he didn't just want to bed Stacia. He was impatient to take her home to Rosewood and start a life with her.

Home.

When was the last time he'd thought of Rosewood that way? Had he ever?

The nine days might have been a hellish wait, but there was no denying that his feelings for her had grown exponentially as they'd come to know each other better.

For the first time in his life, he hadn't wanted his solitary morning rides; he'd wanted Stacia with him. He'd wanted to tell her about Rosewood, about the stud farm—about everything—and he'd wanted to hear her opinions and ideas about everything.

It had struck Andrew—when he and Stacia had been discussing the possibility of resurrecting the long disused dairy at Rosewood—that a good marriage was also a partnership, two like-minded people pulling together in harness.

Who would have believed he would ever entertain such a domestic thought?

Was it possible that what he felt was not just sexual attraction and deep affection but...

Love?

Andrew stared without seeing, his already disordered thoughts now in utter disarray.

Damnit! Love? Could that be it?

He looked up dazedly from his roiling thoughts to find the Duchess of Chatham regarding him with her usual unreadable gaze.

Andrew had been startled—but pleased—when Stacia had asked his cousin's wife to stand as her matron of honor. Her choice ought not have surprised him as the normally reserved duchess had exhibited an almost solicitous interest in Stacia ever since freeing her from the priest hole.

"Sylvester forgot the ring and had to go back for it," the duchess explained in a quiet voice. "I believe he is almost as nervous as you."

"Ah." What else could he say? He *was* nervous; nervous that Stacia would come to her senses and abandon him at the altar.

"I like Miss Martin," the duchess said.

Andrew couldn't help grinning. "So do I."

His humor did nothing to melt her icy façade. Or perhaps that *was* the duchess? Ice, through and through. But Andrew didn't think so. Especially considering the way she sometimes stared at Sylvester when she thought nobody else was looking: as if she wanted to consume him.

"Chatham believes you will do right by her," she said.

Andrew bristled at her carefully worded comment, which implied that *she* did not think the same thing. "That is certainly my intention," he said stiffly.

After a long, uncomfortable moment, she said, "I agree with him."

Andrew's eyebrows leapt at this unprecedented sign of approval.

Before he could come up with something to say—and probably irritate her again—the doors opened and Sylvester and Stacia entered the nave, arm in arm.

He gawked like a star struck youth.

She was…radiant.

Her gown of emerald-green velvet made her look like a burst of spring on a frigid winter's day. She held a bouquet of white hydrangeas with a few sprigs of prickly holly and bright red berries in the middle.

He lifted his gaze higher, until their eyes met.

Her loving smile touched off an explosion inside him to rival a pyrotechnic display at Vauxhall Gardens.

Andrew was far too addled to identify all the emotions that filled him to near bursting, but the cumulative effect was a feeling of…rightness.

Was that normal? Was *rightness* a proper feeling to have for one's prospective bride?

It feels right *because it is love, you dolt.*

Andrew blinked and looked up from the revelatory thought—doubtless grinning like an idiot—and saw mild puzzlement in Stacia's eyes.

He knew he should at least acknowledge his cousin, but he could not look away from her, more engrossed than he'd ever been in his life.

The vicar's words all ran together. Andrew was impressed that he was able to speak his responses when it was time for him to do so.

"—you may kiss your bride."

Those words shook him from his fugue.

Stacia gazed up at him with love. Not adoration for the handsome face and body the rest of the world saw, but love for *Andrew*, the flawed, damaged man inside who had made one disastrous decision after another.

Until her.

Her lips twitched and he realized he was staring. Andrew collected a few of his remaining wits and gently claimed her upturned mouth with a chaste kiss while promising, with his eyes, much, much, much more later.

The Bellamy siblings and their spouses made enough racket for three times their number when Andrew and his new wife walked down the aisle. The short journey to the dining room was a raucous, laughter-filled pilgrimage.

Lord and Lady Needham had orchestrated a magnificent wedding breakfast. True to form the seating defied convention and Andrew found himself between Mrs. Nora Walker and Kathryn.

"Congratulations, my lord," Mrs. Walker said, her beautiful face shining with a sort of serenity that seemed strange to him, given that she was at the family home of her former lover's wife.

"Thank you, ma'am," he said.

"They are a lovely family." Her gaze flickered over the Bellamy sisters and lingered on Lady Crewe. "I did not want to come here for Christmas."

Andrew leaned closer to whisper, "Me neither."

They both laughed.

"Why did you?" he asked now that she had raised the subject.

"Because Aurelia convinced me. She pointed out that Guustin would not come here without me, and that Crewe would miss his son at Christmas." She shrugged. "It seemed selfish to say *no*."

"Are you glad you came?"

"Very. I did not have a large family, so this has been lovely."

Chatham, who was on her other side, asked her something and she excused herself.

Andrew took a deep breath and turned to Kathryn.

She was waiting for him. Andrew had not spent any time alone with her since before the priest hole incident. She looked tired and there were dark smudges beneath her brilliant eyes.

The smile she gave him was tentative—un-Kathryn-like, in other words—and Andrew sighed. "I might as well say it, as I've been thinking it for days. Thank you."

Her eyes bulged.

Andrew chuckled at her reaction. "What?" he taunted. "You do not think me a big enough man to admit when somebody else is right and I am wrong?"

"Not when that *somebody* is a girl," she shot back, showing some spirit.

"A woman," he corrected. "You are no girl, Kathryn. You are...formidable."

She looked cheered by that description. "I did not choose Stacia capriciously, you know. Mrs. Leary mentioned more than once how she'd felt dreadful stealing your attention when so many other women would have genuinely liked it. She mentioned Stacia specifically."

Andrew hated hearing that. He hated yet more confirmation that he'd forgotten her. Over and over again.

"You know that you forget things, Andrew."

Andrew waited for the surge of rage he'd felt when she had *poked* at him in the past. But it didn't come.

"I know," he finally said.

"Are you afraid?"

He looked up from his mostly untouched soup. "What do you think?"

She nodded, sympathy in her eyes.

"What happened to you at your aunt's house?" he asked.

Her eyes, so open a moment earlier, shuttered. "I don't know what you mean."

Yes, she did. But it was Andrew's wedding day and the last thing he wanted to do was rub salt in her wound—and there *was* a wound, of that he was sure.

And so he said, "What do you think the chances are that Chatham can make your sister ride the entire way to London in the coach?"

Kathryn snorted. "I'll not take that wager, thank you."

Andrew laughed.

Chapter 39

Andrew led Stacia through the narrow doorway into their 'bridal chamber'.

She couldn't help laughing. "Whose idea was this?" she asked as they paused to admire the familiar scene at the far end of the priest hole.

Andrew grinned. "It seemed…fitting."

"Is somebody going to lock us inside this time, too?"

"Would you mind terribly?"

"Hmm." She thoughtfully tapped her chin. "It depends on what books have been included."

He laughed. "Come," he said, taking her hand and leading her toward the blazing fire. "Needham looked so happy to oblige my request to use this as our bridal suite that I suspect the viscountess will find herself imprisoned up here sooner rather than later."

"Do you think he knows about our first stay in this room?" she asked, taking a seat on the settee while Andrew investigated the hampers.

"He did not give me that impression," he said, pulling a bottle from a bucket of ice. "Champagne?"

"Yes, please. I felt sure that Kathryn's sisters knew."

"Perhaps they decided the rest of their families did not need to hear the truth," he said, removing the cork with a *pop,* filling the waiting glasses, and handing her one before sitting down beside her. He raised his glass. "To us." He paused, grinned, and then added, "Wife."

"To us," she echoed. "Husband."

He laughed and they both drank. Afterward he took her glass and set it down before sliding his arms beneath her and lifting her onto his lap, shifting her until she was exactly where he wanted her.

"There," he said, looking smugly satisfied. "I have been dying to hold you for days. And I've been dying to do this, too." He claimed her mouth with a deep, drugging kiss that left her body limp when he finally released her.

His eyes were dark as they flickered over her and landed on her hand. He lifted it and examined the ring as if he'd not been the one to give it back to her mere hours earlier. "It is lovely, but I cannot believe you will not allow me to buy you a more suitable ring."

"I don't want another one, Andrew, I adore *this* one," she said, admiring the perfect rose.

"But it was a Christmas present—not a wedding ring."

She ignored him. "I still cannot believe you knew how much I liked this."

"I was spying on you that day. Stalking you." He waggled his eyebrows in a villainous manner. "It was to be your secret St. Nicholas gift, but it wasn't ready when I went to the village to fetch it before going to London. I had to take it along to a jeweler I know in town, and he sized it."

Stacia stared for a moment, and then said, "Oh." She suddenly felt like a jealous toad.

"What is that *oh* for?"

"Nothing." The last thing she wanted to do was expose her jealousy to him.

He cocked his head. "*What?*"

"It is just—well, it wasn't a very nice thing."

"What thing?"

"I knew you'd gone to the village before going to London—Mr. Higgins mentioned it—and I thought—" She bit her lower lip.

"You thought what?"

"That you had gone to see Mrs. Johnson," she blurted the words out in a rush, hoping that would make her feel less insecure and foolish. It didn't.

He frowned for a moment and then his eyes widened in comprehension. Instead of being angry, he clucked his tongue. "I told you I wanted to marry you only a few hours earlier! What a filthy mind my new wife has. I shall have to see that she turns it in the appropriate direction henceforth."

"I'm so sorry, Andrew," she said, unwilling to forgive her suspicious mind as quickly as he did.

"You are forgiven. Just promise me you won't think such a thing again?"

"I promise."

"Good. Because I am yours. And you are mine. I don't want any other woman, Stacia." He hesitated, met her eyes with an unsmiling look, and said, "For years I have cultivated a reputation as a heartless rake, but—like so much of my behavior—most of what I did was engineered to irk Sylvester." He lightly stroked her cheek, his eyes flickering over her face.

His expression shifted until he looked almost tentative.

"What is it?" she asked, a tendril of fear snaking through her.

"There is something else. Something I did not want to mention when you told me I had met you before—often. I didn't say anything at the time because it seemed too self-serving." He pulled a wry face. "It is also an unpleasant subject for me. I have known for a long time that I must have sustained more than hearing loss when I, er, got my bell rung. I often forget things, Stacia—people, faces, names. I do better if there is more than just a brief introduction. Conversations of any length seem to—to *set* a person in my mind, for lack of a better term. I should have confessed my problem before we marr—"

She cupped his face with both hands and brought him lower for a kiss.

"*Mmm,*" he hummed when she practiced some of his own tricks on him. When she pulled away, his eyes were heavy-lidded. "What was that for?"

"Because I wanted to kiss you."

He smiled. "That is an excellent impulse. You must always surrender to it. Did I tell you how beautiful you look today?" he asked, his teasing tone telling her that the question was not a memory lapse.

"You did. Twice."

"Here is a third time: you look utterly gorgeous." He cocked his head. "Are you hungry?"

Stacia blinked at the change of subject. "Er, no."

"Do you want to play a game of Dictionary?"

She gave a startled laugh. "No."

His nostril flared slightly. "Are you ready for bed?"

Her face scalded under his knowing look. "Ye—"

He lunged to his feet before the word was all the way out.

Stacia laughed as he carried her toward the bed, all but sprinting.

***

Andrew loved hearing Stacia laugh almost as much as he loved hearing her pant, gasp, and whimper.

He had been looking forward to tonight for days, but he also felt a certain tension. She was a virgin, after all.

"Are you nervous?" he asked, as he set her down on the bed.

"A little. But I trust you."

340

Christ! The woman knew how to grab his heart. Andrew suddenly recalled a conversation they'd had in this very room, in this bed. Lord. How much did she know? How much *didn't* she know? "Are there any, er, questions that I can answer?"

"Oh. You mean about what is going to happen?"

Andrew nodded. "You told me that nobody tells young women about, er, sexual matters."

Her cheeks darkened. "Lady Needham spoke to me last night."

Andrew felt a rush of relief. As much as he adored filthy pillow talk, he had not relished having to describe such an intimacy in practical terms. "Ah. Good. Excellent. I daresay she knows what she is talking about."

She laughed. "Yes. It sounded like it." She swallowed, her amusement dwindling, and then added, "She said there would be a little pain. She also said that you were probably the sort of man who would, er, make sure that discomfort did not signify."

God bless Lady Needham.

"I will make it good for you, Stacia."

"I know you will."

He caressed her face, unable to resist touching her. "I don't usually sleep in most of my clothing as I did those nights we spent together."

She snorted softly. "I did not think you did."

"I don't even sleep in a nightshirt."

"Oh. Is that—is that something you would like for me to do?"

He grinned. "You mean sleep naked?"

She gave him an exasperated look. "You just like making me blush."

"Yes. I do. And *yes* to your first question. I want you to sleep naked. And when I say *sleep*, I mean any time we share a bed. Which will be every night."

"You don't wish to have your own room?"

"We will have our own rooms, but we will share one bed—yours, mine, I do not care which." He took her chin between his fingers and tilted her up for a kiss. "But I want to sleep tangled up together. I like it almost as much as I like sex, Stacia. I want both with you, as often as possible."

She caught her lower lip with her teeth and then nodded.

"Who shall I undress first?" he asked.

"You first," she blurted, making him laugh.

"As my lady commands."

There was a pair of candles on one of the nightstands and he wondered if she would ask to have them snuffed. But her eyes and attention were riveted to his hands as he unbuttoned his dark green tailcoat and the pale gold waistcoat beneath it.

"Will you valet me?" he asked once the coats were both unbuttoned.

She leapt to her feet with an enthusiasm that made him chuckle.

A moment later, after much pulling and tugging, she managed to peel off the tight sleeves.

He caught her arm before she could return to the bed and pulled her close, kissing her soundly. "You are such an excellent valet that I almost regret engaging Thomas."

"You cannot change your mind now—Dora would not allow it," Stacia said.

He laughed. "No, I daresay she would not."

The young lovers had approached Andrew when they'd learned he was engaging a valet and personal maid, offering their services. Thomas had waited on Andrew several times during his stay and Stacia seemed fond of Dora, but he had needed to talk to Needham before poaching his servants. Naturally, the viscount—one of the most generous men Andrew had met—was as gracious about losing two excellent servants as he had been about everything else.

Andrew released her and then sat down on the bed. He was tempted to ask for help with his hessians—his cock throbbed just imagining the sight of her straddling his leg—but something told him he needed to save his more playful impulses for a later date.

Once he'd shed his boots and stockings he stood and tugged off his cravat, holding it out to her. "Will I need this?"

Her hand twitched and he thought she might reach for it, but she just shook her head.

Andrew tossed it aside, pulled off his shirt, and then pushed down his tight pantaloons and drawers in one motion.

When he stood, her eyes arrowed directly to his cock, which was delighted to be on display and already standing at attention and slick with need.

He held out a hand. "Come here and let me undress you."

She swallowed but stood.

Andrew turned her back to him and slowly worked on the row of small buttons, dropping kisses on her exposed nape. "Have I told you—"

"Yes."

He laughed softly. "You don't know what I was going to say."

"What were you going to say?"

"How beautifu—"

"Yes, you've told me."

"Don't you like hearing that?" he asked, slipping his hands beneath the shoulders of her loosened gown and pushing it to the floor before turning her.

"I am not beautiful," she said as Andrew stooped to pick up her dress while she stepped out of it.

He laid the garment carefully on the bench at the foot of the bed before turning to her and setting his hands on her shoulders. "You are beautiful to me." He forced her to meet his gaze. "I will keep saying it until you believe me." Her lashes lowered and he tilted her face up. "I'm serious, Stacia." He kissed her. "You are the most beautiful woman of my acquaintance." He smiled wryly. "And that includes the many I've probably forgotten."

Rather than laugh or smile, she merely looked pained.

"What is it, darling? You need to talk to me. Always. I am terrible when it comes to reading your mind—it is all I can do to read my own."

"It is nothing."

"It is something. Come. Tell me."

She closed her eyes. "You said once before that M-Mariah was the most beautiful woman you'd ever seen. I suspect that was probably more truthful. I know full well that I am passable, at best."

There could only have been one time when he might have said such a thing, not that he could recall his exact words. "Open your eyes, darling. I need to tell you something that shames me." When she complied, he continued, "I cannot recall Mariah's face. I know she had blue eyes and blonde hair, but that is all I remember. I don't know if I have forgotten because of"—he made a vague gesture toward his head—"or because the memory has simply faded because of time. For more than a decade I romanticized a relationship which lasted less than two months. An *affair*." He held her gaze. "If I said she was the most beautiful woman I had ever seen, it was because that is one of the few things I recall feeling." He cupped her face. "I don't see her face, Stacia. When I close my eyes, I see *yours*."

***

Stacia felt like a needy, insecure fool for bringing up such a matter—especially when she heard the truth.

"You told me to forget the past—to forgive myself—and to move on. You have to allow me to do that, darling. I am ten years your senior and there have been women in my life. But now—and for the rest of my days—there is only *one* woman." He kissed her and then pulled back and frowned. "What is this?" he murmured, brushing away a tear she hadn't realized she'd shed.

"They are happy tears. I don't understand why I am feeling so emotional."

"I think that is understandable; it has been a hectic few weeks. Let me relax you." He kissed her lightly and resumed undressing her with a practiced ease that still gave her qualms, as much as she tried not to think of his past.

"Sit," he said, once he'd slipped off her stays.

He took her foot and set her slipper on his knee.

Stacia's eyes slid over to his membrum virile. It was not as erect as it had been a few minutes ago, but neither was it completely...quiescent.

"Other foot, sweetheart."

Stacia blinked; he'd removed her slipper, garter, *and* stocking while she had been staring.

"I like your eyes on me," he said as he slipped off her other shoe.

Stacia swallowed at his hot, hungry look and resumed her unmannerly gawking.

A moment later all she wore was her shift. She tensed, waiting for him to pull away her last defense.

Instead, he lightly caressed her cheek and said, "Lie back, sweetheart."

Stacia lifted her feet onto the bed and pushed away from the edge before lying down.

He lowered onto the mattress and bracketed her shoulders with his hands, his knee nudging at her tightly clenched thighs. "Open for me, darling."

When she did, he laid down between her legs. "You remember what I did before?"

Stacia gave a slightly hysterical giggle. "As if I could forget."

"It was pleasurable?"

She nodded, not trusting her voice.

"Close your eyes if it helps you relax, darling."

344

Stacia was about to do exactly that when her inner voice suddenly woke up. *Begin as you mean to go on.*

Indeed.

She forced down her embarrassment and pushed up onto her elbows. "I want to watch."

The slow, sinful smile that spread across his face told her how much he liked that answer.

***

Unlike the last time, when it had been too damned dark to see anything, Andrew groaned when he parted her lips, his mouth flooding at the sight of her slick, swollen sex. "So lovely, Stacia." He looked up and smiled at her wide-eyed face. "I wish you could see how beautiful you are."

"I—what—why—"

He chuckled. "But we will save that for another night, my love." Holding her gaze, he lowered his mouth, his eyelids fluttering with pleasure at the taste of her.

"Andrew," she whispered through slack, parted lips.

He slid a finger inside her tight sheath while he tongued and sucked, taking his time working her toward her climax.

Or at least he tried to take his time, but her body soon tensed and her hips lifted higher and higher, until she was pushing against his mouth, bucking and writhing, her skin sheening with sweat.

Andrew marveled at the feel of her tight cunt as she contracted around his finger, her orgasm rolling through her in powerful waves.

When she began to come back to earth Andrew slid a second finger inside her.

She made a soft sound of surprise and her snug passage squeezing him like a vise.

"You are so deliciously tight," he said, smiling at her expression of dazed mortification. "I need you to come for me one more time, love." He lightly kissed her bud. "Will you do that? For me?"

She nodded, her breathing becoming rough when he eased a third finger alongside the first two.

"Relax, Stacia," he murmured, carefully stretching her silken sheath a bit more with each stroke. Only when she began to meet his thrusts did he lower his mouth, fucking her harder and deeper, not stopping until her back arched off the bed as a second orgasm wracked her small body.

Only when the last ripple of pleasure had faded did he reluctantly withdraw and rise up to his knees.

He smiled down into her heavily-lidded eyes and used the head of his cock to stroke her, slicking his shaft with her juices before positioning himself at her opening.

"Ready?" he asked.

She stared up at him through sated, slitted eyes and nodded, spreading wider for him.

"Such an eager darling," he praised, hissing in a breath when he pulsed his crown past the outer ring of muscle. "Christ but you're tight!"

She bit her lip at his crude words, but her hips lifted to take him deeper, pain creasing her eyes.

"Fast or slow?" he asked in a strained voice.

She swallowed. "Fast."

Andrew gritted his teeth and sank into her until he could go no deeper. He thought he felt some barrier give way, although he strongly suspected that was only his imagination.

She was breathing harshly.

Andrew kissed her, his hips not moving. "I'm sorry, sweetheart."

"I know," she said. Her hands, which had been limp at her sides, slid over his back. And then lower.

Andrew raised his eyebrows when they froze.

"May I touch—"

"Anywhere," he said emphatically. "You may touch me anywhere. In fact, it is mandatory." He smiled so that she knew he was speaking in jest. Well, mostly.

Her small, cool hands slid south until one rested on each buttock.

"Oh," she said, catching her lip with her teeth before squeezing him so lightly he might have thought he'd imagined it if not for her shy smile.

He withdrew while she was distracted.

Her brow creased and her hands stilled.

"Am I hurting you?" he asked.

"It—it doesn't hurt, but it's..."

"Yes?"

"It feels bigger than I thought."

"Flatterer," he teased. "I would say that you are too tight, but..." He kissed the tip of her nose. "I would be lying."

When the tension drained from her face Andrew sank back in, filling her all the way.

The lines on her forehead smoothed and she met his gaze. "It doesn't hurt this time."

"Good. Because I'm going to do it again." He matched deed to word. "And again."

Andrew worked her slowly but deeply, giving her every inch with each stroke, watching her closely for signs of discomfort. But when her hands began to move on his arse—squeezing and cupping him like a pair of cabbages she was contemplating buying—he transferred his weight to one arm, slid a hand between their sweaty bodies as he sped up his thrusts.

She squirmed, her fingers digging into his buttocks as his hips drummed harder and harder.

She exploded just as he lost control and gave in to his need, his last few thrusts wild and savage before he thrust deep and flooded her with his seed.

"Stacia," he muttered as his hips jerked, her tight body squeezing his cock with the echoes of her orgasm, milking him until he had nothing left.

***

Yes. It had hurt.

But what her brief, embarrassingly frank conversation with Lady Needham had not prepared Stacia for was the emotional impact of such a raw, physical joining. Never would she have expected the sensation of completeness she felt.

Andrew was inside her.

And it was glorious.

Stacia reveled in the hot, heavy feel of him and was disappointed when he began to pull away.

"I am crushing yo—"

She dug her fingers into the tight globes of his bottom and held him in place. Or at least, he allowed her to stop him from leaving.

His chest rumbled with laughter. His laugh was one of the things that she loved most about him. And his teasing sense of humor. And the way his eyes lit up when he was amused or delighted. And his—well, there was not much she did not love. And if he did not love her? Well, *this* right now, and the past nine days of companionship, joy, and affection were all far, far more than she had ever hoped for.

"I take it you want me to crush you?" he asked.

She squeezed his buttocks harder in answer.

Again, he chuckled. "This suits me to my toes," he murmured, and then his manhood flexed inside her.

Stacia sucked in a breath. "Was that—did you do that?"

This time, his laughter shook the bed. "Who else would be doing it, sweetheart?"

He did it again and again, until he began to harden inside her.

He groaned. "Now see what you have done, Lady Shelton?"

"I didn't do anything. That was all *you*."

"You are heaven," he said. "Utter heaven. I have been dreaming about being inside you for weeks."

Just what did a woman say to such a thing? Not that she didn't adore hearing it.

He pushed up onto his elbows and smiled down at her. "You are so wet and tight that I want to take you again. And again. But I will not. I know you must be terribly sore."

There was an undeniable ache underlying the pleasure she felt having him inside her. "A little," she admitted. "Are—are you?"

He stilled, his expression arrested. "Er, am I what?"

"Sore."

"No," he said after a long moment. "Men are fortunate that way," he added in a suspiciously level voice.

She squinted at him. "You are teasing me, aren't you?"

"I would *never!*" he said, opening his eyes comically wide.

"You are horrid."

He laughed. "I am," he agreed, slowly withdrawing from her body. "But you love me anyway, don't you?"

A hiss escaped her, and not just from the slight physical burn. "Yes, Andrew. I love you anyway."

He backed down her body, until he was once again between her thighs. "I am relieved to hear it, darling, because I love you, too."

Stacia's eyes, which had begun to close, flew open. "What?"

He grinned up the length of her body, his skilled fingers lightly caressing her sex. "Heard that part, did you? And here I thought you had fallen asleep." He lowered his mouth and kissed her thigh. "I wanted to tell you earlier, but it is bad form to tell one's lover such a thing at the peak of passion."

"But…since when?" she asked.

"Your new husband is a terrible dunce, Stacia. It took me until this morning in the chapel to finally put a name to what I was feeling. But today is not the first time I experienced the emotion."

"It—it wasn't?"

He shook his head. "Somewhere along the way, without me even realizing it, my enchantment turned to love. I wish I could recall when the feeling took hold, but I *do* know that I was enchanted and fascinated by you since the night I said such horrid things about you and you gave me a cool tongue lashing outside the drawing room, instead of doing what I really deserved and shoving me down the stairs."

"Oh, Andrew," she said, her vision suddenly blurry.

"I love your laugh, my sweet, serious, darling Miss Martin." He gave her a rueful smile. "I am sorry it has taken me so long to tell you what I felt. For the longest time I thought there was only room for one sort of love in my heart. I convinced myself that is what my vendetta was all about: my love for Mariah. I am not saying that I didn't love her, but what I did in the years after her death was not about her, but about my obsession with hurting Sylvester. Will you forgive me for being such a dolt for so long—for not telling you what I felt when you shared your love with me?"

"I am glad you didn't tell me then, Andrew. I might have thought you were just being kind, rather than telling me what you truly felt."

"You are too good to me; you have been from the very beginning. I will strive to make my idiotic behavior a thing of the past, darling. And you—you are my future. My future and my love."

She gave a watery laugh when he kissed her. "Don't become *too* perfect. I rather like some of your idiotic behavior."

He laughed. "I can safely say that is a given." His eyelids lowered and he gave her a look that could only be called carnivorous. "But enough *talking* about how much I love you," he said, his lips curving into the sinful smile she loved so much. "Now let me show you."

And then he proceeded to do exactly that.

The End

Epilogue

Stacia hurried up the steps to Chatham House and nodded her thanks to the footman who opened the door for her.

She had spent the morning with Selina and Aurelia, the three of them having the final fittings for their court gowns.

Stacia had never dreamed that she would be presented. It had been Chatham who'd suggested it.

"Shelton is my heir and there is a great deal of curiosity about his new wife. Because this is something I am asking for, I would be honored to purchase your court gown, Stacia," the duke had assured her. "It is a garment which you will never wear again, after all."

"That is a kind offer, Your Grace. But Andrew would, I think, be very unhappy if I were to accept your gift, Your Grace."

Chatham had pulled a face. "He is too proud by half."

"Perhaps," she had agreed with a smile. "I will agree to a presentation, but…on my own terms."

Andrew had not been happy when Stacia refused to allow him to purchase the expensive, ultimately useless, garment—at least not a brand new one.

"Lord, Stacia—when I told you that I was not wealthy, I did not mean that I was so below the hatches that I couldn't afford a *gown*! I told you that Chatham has managed my inheritance so skillfully these past eleven years that we have no need to live like paupers. A gown, no matter how dear, will not beggar us. Nor will it deprive our tenants and servants at Rosewood."

"I know that, Andrew," she had soothed. Stacia had been proud that her husband's first action when he'd discovered the scope of his inheritance had been to write to the steward at Rosewood and give the man instructions to commence much needed improvements. "I have happily agreed to spend money on new clothes—"

"Happily?" Andrew had scoffed. "I recall having to threaten you with husbandly discipline if you did not comply with my command and purchase some new dresses."

Stacia laughed. "Yes. And I distinctly recall you *disciplining* me even after I complied." Indeed, just recalling her husband's interesting brand of *discipline* made her thighs clench. "But I am adamant about the court gown, Andrew. I hate the thought of spending so much money on something that will only be used for a few minutes."

"So, what are you going to do, then? Chatham seems set on this foolishness."

"I have decided to purchase a used gown from the modiste who is making dresses for Aurelia and Selina."

"A *used* gown?" he'd demanded, his face screwed up in horror.

"Don't be such a horrid snob. The gown was worn one time for only a few hours."

After a bit more squabbling—and after Stacia had told him the cost of a *new* court gown—he had grudgingly agreed.

The presentation was in three days. Stacia was relieved she would not be alone. Not only were Selina and Aurelia going, but so was Hyacinth—although with considerably less exuberance than her sisters.

Today's fitting had run over and Stacia had agreed to meet Andrew afterward. Evidently he had some *surprise* that he wanted to give her. She hoped it was not a new wedding ring—which he'd threatened to buy more than once. She loved her silver rose, even though he insisted it was not grand enough.

"Ah, there you are!" Andrew said when Stacia entered the foyer. He was already dressed to go out, Scrapper dancing around his feet.

"Shall I go and change my—"

"You look perfect," he said. "Come along. We don't want to be late."

Stacia stared up at him suspiciously as she took his arm. "Where are you taking me?" She glanced down at the little dog. "And should we leave him here?"

"You will see where we are going. As for Scrapper, he can wait in the carriage." He coughed. "Er, Bently has taken to putting a lap rug and warming pan on the bench for the little beast."

"Oh. *Bently* has done that, has he?" she taunted, knowing full well who was responsible for spoiling the dog.

Andrew shrugged guiltily but didn't bother to deny it.

"One moment," he said to Stacia after handing her into the carriage. She heard him murmur something to the coachman and then climbed in beside her.

"What is all this mystery about?" she asked, their bodies pressed together even though there was at least four inches of unused seat on his other side.

"I cannot tell you, my love, or it would not be a mystery," he said. And then scooted even closer.

Stacia laughed. "I know you have more seat—I can see it."

He grinned down at her and slipped his arm around her. "How did your fitting go?"

"It is the last one, for which I am very grateful."

"I am eager to see you in the gown."

"You will laugh," she assured him. "I resemble a short, squat toadstool with legs." He laughed, but Stacia was serious. "I will just be glad to get the affair over with," she said, and then looked up at him. "And then I want to go Rosewood."

"Are you sure you don't want to spend at least a few weeks enjoying the Season?"

"I do not." She hesitated. "Unless you do?"

"I do not," he said emphatically.

Stacia sighed with relief. "Good."

He took her hand and gently squeezed it. "You know there will be no rest when we get there? A mountain of work awaits you at Rosewood."

"You have already warned me, Andrew." More than once. More than *five* times. Her husband harbored a great deal of guilt toward his estate. The sooner they could put it to rights the sooner he could stop flogging himself.

The carriage rolled to a gentle stop in front of one of the newer mansions on Russell Square. The houses were huge, and, in Stacia's opinion, had sacrificed elegance for sheer size.

"Who lives here?" she asked as the carriage door opened and the footman put down the steps.

"You will see," he said, handing her down from the carriage and then placing her hand on his arm.

"You certainly have a flair for the dramatic, Andrew," she groused as they mounted the few steps to the house.

"It is something I learned during my brief time on the stage."

Her head whipped up. "Are you—oh," she said, scowling when she saw his grin. "You are so odious!"

"I cannot help myself, darling. You snap at the lures I cast so readily."

"*Hmmph.*"

Still smiling, he lifted a hand to the knocker and rapped twice.

After a long moment the door was opened by a footman wearing a powdered wig and the sumptuous blue and gold livery of an older age.

"The Marchioness and Marquess of Shelton to see Lord Clayton. He is expecting us," her husband said, using a haughty tone that Stacia had never heard him employ before.

It took her a second to realize the name he'd just spoken.

Again her head whipped up. This time Andrew was looking straight ahead, his expression of aristocratic ennui so complete she would have laughed if she'd not been so thunderstruck.

The footman hastily stepped back, bowing low as he admitted them into a gaudy foyer, the gilt and mirrors like something from Versailles.

"What are we doing here?" she hissed at Andrew as they followed the servant up the broad white marble stairs.

He merely smiled. "You will see."

"I am going to discipline *you* for this, my lord."

He grinned.

The servant stopped outside a pair of white and gold doors and opened the left-hand one. "Lord and Lady Shelton."

"Show them in," a voice Stacia had not heard for four years called out, although it sounded slightly different, more…nasal.

The moment Andrew guided her into the room Stacia gasped at the reason for her cousin's altered tone. There was a large bandage where his nose should be and his left eye was black and swollen shut.

Geoffrey Martin, the sixth Viscount Clayton, gave a sickly smile and gestured to the chairs in front of his desk. "Please, have a seat."

Once they were seated Geoffrey gingerly took his own seat, moving like a man who was in pain. "You are looking well, Stacia."

"I wish I could say the same for you, Geoff. What in the world happened?"

His eyes—or at least the one that still worked—slid toward Andrew and then rapidly back. "I, er, ran into a door."

Stacia did not comment on his improbable answer.

Geoff cleared his throat. "Er, thank you so much for coming. I regret I have not been able to see you sooner." Again he glanced briefly at Andrew before swallowing and gesturing to a large lacquer box on his desk.

Stacia had not noticed it until then. "Oh! It is Papa's jewelry casket." She looked inquiringly up at her cousin and then at her husband—Andrew still wore his haughty mask and was staring straight ahead. "What is this about, Geoff?"

He leaned forward and pushed the chest closer to her. "This is yours, Stacia. I—er, everything is still as it was when, er, your father died." He cleared his throat again and gestured to a stack of crates beside his desk. "Those are your father's books. Er, most of them. I have sold one or two items. The money I received—and the names of the buyers—is in here." He slid a fat packet tied with string across his desk.

Andrew cleared his throat.

A look of terror flitted across Geoff's face, and he hastily added, "I am deeply sorry for keeping these items from you four years ago, Stacia."

Andrew coughed.

"I have had my man of business contact Lord Needham," Geoff said, speaking so fast his words were tripping over each other. "It would be my pleasure, and my honor, to make good on the settlement he negotiated on your behalf."

"Oh." She blinked rapidly and frowned, looking from her cousin to her husband, who still looked like a stranger with his reserved, languid air. "Erm, thank you, Geoff, that is remarkably handsome of you." Stacia ignored the slight snort that came from beside her.

Geoffry nodded stiffly. "I shall have all these crates delivered to Chatham House unless you have another direction?"

"Chatham House will be perfect, thank you."

They stared at each other in silence for a moment, Geoff looking like a cornered rodent.

"Thank you for receiving us at such short notice Clayton, but I'm afraid we must be on our way," Andrew said, his words causing the other man to jolt and make a small squeaking sound. "No need to bestir yourself," he said, even though Geoff appeared to be frozen to his chair. "We can see ourselves out."

"Goodbye, Geoff," Stacia said, taking Andrew's arm when her cousin merely nodded.

Not until she was bundled in rugs in the carriage, Scrapper snoozing on her lap, and they were rolling along did she look up at her husband. "I take it you were the door my cousin ran into?" she asked.

Andrew gave her the same haughty look he had used to make Geoff squirm. "I am sure I don't know what you mean, my dear."

"That was very bad of you!" Stacia shook her head but couldn't help laughing. She took his hand in both of hers and gazed up at him, her eyes brimming with tears. "It was bad, but it was also the nicest thing anyone has ever done for me. Thank you, Andrew."

He gently squeezed her hand. "I think that is only fair as you've done the nicest thing anyone has ever done for *me*, my lady."

Stacia's lips were already curving in anticipation of his likely teasing, possibly scandalous, answer. "And what is that, my lord?"

"Loving me."

Stacia caught her breath as she stared into his eyes. "Oh, Andrew."

"No crying," he said with mock sternness, wiping a tear from her cheek and then adding, with a boyish grin, "I can't say that my behavior in this instance was entirely unselfish."

"What do you mean?"

"I mean that thrashing Clayton was one of the more pleasurable activities I've had in town this Season."

"*Andrew!*"

"I'm sorry, my love. Was that a terribly vulgar thing to admit?"

"Yes. But mostly I am upset you did not invite me to watch."

Andrew gave a loud hoot and pulled her into an embrace, kissing her soundly. "And here I thought I could not love you more than I already do, my bloodthirsty little wife."

Really The End

Dearest Reader:

Well! Whatever made me think THIS story was going to be a novella, lol? I hope you enjoyed the gentle pace of Andrew and Stacia's romance.

This is not my first Christmas book (I think I've written three Christmas novellas and one Christmas book) but it is the first time that I really wanted to give characters from prior books, in addition to the central couple, some page time.

Not only did I want to give a little update on Phoebe, Hyacinth, Selina, and Aurelia, but I wanted to introduce Kathryn. She really came alive for me while I was writing this, to the point that I have already started her book even though it is months away.

There will be a time jump for Kathryn, Doddy, and Lucy, although I'm not sure just how many years. Yes, I've decided that Lucy will get a book, and I already know who her hero will be and I am so excited!!

So, anyhow, this was a real Cecil B. DeMille, cast of thousands, sort of book, lol. So many scenes hit the cutting room floor that I might make some available at some point. Do I say that a lot? I always think I will get around to cleaning up some of the cut stuff and offering it, but then I find myself running behind schedule and it never happens. Maybe I can make that my New Year's resolution?

If you have read a few of my books you might have noticed this one was especially low angst. Given the current state of the world, I wanted this to be a warm, fuzzy blanket of a book. And, in all honesty, that was as much for me as my readers. I simply could not force myself to write something heavy and angsty.

Although it is fluffy, I still deal with some important themes. Specifically, Post-Concussion Syndrome (PCS). I've had three concussions in my life, so the relatively recent identification of PCS is something that is of interest to me. Knock on wood that I don't seem to have any problems.

Would Stacia have put 2 and 2 together and linked Andrew's memory problems to his head injury? Who knows? Maybe, maybe not. I like to think she was observant enough and thoughtful enough that she could have made that connection.

Incidentally, I got the idea for Andrew's injury after reading about an accident the Duke of Wellington suffered. Except in his case his eardrum burst, and his personal doctor compounded the problem by pouring a solution of 'caustic' into his ear, making it all worse—not to mention horrifically painful.

So, why did I want to make Andrew so damned attractive and irresistible? And who did I have in mind when I wrote his character?

He is introduced in the book SELINA as being Selina's male counterpart in the looks department. I had a lot of fun with Selina and it made me think about appearances and how extreme beauty might not always be the blessing everyone thinks it is. That doesn't mean I'd say *no* to looking like Grace Kelly, lol.

I wanted him to be the sort of guy who was so good looking that he scrambled women's wits and elicited a "screaming, crying Beatles fan" reaction from females of all ages. That said, I didn't really have anyone specific in mind as I wrote him. Although I find it difficult to compare my mental vision of my characters with real people, I will give it a shot...

While I was writing this book I thought often about Brad Pitt in the movie Thelma and Louise. Yep, I just really dated myself... Anyhow, remember that scene when he's not wearing a shirt, on the bed, with Gena Davis? I do. I remember it vividly after all these years. I remember thinking at the time, "No way this guy is real!"

So, anyhow, I imagine Andrew as looking like a cross between Brad Pitt and a not quite so huge Chris Hemsworth. That's a lot of blond gorgeosity to contend with, isn't it?

As for Stacia, I imagined her as looking a bit like Helena Bonham-Carter in *A Room with a View*, but with more hair and drab, Regency clothing.

I've received quite a few emails asking when Ma and Pa Bellamy were going to get their comeuppance. They are such a pair that I felt there wasn't room for both of them in the same book. Don't worry, the Earl of Addiscombe will get what is coming to him. It just might take a while.

So, what is up next for me?

I've got the last two books in **THE ACADEMY OF LOVE** coming up. That is *A STORY OF LOVE* on December 17, 2024, and *THE ETIQUETTE OF LOVE*, which is set for January 28, 2024 but don't be surprised if I have to bump that one to February. I will certainly know if that is the case by December 17th.

Because I can't stop myself, I've started at least three new **VICTORIAN DECADENCE** books, a Georgian series, a new "alien romance", and I've got another **HALE FAMILY** book, *ARES: THE RAKE* on the schedule. All that is in addition to *KATHRYN*, of course.

As always, I love hearing from readers. Drop me a line about what story you'd like to read next, I do actually pay attention!

Until next time, happy reading!

Xo

Minerva

Who are Minerva Spencer & S.M. LaViolette?

Here I am with Mr. Spencer and Lucille (on my lap) trying to wrangle Eva and Winston for a Christmas photo.

Minerva is S.M.'s pen name (that's short for Shantal Marie) S.M. has been a criminal prosecutor, college history teacher, B&B operator, dock worker, ice cream manufacturer, reader for the blind, motel maid, and bounty hunter. Okay, so the part about being a bounty hunter is a lie. S.M. does, however, know how to hypnotize a Dungeness crab, sew her own Regency Era clothing, knit a frog hat, juggle, rebuild a 1959 American Rambler, and gain control of Asia (and hold on to it) in the game of RISK.

Read more about S.M. at: www.MinervaSpencer.com

Follow 'us' on Bookbub:

Minerva's BookBub

S.M.'s Bookbub

On Goodreads

Minerva's OUTCASTS SERIES

DANGEROUS

BARBAROUS

SCANDALOUS

THE REBELS OF THE *TON:*

NOTORIOUS

OUTRAGEOUS

INFAMOUS

AUDACIOUS (NOVELLA)

THE SEDUCERS:

MELISSA AND THE VICAR

JOSS AND THE COUNTESS

HUGO AND THE MAIDEN

VICTORIAN DECADENCE:

(HISTORICAL EROTIC ROMANCE—SUPER STEAMY!)

HIS HARLOT

HIS VALET

HIS COUNTESS

HER BEAST

THEIR MASTER

HER VILLAIN

THE ACADEMY OF LOVE:

THE MUSIC OF LOVE

A FIGURE OF LOVE

A PORTRAIT OF LOVE

THE LANGUAGE OF LOVE

DANCING WITH LOVE

A STORY OF LOVE*

Minerva Spencer & S.M. LaViolette

THE ETIQUETTE OF LOVE*

THE MASQUERADERS:

THE FOOTMAN

THE POSTILION

THE BASTARD

THE BELLAMY SISTERS

PHOEBE

HYACINTH

SELINA

A VERY BELLAMY CHRISTMAS

THE HALE SAGA SERIES: AMERICANS IN LONDON

BALTHAZAR: THE SPARE

IO: THE SHREW

THE WICKED WOMEN OF WHITECHAPEL:

THE BOXING BARONESS

THE DUELING DUCHESS

THE CUTTHROAT COUNTESS

THE BACHELORS OF BOND STREET:

A SECOND CHANCE FOR LOVE (A NOVELLA)

ANTHOLOGIES:

THE ARRANGEMENT